ELLIE PRIDE

Annie Groves lives in the North-West and has done so all of her life. This is her first saga, for which she has drawn upon her own family's history, picked up from listening to her grandmother's stories when she was a child. Her grandmother's great pride in her hometown – Preston – inspired Annie when naming her heroine, who is also a butcher's daughter, just like Annie's grandmother was.

ANNIE GROVES

Ellie Pride

HarperCollins*Publishers*

HarperCollins*Publishers*
77–85 Fulham Palace Road,
Hammersmith, London W6 8JB

www.harpercollins.co.uk

Published by HarperCollins*Publishers* 2003
1 3 5 7 9 8 6 4 2

A catalogue record for this book
is available from the British Library

ISBN 0 00 714955 7

Typeset in Sabon by Palimpsest Book Production Limited,
Polmont, Stirlingshire

Printed and bound in Great Britain by
Clays Ltd, St Ives plc

I would like to thank the following for their invaluable help:

Lynne Drew, who gave me the opportunity to write this book.

Maxine Hitchcock, Jo Craig and Yvonne Holland, my editors and my support system.

My brother for providing me with our family tree.

My parents who giving me so much information about Preston.

Tony without whose driving I could not have done my research in Liverpool and Preston.

And last, but certainly not least, my fellow writers and friends for supporting me through *Ellie Pride*'s birth pangs.

To my grandmother who was the inspiration for this book, and to my lovely husband who was there at its beginning but did not live long enough to see its end.

PART ONE

ONE

'Ellie, why can't we go without them? If we don't get to Fishergate soon, there won't be any places left!'

'John Pride, we can see everything in the procession just as well here at home on Friargate as we can from Fishergate,' Ellie reminded her younger brother with neighbourhood loyalty. And it was true. As Ellie looked out of the parlour window of their home above their father's butcher's shop, she could see down into the street decorated with hundreds of yards of bunting to celebrate this, the first Preston Guild of the new century – and the first in the reign of the new King.

'But the procession will be here soon and I'll never see everything on the Textile Trades' drays from inside! And everyone wants to see them,' John protested, his lower lip protruding mutinously as he glowered at Ellie. 'They're going to have real

3

working machines, and they're going to be the best displays in the whole parade –'

'John Pride, how can you say that?' Connie, the middle one of the three Pride children, cut him off challengingly. 'Our dad's lot, the Master Butchers, is going to be the best. *They* are going to have two bullocks, sheep, shepherd boys leading collie dogs, journeymen in butchers' attire, *and* boys on horses,' she announced triumphantly, ticking off the list on her fingers.

'Oh, I know all about that,' John fought back scornfully, '*and* I knew about it before you did, because our dad told me first and not you . . . and –'

'No he did not,' Connie denied hotly.

'Yes he did.'

'Will you two stop it?' Ellie Pride demanded, a quick elder-sister frown creasing the smoothness of her pretty face. 'Now, John, is that a dirty mark on your collar already? And just look at your new suit! You know what Mother said . . .' As she tutted and fussed, secretly, and despite her newly grown-up sixteen-year-old status, a part of her positively itched to be out on the street with the rest of the excited crowd. But, of course, she wasn't going to admit as much to her younger sister and brother. Their mother had left Ellie in charge.

A little self-consciously she touched the pins holding up her hair. She had been practising putting it up for weeks now, but this was the first time she had been allowed to appear in public with it worn in such an adult way.

Her new dress was also more grown-up than that of one fourteen-year-old Connie, who was still wearing a girl's starched white pinafore over hers, her long hair curling loosely down her back as she kicked impatiently at the strut of the wooden chair on which she was sitting.

Stifling her own longing to be outside joining in the fun, Ellie reproved John. 'You know that we are to stay here in the house until our Aunt and Uncle Gibson and our cousins come round from Winckley Square, and then we are all to watch Father leading the Master Butchers in the Guild parade. Once they have gone by we'll go to Moor Park to see the Earl of Derby open the agricultural show.'

'Well, I agree with John. I don't want to wait for our Aunt and Uncle Gibson either,' Connie announced rebelliously. She considered herself far too grown-up to be told what to do by a mere sister.

John pulled a mutinous face at Ellie. 'Why do we have to go to the showground with Aunt and Uncle Gibson, anyway? I don't like them. Just because they live in Winckley Square and Uncle Gibson is a doctor, they think they're better than us. Father doesn't think so. He says it takes more skill to butcher a beast properly than it does to –'

'John Pride!' Ellie stopped him warningly.

John looked warily at her. He knew that there

was nothing his sisters hated more than him talking about the more gory aspects of their father's trade, though it regularly proved to be an excellent way of reinforcing his male superiority over them. Even if he was just ten, and the youngest of the family, he was still the only son, the one who would in time inherit the family business.

Ellie, however, despite her own delicate and feminine appearance, was not someone to be recklessly baited or disobeyed. She might be all dressed up in a new frock made for the occasion by their mother's dressmaker, and be wearing her hair up in a way that made her look disconcertingly grown up, but, as John had good cause to know, she could still outrun him and deliver a smart buffet that would leave his ears stinging.

'Anyway,' John added, 'they haven't got so much to be high and mighty about now, not with our dad being President of the Master Butchers this year, and being on the Guild Committee.'

Preston's famous Guild celebrations went back to the time when the town had been granted its Guild Merchant charter. As the Guild ceremonies were only re-enacted and celebrated once every twenty years their occurrence naturally generated intense excitement in the town.

'You know that Mother wouldn't like it if she could hear what you are saying,' Ellie reproved her brother. 'Aunt Gibson is her sister, and you know that Mother was –'

'One of the beautiful Barclay sisters,' Ellie's siblings chanted in unison.

'Quickly, Connie, Ellie. Come and look,' John demanded, scrambling from the chair he'd pulled up to the window to stand on the windowsill itself and crane his neck so that he could look down the street. 'There's a photographer waiting. I bet the procession won't be long now.'

'John Pride, come down from that window right now,' Ellie began, but John wasn't listening to her.

'When I grow up I'm going to be a photographer,' he continued importantly.

'You can't be,' Connie objected. 'You'll have to be a butcher like Dad. All the Prides have been butchers.'

'Not all of them,' John argued. 'Uncle William isn't.'

'No, well, that's because he was the younger brother and, anyway, he's a drover and not a photographer and you can't be either –'

'Yes I can!'

'No you can't.'

'Can, can, can . . .'

As John jumped down from the window and reached out to tug on Connie's hair she let out a shriek and tried to box his ears.

'Stop it, both of you,' Ellie commanded. 'Otherwise I shall send you to your rooms and you will miss the parade completely.'

'You can't do that; you aren't our mother,' Connie objected fiercely. 'Anyway, I don't think it's fair that we aren't allowed to go to any of the balls,' she announced, strategically changing the subject, but not before she had aimed a quick triumphant hidden kick at John's shin. 'Two of the girls from school were both going to private dances.'

'Private dances are different from public balls,' Ellie reminded her sister wearily.

Connie was like quicksilver, her moods and reactions changing so abruptly that it could be exhausting just trying to keep pace with her.

'You know that Mother and Father can't have a party of their own because they will have to attend the official ball, with Father being President of the Master Butchers this year, and on the Guild Committee. And because of that he will be too busy to take us to any of the subscription balls,' Ellie explained patiently, though she was aware that Connie knew this as well as she did.

'Aunt and Uncle Gibson are having a private party, though. I heard cousin Edward talking about it after church last week. Why can't we –'

'Quick, quick. The floats are coming!' John's excited cry brought his sisters hurrying to press their noses up against the glass.

A roar of excitement from the crowds massed on the pavements below greeted the arrival of the procession. Ellie was every bit as excited as her younger brother and sister, even though she tried not to show it. After all, this was her first Guild celebration too.

For the first time in the Guild's history, because

of the huge number of displays, the procession had been split into two parts: the Textile procession and the Trades procession. The Textile procession was the first to parade down Friargate.

The Prides had been butchers in Preston for close on four hundred years, and Robert Pride was every bit as proud of his family tradition as his wife Lydia's family were of their more 'gentrified' professional status.

'Just look at that,' John cried out as a huge horse-drawn dray lumbered past, filled with pretty female millworkers in immaculate outfits weaving at their loom.

A little hesitantly Ellie peered over her brother's shoulder.

The cotton millworkers were considered to be lowest in the town's workers' pecking order, and Lydia Pride had never allowed her own children to mix with them. Some of the millworkers had been foundlings, and the threat of being condemned to the workhouse was never far away from the poorer paid.

Ellie had been warned by her mother that she must behave in a grown-up and ladylike way; that she must always remember that she would be judged by her behaviour as well as by her position in the town's society. She must never forget, Lydia Pride had told her daughter, that although her father was a tradesman, she, her mother, came from the town's professional class.

Ellie's grandfather had been a solicitor, and his

9

elder brother had been a judge. Lydia's sisters had all married within their own class, and Lydia was determined that her two daughters would be brought up as 'young ladies', as she had been.

Beneath the window, Friargate was thronged with people: those standing watching the procession and those following it, the latter being a boisterous crowd of apprentices and schoolboys, in the main, out for the kind of mischief her younger brother was quite obviously itching to take part in, Ellie recognised.

Their maid, Jenny, was standing outside on the pavement with several other girls. Lydia Pride had taken Annie, her cook, with her when she had left to go to Moor Park, where she and the other wives were in charge of organising one of the refreshment pavilions, in this, the hottest Guild Week in living memory.

Ellie had noticed the thin curl of her Aunt Gibson's lip when her mother had mentioned her refreshment pavilion duties.

'My dear Lydia,' she had exclaimed fastidiously, 'surely it would have been better to have brought in caterers! Alfred insisted that I have our small party catered.'

'Robert wanted to make sure that the meats that were served were of the highest quality,' Ellie's mother had responded in her gentle, well-modulated voice, 'and he says that the only way to do that is to oversee the ordering and cooking ourselves. It seems that some of the more unscrupulous

10

caterers provide very inferior food. And, after all, in view of Robert's trade . . .'

'Ah, yes . . . trade,' Ellie's aunt had sighed disdainfully. 'It is such a pity, my dear –' she had continued, stopping when she realised that Ellie was listening. But Ellie knew what she had been about to say. It was no secret to the Pride children that their mother's sisters felt she had married beneath her.

Absently Ellie glanced at the float passing beneath the window. The young workers on it might be immaculately dressed today in their pinafores and caps, but everyone knew about the unpleasant, often dangerous, working conditions and low pay that these women had to endure, whilst those who owned the mills lived in the town's biggest and finest houses.

A group of rough-looking young men were running alongside the float and, without meaning to, Ellie discovered that she was staring at one of them. The sun was shining down on the thick dark curls of his capless head. She could see the sinewy strength of his muscular arms through the soft cotton of the shirt he was wearing – open at the neck, she noticed, before her face coloured in self-consciousness. There was something about him that made her feel odd . . . excited, nervous, tingling with the sudden rush of unfamiliar sensation invading her body. That feeling made her angry with herself and even more angry with him for being the cause of it. His skin was warmly

11

tanned, as though he worked outside. Was he perhaps one of the railway workers who had been responsible for adding the extra platforms to the station to cope with the influx of visitors come to enjoy the Guild Week celebrations?

Preston's Guild Week was famous throughout the country – and even further. It had been in the papers that visitors were expected from as far afield as Canada, Australia, and even New Zealand.

It had taken the committee organising the celebrations nearly two years to plan everything. Ellie could well remember her father returning from his meetings in either a state of high exultation and triumph, or deep despondency, and one of the committee's most spectacular achievements had been to obtain the offer by the new electric company of free electric lighting for the event. People would come from counties away just to see that, Robert Pride had forecast excitedly.

Leaning a little closer to the window, Ellie gazed at the young man below her, her dark blue eyes becoming darker, and her soft skin a little pinker, her lips parting as she breathed faster, caught up in a sensation she herself did not understand.

As though somehow he had sensed her curiosity he suddenly stood still in the street and looked up at the window.

His eyes were a curiously light silver grey, and there was something about him . . . Ellie gave a tiny little shudder before snatching her gaze away from his. He had no right to look at her in that . . .

12

that openly bold and . . . and dangerous way. No right at all.

'Ellie, why is that man staring up at us?' John demanded.

'Silly, it's because we're girls,' Connie answered him, preening as she tugged on her ringleted curls and coquetted openly, giggling when the stranger suddenly swept her a deep bow, and then reached into his pocket to remove three coloured balls, which he proceeded to juggle expertly.

'Oh, look at him, isn't he clever? Ellie, I want to go down and give him a penny.'

'No, you mustn't!' Ellie protested, horrified.

'Mother would want me to. You know she's always saying that we should be charitable,' Connie insisted smugly. 'Come on, John.'

'What? Waste a penny on him? No fear,' John refused sturdily. 'I want to buy myself a toffee apple at the park.'

The procession was moving on, and the 'juggler' was being urged to join it by his companions. Connie laughed and clapped her hands together as he returned the juggling balls to his pocket and swept the Prides another bow.

Someone was knocking on the back door to the house, and Ellie could hear Jenny, who had obviously returned to her duties, going to answer it. She knew that the arrivals would be their aunt and uncle, who would have taken a short cut through Back Lane to reach them. Her brother and sister, obviously sharing her thoughts, both ran towards the door, anxious to join in the celebrations.

As Ellie lingered, the young man stood watching her. Just before she turned away he suddenly gave her a look so undisguisedly bold that it shocked her, his gaze lingering on the bosom of her gown before he deliberately blew her a cheeky kiss.

Scarlet-cheeked, Ellie hurried away.

Tiredly, Lydia Pride started to remove the feathers from her headdress. In the mirror she could see her husband, Robert, walking up behind her. Bending down, he brushed his lips against the bare skin of her shoulder.

'You looked beautiful tonight,' he told her approvingly. 'I did very well for myself the day I married you, Lydia.'

Silently Lydia watched him. He had been outstandingly handsome as a young man and very confident. He was still handsome now, at close to forty, and, if anything, even more confident. He had told her the first time they met that he intended to marry her. She had laughed at him then. Her father was a solicitor, and her parents had a large house in Winckley Square. Robert lived over his butcher's shop in Friargate, with his widowed mother, his younger brother and his two sisters, and there was no way Lydia could ever see herself marrying someone like him.

'Did you see the Earl talking with me, Lydia?' Robert demanded. 'He spent longer with me than with anyone else,' he boasted. 'He said that beef you served him was the finest he had ever tasted. See if I don't get a good deal of extra business from this. We could even open a second shop. My, but that sour-faced brother-in-law of yours looked put out when he saw how much more interested in what I had to say the Earl was than in him. I can never understand what your sister saw in him. He's about as much use as a pocket in a shirt.'

'He's a doctor, Robert,' Lydia replied a little tartly. Self-confidence was all very well, but there was such a thing as reality! And in the eyes of the world at large, there was no way a butcher could be considered on an equal social footing to a doctor. Or a butcher's wife and family's status equivalent to that of a doctor's – a fact that was beginning to prey with increasing frequency on Lydia's private thoughts. 'They live in a fine house in Winckley Square.'

Frowning, Robert looked at her. 'What's to do, lass?'

As always at times of emotion, the strong Preston burr of his accent intensified. Lydia made a mental note to ensure that John would be sent to Hutton Grammar School once he was old enough. There he would be mixing with boys of the same social standing as her sisters' sons and would lose that accent.

'Nothing. Nothing is wrong,' she denied, answering Robert defensively. 'Why do you ask?'

'Well, it's just that lately you seem to be forever comparing our life to that of your sisters – and finding ours wanting. Do you find it wanting, Lyddy?' The simple directness was so much a part of his character and his strength.

Lydia felt a touch of shame and remorse. 'Oh, Robert, I'm sorry. I didn't mean . . . it's just that with the girls growing up, especially Ellie . . . Robert,' she swung round eagerly to face him, 'she is so very pretty. Prettier than any of her cousins – prettier, I think, than I was myself, and she could have so much. I don't want her to . . .'

'To what? To marry beneath her, like you did?'

Lydia bit her lip.

'Lyddy, I don't know what's happened to you just lately. I thought I'd made you happy; seen to it that you wanted for naught. Why, I've built the business up to four times what it was, and you wait and see, we shall see it increase even more after today.'

'Oh, Robert,' Lydia protested guiltily, 'it isn't for myself that I . . . worry. It's for the girls. I want them to be –'

'Young ladies! Yes, I know. But they are a butcher's daughters – my daughters – and that should be good enough for anyone. And all these airs and graces you've insisted on giving them! Piano lessons; dancing lessons . . .' He shook his head.

'It's no more than my sisters' daughters have. No more than I had myself!' Lydia pointed out passionately. 'I don't want to see either Ellie or Connie wasting herself on some . . . some going-nowhere apprentice, Robert. I wouldn't be doing my duty to them as their mother if I allowed that to happen.'

'Has it occurred to you that who or where they marry will be out of our hands? Love's like that, Lyddy, as you and I have good cause to know.'

'Love . . .' Lydia moved restlessly in her chair. Yes, she had loved Robert. Passionately, violently, wildly. But the experience of those emotions, of being held in thrall to them and being overwhelmed by them, was not something she wanted for her daughters. No, for them she wanted what she herself had disdained – especially for Ellie, whose beauty, even if Ellie herself was unaware of it as yet, was truly out of the ordinary.

'Yes, love,' Robert repeated, his voice thickening. 'Our kind of love, Lyddy, and I'll bet that that is something that those posh sisters of yours won't ever have had!'

Lydia stiffened a little as he slowly edged her low-necked, lace-trimmed ball gown even lower down her arms to expose the soft flesh of her breasts.

'Robert!' she protested. 'You know what we were told, what Alfred said the specialist said. That I should not have another child.'

She had lost a child at birth eight months after

17

Robert had first learned he was to be on the Guild Committee, and they had been told then that it would not be safe for her to conceive again. The lost baby, a boy child, had damaged her inside. Since then Robert had been acutely careful but Lydia still worried.

'There won't be a child,' Robert assured her thickly. 'I shall see to that. God, but I want you, Lyddy . . .'

He had always been a vigorously sexual man, which was part of what had attracted Lydia to him in the first place, even if she had been too naïve then to recognise her feelings for what they were. He had been very different from the other young men she had known: the sons of her parents' friends, destined to enter either the legal or medical professions, like their fathers and their grandfathers. Robert had been a breath of dangerously exciting fresh air, blowing through her sheltered world and catching her up in it.

'Marry Robert Pride! My dear, no, you can't mean it!' her mother had protested, shocked.

But Lydia had meant it. She had been of age, and she had had her little bit of money left to her by her grandmother and, more important so far as she had been concerned, she had had love and Robert.

And, of course, she still loved him, but now she had her daughters' futures to think of, and now, ironically, she understood just how her own mother must have felt because there was no way she wanted her daughters to follow her example.

18

No! What she wanted for them was what she herself had so recklessly disdained: the house in Winckley Square like her elder sister, Amelia; or the elegant vicarage like Jane, her second; or the handsome mansion in Hoylake on the Wirral, like the elder of her twin sisters, Lavinia, who had married a solicitor. Her twin Emily's husband was the headmaster of Hutton grammar school twenty miles away.

The futures of their sons and daughters, unlike her own, were assured. Their sons, unlike her John, would automatically go to Hutton, as her father had done; her daughters, like theirs, might have been educated at Preston's Park School, but, once adult, the world of their cousins would be closed to Ellie and Connie, unless they married into it.

Robert's hungry, demanding kisses distracted her. It was a hot night; the sounds of the revelry outside echoing into their bedroom.

'Robert, please be careful,' she pleaded with him as he slipped her dress off her shoulders and started to unlace her.

She always worried when, as now, he was in one of his ebullient, boisterous moods, filled with energy and excitement, just in case he should forget himself and the precautions they were obliged to take. She gave a small moan as she felt him touching her, her body tensing and then quivering as the aching sensation of wanting him began its familiar dance with her fear. Outside, the raucous laughter of some late revellers masked the small groan of pleasure she gave as her own need overwhelmed her fear. It had always been like this between them for her; her own secret cause of joy and shame. She had no idea where it had come from, this deep, dangerous chord of sensuality, so strong that it could override everything else.

Calling out to Robert, she dug her nails into the strong muscles of his arms, lifting her body against his, driven by her own hunger. Wrapping herself around him, she drew him down against her and into her body, glorying in the hot, strong feel of him inside her.

No, her sisters would never have known anything like this. Even now, Robert still had the power to make her want him with a ferocity that shocked her in the cold light of day as much as it thrilled her in the sweaty, secret, dark heat of night.

And it had been so long. Weeks . . . Passionately she bit at his mouth, and felt him shudder as she urged him to thrust deeper.

'Lyddy . . .' Robert tried to protest, but he ached so much for her – as much now, after nearly twenty years of marriage, as he had done when they had first met. But they had to be careful. There must be no child . . . he must not . . .

Gritting his teeth, Robert made to withdraw from her, but Lyddy refused to let him, moaning in protest, clinging to him, locking her muscles and writhing frantically against him.

'No. Lyddy . . . we must not . . .' Robert repeated,

but the words were lost, torn from him by Lydia's passionate kiss.

It had always been like this between them, and Lydia desperately hoped that she might not have passed on to her daughters this wanton strain in her nature of which she was so ashamed.

As the sensation inside her swelled and grew, it became impossible for her to think any longer – only to feel, to ache, to want . . .

She was almost there. Almost . . .

'Robert!' As she cried his name and clung to him she felt him groan and jerk back from her.

The spill of his completion fell hot and sticky against her thigh.

Shuddering, and gripped only by her own sense of aching frustration, Lydia reached out to guide his hand to her body so that he might complete what he had started.

TWO

'Now remember, we are all to stay together,' Robert warned his family as they stepped out into the street to join the crowds already there, intent on watching the final torch-lit procession of the Guild celebrations as it made its way through the streets to the barracks.

It had been a long day. After attending a sub-scription lunch they had seen the matinée perfor-mance of *The Yeomen of the Guard* at the Thea-tre Royal in Fishergate. From there Robert had taken John to watch the traditional football match played by the Guild against Woolwich Arsenal. And now they were joining the crowds pouring through the streets to watch and follow the pro-cession.

Just the noise from the revellers was enough to make Ellie want to cover her ears.

'I don't think there's any point in trying to get to Fishergate,' her father was saying. 'There's even more people here than I expected. They're saying that the shopkeepers in Fishergate have made hundreds of guineas letting out viewing space from their windows.'

'Well, we have had just as good a view from our own home,' Lydia told him, 'and it hasn't cost us a single penny!'

She gave a small gasp and clung tightly to her husband's arm as the crowd swirled round them. 'Stay close together, children,' she urged them anxiously. 'Connie, you hold on to me and, Ellie, you take charge of John and keep close to us. Robert, are you sure it's safe to be out?' she asked uncertainly. 'The street is packed so close with people that in the heat I feel I can hardly breathe.'

'They are saying that it is the best-attended Guild on record,' Robert confirmed happily. 'And we shall be perfectly all right just so long as we stay together.'

'Dad, just look at that,' John called out excitedly, as a group of ghostly looking grotesques walked past, their torches held aloft to illuminate their eerie masks and costumes.

Ellie shuddered, as repelled by their appearance as her younger brother was admiring.

The noise from the revellers watching and the participants in the procession was ear-shatteringly strident: young children blew shrill toy trumpets, girls screamed, and each group participating in the parade seemed to have its own musical accompaniment. A group of boisterous young men, shouldering their way through the crowds, were singing bawdy music-hall songs, whilst another group sang a rousing military anthem.

All around the Prides the warm night air was punctuated by the sounds of people's enthusiastic excitement, and as for the smells . . . ! Ellie wrinkled her nose as one of the Southport shrimpers walked past in her distinctive local dress, carrying a tray of her wares. The wings of her white hat were so wide that Ellie marvelled they weren't crushed by the crowd, but then everyone knew that the shrimpers were a formidable band of women and took care not to jostle them.

John started to beg for some, but Lydia shook her head. It had been a hot day, and heaven alone knew just how long the shrimps had been on those trays. A scuffle broke out amongst the crowd and Robert started to move his family out of the way.

'Ellie, let go of me,' John demanded. He had seen a school friend a few yards away and was determined to boast to him about how close he had been able to get to the balloon in Avenham Park before it had begun its ascent.

'John!' Ellie protested, as he finally broke her hold and darted into the crowd. 'Come back here.'

She went after him, calling crossly to him as she did so, but he refused to pay any attention to her.

Having gained his freedom, John quickly abandoned his original goal of reaching his friend and instead started to make for the front of the street, intent on getting a better view of the procession.

He thought it a poor thing that his father had refused to allow him out on his own or, at the very least, agreed that they could walk alongside the procession.

For an agile ten-year-old, wriggling through the tight-packed mass of people was relatively easy; for Ellie, following furiously in his wake, it was very much more difficult.

With her hair up and her new dress on she was not a young girl any more but a young woman. Disapproving matrons and high-spirited young men both commented on her progress through their midst in terms that brought a hot sting of colour to her face, although for very different reasons.

When one young gallant actually dared to refuse to let her pass until she had allowed him a kiss, she gave him such a look of fulminating fury and disdain that he immediately stepped back. Where on earth was John? Despairingly Ellie searched the crowd. She had come only a few yards down Friargate, but the press of people was such that she felt almost as though she was in an alien land. All around her she could hear the hum of unfamiliar accents mingling with those of the townsfolk.

'John!' she called out, relief filling her as she suddenly saw his familiar tow-coloured head only feet away from her.

The procession was almost out of Friargate now and, as Ellie plunged into the crowd to grab hold of John, it suddenly became a dangerous maelstrom of humanity as it poured into the space left by the procession and surged down the street behind it. To Ellie's shock she suddenly found herself being lifted off her feet by the sheer force of the tightly packed bodies and carried forward, totally helpless. She started to panic, frantically trying to turn round and make her way back to where she had last seen John, but the press of the crowd made it impossible for her to do so. It was the most frightening sensation she had ever experienced.

She gave a small cry of pain as her new straw hat was tugged off, causing its pins to pull on her hair. She could hardly breathe, let alone move. She could hear other women screaming and men calling out but somehow she felt oddly distanced from the sounds. Her chest felt so tight, she could feel her own heart pounding, and her head too. Someone's elbow jarred accidentally into her body but she barely felt the blow. She wanted her father! Her mother! She tried to call for them but could only make a tiny pitiful mew of sound, it was becoming so hard for her to breathe. There was a dreadful pain inside her chest, as though it was being crushed . . .

Gideon Walker had seen Ellie as he made his way through the crowd and had immediately recognised her as the pretty blonde girl he had seen standing in the upper window embrasure of Robert Pride's Friargate butcher's shop. His eyes had been drawn to her. She was very pretty, and he had spent more time than he wanted to admit thinking about her since then.

He had seen what was happening to her, but by the time Gideon, who had been less than ten feet away from her, finally managed to push through the crowd to reach her, she was in very grave danger of being trampled by the crowd as it surged after the procession.

Terrified and scarcely able to breathe, Ellie was at first too relieved to be aware of just who her rescuer was when a pair of strong male hands grabbed hold of her and dragged her upright, but by the time Gideon had guided her free of the crowd she was acutely conscious not just of the fact that he had probably saved her life but also of his identity. Now that she was standing so close to him she could see just how tall and broad-shouldered he was, and how mesmerising those silver-grey eyes of his actually were.

'You shouldn't be out alone. It isn't safe,' Gideon told her, his voice gruff with the mixed emotions of protectiveness and desire that she was arousing in him.

'I was trying to find my brother,' Ellie defended herself. Her head ached, and her hands were shaking as she reached up to try to straighten her hair. She knew how dishevelled and untidy she must look. There was a tear in the flounce of her new dress and several grubby stains marked its original pristine freshness.

'Ellie! There you are! Thank goodness!' Robert Pride was frowning at Gideon as he studied him.

'Father, this young man has just been kind enough to help me,' Ellie explained, guessing what her father was thinking. 'John ran off and I was trying to find him and . . . and the crowd . . .'

As her emotions overcame her, Gideon stepped forward. 'I saw Miss Pride. And fortunately I was close enough to be able to go to her assistance.'

Robert's frown deepened. 'You know my daughter?' he demanded suspiciously.

'I know your brother, William Pride, the drover. I have been working for him. He pointed out your shop to me and Miss Pride happened to . . . to be there,' Gideon responded equably.

'I see.' Robert's frown relaxed. 'Well, we are indeed indebted to you, Mr . . . ?'

'Walker. Gideon Walker.'

'And you say you work for my brother?'

'Only on a temporary basis. I was apprenticed to a master cabinet-maker in Lancaster.' Gideon gave a small shrug. 'He has three sons of his own to follow him into the business. Now that I am out of my apprenticeship, and have done my time as a journeyman, it is my intention to set up in business on my own.'

'So you come from Lancaster. Do you have family there?'

'Robert, I want to get Ellie inside,' Lydia interrupted her husband. 'She is very much shocked.'

'Of course,' Robert agreed.

'Oh, it is too bad,' John was complaining. 'I wanted to go all the way to the barracks with the parade and buy myself some souvenirs.'

'I'm sorry, son, but with this crowd it would be far too dangerous.'

Sensing that John was about to argue, and aware of Ellie's need to get inside, Gideon shook his own head. 'I must say, I would not want to do anything so foolhardy. I dare say there must be a hundred pickpockets in that crowd and –'

'Pickpockets?'

Over his son's head Robert gave Gideon a grateful look. John cared far more for his pocket than his person and Gideon had hit on exactly the right means of dampening his eagerness to follow the parade.

'I don't know what your plans are for the rest of the evening,' Robert smiled at Gideon, 'but you would be more than welcome to join us for supper.'

'That would be very kind,' Gideon responded, 'but I wouldn't want to impose.'

'There would be no imposition,' Robert assured him, 'and, besides, you will be able to furnish me with the latest news of my brother.'

The two men exchanged a complicit look and Gideon recognised that it was no secret to Ellie's father that his brother had a woman in the town whom he visited when he was there, as well as a wife in Lancaster.

*   *   *

'So, Gideon, tell me a little bit more about yourself,' Robert insisted, as they all took their places around the supper table.

'There is very little to tell.'

Ellie had disappeared upstairs with her mother once they had returned to the house, but Gideon was pleased to see that she was feeling well enough to sit down to supper, even if she was still looking very pale.

'My father was one of Earl Peel's gamekeepers until his death some years ago. He had met my mother originally when she was a personal maid to the Countess of Derby. Later she worked here in Preston, I believe, but moved back to the country when she married. My mother only survived my father by a few months and I was very fortunate in that the Earl paid for my indenture for me.'

'So both your parents were in service then, Mr Walker?' Lydia stated coolly.

Calmly Gideon inclined his head in assent.

It was already plain to him that Lydia considered herself to be something above the common run. The china from which they were eating was of high quality, the tablecloth elegantly embroidered Irish linen – Gideon knew that because he had been taught to recognise and appreciate such things by his mother. There was no snobbery as sharp and keen as that of the nobility's household servants.

'Well, Preston is a thriving town,' Robert assured

him, apparently oblivious to his wife's coolness towards their guest.

'But it won't be easy for you, Mr Walker, to establish yourself in such a business without any financial or family support,' Lydia was quick to point out.

She was already aware of the discreet interest Gideon was showing in Ellie, and she was determined to make it plain to Gideon that Ellie was beyond his reach. When she had married out of her own class, at least Robert had had a thriving business, and she her own inheritance. Gideon, it was obvious, had nothing. She might have ignored the warnings of her own mother, but she did not want either of her daughters to copy her mistakes. Love was all very well, and she did love Robert, but she also felt many sharp pangs of envy and regret whenever she visited her sisters and compared their lives to her own.

'It won't be easy, no,' Gideon responded, 'but certainly it is not impossible either.'

There was no way he was going to reveal his childhood dreams to Lydia. He could still remember how his mother had reacted when she had found him meticulously drawing a plan of Earl Peel's house.

'Gideon, what are you doing?' she had asked him in an angry scolding voice. 'You are supposed to be practising your handwriting, not wasting time drawing.'

'But, Mam, just look at this. See how this part

of the house comes out here – well, if it were to be brought out further and –'

'Give that to me!' his mother had demanded, tearing in pieces the sheet he had been drawing on, her mouth compressing and her face very red. 'Don't let me catch you wasting time on such silliness again, otherwise your father will be taking his belt to you.'

Gideon had loved his mother and he knew that she had loved him, but he had often felt that she did not understand him, and as a child that had both confused and hurt him at times. To him, the drawing that she considered to be a waste of time was as instinctive and necessary as breathing, but he had quickly learned that it was a pleasure it was best to keep hidden.

He had been twelve when he had realised that he wanted to be an architect – having read about the profession in one of the Earl's discarded newspapers – and not very much older when he had recognised that for someone like him, this was an impossible dream. At least as a cabinet-maker he was able to satisfy in some small measure his hunger to create and build.

Was Gideon Walker challenging her, Lydia wondered, as she absorbed both his answer and the thoughtful look he had given her. If so . . .

A quick glance at her daughter's still-pale face assured her that Ellie was in far too distressed a state to be aware of the young man's interest in her, never mind return it.

'Robert, we have all had a tiring day,' she began firmly. 'Ellie in particular. Perhaps it might be a good idea if you took Mr Walker into your office, if you wish to talk further with him.'

Ruefully, Gideon accepted her hint and got to his feet, calmly thanking her for her hospitality.

Ellie could feel herself flushing slightly when he shook her hand. She wanted him to keep on holding it, but at the same time she wanted to pull away. Without meaning to she looked at his mouth and then sucked in her breath as she suddenly felt hot and giddy. But that was nothing to how she felt when she realised that Gideon was looking at her mouth.

Gideon whistled happily as he made his way back to his lodgings. The crowd had dispersed and the late evening air was softly balmy.

Ellie Pride! One day soon, very soon, if he had his way, she was going to find out just what happened when a girl looked at a man's mouth the way she had looked at his tonight!

Ellie Pride . . . Ellie Walker!

THREE

'And Gideon said the next time he comes down with our uncle he will bring me a sheepdog puppy of my very own, and . . .'

Lydia frowned as she listened to John's excited chatter. It was nearly five months since the Guild festivities, and in those months Gideon Walker had become a far more frequent visitor to Friargate than she liked.

Right now, though, she had other things to concern her in addition to her anxiety about the dangerous effect such a handsome and masculine young man was likely to have on her vulnerable sixteen-year-old daughter.

Automatically she put her hand on her stomach. The child she had conceived the night of Robert's Guild parade was already swelling her body. Robert had been shocked and contrite when she told him. Looming over both of them was the warning she had been given after the stillbirth of her last child.

'Are you sure you want to go to Aunt Gibson's, Mother?' Ellie asked anxiously.

Her mother had told her earlier in the week that she was to have another child, and this confidence had confirmed to Ellie her status in the household of a grown-up and adult daughter, and not a child. She had automatically begun to mother Lydia in much the same busy way she did her own younger siblings, and Lydia, exhausted by the sickness of her early months of pregnancy and her fear, had wearily allowed her to do so.

She still had her sisters to face. By now Amelia's doctor husband was bound to have informed his wife of her condition. Which was, no doubt, why Amelia had summoned her to take tea with her this afternoon.

'The walk will do me good,' Lydia responded.

They were almost in February, and the cold air misted their breath as Ellie and her mother stepped out into the street.

'Gideon is so good, offering to bring John a puppy,' Ellie commented happily to her mother as they walked towards Winckley Square.

'He is certainly a very handsome and determined young man,' Lydia agreed coolly, 'but as to him being "good" . . .'

Ellie gave her mother a surprised look. 'I thought you liked him.'

'I do,' Lydia agreed. 'But . . .' She paused and shook her head.

'But what, Mother?'

But Lydia refused to be drawn.

They had reached Winckley Square now, and stopped in surprise at the comings and goings at the large mansion on the opposite side of the square to the Gibsons.

'It looks as though someone is moving into Mr Isherwood's old house,' Ellie commented.

It was over a month since the elderly widowed mill owner, who had lived in the house, had died, and despite the busyness of the removal men, the house still had an air of bleakness about it.

Ten minutes after they had been shown into Amelia Gibson's parlour, Lydia asked her sister, 'Has the Isherwood house been sold, only we saw someone moving in when we walked past?'

'No,' Amelia replied. 'It seems that Mr Isherwood's daughter has decided to return to Preston. She was his only heir and, despite the fact that they quarrelled so badly that she left home, he left everything to her, apparently. I shall call and leave a card, of course, but I must say I always thought her rather odd. I mean, going off to London like that to live virtually on her own . . .

'You look very pale, Lydia,' she announced, changing the subject. 'How are you feeling?'

'I am well enough,' Lydia replied.

As she stood protectively beside her mother, Ellie saw the sisters exchanging looks.

'Ellie, why don't you go upstairs and join your cousins?' Amelia suggested firmly.

A little uncertainly, Ellie looked at her mother.

'Yes, Ellie,' Lydia agreed. 'Do as your aunt says.'

Obediently, Ellie got up, but once she was outside the parlour door she hesitated. From inside the room she could hear her Aunt Gibson's voice quite plainly.

'So it is true, then?'

Ellie could discern the anger in her aunt's voice, but before she could learn any more her cousin Cecily suddenly appeared on the stairs.

'Ellie, come up quickly. I can't wait to show you the trimmings I have got for my new hat. Mother and I saw them last week in Miller's Arcade.'

Reluctantly, Ellie started to climb the stairs.

In the parlour Amelia Gibson shook her head as she looked at her youngest sister.

'Lyddy, Mr Pride knew you were not to have another child. He was told that it would be too dangerous. Alfred is most concerned. He has sought the advice of an eminent specialist on your behalf but he confirms what has already been said.'

'Yes, I know,' Lydia replied wanly, before bursting out in a panic-stricken voice, 'I am so afraid, Melia, and not just for myself. I have my girls to think about, especially Ellie. If anything were to happen I would want them –'

'Lyddy, please, you must not distress yourself

like this,' Amelia said firmly. 'You may rest assured that we, your sisters, shall always do what is right and proper for your daughters. Even though you defied and hurt our mother when you went against her to marry Robert Pride, I know she would want and expect us to treat your daughters as our own.'

'He has provided well for us,' Lydia defended her husband quickly. 'He has a good business and –'

'He has got you with child again, Lydia,' her sister interrupted, speaking with unusual bluntness. 'And he was warned the last time. Had you married a man of our own class such a thing would not have happened. I'm afraid that men of Mr Pride's class have . . . appetites that should never be inflicted on a lady!' She added delicately, 'Alfred made it quite plain to him that if he wished to indulge in . . . marital relations he must adopt certain . . . safeguards.'

Lydia bowed her head, unable to make any response. How could she possibly tell her sister that she had been the one to urge Robert on?

A dull smog from the factory chimneys was thickening the air when Ellie and her mother finally left Winckley Square.

Ellie had noticed a tremendous difference in her mother these last few months. She no longer smiled and sang about the house, but had become critical and cross. Ellie couldn't remember the last time she had seen her father come into the parlour and pick her mother up off her feet, as he had once frequently done, whirling her round in his arms and planting a kiss on her lips, whilst Lydia mock-scolded him for his boisterousness.

Yes, there was a very different atmosphere in the Pride household now, and although Ellie, growing quickly to womanhood herself, longed to know if in some way the baby her mother was carrying was responsible for the change in her, she knew better than to ask such an intimate question.

Ellie wasn't ignorant of the way in which a child was conceived; their father's family, for one thing, had a much more vigorous and salty approach to life than her mother's, especially their Uncle William, the drover for whom Gideon sometimes worked.

William Pride was the black sheep of the family; a rebel in many ways, who had still managed to do very well by himself materially. And in doing so he also ensured that their father was supplied with the best-quality meat on offer, since it was William who went to the northern markets to buy fat lambs and beasts, as well as poultry in season, driving the animals back from the Lakes and Dales markets to sell to several butchers, including his brother.

Ellie knew that her mother did not approve of her husband's brother, and she always tried to discourage her husband from spending any more time than necessary with him when he was in town.

As they hurried through the smog-soured streets,

keeping their scarves across their faces to protect themselves from its evil smell, out of the corner of her eye, Ellie saw a group of young millworkers huddled in a small entry that led into one of the town's 'yards'.

The houses, crammed into these places to accommodate the needs of the millworkers at the beginning of the Industrial Revolution, before the mill owners themselves had put up new terraces of cottages to house their workers, had no proper sanitation and were deemed to be the worst of the town's slums. Even through the thick choking smog, Ellie had to wrinkle her nose against their nauseating smell.

A man crossed the street in front of Ellie and her mother, causing them to step into the gutter to avoid him as he stood in front of the girls, leering at them. Drunk and unkempt, he made Ellie shudder in distaste. Her mother tugged sharply on her arm, drawing her firmly away. But Ellie already knew that the place they had just passed was one of the town's most notorious whorehouses.

Grimly, Mary Isherwood studied the dark and dank hallway of her childhood home in Winckley Square. Despite his wealth her father had been a notoriously mean man. Fires were only to be lit when he himself was at home, and her mother, the poor thin-blooded woman he had married when he was in his fortieth year, had shivered ceaselessly from November until April, her hands red and blue with cold.

Mercifully, Mary had inherited her father's sturdier physique. It had been common knowledge that her father had only married her mother because of her connection with the landed gentry – and that having done so he had mercilessly bullied her and blamed her for the fact that she had not given him a son.

Mary had grown up hating her father even more than she had despised her mother. Naturally scholastic, she had infuriated her father with her ability to out-argue him, shrugging aside his taunts that she was too clever for her own good and that no man would ever want to marry her unless he himself paid him to do so.

She had never let him see how much that jibe had hurt her, but she had made sure that he paid for it. Only through her could he have grandsons, the male heirs he longed for, and she had decided that he would never have them. She would never marry; never put herself in a position where he could boast and torment her that he had bought her a husband. Mary was every bit as stubborn as her father had been, and she had stuck to her resolution.

It had shocked her to learn that he was dead, and it had shocked her even more to discover that she was his sole heir. She had expected that he would cut her out of his will – that he would rather leave his wealth to the foundling home, whose occupants he so brutally used and destroyed working in his

41

appalling factories, rather than allow her to see a penny of it.

The factories were sold now. Horrocks's had made her father an offer he couldn't refuse, and Mary was glad of it. They represented everything she most hated.

Perhaps her father would have redrafted his will if he had realised that he was facing death. Mary felt ironically amused to learn that he had died of a chill on the lungs. Her mother had suffered a long agonising decline and a painful death from tuberculosis, brought on, Mary was sure, by her husband's refusal to allow her any home comforts. She had lived as poorly as any of the workers in her husband's mill.

Yes, Mary reflected, her father had been a hard man and a cruel one, but now he was dead, and she had decided to move back to Preston. She knew people would question her decision, but she had her own reasons for being here.

Frowning, she studied the huge oil painting of her father that hung at the top of the stairs.

'I want you to take that down,' she instructed the removal men.

'That's fine, missus, but where will you be wanting us to put it?' the foreman asked her.

'Anywhere you like, just so long as it is gone from this house,' Mary responded coolly.

She had ordered coal to be delivered ahead of her arrival, but it seemed that her late father's housekeeper had not received her instructions to light fires in every room. Ringing for her, Mary stood in the hallway and watched as the men struggled with the huge gilded frame.

She had been eighteen years old when the portrait had been commissioned and her father had been at the height of his power. He had paid the man who had painted it more than he had spent in feeding and clothing her mother and herself in a dozen years. Mary knew because she had seen the bill.

'You rang for me, miss? Oh, the master's portrait . . .' The housekeeper, Mrs Jenkins, placed her hand to her throat in shock as she saw what the men were doing.

'Yes I did,' Mary confirmed. 'It seems that a letter I sent you from London, requesting that you have fires lit in all the rooms, went astray. And –'

'Oh no, I got the letter, miss,' Mrs Jenkins confirmed, 'but the master would never have allowed anything like that. Why, even in the week he died he refused to have a fire lit in his bedroom, despite the doctor saying that he should.'

Mary could tell from her accent that the housekeeper was a countrywoman, and she suspected that, like everyone else who had ever worked for her father, she had been in terror of him.

'My father is dead now, Mrs Jenkins, and I am mistress here,' Mary replied. 'You will, I hope, find me a good and a fair mistress, just so long as you understand that it is I and not my father who now gives the orders. As soon as you have a maid free you will instruct her to light all the fires, please.'

'Very well, miss . . . but you cannot mean to remove your father's portrait,' the housekeeper blurted out. 'He was that proud of it; used to stand and look at it every day, he did, before he got poorly.'

'Thank you, Mrs Jenkins, I am aware of my father's pride in himself.' And of every other aspect of his unpleasant personality, Mary could have added.

She still bore the faint scars on her back where he had whipped her as a child. She was forty now, but sometimes at night, when she couldn't sleep, they still ached.

'But what is to go in its place?' the housekeeper was fretting. 'The wallpaper will have faded, and in such a large space –'

'If it has then we shall have new wallpaper, Mrs Jenkins. In fact, I believe we shall have new wallpaper anyway. Something light and modern. Now just as soon as the men have finished, I want someone to take them down to the kitchen and give them a good hearty meal before they leave.'

The housekeeper was staring at her, and Mary guessed why. She doubted that anyone in the household knew what a good hearty meal was. Well, they were soon going to discover.

She might have particular plans for the huge inheritance she had received, but that did not mean that she didn't fully intend to enjoy some of its benefits immediately. Starting with doing something about the house.

As the men brought the painting down the stairs, the artist's name glittered under the light of the chandelier. Hesitantly, Mary reached out and touched it, running her fingertips over the slightly raised surface of the paint.

Richard Warrender.

Very briefly she closed her eyes. Some memories were too painful for her to recall, even now.

FOUR

'A puppy for John, is it, or more like a sweetener to win the favour of young Ellie?' William Pride laughed as he watched his young helper button the collie pup he had brought with him from the borders inside his jacket.

'You're wasting your time there, my lad,' William told Gideon, shaking his head. 'She's a fine-looking girl, I'll grant you that. Got her mother's looks and her fancy airs and graces as well. Lyddy will never allow any daughter of hers to get sweet on a working lad like you. Thinks too much of herself for that, she does.'

'Mr Pride has always made me very welcome in his home,' Gideon said stiffly.

'Oh aye, our Robert – Mr Pride – he will, but we're talking about Mrs Pride now, lad, 'er as was "a Barclay" before she wed our Robert. I remember how it was when they first met. Let us know that she thought herself well above us, she did, allus talking about her father the solicitor in

that posh voice of hers. Of course, our Robert was
well fixated on her. Daft as a tuppence-halfpenny
wristwatch he was – dafter! I could never see the
sense in it m'sel'. Never catch me allowing any
woman to rule my life. Good enough in their right
place, women is, but only that place!' He winked
meaningfully at Gideon. 'What tha' wants, lad, is
some willing wench – but make sure she's clean,
mind. I don't mind telling you I had my problems
in that way when I was a young green 'un. Don't
you make the mistake of settling for one before
you've sampled a few like I did, either. Naught
wrong with our Gertie, mind, but a bit of choice
isn't a bad thing, if you know what I mean.' He
grinned, tapping the side of his nose.

Grimly, Gideon forced himself not to object.
He knew exactly what his employer meant, and
he knew too that once they had parted company
William would make his way first to the pub, where
he would garner the current gossip, and then to the
home of the woman who was his 'wife' whenever
he was in the town, and by whom he had three
tow-headed sons.

Gideon wasn't finding it as easy to get work as
he had hoped – but William Pride paid a fair wage
to his men, even though the work itself wasn't what
Gideon really wanted to do.

Every time they visited Preston, as well as calling
at Friargate, ostensibly to update John on the progress of his pup, Gideon combed the town's streets,
looking for somewhere to set up his business.

So far his search had been disappointing. Those townspeople rich enough to employ a cabinet-maker, instead of buying ready-manufactured furniture, automatically looked to tradesmen they knew and believed they could trust, many often going as far afield as Gideon's own ex-master in Lancaster.

He had had one small but potentially lucrative job, which had set his hopes soaring – the restoration of a carved banister in a tumbling-down manor house in Lancashire, which had been bought by a newly rich railway shareholder, but the man had refused to pay Gideon the full amount they had agreed, and he had been lucky to cover his costs for the job, never mind make a profit.

He was not about to give up, though. The struggle he was having now would make his eventual success very sweet, and even sweeter if he were able to have Ellie to share it with him.

Ellie. How she teased and tantalised him, giving him bold, tormenting looks one minute, and the next blushing a softly delicious pink just because he had happened to comment on her mother's pregnancy.

Gideon frowned as he thought about Lydia Pride. There was a very different atmosphere in the Pride household now, in April, than there had been when he had first been invited there in Guild Week.

Robert Pride himself had changed, Gideon believed. He no longer seemed to laugh as easily or as heartily, and there was a hangdog, sheepish look about him whenever he was around his wife.

Even Ellie seemed to be affected by the change in her parents' relationship, and Gideon had seen how very protective she had become of her mother.

The pup inside his jacket struggled and yelped, reminding him of its presence and his plans. He had first to take his bag to his lodgings – a small but reasonably clean room tucked away at the back of a small courtyard – and then he would deliver the puppy – and set eyes again on Ellie.

'Show me again, Gideon,' John pleaded as the balls he had been trying to juggle refused to move as dextrously in his hands as they did in Gideon's.

Laughing, Gideon did so. They were standing outside Robert's shop in the sharp spring sunlight, waiting for the rest of the Pride family. Robert had invited Gideon to join them for the traditional Easter Monday egg rolling in Avenham Park, and Gideon had accepted gratefully, only too pleased to have a legitimate excuse to spend some time with Ellie.

'If you don't want to go to the park, Mother, would you like me to stay here with you?' Ellie offered anxiously.

'No, you must go, Ellie, if only to keep an eye on

John and that wretched dog of his,' Lydia sighed tiredly.

The combination of a boldly inquisitive and danger-prone ten-year-old and an equally adventurous collie pup was not one that was designed to soothe a mother's natural fears.

John had become devoted to his pet. They went everywhere together, and virtually every day he insisted that they all watch whilst this wondrous creature performed some new trick he had taught it.

'And look out for Connie too. You know what she's like.'

The closer it got to her due date, the more haunted Lydia was becoming by the warnings she had been given. It was all very well for Robert to say that doctors always tended to look on the black side, and to remind her that she had already produced three healthy children with no risk to herself whatsoever. Sometimes in the night she dreamed that she was a girl again, her body slender and empty, and she would wake up full of relief until she realised the truth.

Her sisters, she knew, blamed Robert, and so increasingly did she.

As the youngest child of the family she had perhaps been indulged rather more than the others – she had certainly been far more rebellious. Also her marriage, Lydia knew, was different from those of her sisters, just as her nature was different. If her daughters had inherited that streak of sensuality from her they would need to learn to guard against it, otherwise . . .

'Are you sure?' she heard Ellie asking her.

'Yes. You go, and, Ellie . . .' But as Ellie turned back, Lydia shook her head. 'It doesn't matter.'

To warn her daughter at this stage against Gideon Walker might do more harm than good. Ellie was a young girl, after all, and Gideon was an extremely handsome young man. Lydia was not so old that she could not remember the way she had felt when Robert had first looked at her with his bold, laughing eyes and his warm smile . . .

Sunshine danced on the crystal bowl in the middle of the table, and suddenly Ellie was impatient to be outside. Giving her mother a swift kiss, she hurried to the door.

'John, if you are not careful you will break all your eggs before we even reach the park,' Ellie scolded, as John, growing bored with his family's leisurely progression, began to swing his basket of eggs.

The town's Easter Monday festivities at Avenham Park was a popular and well-attended event, especially the egg-rolling race.

But much as John wanted to hurry them towards what he considered to be the most important and exciting part of the day, his sisters obstinately refused to listen.

'Oh, Ellie, do look. There is Sukey Jefferies from school. Just look at her dress.' Connie was tugging on Ellie's arm.

Judiciously Ellie studied the other girl, who, like them, was accompanied by her family. The Jefferies family were involved in the cotton trade, and considered to be well-to-do, even though they did not actually own any of the town's mills.

'The silk is far too rich for a daytime outing,' she pronounced, 'and as for all those lace frills and flounces . . .'

'It looks very grand,' Connie breathed enviously. 'I wish that Mother would allow me to wear a proper grown-up dress, instead of making me wear these stupid pinafores, like a child. After all, Sukey is only a year older than me.'

'She is two years older,' Ellie corrected her, 'and her dress is far too fussy.'

It wasn't just their beauty that the Barclay sisters were renowned for, it was their taste and stylishness as well, and Ellie knew instinctively just what her mother would have thought of Sukey's gown, with all its fanciful, overdone trimmings.

Her own dress, for all its simplicity, was, Ellie knew, far more stylish and elegant, but before she could say as much to her sister, John was rudely interrupting their conversation, demanding, 'Oh, why must we waste time talking about such stuff? If we don't hurry we won't get a decent place.'

'There is plenty of time, and I know the exact

spot we need,' Ellie reassured him, unaware that she was being observed keenly by Gideon, walking slightly behind them with her father, as she gave John an impishly droll look.

'What, you mean you will show me the spot you've won the egg race from three years running?' John exclaimed in excitement.

This awesome feat by his elder sister had become a part of their family history, and secretly it was John's goal not just to match it but, with luck, to better it.

'What's this? I hadn't realised that we had a champion egg roller in our midst!' Gideon exclaimed, joining in the fun.

Flushing a little, Ellie nevertheless held his gaze.

'I think we shall have to put your skills to the test,' Gideon announced, 'since I consider myself to have some sporting skill.'

'Yes! Yes!' John encouraged, dancing up and down.

'What do you say, Miss Pride – will you allow me to challenge you?' Gideon laughed.

A little uncertainly, Ellie looked at her father, half expecting and even half hoping that he might object and insist, as she suspected her mother would have done, that such behaviour on her part would be unseemly, but to her consternation he just laughed and said, 'You will have to be very good, Gideon, if you are to best Ellie. Had she been a boy I dare say she would be captaining the Hutton cricket team by now.'

They had nearly reached the end of the elegant colonnaded walk that led into the park. Several family groups had paused to chat, and Ellie recognised her cousin Cecily in one of them, with her fiancé, but she didn't draw her father's attention to their presence, sensitively aware that Cecily might not want to acknowledge them if she was with her fiancé's family.

Cecily's father-in-law-to-be was, as Aunt Gibson had proudly informed her sister, a very senior Liverpool surgeon, Sir James Charteris, who, through his wife's family, was connected with the nobility!

A group of girls of around her own age hurried past them, and Ellie guessed from their loud voices that they must work in one of the town's mills. Everyone knew that the noise inside the weaving sheds turned people deaf and that the millworkers had devised their own sign language for communicating with one another.

One of the girls suddenly stopped. Taller than Ellie, with a wild mane of thick curly red hair and a pale complexion, she gave Ellie an astutely assessing female look before tossing her head dismissively and going boldly up to Gideon, throwing him a look that was openly flirtatious, as she exclaimed in the thickest of the town's dialect, 'Well, if it isn't Mr Gideon Walker . . .'

'Good afternoon, Miss Nancy,' Gideon responded with an easy openness that shocked and dismayed Ellie. Immediately she drew herself up to her own full height and pursed her lips every bit as disapprovingly as her mother would have done.

'Miss Nancy!' the redhead emphasised, and laughed.

'Come on, Nance.' One of the other girls tugged on her skirt. 'There's free refreshments for them as gets there first, and I'm fair clemmed . . .'

Watching the girls hurry away, Ellie had to admit that the cheap dress worn by 'Miss Nancy' had far more style about it than those of her companions. Did Gideon find the redheaded mill girl attractive? Did he think her pretty . . . prettier than she? Did he want to kiss her? Had he perhaps already kissed her?

Ellie's mother considered that red was not a suitable hair colour for a young lady, and Ellie had been brought up to be proud of her own soft golden curls, but now suddenly she was sharply aware that a woman did not necessarily have to have blonde curls and ladylike manners to attract a man.

'Who was that?' John demanded, too young to feel any need to conceal his curiosity.

'Miss Nancy and some of her co-workers rent rooms in the house next to where I rent my own,' Gideon explained easily. 'She came to me for assistance some time ago, when . . . when one of the girls had . . . had fainted. I believe that underneath her brash manner she is a good sort, and –'

'These mill girls have a very hard life,' Robert Pride interrupted. 'Every year so many are killed in accidents with the heavy looms. There is much talk of the need to reform the conditions under which the mills are run.'

'There is always talk,' Gideon replied sharply, 'but very rarely any action, and even when there is, the mill owners seem to find a way to circumvent it. I was called into one of the mills the other day to repair a piece of machinery – I think I would go mad had I to work there permanently. The noise alone, never mind anything else.'

Ellie could feel the heaviness that had enveloped the two men as they talked. The looks on their faces reminded her of the man she had seen in the fish market the previous Friday when she had gone there with her mother.

He had gathered a small crowd around him, and Ellie had been forced to wait until a pathway had been cleared before she could follow her mother past him. Whilst she had done so, she had heard the man declare, 'These mills are a running sore on the face of our town, and worse, the running sore we can see. But what of those other sores which are hidden shamefully from view, the plight of those who work in such abominations? The plight of our womenfolk, our sisters, our daughters, our mothers . . .'

Ellie's mother had dragged her away before Ellie could hear any more.

Now suddenly she felt angry with 'Miss Nancy' for intruding on the happiness of her day.

'Come on,' John was urging them all. 'Hurry up . . .'

'Are you sure you haven't changed your mind?' Gideon demanded teasingly as he and Ellie stood side by side at the top of the hill.

All around them children were rolling their eggs, their cries of disappointment or triumph filling the air.

Since neither she nor Gideon had come equipped with eggs to roll, Gideon and her father had purchased some from one of the booths set up in the park. Surreptitiously Ellie checked them. In her experience the right consistency of hard-boiled egg was essential if they were to roll any distance – and not just the consistency of the inside of the egg. She had always painted hers with a special paint she had mixed herself, which had helped to bond the shell together. But these eggs . . .

'Chicken?' Gideon demanded, laughing.

'Chicken . . . eggs,' John laughed, hugely delighted with his wit.

'I don't know why you are laughing, John Pride,' Connie taunted him. 'All your eggs are broken – apart from those eaten by your dog!'

With the two of them squabbling amicably as a backdrop, Ellie picked up her first egg.

Childishly she held her breath a little as it rolled down the hill, only letting it out when she saw that the egg had gone a respectable distance and remained unbroken as it lay in the small dip in the group that had trapped it.

'Ah-ha. That is good, but I believe I can do better,' Gideon boasted.

He had seen the look of smouldering female resentment that Ellie had given Nancy, and it was that rather than any desire to win the egg-rolling race that was responsible for his high spirits. Ellie had been jealous!

Carefully, Gideon reached for his first egg.

'No, you can't do that,' Ellie reproached him firmly, as he gently threw the egg several yards before it dropped to the ground and rolled with great speed down the hill.

'Why not?'

'It's against the rules.'

'What rules? I haven't seen any rules,' Gideon protested, mock innocently.

He loved the way Ellie's eyes darkened with emotion, the way she threw herself so whole-heartedly into everything she did. Was she herself aware of the passionate intensity of her own nature or had her mother succeeded in hiding it from her beneath the smothering strait-jacket of ladylike behaviour she imposed on her?

'Gideon's egg has gone further than yours, Ellie,' John sang out.

Ellie reached for her second egg, giving Gideon a challenging look of determination.

This time it was Connie who was dancing up and down in excitement as they watched Ellie's second egg roll triumphantly past Gideon's.

'Right!' To John's delight Gideon immediately took up a very determined male stance, rubbing his hands together lightly before picking up his own second egg.

Once again Ellie discovered that she was holding her breath whilst willing Gideon's egg not to match the distance achieved by her own.

Judiciously, Gideon mentally measured the distance from where he was standing to where Ellie's egg lay.

'Come on, Gideon,' John shouted. 'You can't let her beat you. She's a girl.'

She certainly was, Gideon acknowledged, trying not to let himself think about the way the bodice of Ellie's dress moulded the soft curves of her breasts.

There was something distractingly enticing about the demure, daintily pleated neckline against her throat. And as for that enchantingly ridiculous nonsense of straw and ribbons she was pleased to call a hat – did she have any idea just what she was doing to him when she looked up at him from beneath its brim, or when he looked at her and could see only the straight sweetness of her nose, and the full promise of her mouth?

If he allowed her to win, John would never let him hear the end of it, but if he beat her . . . He too was holding his breath as he watched his egg roll down the grassy slope.

Just a few feet short of her own, Gideon's egg came to a stop. Exhilarated colour warmed Ellie's face. She started to turn towards Gideon and then stopped as out of the corner of her eye she saw Rex, John's pup, suddenly rush past her in pursuit of the egg.

'No . . . he mustn't touch it!' she cried out, but Gideon, guessing what the pup had been instructed to do, was already lunging down the hill. Angrily, Ellie followed him, whilst Robert Pride firmly held John back, demanding that he recall his errant accomplice.

The pup had already reached the egg, which he had picked up, but the moment he saw Nemesis in the shape of both Gideon and Ellie bearing down on him, he dropped it and headed back to his master.

The egg, given fresh impetus, rolled happily forward, quickly overtaking the others, before dropping out of sight into a small hidden grassy dip.

'Oh no!' Ellie cried out hotly, and then gasped, as she suddenly lost her footing and pitched forward.

Immediately, Gideon turned to try to help her, his arms wrapping protectively around her, and somehow ended up also slipping on the steep slope. Body to body they followed the path of the egg and, like it, came to rest in the secluded grassy dip.

'Oh, that John,' Ellie condemned her young brother, as she lay against the protective warmth of Gideon's body, trying to get her breath.

'He is a mischief,' Gideon agreed in amusement, the expression in his eyes suddenly changing as he looked at Ellie. 'But right now,' he murmured, 'it is his sister I am much more interested in.

Has anyone ever told you, Ellie Pride, just how beautiful you are? How adorably sweet your nose is. How irresistibly kissable your lips are . . . ?'

With every word he uttered Gideon's voice became thicker and softer, and with every word Ellie's sense of excitement and wonder grew. She could feel her heart beating so fast beneath the bodice of her dress that it was a wonder she could still breathe.

As he looked down at her, into her eyes and then at her mouth, before lifting his gaze to her eyes again, Gideon groaned softly.

'Ellie,' he whispered. His fingertips touched the side of her face, and he marvelled at the softness of her skin, its purity and perfection, whilst Ellie shuddered in pleasure that such a little touch should do so much!

She could feel the warmth of Gideon's breath against her face, her lips. His eyes were no longer a cold silver grey, but a hot liquid gunmetal colour that made her insides feel as though they were melting.

His lips touched hers, brushing them gently. Ellie gave a small gasp and then a soft sigh.

Boldly, Gideon kissed her with more pressure. He could feel his longing for her, his love exploding inside him. Unable to stop himself he ran the tip of his tongue along the soft, closed virginal innocence of her mouth. Her lips felt so soft, so warm, so Ellie . . . Cupping her face in his hands, Gideon forced himself to remember where they were.

'I know it may be too soon to say this to you, Ellie Pride, but let me tell you this,' he began, his voice husky with emotion. 'I love you and I will always love you. And just as soon as I am able to do so I intend to claim you for my own. For my wife,' he emphasised, just in case Ellie might mistake the seriousness of his intentions.

Her eyes shining with emotion, Ellie gazed wonderingly back at him. Gideon loved her. And she knew that she loved him. Hadn't she spent far too many nights lying in the bed she shared with Connie, secretly thinking about him and dreaming of a moment like this, even to think of doubting it?

'Nothing can stop what's happening between us,' Gideon told her fiercely. 'Nothing . . . and no one.'

'If the ladies are ready, I suggest that we start to make our way back to Winckley Square.'

Courteously Stephen Simpson waited for the female members of his party to agree with him. It had been at his suggestion that they had gone to the park to watch the local children rolling their eggs. He had a house party this Easter, and his guests had clamoured to witness such an unusual custom.

As she joined the other ladies of the party, Mary Isherwood smiled at her host. The Simpson family had owned their gold thread works in Avenham Lane for several generations, and were a sociable family, who, Mary knew, had been very fond of her mother. It had been kind of them to invite her to join this party. The ladies of the family had been the first hostesses to leave a calling card on her return to Preston.

'I understand that you are having a great deal of work done on your late father's house.'

Mary turned towards the woman speaking to her. They had met for only the first time today, and it was tempting for Mary to reply that she must have come by her information from someone else, since Mary herself had made no mention of Isherwood House.

Almost as though she guessed what Mary was thinking, the other woman explained, 'I live across the square from you. My husband is Dr Gibson.'

'Yes, of course,' Mary acknowledged, fibbing politely. 'I believe I have seen you in the square with your family.'

'My daughters,' Amelia informed her proudly. 'My eldest, Cecily, has recently become engaged to Mr Paul Charteris. His father is an eminent surgeon and Mr Charteris hopes to follow in his father's footsteps.'

Mary was able to place the other woman now and to realise who she was. 'Ah, yes. I see that your daughters have inherited the Barclay family looks. They are both very pretty girls.'

Amelia beamed and preened herself a little. 'Well, yes, it is true that they have. That is . . . my sisters and I . . . and luckily all our daughters have . . .'

She trailed off as she saw the direction in which Mary was looking.

'I see that you are admiring Mr William Ainsworth's villa,' she smiled.

'Admiring it!' Mary's voice hardened. 'I could never do that, knowing the nature of the man who built it. My father had the reputation of being a hard employer – he was certainly a very hard father – but his lack of regard for his workers was nothing to that of William Ainsworth. The cruelties and injustices he inflicted on those who worked for him!' Mary's mouth compressed. 'It is an open secret that the fines he imposed upon his wretched workers for his own cleverly thought-up "offences" rendered them unable to live on what was left of their wages, to the extent that the female workers were forced to –'

'My dear,' Amelia intervened hastily, her face flushing, 'I have no wish to offend you, but as an unmarried woman, I do not think –'

'You do not think what?' Mary challenged her sharply. 'That I should have been indelicate enough to discuss the fact that members of our sex have to sell their bodies on the streets of our town simply to feed themselves? No, shameful indeed that I should dare to do so! But how much more shameful is it that such a situation should exist and that we as women should turn our backs on it?'

Without waiting for Amelia to respond, Mary turned away and went to take her leave of her host.

It was perhaps unfair of her to let rip at her neighbour in such a way, but it infuriated her that women of Amelia's ilk should so easily and so damagingly turn their backs on the misery that lay so close to their homes. But then who could blame her for her attitude when the law of the land itself denied her any say in the way the country was run? It was inequitable that in a country like Great Britain, which considered itself to be the foremost and most advanced, politically democratic nation in the world, that its women should be denied the most basic and most important political right – that of being allowed to vote.

The sooner that situation was changed the better, so far as Mary was concerned, and she knew that she was not alone in her desire.

FIVE

'And this year I am going to enter Rex in the agricultural show, and –'

'Oh, do stop going on about your wretched dog,' Connie commanded her brother impatiently. 'Have you spoken to Mam yet about my new dress, Ellie? I'm old enough now to have a proper grown-up outfit. All the other girls in my class –'

'Connie!' Ellie stopped her sister angrily. 'You know that Mother does not like us to speak like that. We are to call her Mama or Mother.'

'That is because she is a snob. That's what Jimmie Shackleton three doors down says his mam calls her. Oh, look, here is our aunt arriving.'

As Connie made to slide off the piano seat, Ellie informed her firmly, 'I shall see to our aunt, Connie, whilst you continue with your piano practice.'

'You cannot tell me what to do, Ellie,' Connie declared sulkily. 'Just because you are walking out with Gideon, that does not mean –'

'I am not doing any such thing,' Ellie protested, pink-faced.

'Oh, yes you are,' Connie insisted. 'You are sweet on him, and don't try to pretend that you are not. Your voice goes all gooey and funny whenever you speak about him.'

Ellie could feel her colour deepening.

Since Gideon had declared his feelings for her, they had spent as much time together as they could, but it had not been easy, as her mother was increasingly dependent on Ellie's help, and increasingly insistent on keeping her close at hand.

Gideon had told Ellie that there was no way he could approach her father to ask for her hand until he had established his business and was able to provide her with a proper home.

'I know that you can do it, Gideon,' Ellie had whispered lovingly to him, her eyes warm with pride and dreams. 'I can see it now. Everyone will want to commission you to make them furniture, including the Earl. All you need is the opportunity to prove to people how good you are.'

'I hope that you are right,' Gideon had responded.

By taking on extra work for William Pride he was managing to save some money, but the extra work he was doing meant that he had less free time to visit Preston and see Ellie, never mind look for premises for his business.

Ellie had urged him to seek help from her father. 'Since he is in business himself he is bound to know if the right kind of shop premises become available,' she had counselled Gideon practically.

But Gideon had told her stubbornly, 'No, Ellie, I do not want to go cap in hand to your father for help. I want to show him that I can establish myself, that I am fit to be your husband. And besides, we have plenty of time. You are still only sixteen.'

'Seventeen soon,' Ellie had reminded him.

Putting down the nightgown she had been sewing for the expected baby, she checked Connie with a stern frown before going to greet her Aunt Gibson.

'Ah, Ellie, I am come to see your mother.'

'She is upstairs in her room,' Ellie informed her aunt.

There was something about her mother's eldest sister that Ellie had always found slightly daunting. And now, for no reason at all, she discovered that she was fidgeting slightly as Amelia subjected her to scrutiny.

'I know the way, Ellie. You do not need to accompany me,' she informed her niece firmly, as she swept towards the stairs, obliging Ellie to stand to one side.

Ellie waited until she had heard her mother's bedroom door open and then close again before returning to the back parlour to oversee Connie's piano practice.

'Lyddy, my dear, I came as soon as I had your message. What has happened? Is it the baby?' Amelia demanded anxiously as she hurried to embrace her sister.

Lydia shook her head. 'No.' Her pregnancy still had some three or so weeks to run, and the enforced rest Amelia's husband had insisted she must take was making the time hang heavily. She would much rather have been active, the chatelaine of her home as she had always been, rather than being obliged to leave so many of her duties in the hands of her elder daughter.

Not that Ellie was not fully capable of running a home. No, Lydia had seen to it that both her daughters knew how to maintain and order a household.

'Then what is amiss?' Amelia asked her.

In contrast to the obvious swollenness of her belly, Lydia's face looked alarmingly thin, her eyes sunken in its paleness, her flesh stretched almost painfully over her elegant bones, but it was the look of fear in her eyes that affected her sister the most.

Lydia was ten years Amelia's junior, the baby of their family, the prettiest of all of them, the spoiled precious youngest child, who had been adored and fêted all her life until she had so foolishly and disastrously married Robert Pride. And now look at her!

'It's Ellie, Amelia,' Lydia told her sister tiredly. 'I am so concerned about her.'

'Concerned? In what way?'

'She has become involved with this Gideon

Walker – I have told you about him. Oh, she says nothing to me, but I know what has happened. She thinks herself in love with him. I can see it in her eyes, hear it in her voice every time his name is mentioned. I have tried to talk to Robert about it, but he will not listen. He does not understand – how can he? Melia, Ellie must not do as I have done. She is worthy of so much more. But what is to be done? Robert is allowing Gideon the run of the house as though . . . as though he were already a member of our family. John worships him, and I am not well enough to keep a check on what is happening.'

'Ellie must be sent away before any more harm can be done,' Amelia announced grimly. 'The best place for her to go would be to our sister in Hoylake. Lavinia and Mr Parkes live a very social life there. Mr Parkes has several wealthy ship-owners as clients, and I dare say that after attending a few parties where she may meet some proper young gentlemen, Ellie will soon forget any foolishness over this . . . this Gideon.'

'Oh, Amelia, do you think so?' Lydia's expression brightened. 'But Hoylake! I don't know . . . I need Ellie here and –'

'You need do nothing for the present,' Amelia assured her comfortingly. 'I shall write to our sister, and just as soon as you have been confined and safely delivered, Ellie may be sent to stay with Lavinia in Hoylake until the danger of her fancying herself in love with Master Gideon is completely over.'

'When?' Lydia cried bitterly. 'Oh, Amelia, I am so –'

Hastily Amelia interrupted her. 'Alfred says that you may expect to be confined before the end of the month.'

'Yes. He has said as much to me.'

Lydia's lips trembled. She had not been able to bring herself to ask her brother-in-law if he still believed her life to be at risk. She had been too afraid of what he might say, and so instead she had allowed herself to believe Robert when he insisted optimistically that she had nothing to worry about. But sometimes in the dead of night, she woke sweating and trembling, her heart racing and her mouth dry, overwhelmed by fear.

Making plans for Ellie's future, and the ways in which she could thwart Gideon Walker's intentions of ruining her daughter's life, gave her a means of escaping those fears.

'Cecily is to put off her wedding until next year so that you will be able to attend. She is determined to be a June bride,' Amelia informed her sister.

What she could not tell Lyddy was that she herself had had to suggest discreetly that her daughter plan her wedding more than twelve months hence, just in case they should be overtaken by events. She certainly had no wish to wear mourning at her own daughter's wedding.

And neither had she any wish to lose her youngest sister, but Alfred had refused to offer her much hope.

'The damage caused by the birth of her last child is such that I do not believe she can survive this birth. I pray that I may be wrong,' he had said to his wife when she had questioned him.

'You must not tax your strength, Lyddy,' Amelia told her now. 'Whatever happens, you can trust us, your sisters, to do whatever is necessary for your children. We have already discussed this.'

'Yes, I know that, Melia, and I am grateful to you all . . .' Tears welled in Lydia's eyes.

Quickly Amelia bent and kissed her cheek. 'I must go. But remember, Robert is to send for Alfred the moment you need him.'

Wanly, Lydia agreed.

The forthcoming birth of Lydia's child was also the subject of discussion in Alfred's handsome consulting room in the Winckley Square house.

'But if the risk to Mrs Pride is so great,' Paul Charteris was saying earnestly, 'then surely there can be nothing to lose and everything to gain by adopting such a procedure.'

'Have you discussed this with your father?' Alfred challenged his son-in-law-to-be.

Paul sighed. 'I have, but he believes there are too many risks involved.'

'Exactly,' Alfred pounced. 'To perform a Caesarean operation to remove the child might seem to be a solution, but in my view it is one that carries far too much risk, not just to mother and child, but also to the reputation of the surgeon who carries it out, to make it a responsible or viable option.'

'But if it is the only means of saving the mother and her child, surely it is better to take that risk than to stand by and –'

'Paul, Paul, your ardour does you credit,' Alfred told him sombrely, coming round his desk to place a consoling arm about the younger man's shoulders, 'but I fear you are permitting your emotions to overrule your judgement, and that is something no physician should allow to happen.'

Bewildered, Paul watched him. His own father had been as loath to acknowledge the potential benefit of performing a Caesarean delivery as his prospective father-in-law was.

Caesarean deliveries were performed, of course, when the mother's life was agreed to be of less value than that of the child she was carrying, or where a choice had to be made between mother and child, but to perform one where both mother and child were expected to survive was a dangerous medical procedure. And yet the operation had been done – and successfully. It was Paul's dream that one day such operations would be a matter of course, and that he would be performing them; that he would be at the forefront of his profession, not content, as his father was, to rest on his reputation and accept a knighthood, but to push back the medical barriers as far as they could possibly go; to conquer the perils of infection, surgical trauma and blood loss.

Reluctant to abandon his dream he burst out, 'Perhaps if Mrs Pride were to be consulted . . . If she were told, offered the choice . . .'

Alfred looked outraged. 'How can you suggest such a thing? No! Poor woman, she already has enough to bear. She should be left at peace now, to compose herself for what lies ahead. That is our most solemn duty and responsibility to her.'

'But surely, sir, our first and foremost duty is to try to save her life and that of her child,' Paul insisted doggedly.

'Do you think that I am not aware of that? Lydia Pride is not just my patient, she is also my wife's sister,' Alfred reminded Paul sternly. 'And, besides, I am not convinced that such an operation, even if it were successful in saving the child, could save her. She should never have conceived again. It was only by good fortune that she was spared last time.'

Paul took a deep breath before asking, 'Then would it not perhaps have been better for the pregnancy to be terminated in its early stages?'

The words fell into a heavy silence that suddenly filled the room. Alfred's face grew stern. 'I shall pretend that you did not utter that remark, Paul.' When Paul said nothing, Alfred burst out angrily, 'You know as well as I do that such a course of action is against the law.'

'Yes I do, which is why women, poor creatures, are forced to resort to the desperate measure of paying some filthy harridan to maim and murder them.'

'I will not listen to this, Paul. You are not talking

about our own womenfolk here but a class of women you should know better than to discuss. If a woman has a need to resort to . . . to the solution you have just allowed to soil your lips, then it is because she herself has sinned and is seeking to hide that sin from the world and escape her just punishment for it!'

Paul gritted his teeth. The older man was only echoing the view shared by his own father, he knew, but it was a view that Paul himself did not find either acceptable or honest, never mind worthy of his Hippocratic oath. It was on the tip of his tongue to remind Alfred that, far from sinning, Lydia Pride had been an admirably dutiful wife, but he could see from the florid, bellicose expression on Alfred's face that such an argument was not likely to find favour.

'I have done my best for Lydia. I –' Alfred coughed and looked embarrassed, '– I have discussed with Robert the . . . benefits of, ahem, not completing the . . . the act . . .'

'But there are far more modern and reliable ways of preventing conception than that,' Paul burst out, unable to contain himself.

Once again his frankness earned him a disapproving look. 'I have no wish to continue this discussion, Paul.'

Frustrated, Paul turned away to look out of the window.

*   *   *

'There is a gentleman to see you, ma'am, a Mr Dawson.'

'Thank you, Fielding. I am expecting him. Please show him into the library,' Mary instructed.

She had been advised to hire a manservant by the friends who had been so kind to her when she had originally left home to seek employment – and freedom – in London. A woman in her position needed to have the protection of a male retainer, they had insisted.

'I'm not so sure about giving me protection, but he certainly adds an aura of grandness to the place,' she had laughed to one of her neighbours, Edith Rigby, when she had invited Mary to take tea with her.

'Good afternoon, Mr Dawson,' Mary greeted her visitor as she hurried into the library. 'Will you take tea? You have had a long journey here, I suspect.'

'Tea would be very welcome,' her visitor confirmed, his accent betraying that, unlike Mary herself, he was neither a member of the upper middle class, nor a local. His accent had a distinctly cockney twang to it, which was explained by the fact that Mary had originally recruited him via her contacts in London.

'So,' she sat down behind the huge partners' desk, which had originally been her father's, indicating to the waiting man that he was to take a seat, 'what news do you have for me?'

Her heart sank as she saw the expression on his face.

'I very much regret to have to tell you, Miss Isherwood, that the woman you wanted me to trace – your nurse, I believe you said she was – passed away some time ago. She was predeceased by her husband, and, as you informed me, she was in the employ of Earl Peel of Lancaster.'

'Yes . . . yes . . . I . . . I understand.'

'I have brought you bad news, I can see, and I am sorry for it.'

Mary gave him a wan smile. 'You must think me foolish, Mr Dawson, but Emma was very dear to me. She was my nurse, you see, and my closest companion after the death of my mother. She was less than a dozen years older than I, and had been hired originally as a nursery maid.'

Frank Dawson remained quiet. He had experienced many scenes likes this one in his work as a private investigator, but something about Mary Isherwood's quiet dignity elicited his highest accolade – his rarely given respect.

'Emma was everything to me,' Mary told him simply. 'But then she . . . she had to leave. My father decided that I was old enough not to need her services any longer, and so Emma took employment elsewhere, which was how she met her husband. We kept up a correspondence for a while, until . . . until I quarrelled with my father and . . . and left home to go and live with friends in London.'

'I am sorry if my investigations have brought you

unhappiness.' Frank Dawson gave a small cough. 'There is, of course, the matter of my fees, but –'

'No, no . . . I shall pay you now,' Mary insisted firmly. 'Do you have your account?'

Relieved, Frank Dawson reached into his pocket for the invoice he had written before coming north. It wasn't that he didn't trust Mary, it was just that he knew the way that rich folk could take their time about paying bills.

'Oh . . .' she began, and then checked. 'I had heard that Emma had had a child, Mr Dawson, a son. I don't know if . . . ?' Mary's face had become slightly pink and she sounded a little nervous.

'Oh, yes, I almost forgot,' Frank Dawson responded. 'I was that concerned about telling you that your nurse had passed away that I nearly overlooked the boy. It's all here.' He proudly removed a notebook from his pocket and tapped it with one thick forefinger. 'A son born not a year after they had wed, he was.'

'I see. And what do you know of this son, Mr Dawson, if anything?'

'There is not much to know, ma'am, other than that he visits this town in his line of business. Well, not exactly his line of business, since he was apprenticed to a master cabinet-maker in Lancaster, but it seems that Master Wareing could not find work for the young man, having three sons of his own to take into the business, and so currently by all accounts Mr Gideon Walker is working for William Pride, a cattle drover, whilst he tries his luck at setting himself up in business as a cabinet-maker.'

'A cabinet-maker . . . and he visits Preston regularly, you say? Goodness, you have been thorough and clever, Mr Dawson,' Mary complimented him. 'You wouldn't happen to have an address where I might find him, would you? I may have come into my inheritance too late to do anything to reward Emma for her care of me, but perhaps I shall be able to benefit her son – for her sake and her kindness to me.'

'Very worthy sentiments, if I may be so bold as to say, ma'am. As to the young man's address, I shall do my best to discover it, ma'am, and once I have done so I shall send you a note of it,' Dawson promised.

'You are every bit as efficient as my friends promised, Mr Dawson,' Mary smiled, discreetly adding an extra guinea to the money she was placing on the table in front of her. 'And I am very grateful for what you have done.'

After Frank Dawson had gone, Mary frowned into the silence of the room.

There had been a time when Emma had been everything to her: mother, sister, friend, protector.

The genteel poverty in which Mary had lived during her father's lifetime, scraping a living giving private French lessons, had made it impossible for her to do anything to repay Emma for her care of her as a child, but now things were different.

With so much renovation needing to be done on

the house she could easily find work for a skilled cabinet-maker. And surely she owed it to Emma to do for her son what she could no longer do for Emma herself.

SIX

Newly returned from Lancaster, as always when he walked past the huge bulk of the Hawkins cotton mill on his way to his lodgings, Gideon was struck by its gauntness and the dark, sour shadow it threw across the narrow street. Not for anything would he want to work in such an environment, and he sincerely pitied those who must. As he turned off the main street and in through the ginnel that led to the yard that housed his lodgings, he saw Nancy walking towards him.

'Still seeing that posh lady friend of yours, are you?' she demanded, giving him a bold-eyed look. ''Cos if you ain't . . .'

A meaningful smile accompanied her words, but as she deliberately reached out and touched his bare forearm with her work-roughened hands, Gideon had to stop himself from protesting. Her touch was nothing like Ellie's and it was almost a profanity even to think about his beloved in close proximity to a woman like Nancy.

'Just wanted to thank you, like, for helping us out wi' poor Peggy. Snuffed it, she did, of course. Best thing for her really. She was too far gone to risk what she did. Fair butchered her, that old Jezebel who calls herself a wisewoman did. Better she had had the brat and then left it on the doorstep of the foundling home – or, better still, with its father.' Her face twisted into an ugly bitterness. 'Not that he'd care to acknowledge it, nor what he gets up to wi' lasses who can't afford to say no to him.'

Gideon didn't know what to say. He had guessed what had happened to the girl. William Pride had spoken openly to him about the way some of the mill girls were forced to supplement their small incomes, and their resultant need of the illegal services of the town's notorious 'wisewoman', who for a fee was willing to help terminate their unwanted pregnancies.

'Poor little sods might just as well throw 'emselves int' Ribble!' he had told Gideon wryly. 'At least that way 'ud be quicker and less painful.'

Gideon had kept his own counsel, although he had found what he had been told disturbing.

His landlady approached him as he walked into the house.

'There's a letter for you,' she told him. 'It came a couple of days back. Shall I fetch it?'

Nodding, Gideon tried to conceal his impatience as he waited for her to return. He had made enquiries about a couple of shop premises, and maybe the letter was about one of them.

When his landlady returned with a sealed envelope with his name written elegantly on it, Gideon resisted the temptation to tear it open straight away. She was watching him with open curiosity, but, sidestepping her, Gideon made for the stairs.

Once inside his own room he ripped open the envelope, frowning a little as he read its contents.

Disappointingly, it wasn't about either of the shop premises he had visited. Instead, the letter declared that its writer was aware that he was a skilled cabinet-maker newly come to the town, and that she had some work she wished to discuss with him if he could make himself available at the address given on the letter when he was next in Preston.

Ruefully Gideon reread it. Well, at least he had a potential offer of work, even if he did not have any premises, but he was warily conscious of the work he had done that had still not been paid for. This time he would behave a good deal less naïvely and trustingly when he visited his would-be customer.

He studied the address. Winckley Square. Very posh. What exactly was it that Miss Mary Isherwood wanted him to make, he wondered.

At least he would have some good news to tell Ellie. Whistling cheerfully under his breath, Gideon washed quickly and then put on fresh clothes. The last time he had been in Preston he had promised that he would take Ellie boating on the river. The thought of being with her made his heart lift in anticipation.

*   *   *

'Oh, my poor head. What on earth is that dreadful noise?'

Ellie sighed, trying not to betray either her impatience or her longing for Gideon's promised arrival and her escape from the stuffy, claustrophobic atmosphere of her mother's room and company.

'It is the men who have come to install the new telephone,' she replied as patiently as she could.

Fretfully Lydia Pride pressed her hands to her temples. 'I cannot understand why your father should have been so unthinking as to have them come round now when he knows that I am suffering from a bad headache.'

Ellie said nothing. The truth was that her mother had been suffering from 'a bad headache' and an even worse temper on and off now for weeks, and Ellie couldn't help fidgeting a little and glancing longingly towards the window through which the late spring sunshine was shining in intoxicating temptation.

'You must go and tell them to stop, Ellie,' Lydia announced. 'I really cannot stand any more of this noise. And whilst you are downstairs, tell Cook to prepare me a tisane. It might soothe my poor aching head. No, you had better make it yourself, Ellie, I am sure that Cook did not use newly boiled water yesterday when she made me one. It had a distinctly sour taste, and she had used far too much ginger!'

The taste of her mother's tisane could not be any sourer than the air in this room, Ellie decided rebelliously, and certainly nowhere near as sour as her mother's mood. Ellie scarcely recognised her gentle, laughing mother in the cross shrew she had turned into these last few weeks.

'The men are almost finished,' she tried to placate her.

'But why could they not wait a little?'

'Mother, you were the one who insisted that Father had a telephone installed as soon as he could, remember?' Ellie couldn't prevent herself from challenging. 'You said that if all your sisters had telephones then you must have one too. You said that Father would find that it increased his business,' Ellie pressed on, ignoring the protective little voice inside herself that was urging her to remember that her mother was not well, and that the pregnancy must be making her feel uncomfortable. Ellie couldn't wait for the next few weeks to be over. In fact, she decided crossly, she wished her mother would have the baby now and then perhaps the Pride household might get back to normal!

'Ellie, I wish you would not speak to me in such a way,' Lydia responded sharply. 'Did you tell Jenny about the sheets, like I asked you to? They must be sent straight back to the laundry, and no bill paid until they are returned properly laundered – and whilst we are on the subject, you must take care to watch what Jenny is doing on washdays. She cannot be left alone in the wash

85

house with the copper. If she is she will skimp on her duties!'

Ellie bit on her bottom lip. Gideon would be here soon. He had promised her that he would make all speed to come round to Friargate the moment he arrived in Preston, and her uncle had already been round to the shop to try to persuade her father to join him in one of his favourite drinking haunts.

Gideon! Ellie was longing to see him again. Would he kiss her as he had done before? A delicious sense of anticipation was filling her, increasing her impatience with her mother.

'Ellie! Pay attention! You are not listening to me! Jenny –'

'I'm sorry about the washing, Mother, but you said that the things for your lying-in had to be prepared, and because of the rain it took longer to get everything dried.'

'You must not make excuses for her, Ellie. Like all domestics Jenny will try to take advantage, if you let her – Ellie, why do you keep looking towards the window?'

'It is nothing, Mother, only that Gideon Walker has promised to take us all boating on the river. John is so excited, and –'

'Gideon Walker?' Lydia interrupted her sharply, struggling to control the surge of fear and hostility that drove the dull ache in her temples into a hammering crescendo of pain. Just recently she had begun to sense a change in Ellie, a new wilful stubbornness that reminded her all too painfully of the way she herself had been at the same age. 'Ellie, I need you here with me. You know that I am not well.'

'You said that you wanted to be left alone to sleep,' Ellie reminded her mother, aching with impatience to be gone. 'And besides, I have already promised John that we are to go on the river. Father said it would do us all good to get out in the fresh air,' she could not restrain herself from adding.

'Ellie, I do not want you to go. I want you to stay here with me,' Lydia stopped her angrily as she turned to the door.

Ellie stared at her mother. 'But . . . but why?' she demanded. She could feel the whole of her stomach cramping in anger and disbelief. Hadn't she done everything she could to make her mother comfortable, and to do as she was bidden these last difficult weeks? 'You are just being mean because you are cross, and –'

'Ellie, how dare you speak to me like that?' Lydia demanded angrily. 'And as for you going anywhere with Gideon Walker, I absolutely forbid you do so!'

Ellie could not believe that this was her gentle, loving mother speaking to her so.

'No,' she denied fiercely, 'no, I won't stay. I won't!' Tears of confusion filled her eyes as she heard the rebellion in her own voice, and her legs trembled a little at her defiance, but that didn't stop her from hurrying towards the door and wrenching it open.

Lydia watched Ellie leave in shocked disbelief. Had she behaved in such a way as a girl her mother would have had her whipped! Of course, Lydia knew exactly who to blame for her daughter's behaviour. Gideon Walker!

What had happened to the mother she loved, Ellie wondered angrily, distressed flags of red flying in her cheeks as she hurried downstairs. For weeks now Ellie had dutifully acted as a go-between for her mother, conveying her increasingly demanding instructions to Annie and Jenny, and doing all she could to appease both of them as well as her mother. If anyone should have a headache, she decided rebelliously, it should be her.

Not that she was the only one to suffer from her mother's suddenly sharp tongue. Only the previous day, Lydia had shocked them all when, at supper time, she had been discussing Cecily's wedding.

'It will be a very grand affair,' she had announced. 'My sister says that Cecily's fiancé's family are very well connected, and can trace their ancestors back to the reign of our late queen's grandfather!'

'Well, that is nothing,' John had boasted immediately. 'There were Prides keeping a butcher's shop in the Shambles for hundreds and hundreds of years, weren't there, Dad, before they were knocked down to make way for the new Harris Museum?'

'John, I wish you would not mention such a place

as the Shambles!' Lydia had complained sharply. 'And as for boasting about your father's family's connection with it, I would have thought I had taught you better.'

There had been a small uncomfortable silence whilst the siblings had looked at one another, and then their father had said quietly, 'I seem to remember, Lydia, that when we first met you liked to hear stories about the origins of my family and the business.'

When Ellie had glanced across the table at her father she had seen a look in his eyes, a sadness that had made her heart ache.

And then he had got up and had left the table without finishing his supper, and her mother had sent John to bed.

But now, as she hurried downstairs, Ellie could hear John calling out excitedly, 'Gideon's here!'

Her heart was beating so fast she felt giddy. And even in the darkness of the narrow passageway Ellie felt as though she could feel the warmth and brilliance of the sun.

'What on earth is happening?'

Ellie felt her whole body quiver at the sound of Gideon's voice from across the small room at the back of the shop, where he was standing, with John and Connie both trying to out-do one another to engage his attention. At the same time, the dog, Rex, was barking his head off, as eager for Gideon's acknowledgement of his presence as the others.

Ellie's shy gaze met Gideon's much bolder one. For a few seconds her feelings were so intense that it was impossible for her to answer his question, and even more impossible for her to tear her gaze from his.

'The noise?' Gideon prompted her, and Ellie shook her head, laughing, as Gideon waved in the direction of the workmen.

'They are installing one of the new telephones,' she informed Gideon.

Immediately, John chimed in, 'Yes, and we went to the telephone company's offices and saw how they worked, and they told Ellie that she could have a job working in the telephone exchange any time she wished.'

'Did they indeed!' Gideon marvelled, but it was the look in his eyes as his gaze met Ellie's over the head of her younger brother that made her colour up so prettily, her argument with her mother already almost forgotten. Almost, but not quite.

'Gideon, if you don't mind I should like to call at Miller's Arcade on our way back later. I want to buy some sweets for my mother. And there is a shop there that sells her favourite ginger pieces dipped in chocolate.'

As Gideon inclined his head, Robert Pride gave his elder daughter a pleased look. He was aware of just how much responsibility had been placed on Ellie's shoulders recently, and just how much more there would be if things went wrong with the coming child's birth, as had been so gravely forecast.

Sombrely he waited until the chattering quartet had moved out into the street, before giving his assistant instructions to mind the shop and hurrying up into the house.

Lydia looked up expectantly as the bedroom door opened. Ellie had obviously realised how badly she had behaved and had come back to beg her forgiveness. Mentally Lydia rehearsed what she intended to say to her erring daughter, but to her irritation it was her husband who was coming into the room.

'Where is Ellie?' she demanded peremptorily as Robert closed the door behind him.

'She has gone off to the river with Gideon and the children.'

'And you permitted her to go?' Lydia's mouth thinned. 'I wish you would not encourage that young man to believe himself welcome here, Robert.'

'But he *is* welcome,' Robert told her easily. 'He is a hard-working lad, and –'

'He has no prospects! No family! Can you imagine what my sisters will think if Ellie should be foolish enough to walk out publicly with him?'

'Your sisters?' Robert's genial expression gave way to one of anger.

'Robert, listen to me,' Lydia stopped him. 'If

anything should . . . should happen to me, I want your promise that Ellie will not throw herself away over someone like Gideon Walker. She is worthy of so much better. Surely you can see that?'

'Lyddy, nothing is going to happen to you,' Robert tried to reassure her, going over to stand behind the chair on which she was seated, placing his hands tenderly on her tense shoulders. 'Even that old woman your brother-in-law has admitted that he does not know . . .'

'That he does not know what?' Lydia demanded tearfully. 'That I shall die in childbed? Why didn't I listen to my own mother? Why didn't I realise how much wiser she was than I, and that she was only speaking in my own best interests when she tried to dissuade me from marrying you? It is easy enough for you to speak, Robert! You should have taken more care,' she told him bitterly.

Behind her Robert's face went white. He already knew that Lydia blamed him totally for her pregnancy and he had been too concerned for her to want to remind her that she had been the one to urge him on.

He ached to hold her in his arms and tell her how much he loved her, how afraid he was for her, and for himself, but he knew already that she would reject him and pull away from him. From the moment she had known she was pregnant she had erected a barrier between them, turning for consolation and comfort more and more to her sisters, especially her eldest sister in Winckley

Square, and increasingly excluding him from her life.

It hurt him unbearably to know not only that she blamed him for her plight but also that she felt so contemptuous towards him, so angrily resentful, that she now allowed the love she had originally felt for him to be deemed secondary to her mother's wishes.

'I cannot bear to think that Ellie might make the same mistake that I did, Robert. You must promise me that you will not allow her to do so! Promise me!' Lydia insisted, her voice rising with emotion. 'You owe it to me and to Ellie to do so!'

Robert hesitated. 'Lydia,' he began gently, 'you are overwrought and upset –'

'Why won't you listen to me? I intend to forbid Ellie to ever see Gideon Walker again, and you must do the same, Robert. Promise me!'

'Lyddy . . .' Robert tried to soothe her.

'Promise me!'

Shaking his head, unable either to calm her or accede to what she was demanding, Robert stepped back from the chair.

Immediately Lydia got up and turned to confront him. 'I want your promise, Robert,' she began, and then stopped, giving a sharp gasp and clutching her body.

'Lydia, what is it?' Robert demanded.

Lydia shook her head. 'Nothing,' she denied stubbornly, but the sickly pallor of her face betrayed her.

The truth was that she had been having slow

labour pains for several hours, but she had stubbornly refused to acknowledge them, suffering in an increasingly terrified silence as she fought against them and against what lay ahead.

'The baby?' Robert guessed immediately. 'Lydia, come and lie down. Shall I send for the midwife?'

'No, not yet,' she gasped, as a fierce pang of pain gripped her. 'Send to Winckley Square, though, Robert, for my sister . . .'

As the pains rose and fell, searing her, savaging her, she was dimly aware of Robert opening the door and calling for Jenny.

'Sit here with your mistress, and don't leave her,' she heard him telling the maid tersely. 'I am gone to Winckley Square for her sister.'

'I don't want today to ever end,' Connie declared passionately, pouting as Gideon began to steer their hired boat back to Mr John Crook's premises on Ribbleside.

'Neither do I,' Gideon murmured to Ellie, the soft warmth of his breath tickling her ear and sending a rush of sweet pleasure through her.

Whether by accident or design, Gideon had managed things so that both John and Connie were seated facing away from them in the boat, leaving Gideon free to indulge in all manner of lover's secret looks and whispered words to Ellie without her younger siblings knowing.

Only Rex the dog had threatened to spoil things,

by suddenly jumping into the river to swim after a duck, and then having to be hauled back in to the boat again, whereupon he had shaken himself, covering them all in Ribble water. But even that incident Gideon had managed to turn to his own advantage, solicitously offering Ellie his brand-new handkerchief to dry off her dampened gown and arms.

'I shall keep this for ever,' he had whispered passionately to her when she had handed it back to him, causing her eyes to sparkle with the feelings she couldn't manage to hide.

'We must not forget to call at Miller's Arcade for Mother's sweets,' she reminded Gideon now as they reached the shore.

'No indeed, and I must not forget that I have some special news to share with you,' Gideon responded.

'You have found a shop?' Ellie demanded excitedly. 'Oh, Gideon . . .'

'No, not that, I'm afraid, although I hope that I soon shall do so, especially now that I may be about to receive a new commission.'

'A commission?'

'Yes. There was a note waiting for me at my lodgings from a Miss Isherwood of Winckley Square. She has requested me to call on her so that she may discuss her requirements regarding some work.'

'Miss Isherwood?' Ellie frowned. 'Oh, but she –'

'You know her?' Gideon was frowning himself now as he saw the discomfort on Ellie's face.

'Well, I do not exactly know her, no, but I know of her. My mother and my aunt were talking about her some weeks ago. She has recently returned to the town to take up her inheritance.'

'And that causes you to frown?' Gideon teased her.

'No, of course not! It is just that my aunt said that . . . that Miss Isherwood – well, it seems that she quarrelled with her late father and then left home to go and live in London. Very little is known about what she did when she lived there.'

'A mystery! I shall have to do my best to unravel it for you,' Gideon laughed.

'I wonder how she comes to know of you?' Ellie mused.

'I don't know. Her note simply asked me to call.' Gideon shrugged. 'I dare say I shall know more once I have spoken with her. Perhaps someone recommended me to her. If so, I hope it was not the railway magnate who cheated me out of my fee.' He paused and looked at her before revealing diffidently, 'Had it been possible I should have liked to have studied to become an architect.'

He waited tensely for Ellie's reaction. If she were to laugh and deride him for being foolish enough to have cherished such an impossible ambition he knew it would damage for ever that secret vulnerable part of himself he had learned to hide away from others.

'An architect!' Ellie's eyes rounded in awe. 'Oh Gideon!'

'It's not possible, of course. But, oh, Ellie, if it had been I would have built such buildings, and the most wonderful of all of them would have been the house I would have built for you.'

The passion in his voice sent a quiver of fiercely protective emotion shivering through Ellie, the brilliance of her eyes and the tenderness of her expression revealing to him what she was feeling.

'I am just a foolish man with even more foolish dreams,' Gideon mocked himself.

'No, you are anything but foolish,' Ellie told him sturdily, 'and as for your dreams –'

'Ah, but I have another dream now,' Gideon whispered softly to her, looking deep into her eyes. 'You are my dream now, Ellie. You and the future I hope we shall share together.'

'As you are mine,' Ellie responded shyly.

'I shall be a good husband to you, Ellie. I shall work hard for you. A cabinet-maker may not be as grand as an architect, but he can still make a good living for himself. There is wealth in Preston,' he told her enthusiastically, 'and I aim to make sure that my name gets known in all the right quarters, and that I am the first choice of those wealthy residents looking for the best craftsman. And I shall be the best, Ellie.'

Just listening to him made Ellie's heart swell with love and excitement, and a sharp sweet longing for the future he was drawing for her.

They had reached land, and Gideon busied himself helping his charges out of the boat, deliberately making sure that he placed the two younger ones, and the wretched Rex, on dry land first.

'No, Gideon!' Ellie protested breathlessly when he finally turned to take hold of her carefully, swinging her into his arms. 'I can manage. You do not need . . .'

'Oh, but I do need. Have you any idea just how much I want to kiss you, Ellie Pride?' he demanded huskily.

His lips were only inches from hers and Ellie couldn't stop herself from looking betrayingly at his mouth, her own lips parting slightly, her pretty pink tongue unknowingly revealing her feelings as she touched it against them.

She heard Gideon make a strangled sound, and saw his eyes darken, his grip on her tightening as he lowered her slightly.

'Ellie . . . Ellie . . . I want you so much!'

Ellie shuddered excitedly at the passionate words.

'If only I had you to myself right now . . .' Gideon continued.

Silently they looked at one another in mutual longing, their rapt concentration broken only when John, tired of waiting for them, called out to them to hurry up.

With Connie, John and Rex walking ahead of them, Gideon surreptitiously took Ellie's hand in his own. Flush-cheeked, Ellie looked at him, but made no attempt to pull away.

'John! Connie!'

Ellie jumped a little as Gideon called her brother and sister. As they turned round and came over, Gideon released Ellie's hand.

'Ellie is feeling rather tired, so if I give you a penny each, can you run to Miller's Arcade and buy some chocolate-covered ginger for your mother, and, of course, a treat each for yourselves? We will meet you back at Friargate.'

'Gideon, you should not have done that,' Ellie reproached him, as John and Connie sped off, clutching their money.

'Perhaps not,' Gideon agreed, 'but they will come to no harm, and it was the only way I could think of to get you to myself.'

Very gently he led her towards a secluded part of the shrubbery, and then took her into his arms.

Helplessly Ellie allowed him to do so, blindly raising her face to his, her eyes closing, her body quivering with excitement and longing.

'Ellie, Ellie . . . you are the most beautiful girl in the world. I think I fell in love with you the moment I saw you.'

'Fell in love with me?' Ellie managed to challenge him breathlessly. 'You certainly looked at me very boldly.'

'Boldly?' Gideon laughed. 'Is that what you thought? No, I felt anything but bold when I looked up at your window and saw you standing there, Ellie.'

'So what did you feel?' Like any woman newly

and deeply in love she wanted to possess herself of every single small detail of her lover's reaction to her.

'I felt . . .' Gideon paused, looking away from her, his eyes narrowed against the sun, 'I felt that I had met my fate. I looked at you, Ellie, and I knew that my life could never be the same again. That I could never be the same again. That that one single look had changed everything. I love you, Ellie.'

In between each passionate word Gideon paused to kiss her, each kiss taking them both a little further away from the calm waters of sedate courtship and into the much deeper and dangerous ones of intense desire.

Protected from prying eyes by the shrubbery, Ellie pressed ever closer to Gideon, shuddering fiercely when she felt the tentative touch of his hand on her breast. She could feel the heat of his hand right through the fine fabric of her summer dress.

'Ellie . . .'

A thrill of female satisfaction shocked through her when she heard the taut male agony in Gideon's voice. The kisses he pressed on the soft skin of her throat, and then along the neckline of her dress, set off a fierce ache deep down inside her body.

'I want you, Ellie! I want you now!' Gideon muttered as he started to push the neckline of her dress out of the way.

The feel of his hand against her almost bare breast made Ellie cry out in awed pleasure. But instead of encouraging him to press her to further intimacy, her helpless sound of arousal made Gideon tense and then gently put her away from him, reminding himself that it was his duty to protect and be responsible for them both, even though that meant denying himself. She was his love, his life, his Ellie. *His!*

'Come on. It's time I took you home,' he told her huskily, 'before I truly forget myself.'

SEVEN

The minute they turned into Friargate and Ellie saw her brother and sister standing huddled together outside the closed shop door, she knew that something was wrong. Anxiously she started to walk faster.

'Ellie, you've been ages . . .' Connie's face started to crumple, and she suddenly looked much more like a young girl than the young woman she was always claiming herself to be.

'What is it? What?' Ellie began, and then stopped as the door opened and her aunt stood there eyeing her coldly.

'So you have finally returned, have you, you wretched creature?' Aunt Gibson hissed bitterly. 'Do you know what your disobedience has done to your mother?'

Horrified, Ellie looked past her aunt towards her father.

'That's enough, Amelia,' he said quietly. 'It's not fair to blame Ellie. She –'

'Not fair?' Amelia gave Ellie an angry look. 'Is it fair, Robert Pride, that my poor sister should go into labour ahead of her time because her daughter defied her?'

'No!' Ellie protested. What her aunt was saying couldn't be true. It mustn't be. She started to tremble, cold now where just a few minutes earlier she had been sweetly warm with the intoxicating memory of the illicit pleasure she and Gideon had just shared, delighting in the precious secret world of their love.

'Yes!' Amelia insisted sharply. 'You are a wicked, wicked girl, Ellie Pride, and if your poor mother and this baby die, then it will be on your conscience.'

'Amelia, that's enough,' Ellie's father said sternly. 'I know how upset you are, but if anyone's to blame for this . . .'

Her mother die? What on earth was her aunt saying? Frantically Ellie looked towards the stairs.

'Ellie, no!' Robert Pride blocked her path. Grasping her arms, he told her in a gentler voice, 'No, you cannot go up there right now. The midwife is with your mother, and . . . and your Uncle Alfred.'

'So it is true,' Ellie whispered, her eyes huge with distress and despair. 'The baby is coming.'

'Yes.'

Glancing past her Robert could see through the still-open door that Gideon had quick-wittedly drawn the two younger children out of earshot and was entertaining them with one of his tricks.

Releasing Ellie, Robert strode out to them, closing the door behind him.

'Gideon, lad, I wonder if you would be kind enough to take our Connie and John over to Winckley Square? They are to stay there until . . . for the time being.'

'What? Why have we got to go there?' John demanded indignantly.

'Is Mother really having the baby?' Connie asked excitedly.

'Aye, lass, she is,' Robert confirmed. 'Now be good children and go with Gideon. Your aunt has sent instructions home that beds are to be prepared for you.'

'Well, I hope Mother doesn't take too long to have this baby,' John grumbled. 'I don't like it at Winckley Square. You have to be quiet all the time and not touch things.'

Awkwardly Robert patted his shoulder, but his concentration wasn't really on his two younger children.

As Gideon ushered them away, Robert glanced up at the closed bedroom window above, his face tight with anxiety and despair.

In the hallway, Ellie was pleading tearfully with her aunt to be allowed to see her mother.

'Certainly not, miss. It would not be at all proper, and besides –'

Amelia broke off as they both heard the long tortured cry of primeval pain that came from the room above them. Then Ellie pulled free of her aunt and raced up the stairs, pushing open her parents' bedroom door.

A strong smell of carbolic filled her nostrils, making her catch her breath. The room was hot and lacking in fresh air.

Her mother was lying in bed, her hands gripping the bars of the brass bedstead, her teeth clenched over the twisted piece of cloth in her mouth, her head twisting from side to side as she tried to escape the pain tearing at her.

Ellie froze in shock. Surely this was not her fastidious, elegant mother, this woman who bared her teeth in a feral grimace before uttering a low panting animal grunt of mingled pain and endeavour?

Sweat caked her mother's hair, which clung stickily to her face. As another wave of pain struck, she began to pant, her fingers gripping the arm of the midwife.

Was this what giving birth was? This primitive agony that filled the air with sights, sounds, scents from which Ellie recoiled, shocked by their visceral rawness.

But beneath her shock there was still her love for her mother; and her guilt. She was responsible for this, for her mother's agonisingly hard labour; that was what her aunt had told her. She, by arguing and quarrelling with her mother and going against her wishes, had somehow brought on the arrival of the baby before its due date.

Unable to think logically, Ellie was filled with fear and remorse. She took a step towards the bed, barely aware of her aunt grabbing her arm to pull her back as her mother went rigid, beads of sweat glistening waxenly on her forehead as she began to moan.

'Get that girl out of here. She has no business being here,' Uncle Gibson demanded curtly, no longer the familiar, slightly pedantic figure Ellie knew, but a grim-faced stranger, whose presence cast a dark shadow over the bed.

As her aunt pushed her towards the door, Ellie suddenly tensed and turned round to look imploringly towards her mother, mentally begging her for forgiveness.

'I'm so sorry, Mama,' she whispered, adopting the baby form of address she had long ago grown out of. 'I promise I will never ever disobey you again . . . never.'

As Ellie looked at her it seemed to her that her mother had changed; that her skin had somehow gone grey, her eyes become sunken. Instinctively Ellie wanted to go to her, but then suddenly Lydia's whole body convulsed and she started to scream.

Ellie only realised that *she* was screaming as well when her aunt slapped her face briskly the moment she had her outside the bedroom door.

'It is your mother who is in travail, you stupid girl,' she told Ellie bitingly, 'not you.'

Ellie couldn't make any response. She was shivering, her teeth chattering. She desperately wanted to beg her aunt to reassure her that having a child was not always like this – that her mother's agonising pain would never be her own. How could her aunt not be as shocked and appalled as she was herself? How could her uncle not do something to alleviate her mother's agony? How could her father have allowed this to happen?

How could *she* have so cruelly and heedlessly disobeyed her mother?

All through the warm May evening it went on, until Ellie did not know which was the worst to bear – her mother's screams or the oppressive silences between them when she kept her own body as still as she could in the emptiness of the parlour, listening, waiting . . . doing her self-imposed penance for her sin of disobeying her mother.

Her father had gone out, unable to endure the sound of his wife's agonising distress; her aunt was still upstairs, assisting her husband and the midwife.

Ellie tensed as suddenly a thin, high scream split the thick silence, followed by the sharp mewling cry of a newborn child.

Picking up her skirts, she ran up the stairs, but before she could enter the room her aunt came out, firmly closing the door behind her and barring Ellie's way as she gripped hold of her.

'I want to see my mother,' Ellie begged frantically.

Refusing to let go of her, her aunt dug her fingers painfully into Ellie's arm.

'No. You cannot. Your mother has given birth to a son. You have a new brother,' her aunt told her tonelessly. 'She is resting now and must not be disturbed.'

'Resting!' Ellie sagged against the banister in relief, closing her eyes as hot tears of release burned onto her skin, too innocent to recognise just what the grim, flat defeatedness in her aunt's voice really meant. Her mother was alive!

Below, the front door opened and her father came hurrying up the stairs, bringing with him the smell of strong ale.

Amelia recoiled in distaste and shot him a bitterly contemptuous look.

'Lyddy?' he demanded thickly.

'You have another son,' Amelia told him curtly.

'Mam is resting, Father,' Ellie told him softly. 'They are both all right.'

As she brushed away her tears, Ellie missed the looks her father and her aunt exchanged, her father's questioning and anxious, her aunt's grim and negative. When she looked up Ellie saw the dark tinge of colour burning her father's face as he turned away from her aunt, and puzzled over it. Surely now that her mother had been safely delivered and both she and the new baby were alive, there was no need for her aunt to continue to be so angry.

Ellie ached to ask if she might see her mother but her uncle and the midwife were still in the bedroom with her, and Ellie gave the closed door a helpless stare before accompanying her aunt downstairs.

'It will be better if Connie and John stay at Winckley Square until . . . for now,' Ellie's aunt said as she paused in front of the hall mirror to pin on her hat.

Aunt Amelia looked as though she had been crying, Ellie suddenly recognised, as she inclined her cheek for Ellie to kiss before opening the front door.

It was a soft late spring night, with the sky full of stars. A lovers' night. Shame and guilt filled Ellie. She longed to be able to see her mother and to beg her forgiveness; to promise her once more that she would never disobey her again! She felt sick and shaky, overwhelmed with love for her mother, and overwhelmed too by her own intense remorse. Her guilt would be branded into her for ever, Ellie told herself.

Robert Pride looked down into the sunken face of his wife. Tears filled his eyes and his shoulders began to shake. Carefully he reached for her hand, hardly daring to touch it. She looked so fragile. So frail!

'Robert?'

He tensed at the thin, whispery sound of her voice. She had opened her eyes, and even they looked different somehow: opaque, almost devoid of their normal rich colour.

'Lyddy, don't try to talk. You have to rest.' His voice broke as he tried to control his emotion. Curling her cold hand into his own he lifted it to his lips, kissing her icy fingers, as though he was trying to breathe warmth – and life – into them.

'She cannot survive, Robert,' Alfred had told him after the midwife had finished her business and left them on their own.

'But she is alive,' Robert had protested, 'and the birth is over.'

'The child has been born, but Lydia is . . .' Alfred had coughed, plainly uncomfortable discussing something so intimate. 'But there was . . . she . . . she is bleeding badly, Robert, and we cannot stem it. I had feared that this would be the outcome of her pregnancy.'

'Bleeding? But surely you can do something to stop it.' It was inconceivable to Robert that, having survived the appalling agony of the birth of their child, Lydia should not be safe.

'We have done all that we can,' Alfred had told him heavily. 'The midwife and I have raised the foot of the bed and done everything we can do to stanch the flow, but I'm afraid . . .'

As he spoke, Robert's stomach had lurched. He had been vaguely aware of the midwife removing a pile of soiled bed linen, but he had not understood just what it meant.

'I did warn you that this could happen,' Alfred had reminded him sternly. 'There was a similar problem with her previous birth, but then the

110

child was not full term, and small. I must go now. There is nothing more I can do here. You must keep her quiet and still. The less she moves . . .' He had shaken his head. 'I'm afraid that it is only a matter of time, Robert. I shall return in the morning, but if . . . if you need me in the meantime . . .' Awkwardly, he had patted Robert's shoulder, sighing as he added, 'I am afraid that Amelia is taking this very badly. Lyddy was . . . is her favourite sister and she feels . . .'

Numbly, Robert had let him go.

'Robert, I want to see Ellie. Where is she?' As she spoke Lydia was struggling to sit up.

Panic-stricken, Robert urged her to lie down. Beneath the covers she was swaddled in old sheets, wrapped around her to soak up the life draining from her.

'Ellie . . .' Lydia demanded weakly.

'I shall bring her to you,' Robert promised her. 'Only lie still, my beloved. Please.'

'Mother wants to see me?'

It hurt Robert unbearably to see the relief and happiness brightening Ellie's pale face.

'Oh, then she is getting better!' Eagerly she followed him upstairs, pushing open the bedroom door and hurrying to her mother's side.

The strong smell of carbolic still hung on the air but now it was overwhelmed by another smell, one that Robert recognised, but that he prayed both his wife and his daughter could not. How many times in the slaughterhouse had he breathed in that scent of hot blood? His throat closed and surreptitiously he wiped his hand over his eyes.

Briefly, Ellie glanced at the baby as she sat down beside her mother.

Robert followed the direction of her glance. The child at least was healthy in spite of its early arrival – a six-pound boy with a strong pair of lungs.

As he looked towards Lydia, Robert thought he could already detect signs of death in her still features. Ellie, though, thank goodness, was oblivious to her mother's real condition as she bent her head to kiss her tenderly.

'Oh, Mama, Mama, I am so sorry that I made you angry,' she whispered. 'Please, please, say that you forgive me!'

Quietly, Robert left the bedroom.

'Ellie . . . please listen to me . . .'

Tiredly, Lydia closed her eyes and fought to summon what was left of her strength. There was none of the familiar ache she had experienced after her previous live births, none of the deep but satisfying exhaustion that told of hard labour well done; none of the cleansing sense of freedom and euphoria; of maternal joy, only a deep numbing coldness that seemed to seep up her body in a slow tide that could not be escaped. She didn't need to see the tears of her husband, or the anguish of her sister, to know what was happening to her. She had known it from the moment she had felt that dreadful tearing pain, which had seemed to wrench not only the child from her, but her very womb as well. Time was running out for her, and she doubted that she would see another dawn, which made it all the more imperative that she spoke with Ellie.

'I am listening, Mama,' Ellie told her emotionally.

'Ellie, I want you to promise me never to see Gideon Walker again. I ask you for this promise not because I want you to suffer but because I want to protect you. My mother pleaded with me not to marry your father, but I would not listen. I believed that I knew better than she, and now look what has become of me. Your father is a good man and I would not have anyone say any other, but . . . but none of your aunts, my sisters, would ever find themselves in the situation that I am in. Men like your father and Gideon Walker, they . . .' Weakly, she closed her eyes. How could she explain to Ellie the terrible price that women had to pay to appease the hungry sexuality of such men?

'Your aunts, my sisters, know my wishes, Ellie . . . and my hopes for you and your sister. I want you to promise me that you will obey them in all things, and that you will remember that they are carrying out my wishes. I cannot bear to think that you may meet a fate like mine, Ellie . . . Promise me, Ellie . . .'

Ellie started to cry, too overwrought to question logically what was happening, knowing only that right now her love for her mother took priority over everything and everyone else in her life.

'Mama, please,' she choked. 'I will promise you whatever you want, if only you will forgive me . . .'

'You will put Gideon Walker completely out of your life and your thoughts, and you will be guided by your aunts in all things, do you promise?'

'I promise, Mama,' Ellie sobbed.

'Good. I want you to remember always that you have made me this promise, Ellie. To remember it and to honour it, because . . .'

Her mother's voice had become so faint that Ellie could barely hear it, and then suddenly she stopped speaking, her head falling to one side on the pillow.

As she clung to her mother's icy cold hand, Ellie could hear her breath rattling in her throat.

'Oh, Mam, Mam, please, please get well,' she begged heartbrokenly, reverting to the comforting softness of the town's dialect as she clung to her hand.

Lydia's eyes were closing. 'Always remember and honour your promise to me, Ellie.'

The words were so low, little more than a sigh, that Ellie had to bend her head closer to her to hear them.

She saw her mother's chest expand once as she breathed in – sharply – and then went still, her eyes suddenly opening, focusing not on Ellie but into the distance.

Panic suddenly filled Ellie. Releasing her mother's hand she ran to the door and opened it, calling frantically for her father, as Lydia's final breath bubbled in her throat.

EIGHT

Gideon paused as he turned into Friargate. Theoretically he was on his way to see Mary Isherwood, having telephoned to make an appointment, but naturally he wanted to call in at the Prides' house to see how things were. And, of course, to see Ellie!

For once there was no busyness outside the shop, no carefully protected display of choice hams and salted beefs. The door was firmly closed, and there was no sign of either life or light inside, and then as Gideon glanced along the street he saw the sombre black ribbon attached to the front door knocker – a sign that the family was in mourning.

Had the child not survived? Reluctant to intrude, Gideon started to turn away, but as he did so the door suddenly opened and a buxom woman dressed in black emerged, accompanied by a white-faced Ellie, her hair escaping from its pins to curl softly round a face so riven with grief that Gideon caught his breath in anguish for her. The bleakness of

Ellie's expression didn't belong to the girl he had held and kissed only the previous day.

'Thank you, Mrs Jakes,' Gideon heard her saying. 'I'm sorry that my father isn't here, but –'

'Aye, that's menfolk for you. First thing they do is turn to drink when they're in grief. Never met one of them yet who could stomach a laying-out. 'T'ain't natural for 'em, you see. Tell your aunt that I've done the best I can. Allus close to your mother, she was. She'll be sadly missed, will your ma, especially with a new baby to be cared for.'

'My Aunt Jepson is to take care of the baby,' Ellie said in a low, unsteady voice. 'My mother left instructions for . . . for everything. She was afraid that –'

Unable to bear seeing her in so much distress, Gideon stepped forward, causing the departing midwife, who had come to lay out Lydia's body, to give him a speculative look. Gossip was as much her stock in trade as births and deaths, and it seemed that the Pride household had very generously supplied her with all three. Whoever the young man was in such a rush to get to Ellie Pride, he was certainly a good-looking 'un, that was for sure.

'Ellie! What –'

'Gideon!' Ellie stepped back from him immediately, holding up her hands in a gesture of denial, but Gideon had already followed her into the hallway and was closing the door behind him.

'I saw the black ribbon,' he told her, 'but I

thought it must be the child. I had no idea . . . My poor little love. Believe me, I do know how you must be feeling. When I lost my own mother . . . But it will get better, Ellie, I promise you, and you have me and . . .'

Ellie froze. How could Gideon claim to know what she was feeling? How could he say that he understood? No one understood! No one knew what misery and guilt she felt, what pain!

As he saw the emotions chasing one another across her face, Gideon's smile changed to a concerned frown. Swiftly he crossed the distance separating them, taking hold gently of her upper arms.

'Ellie, Ellie, my love, please do not look so,' he begged her, unable to keep his feelings out of either his voice or his eyes. 'What is it?' he demanded when he felt her stiffening against his hold.

'Let go of me, Gideon,' Ellie demanded sharply. The icy tone of her voice was her mother's and as she heard her own words and recognised it, Ellie drew strength from what she felt must be her dead mother's support and approval. Haughtily she drew herself up tall and looked into Gideon's eyes.

'Ellie, sweetheart, don't look like that,' he protested. Had she wept he would have known immediately what to do, but this icy stiffness bewildered him. 'Come here,' he commanded gently. 'Let me hold you and –'

'No!'

The fury in Ellie's eyes as she pulled away from him shocked Gideon into silence.

'Don't touch me!' Ellie told him. 'Don't come anywhere near me! I don't want to see you ever again, Gideon. Ever!'

White-faced, she looked dispassionately at him. Why was he still standing there? Hadn't she told him to go? The icy coldness surrounding her had somehow become a form of welcome protection, and she withdrew herself even deeper into its glacial grip. Here, within it, away from anyone else, she could truly make reparation to her mother for her guilt.

'I promised my mother that I will never see you again, Gideon. And I intend to keep that promise!' she announced.

Gideon stared at her, unable to take in what she was saying. Disbelief, anger, and then pain – oh, such a pain – held him silent! When at last he was able to speak, his voice was raw with emotion.

'No! You cannot mean that! What are you saying? I understand how shocked and upset you must be, but your mother had no right –' he began unwisely, carried away by his feelings of outrage.

Ellie stopped him. 'I will not stand here and let you abuse my mother. My Aunt Gibson is right! If my mother had not stepped out of her class to marry my father she would still be alive now.'

As he listened to her increasingly hysterical outpouring, Gideon's compassion and concern started to change to resentment and anger – not against Ellie, but against her mother.

'You have no way of knowing that,' he told Ellie brusquely, adding curtly, 'And as for the rest – I

119

knew that your mother was a snob, Ellie, and that she was encouraged by her sisters to believe she should not have married your father – your Uncle William has told me as much – but I never thought that you would be foolish enough to allow yourself to become tainted by the same brush.'

'How dare you say that?' Ellie rounded on him furiously. 'How dare you even so much as speak of my mother?'

An ugly silence fell between them.

Ellie's outburst had touched a raw spot on Gideon's pride. Did she seriously believe that he wasn't good enough for her? Had she believed that all along?

Gideon couldn't bring himself to speak. If he did not go soon he would be late for his appointment with Mary Isherwood.

'Ellie . . .' he pleaded eventually, lowering his pride for the sake of their love, but immediately Ellie stepped away from him.

'I promised my mother,' she reminded him stiffly.

'Ellie, Ellie, I understand that right now you are overwrought and upset, but I can't believe you mean this. A deathbed promise! You can't mean to destroy our love, our lives, the dreams we have begun to share, because of that. Your mother had no right!' he exploded again, when he saw the stubborn look on her face.

'I gave her my word,' Ellie told him woodenly.

'Yesterday you gave *me* your love!' Gideon reminded her bitterly.

Ellie looked away from him. 'My promise to my mother comes before anything and everything else, Gideon. I was . . . unwise . . . foolish . . . unknowing. My mother is . . . was right and –'

'And I'm not good enough for you? Is that what you're trying to say?' Gideon challenged her bitterly.

'Please leave, Gideon,' Ellie demanded, her voice thickening in her throat. 'My aunts will be here soon to . . . to . . . see my mother. I should not even be here with you whilst she is alone. You see, even now you are coming between us. Oh! You don't know how much I wish I had never met you!'

Fighting to master his emotions, Gideon looked at her. She had become someone he didn't recognise, a very different Ellie from the one he had fallen in love with. She had become, he recognised bitterly, her mother's daughter. His Ellie would come back, though, he was sure of it. He was not going to give her up so easily!

'Very well then. If that is what you want,' he told her quietly, 'I shall go.'

After she had shut the door behind Gideon, Ellie leaned against it and closed her eyes.

'I have done what I promised, Mama,' she whispered as the tears blistered from her closed eyes and burned an acid trail down her face.

*   *   *

'Edith, I'm afraid that I must go. I am expecting a young man to call round and see me – a Mr Gideon Walker. He is newly come to the town and wishes to set himself up as a cabinet-maker. I am determined to put my own stamp on the library, and I also want to commission some new cupboards for the drawing room.'

Edith Rigby's eyebrows rose. 'I am surprised that you would consider entrusting such a large commission to an unknown tradesman, Mary, especially when Gillows of Lancaster have such a good reputation.'

'Gillows can afford to pick and choose their clientele and take their time about completing their commissions. It seems to me that if this young man has anything about him he will be so grateful to me for giving him a commission that he will put his whole heart and soul into his work, as well as complete it on time.'

As both ladies stood up, Edith Rigby hesitated a little, picking her words carefully. 'It seems from what I have learned about you from certain friends of mine in London that we have a common interest. I do not wish to say too much at this stage, Mary, but if you are interested, I entertain a few. . . like-minded friends once a month. We are rather a serious crowd, I'm afraid, for we discuss in the main not fashion or the goings-on of the King and his friends, but rather more political issues. If you think you would be interested in joining us . . . ?' She looked searchingly at Mary.

Levelly, Mary returned her look. 'I too had heard from my friends that you shared our beliefs and goals.'

Edith sighed. 'A goal which even between ourselves neither of us quite dares to put into words for fear of ridicule and rejection. It is my passionate belief that our sex has been wrongfully and deliberately denied the right that every adult man may take for granted and that it is high time that we were accorded it in full, and given the vote. There, I have said it, and if I have offended you or mistaken the situation –'

Mary shook her head. 'No, and you are right, Edith. I too am passionately committed to that goal. We owe it to our sex to do everything within our power to right what must be one of the most shameful wrongs ever done! For a country that abhors and has abolished slavery, to permit its women to be so disenfranchised is surely a sin against our sex.'

Having given her a fierce hug, Edith released her to say, 'At the moment we are merely straws in the wind, Mary, an ununified smattering of like-minded people, but one day those straws will bind together and when they do we will be a force to be reckoned with. But there, I am lecturing to the converted, and you will be late for your cabinet-maker. If he is as good as you hope, you may instruct him to present himself here. I too have work I should like to have done. Who knows,' she teased, 'between us we may be able to convert him to our cause, and if he

123

has a wife, a mother, a sweetheart or a sister, they will one day, I hope, have good reason to be grateful to us for doing so.'

As Gideon walked through Winckley Square, he was still trying to come to terms with what had happened. That Ellie, his lovely, gentle Ellie, could have spoken to him in such a way had hurt him very badly. Naturally, she was very upset about her mother's death – he could understand that and, of course, forgive her her cruelty to him – but what he could not forgive was the way in which Lydia Pride had played upon her daughter's feelings and tried to turn Ellie against him.

He loved Ellie and she loved him too. He was sure of it. Somehow he would find a way to make her see sense. But perhaps it would be best if he waited until the funeral was over before seeking her out again.

Of course, with her mother's death she would have new responsibilities and would, no doubt, have to take charge of her father's household. Gideon's eyes warmed with a lover's pride as he mentally envisaged his Ellie bustling about her new household duties – duties that might well mean that their married life would have to begin beneath her father's roof, he acknowledged, because he certainly could not see Ellie abandoning her siblings. He would have preferred to have her all to himself, but Gideon was sensitive enough to recognise that Ellie would be needed at home. His spirits lifted by his imaginings, Gideon managed to shrug off his angry despair. All courting couples quarrelled from time to time, he reasoned, and it was far more pleasurable to think about the rosy future he was visualising for Ellie and himself than to dwell on the hurtfulness of her icy words.

He may not have particularly liked Lydia, but, of course, Ellie had loved her mother. Even he had been shocked by the news of her death, so how must his beloved Ellie have felt?

'Well, Mr Walker, you certainly seem to have an excellent grasp of what I'm looking for.'

Surreptitiously, Mary studied him. He was both what she had expected and yet not. The years of his apprenticeship had given him an impressive breadth of shoulder to add to the height he must have inherited from his father – along with that cool and rather disconcertingly direct grey-eyed gaze. The shock of thick dark curly hair she supposed she should have expected, along with the slightly olive cast to his skin. His voice had a soft country burr, and there was a calm sureness about him that also spoke of his being a countryman. But that cool objective ability to assimilate what she required, and the instinctive skill to translate it into quick, economically elegant sketches that showed her just how her room would look as they came to life beneath his hands – that *had* caught her off guard.

And that air of control and authority – where had he got that from? Herding William Pride's livestock? Mary doubted that.

Determined not to let Mary see how anxious he was about her reaction to his drawings, Gideon sought to assume a nonchalant confidence he was actually far from feeling. He ached, like every young man in love, to prove to his beloved that he was worthy of her. He could feel the anxious tension gripping his gut whilst he watched Mary Isherwood studying the sketches he had made following her description of what she wanted. If she commissioned him to make her cabinets then a whole new future could open up for him: a future in which he could afford to provide for Ellie as his wife! And once they were married he would see to it that he made her so happy that she soon forgot about the snobbish aspirations of her mother!

'Mr Walker, I believe we shall be able to do business together.' Mary smiled as she handed back his rough sketches.

Gideon felt his pent-up nervous breath leak jerkily from his lungs. Mary had been studying the drawings for so long that he had begun to fear that they did not suit her. Just wait until he told Ellie! Gideon frowned. Of course, with Ellie in mourning for her mother he could not rush round to Friargate as he longed to do and share his excitement with her. No, he would just have to be patient . . . leave her to grieve for her mother for now, and then see her after the funeral.

'I shall require you to supply me with detailed drawings, of course, and costings, and if I should find that you have attempted to cheat me by substituting inferior wood, or indeed in any other way, I promise you I shall make you sorry for it. I may only be a woman, Mr Walker, but I am not a woman to be underestimated.'

Controlling his excitement, Gideon forced himself to concentrate on what Mary was saying to him, and then frowned as the meaning of her words sank in.

'It is not my habit to cheat, Miss Isherwood,' he told her angrily.

'No, I am sure it is not,' Mary agreed calmly. 'But you are a young man about to set up in business on your own account and there will be those who will seek to cheat you, I'm afraid. So you will do well to be on your guard. Now, how soon can you let me have the detailed drawings and your costings?'

Gideon thought quickly. 'By the end of the week?'

'And the work? When will you be able to begin that?'

Gideon tensed. This was the question he had been dreading.

'I . . . there is a slight problem, Miss Isherwood,' he admitted uncomfortably.

'You have other commissions to complete?'

'No . . .' Gideon told her reluctantly. 'The truth is,' he blurted out, 'as yet I do not have any premises to work from. I have two in mind, but I am waiting for the landlords to come back to me.'

'I see.' Mary looked searchingly at him. 'And where exactly are these premises?'

Hesitantly, Gideon gave her the addresses.

'Well, Mr Walker,' Mary said crisply, 'we must just hope that one of your prospective landlords comes back to you very soon, otherwise I fear we are both going to be disappointed. Mollie will show you out.' She rang the bell for the housemaid who had originally shown him into the room.

'Oh, Mr Walker . . . ?'

Halfway towards the door, Gideon stopped.

'You have a very fine eye for detail,' Mary told him. 'I wonder if when you have finished with them you would allow me to have the sketches you have just done?'

When Gideon stared at her in surprise she gave a small shrug and explained carelessly, 'I am keeping a record of all the work this house has undergone, and I would like to put them in it.'

'Of course you may have them,' Gideon replied.

One foot on the stairs, Mary Isherwood paused to glance at the wall where her father's portrait had hung.

How furious he would have been had he known what she was planning. It had been her mother's relatives, the second cousins who had taken Mary in after she had fled from her father following their bitter

128

quarrel, who had been responsible for her original involvement in the women's movement.

Irene and Amy Darlington, the two spinster sisters, who had been derided by her father for being 'unmarried bluestockings', shared a passionate belief in the cause of women's suffrage and their right to be treated as men's equals.

Now in their eighties, they were still as fiercely dedicated to that cause as they had been as young women, and Mary shared their dedication.

She had heard about Edith Rigby's involvement on the grapevine that linked the small groups of women's rights activists together. The time was coming when those groups were going to have to be melded together, to work together, and Mary already knew that she would be called upon to play her part in this process. That, after all, was one of the reasons she had come back.

One of the reasons. She looked at the blank wall again. Perhaps she would commission Gideon Walker to carve some suitable piece to hang in the portrait's place.

She had already dispatched a note to one of the potential landlords Gideon had mentioned to her, having immediately recognised that he was simply an agent and that the true owner of the business property was herself. Her father had built up a strong portfolio of properties in the town, which were let out, and she could see no good reason why Gideon Walker, and therefore she herself, should not benefit from this.

NINE

Ellie shivered as she stepped out into the cold dampness of the rain-sodden day. The cortège was waiting; her aunts already installed in their barouches with their families, white faces grimly unsmiling, garbed in deepest funereal black.

The horses, bearing their black feathers, their coats as wetly polished as the hired carriages and just as dark, stood sombrely beneath the stinging rain.

Ellie averted her eyes from the sight of her mother's coffin. She was to travel in one of the last carriages with Connie and her cousins. John, though, was to ride in the principal coach with their father, whilst the new baby, who was to be named Joseph according to her mother's wishes, remained behind in the care of her aunt's nursemaid.

'But, Father, why cannot we have the baby here at home with us?' Ellie had protested, desperate to cling to this last human piece of her mother.

'Because it was your mother's wish that he should

be brought up by her sister,' Robert Pride had told her, his face becoming bitter as he'd muttered under his breath, 'No doubt she felt she could not trust me to do so.'

Her father had changed so much in the short time since her mother's death. Her mother's body had not even been cold when he had left the house, only returning once all the funeral arrangements had been put in hand, obviously drunk and maudlin, weeping openly as he grieved for the woman whose death he had caused.

In the space of a few short days Ellie's whole world had changed and she had lost everything that had been safe and familiar. The strong, good-humoured, gentle father she had known and loved had turned almost overnight into a weak, broken man, content to let his sisters-in-law have their way.

In her sleep she dreamed of him holding them all protectively close in his paternal arms, and her father's arms weren't the only ones in which she dreamed of being held fast. But it was wrong of her to think of Gideon.

She had declared passionately, when Connie had asked her why they had not seen Gideon, that she never ever wished to set eyes on him again. And she had meant it!

There was nothing left in her world to give her comfort or hope. Her aunts, she knew, were bitterly vehement in their condemnation of her father. She had heard what they had to say about him as they moved about her mother's bedroom, performing the duties Lydia had requested of them. Deep down inside, Ellie had resented their presence and their assumption of a greater closeness to her mother than she herself was allowed. With them her mother had inhabited a world, known a life in which Ellie had never played any part. In their eyes she had seen grief and anger that excluded her as much as it bound the remaining four sisters together. In death it was as though her old life had reclaimed Lydia, so that the Prides were not only robbed of her physical presence but also of their memories of her. Ellie's aunts had ordered every detail of the funeral – a funeral that would befit a Barclay! Lydia was not to be buried in the plot that Robert had hastily bought, but in the same grave as her parents. Initially Ellie had thought that her father had been going to protest and insist that Lydia be buried where he could eventually join her, and Ellie had held her breath, aware that, for her, more than just the last resting place of her mother was hanging in the balance. If her father should persist, if her Aunt Amelia should back down, then maybe . . .

Maybe what? She could break her word to her mother? Ellie was furious with herself for even permitting such a thought. She would never do that, never.

But then Aunt Amelia had announced that it had been her mother's wish that she be buried with her parents, and Ellie had watched as her father had turned away in silence.

Inside, a vulnerable part of her had ached for him and for herself, and she had longed to run to him; to tell her aunt defiantly that their mother belonged to them and not to her sisters and her parents. Now it was too late.

Their neighbours had come out to stand in respectful silence as the cortège made its solemn, mournful way down the street. Tears pricked at Ellie's eyes, blurring everything around her as they turned out of Friargate and headed for St John's Parish Church.

Gideon's head was aching and there was a sour taste in his mouth. Slowly, like a trickle of rancid milk, memories of the previous evening came back to him.

He had taken Nancy to the music hall, where they had both had too much to drink. They had then made their way back to his lodgings, but when they had got there, and Nancy had offered to come inside with him 'to finish off the evening', Gideon had suddenly sobered up and recognised that the last thing he wanted was to take her to bed.

He had tried to be tactful, but Nancy had a very straightforward attitude to life and she had immediately objected to being denied the end of the evening she had been anticipating. What had begun as a quiet conversation had quickly escalated into a very noisy argument, at least on Nancy's part. Before too long she had been joined by some of the other mill girls, who had gleefully egged her on.

Gideon winced as he recalled their frank and bawdy comments about his refusal to 'show her what he was made of'.

To make matters worse, some of the clients of the nearby whorehouse had objected to the noise and had come out into the street with their whores, whereupon a fight had begun between the two groups of women.

The mill girls, robust though they were in their attitude to sex, considered themselves very much a cut above the whores, who sold sex, and the opportunity to air long-standing offences and give vent to festering insults was not one either party had been readily prepared to relinquish. In the end it had taken the threat of sending for the police to break things up, and even then one of the whores had claimed triumphantly that they would have to get the local sergeant out of her bed first.

After everything had quietened down, Gideon had finally made it into his lodgings to be greeted by his stony-faced landlady, who had informed him grimly that she kept a clean and respectable house, thank you very much, and that if he did not mend his ways and his choice of company he would be looking for new accommodation . . .

Ellie's mother was being buried today. Gideon blinked his gritty eyes at his clock. The service was to be at eleven o'clock. It was nearly nine thirty now.

Quickly he got out of bed, groaning as he felt the alcohol-induced pain thudding in his head. In the yard shared by all the houses, he sluiced himself down with cold water from the pump, gritting his teeth as its cold bite increased the fierce pounding of his hangover.

Upstairs in a neighbouring house, one of the mill girls stood and watched him admiringly. He was a fine-looking lad, that Gideon Walker. No wonder Nancy had warned the rest of them off him.

It was over. Her mother had gone to her rest. Ellie shook with the reaction she was still feeling to that moment of sickening dread when she had thrown her handful of earth down onto the shiny wood of the brass-bound coffin.

Now they were all to go back to Aunt Amelia's where a funeral tea would be served, to fortify the mourners, and the will was to be read to those it concerned.

As they started to make their way back to the waiting carriages, Ellie was conscious of her Aunt Lavinia walking alongside her. Of all her mother's sisters, Aunt Lavinia was the one Ellie knew the least – the one who had married the most success- fully. Her husband was the senior partner in a firm of solicitors based in Liverpool, and they lived in a huge mansion in Hoylake.

Their house had its own separate coach house and stables, as well as a tennis court and a croquet lawn, and their neighbours were the wealthy ship-owners who were clients of Josiah Parkes.

They had no children, a fact that Ellie had heard being spoken about in hushed tones by her mother and Aunt Gibson.

'Ellie, you will ride back with your Aunt Lavinia,' Amelia announced firmly, putting a restraining hand on Ellie's arm as Ellie started to make to join her cousins.

Blank-eyed, Ellie did so. Her Aunt Lavinia had a soft plumpness that the other Barclay sisters lacked, and when she walked she seemed to gasp for breath slightly. She smelled of lavender water, just as Lydia had done. Ellie felt her eyes fill with hot tears.

Numbly Ellie headed for the carriage, and then froze. She had no idea just what had made her stop and turn round to look behind her, to where a group of non-family mourners were keeping a respectful distance as they said their final farewells. There at the back of the small group stood Gideon, his uncovered head bowed as he stood in silence, the wind ruffling his thick rain-slicked hair, the mourning clothes, which Ellie guessed he must have hired for the occasion, suspiciously tight across his chest.

Gideon! Ellie felt her heart leap inside her chest, her emotions churning in wild confusion. What was Gideon doing here after what she had said?

Ellie! Gideon felt his heart soar and then crash as his eyes recognised the truth his heart did not want to accept.

Across the rain-sodden space they looked at one

another. Ellie's face was set, her eyes cold as she focused on him and then dismissed him with a single blank look.

For one wild moment Gideon was tempted to cross the distance separating them, to take hold of her and shake the coldness from her, to demand that she return to being his warm, laughing, gentle Ellie and not this cold, haughty girl-woman who was looking through him as though he were too far below her for her to acknowledge him.

'No!' He wasn't even aware that he had shouted his furious denial out loud until Robert Pride touched him on the shoulder.

Robert had aged dramatically since his wife's death. Gone was the proud jauntiness of his step, his shoulders were stooped and his expression more apologetic than proud.

'Gideon, lad!' he exclaimed warmly. ''Tis good to see you here –'

'I wanted to see Ellie,' Gideon cut him short, his own emotions too sore to allow him the luxury of good manners. 'I need to speak to her.'

The look of pity in Robert Pride's eyes made Gideon's stomach roll in despair.

'Leave her be, lad,' Robert told him wearily. 'It's for the best. I know that you and Ellie . . .' He paused. 'Things are different now, Gideon. You're best forgetting about her.'

'Forget about her? How the hell can I do that?' Gideon exploded, but Robert was already walking away from him to talk with other mourners.

Desperately, Gideon looked past him to where Ellie had been, but she had gone.

He had come to the church in part to pay his respects to Lydia – no matter what she had thought of him or he of her, his parents and especially his mother had given him a lovingly strict upbringing – but, of course, he was here mainly so that he could see Ellie.

Well, he had seen her and she had seen him, even if she had refused to acknowledge his presence.

He knew that she had a stubborn strength about her and he admired her for it, but then he had not realised that that strength and that stubbornness were going to be turned against him, and against their love!

Lydia's will was brief and straightforward.

To her sisters she left those mementoes she had brought into her marriage from the home she had shared with them: the silver dressing-table set she had been given by her grandmother; the pretty golden necklace that had been a confirmation present from her godmother; her personal books and small pieces of jewellery – apart from the rings Robert had given her.

Those, her engagement, wedding and eternity rings, were to be given to her daughters, her will stated – her wedding and eternity rings to Ellie, and her engagement ring to Connie.

Holding them in her cold, closed hand, Ellie

fought fiercely to stem the jealousy she felt at knowing her mother had left the things that were most precious to her not to Connie and herself but to her sisters. The silver dressing-table set in particular had been a favourite of her mother's, and Ellie could picture her now, using it, smoothing the heavy polished metal, for Lydia had allowed no one other than herself to clean it. It had been a family heirloom, given originally to her grandmother by *her* mother, and Ellie ached to be able to pick it up and touch it; to lift it to her face and breathe in any last traces of her mother's scent that might lie hidden in it.

There were, however, letters for Ellie, Connie, John and for the new baby as well.

In Ellie's, her mother told her how much she loved her and how much she hated having to leave her before she was fully grown up.

I have spoken already to my dearest sisters about my fears for you and for Connie, Ellie, and I have spoken to them too of my hopes and desires for you. They have assured me that they will do everything within their power to help you to achieve my hopes for you. You MUST be guided by them in all things, as you would be if they were me. Their words to you will be my words; their experience will guide you as mine would have done. You are to be obedient to them at all times, and in every way, and to remember that they are protecting your Barclay heritage.

When I disobeyed my mother to marry your father I believed I knew my own mind. I have loved your father, Ellie, and I honour him as a good man, but there have been many, many times when I have regretted my wilfulness, and envied my sisters – and never more than where you and your sister are concerned.

Your future now lies with your aunts, and I beg you, for my sake, to be guided always by them.

The plans and arrangements they will make for you have already been discussed with me, and if my worst fears come to be, and I do not survive the birth of my child, then you will read this letter in the knowledge that everything your aunts do for you is with my knowledge and approval. Always remember that I love you and that what I have done I have done in your best interests and out of my love for you.

May God bless you, my darling daughter, and may I rest in peace knowing that you will be dutiful and obedient to your aunts, my sisters.

I am your loving mother,
Lydia Barclay Pride

However her mother may have signed herself, the letter had been written as Lydia Barclay and not Lydia Pride, Ellie recognised bleakly.

People were starting to leave. Dutifully, Ellie

went to say her goodbyes to them, gently guiding Connie with her.

Connie's normally expressive face was blank, her clothes for once uncreased and unmarked, her agile body stiff and unyielding.

'Ellie, what is to happen to us?' she burst out in a frantic whisper. 'In her letter to me, Mam says that I am to obey my aunt and be a good daughter to her, but I am not her daughter, am I? I am Father's daughter.'

Ellie frowned, but before she could say anything, their Aunt Amelia was bearing down on them, firmly dismissing Connie, telling her to go and find her brother, before saying briskly to Ellie, 'We don't have much time, Ellie. Your Uncle Parkes has booked train seats for you to Liverpool so you had best go straight round to Friargate with my sister Parkes and pack your things. You shall be met at the station, and driven to the ferry terminal – your uncle is going on ahead as he has urgent business to conduct. Isn't that right, Lavinia?' she demanded, turning to her sister who was hovering at her side.

'Oh, yes.' Aunt Lavinia gave Ellie a tearful smile, as she added, 'Oh, poor darling Lydia, I never thought it would come to this. But at least she has died knowing that you, her children, will be cared for by us, her sisters. I dare say that it will be late by the time we get home, Ellie, so I have instructed Cook to leave us a cold supper. Mr Parkes does not, generally speaking, approve of suppers, but on this occasion I am sure it is an indulgence he

141

will permit. You have just time to say goodbye to everyone.'

'Say goodbye?' Ellie stared at her aunt in consternation. What was she saying? 'But how can I go to Liverpool?' she protested. 'Surely I must stay here in Preston to take care of my sister and brother, and keep house for my father.'

Aunt Lavinia was beginning to look uncomfortable.

Amelia looked sternly at Ellie. 'What is wrong, Ellie?' she demanded sharply.

'My Aunt Lavinia says I am to go to Liverpool with her on a visit, but surely I am going to be needed here?'

'You are not going to Liverpool on a visit.'

Ellie began to relax, but before she could say anything, Amelia was continuing even more sharply, 'It was your mother's desire that in the event of her death you should go and live with your Aunt and Uncle Parkes. No, Ellie, please do not interrupt me. You are supposed to be an intelligent girl. You have surely read the letter your mother left for you. It makes her wishes plain enough. These matters were all discussed between us at your mother's behest. As much as anything else, I believe she wanted to put as much distance as possible between you and that unsavoury young man your father has so unwisely allowed to ingratiate himself with you all.'

Ellie listened to her Aunt Amelia with growing disbelief and pain. She was to be sent away from her father, her sister and her brother, and it was her mother who had made these arrangements!

'Always remember that I love you and that what I have done I have done in your best interests and out of my love for you,' her mother had written.

Even as Ellie dutifully reminded herself of those words, she still couldn't stop herself from begging shakily, 'But what is to become of Connie and John . . . and baby Joseph?'

'Connie is to make her home with our sister Jane from now on. Your mother, and the rest of us, believe that Connie would benefit greatly from the opportunity this will give her to improve her mind. I am afraid that she has befriended a group of girls at her school whose influence on her is not one that your mother approved of! And as for John, he is to attend Hutton, where Uncle Jepson is headmaster, as a boarder. And the new baby is, of course, to be brought up by your Aunt Jepson.'

'But that means that my father will be all on his own,' Ellie whispered painfully.

'As to that, Ellie, Mr Pride is a man,' Aunt Amelia told her meaningfully, exchanging a look with her sister. 'And men, especially men of Mr Pride's class and . . . inclination, are generally well able to take care of themselves!'

Amelia was not going to say as much, but it was her opinion that a man like Robert would not be long without a woman to order his house and warm his bed.

'Everything is arranged, Ellie,' she told her niece, 'and you must remember these were your mother's wishes.'

'Mother wanted me to go and live with my Aunt and Uncle Parkes?' Ellie whispered, unable to take in what she was being told.

'Yes!' her Aunt Amelia confirmed impatiently.

Ellie looked at her, and then across the room to where her father was standing on his own. A huge lump filled her throat. She wanted to cry out in protest, to run to her father, throw herself into his arms and beg him not to allow them to take her, but she knew she could not do so. She knew she could not argue against or ignore her mother's wishes. And she knew most of all that she could not break the promise she had given her.

PART TWO

TEN

'And I must tell you, dearest sister, how very happy I am to be living with our aunt and uncle.'

Ellie frowned as she reread Connie's short, stilted letter. Try as she might she could find no sign of her giddy, fun-loving sister in the brief, carefully written words, which disappointingly gave her only the same news she had already received in previous correspondence. She had hoped that the long-awaited letter might contain some news of their brothers, John and baby Joseph, and indeed she had begged Connie to send her news of them the last time she had written, but her sister had obviously forgotten. Ellie's early letters to John had been answered not by him but by her Aunt Emily announcing that John was too busy catching up with his schoolwork to have time to write letters.

Even so, it was good to hear from Connie. Letters from Preston were a rare treat now for Ellie. Even her father seemed to be too busy to reply to her own long letters imploring him to write or to telephone her, or, even better, to come and visit her. It was almost twelve months since she had come to Hoylake but Ellie was guiltily aware that she still missed her family as desperately as ever, and that this was a secret she had to keep from her aunt, who would, no doubt, be very upset by Ellie's ingratitude. At Christmas Ellie had been allowed to speak with her siblings by telephone, but only for the merest few seconds, nowhere near enough to appease her ache for them.

As she looked out of the window of her aunt's elegant drawing room, and into the immaculate garden beyond it, a bleak look shadowed Ellie's eyes. Sombrely she allowed her thoughts to drift back over the last year. She felt she was a completely different person now from the Ellie who had first arrived in Hoylake . . .

Twelve months before

'Thank goodness we are home at last. Now remember, Ellie, that Mr Parkes is very particular in his ways and . . .'

Shivering despite the brick beneath her feet to warm them on the journey, Ellie wished passionately that she was at home in Preston and not here in Hoylake. The tears of despair she had cried on the initial stages of their journey had given way to bleak misery. She had tried to respond to her aunt's chatter, inwardly questioning angrily how someone who one minute was claiming to be devastated by the loss of a dear sister could in the next be talking pettishly about the failings of her dressmaker to make her some new garments.

'And I am not talking about going-out clothes, you understand, Ellie, but merely some plain house dresses, the kind one might wear whilst walking in the garden, or instructing the servants, and yet still she has totally ignored my instructions! I shall have to give the dresses to Wrotham, my maid. I could not possibly wear them myself! And Mr Parkes will certainly not agree to pay her bill.'

Ellie was dreading seeing her uncle. She had only the vaguest memory of him from the funeral; a tall, frowning man who had kept himself at a distance from the rest of the mourners, and to whom Ellie had noticed her Aunt Lavinia giving anxious little glances when she thought no one else was watching.

What was her father doing now, Ellie wondered miserably. And Connie and John? She had had to leave her home before the others and had not even had a chance to say a proper goodbye to them.

'Ellie, you must think of them and not yourself,' her Aunt Amelia had chided her. 'It will only upset them unnecessarily to have to say goodbye.'

Aunt Amelia had made it plain that she thought they should all be grateful for what was being done for them, but Ellie ached inside for the comfort of her home, the gruff sound of her father's voice,

149

Connie's unending chatter, John's noisy boyishness, and even Rex's frenzied barking when John played with him. She was even missing the homely familiarity of the small kitchen – yes, and Annie and Jenny too. Had Annie thought to bank up the range and to make sure that her father got a decent meal? He would not think to get one for himself, Ellie knew. Why, she had practically had to stand over him and insist that he ate, these last few days.

The carriage was turning into a wide driveway, and Ellie's eyes widened in awed apprehension as she saw the house looming in front of them. It was far, far larger than her Aunt Amelia's Winckley Square home, and Ellie gave a nervous shudder as she had to tilt her head right back to look up to its high gables.

The carriage came to a halt, and the coachman opened the doors. As Ellie stepped down to join her aunt, the front door to the house was already open. A small rotund woman came hurrying towards her aunt and fussed round her, ignoring Ellie.

'Oh, Wrotham, it is so good to be home,' Aunt Lavinia exclaimed wearily. 'This is my niece, Miss Pride,' she continued, drawing Ellie forward. 'Have one of the maids show her to her room, will you. Oh, and Wrotham, my special tisane . . . I have the most dreadful headache.'

Ellie flushed with discomfort as she was subjected to the dour-faced, middle-aged maid's grimly assessing look. She felt as though Wrotham had mentally calculated the cost and the quality of every stitch she had on and it was plain that she was not impressed. That thin curl of her lip as she dismissed Ellie from her attention and turned back to her mistress was most explicit. Ellie swallowed hard on the painful lump of misery lodged in her throat.

The hallway of the house was so brightly lit that Ellie blinked against the harshness.

A door to one side opened, and Ellie felt her aunt tense as she breathed nervously, 'Oh, Josiah! I hope that we have not disturbed you.'

Ellie could feel her stomach muscles contracting in acute nervousness as her uncle stepped into the hallway.

He was taller than her father, but thinner too, and as he had been at the funeral, he was frowning.

Ellie had removed her hat with its mourning veil in the carriage, and she was conscious of the untidiness of her hair and her travel-stained appearance as Mr Parkes turned to scrutinise her.

'Ellie, you may go straight upstairs to your room,' her aunt was saying. 'One of the maids –'

'No.' Ellie froze as Mr Parkes strode towards her. 'You're forgetting, my love, that our niece has had a long journey and she is most likely hungry.'

Ellie's eyes widened in surprise as she realised that Mr Parkes was actually smiling at her. 'I-I shouldn't want to put the servants to any trouble,' she responded, mindful of her aunt's earlier warnings.

Immediately, Mr Parkes' smile vanished, to be replaced by an intimidating look of disdain.

'You must not concern yourself about the servants, Ellie. They are here to do as they are instructed. Besides, I was just about to partake of some supper myself. You shall share it with me and tell me about yourself so that we can get to know one another.

'You never told me, Mrs Parkes, that our niece was such a beauty,' Ellie heard her uncle commenting as he gave her a wide avuncular smile. The warmth of his hand on her arm as he guided her towards his study somehow reminded Ellie of her father.

Ellie's bedroom was four times the size of the room she had shared at home with Connie, but despite the elegance of its furnishings and the softness of the linen, Ellie ached with misery and longing as she curled herself up into a tight little ball in the bed.

Her uncle's unexpected joviality and warmth had eased some of her apprehension, but this was still not her home, and she felt alien and unhappy.

The sturdy, kind-eyed young maid, who had accompanied her to her room, had announced that she was to be Ellie's personal maid and that her name was Lizzie, and as she had bustled about the room, unpacking Ellie's few belongings, Ellie had ached to be left alone so that she could give way to her tears.

Alone and lonely, she finally succumbed to an exhausted sleep, but in her dreams the events of the day were a distressing, disjointed sequence of blurred images coloured with her own pain and fear. Only one person stood out clearly and starkly in her dream and that person was Gideon.

'Gideon!'

Ellie woke with the sound of his name echoing in her ears and the taste of her tears on her lips.

What was she doing here? Why hadn't her father insisted that she stay with him? Why had her mother done this to her?

A week passed, and then a month, and slowly the sharpness of Ellie's misery gave way to a dull acceptance.

Her aunt and uncle's house, and their way of life, were so different from everything she was familiar with. Her aunt lived the life of a wealthy lady of leisure. Her days were made up of certain strict and set routines.

'I have put off my normal Thursday At Home this month, Ellie,' she informed her niece one morning, 'until we can get you some decent clothes.'

'But, Aunt, I have plenty of clothes,' Ellie protested. 'Aunt Amelia insisted that I was to have two complete sets of full mourning.'

Her aunt looked both uncomfortable and a little impatient. 'Well, yes, of course, my dear, you have clothes, but I'm afraid they simply will not do for Hoylake. Even your uncle has noticed . . . Well, it is on his instruction that you are to have new.

153

He is thinking of me, of course. He knows how embarrassing it would be for me to be shamed in front of my friends, and I am afraid that I would be shamed, Ellie, if you were to be seen in what you have. Which reminds me, I have instructed Wrotham to take you into the dining room this morning and she will go through with you the, er, correct order in which you should use your cutlery. Then this afternoon we shall practise how you must go on when I have my At Home.'

Ellie could feel her face burning with misery and humiliation. She had seen the previous evening the way in which her aunt's gaze had focused on her momentary fumbling with her cutlery. At home their meals had been simply prepared and served; here, well, it still shocked her to see so much waste, to see full courses brought to the table only to be waved away untouched by her aunt and uncle.

Sometimes it seemed as though the new rules she had to learn were unending – but to what purpose?

Her aunt talked confusingly about introducing Ellie to her circle of friends and finding a suitable husband for her amongst Mr Parkes' wealthy clients, but Ellie was no fool. She had neither dowry nor social standing to enhance her value as a prospective bride, and besides, she did not want a husband – ever. The very thought made her shiver in terror, remembering her mother's death. But, contradictorily, her aunt would then talk of how delighted she was to have at long last got a 'daughter', and her great desire to keep Ellie at her side for ever.

And it wasn't just her aunt and uncle's way of life that bewildered her, Ellie acknowledged. The servants were terrifyingly formal and austere, and as different from their own Annie and Jenny as it was possible to be. And the worst of them all was surely her aunt's maid, Wrotham, who seemed to seize every opportunity she could to underline to Ellie how ill-equipped she was to meet the demands of her new life.

'Pay no mind to her, miss,' Lizzie had told Ellie comfortingly earlier in the week, when Wrotham had refused to allow Ellie into her aunt's room, insisting that her mistress be left in peace to allow the tisane she had drunk to ease her headache to take effect.

Her Aunt Lavinia was, Ellie had quickly discovered, a martyr to the most dreadful headaches, all the more so when Mr Parkes was in one of his sharp moods.

But hardest of all to bear was the fact that Ellie had so little contact with her family, despite the many letters she had written to them.

'Oh, there you are, miss. The mistress is asking for you.'

Still holding Connie's letter Ellie turned round in response to Lizzie's words. Sometimes it seemed to

Ellie that she was closer to her maid than to anyone else in her new life.

'Does my aunt wish me to go up to her?' Ellie asked.

'She does that, miss. Said you was to go straight up to her room, if you please!'

Lizzie, a devotee of both the newly fashionable moving pictures and the more traditional music-hall theatre on her afternoons off, had returned from seeing the latest production, straight from London itself, earlier in the month, full of excitement about the hairstyle she had seen the leading lady wearing, and had managed to persuade Ellie to allow her to try it on her luxuriously thick hair.

The result had been so elegant and stylish that even her aunt had commented on how much it had suited her, but all Ellie had been able to think was whether her family would have recognised her in this new, unfamiliar Hoylake young lady she was being turned into. Connie, of course, would have delighted in such fripperies and spoiling – or rather the Connie that Ellie remembered would have done. The brief, lifeless, carefully written letters Ellie received from her sister showed nothing of that Connie.

Did Connie ever see anything of John and the baby? Did she see their father? Gideon?

Ellie froze. She had no right to be letting Gideon Walker into her thoughts.

Ellie could feel the corset Lizzie had laced tightly to give her the requisite eighteen-inch waist digging into her skin as she hurried towards the parlour door.

Picking up the skirts of the new lilac half-mourning dress she was wearing, she hurried up the imposing staircase with its Turkish carpet and intricately carved banister.

Her aunt had told her within a week of her arrival that the house had originally been built for one of Liverpool's shipowners, who, through a succession of unfortunate events, had had to sell it before he had even moved in. 'Mr Parkes was able to buy the house through his business connections,' her aunt had informed her.

At that time Ellie had still been feeling too overwhelmed and daunted by everything that had happened to do anything other than acknowledge inwardly that the house was indeed very imposing and a far cry from her own much humbler home in Preston. But now, twelve months later, she was acutely aware that it wasn't just in their sizes that the home she had grown up in and the house occupied by her aunt and uncle were so very different.

She found her aunt, as she had known she would, lying down on the elegant chaise longue in her boudoir, with Wrotham standing guard over her.

'Oh, Ellie, there you are,' Aunt Lavinia declared in a feeble voice. 'My dear, please do not move so vigorously. It makes my poor head ache! Mr Parkes has informed me that we have now received our formal invitation to your cousin Cecily's wedding.

Thank goodness my sister Gibson had the good sense to put it off until we are all out of mourning. I can think of nothing more dispiriting than a set of wedding photographs showing everyone wearing black, although, of course, as a family we are all fortunate in being so fair and able to carry mourning colours!'

Ellie had been looking forward to attending her cousin's wedding for months, knowing that she would see her family.

'My sister Gibson has secured such a good match for your cousin. I should like to see you equally well married, Ellie, but I fear . . .'

Ellie tensed, knowing already what her aunt was going to say. Her own parentage meant that she could not look as high as Cecily for a potential husband.

Angry tears shimmered in Ellie's eyes. Rebelliously she wished that people might value others for their kindness and their virtues and not for their places in society and the size of their bank accounts. It infuriated and hurt her whenever she heard her father being disparaged, but she knew that she would earn herself a sharp rebuke and, even worse, a reminder of what she owed her mother, if she were to voice those feelings.

'Ellie, please pay attention. You are not listening to me,' Ellie heard her aunt reproaching her.

'I'm sorry, Aunt.'

Ellie had become extremely fond of her aunt, towards whom she had developed a similar sense of responsibility and protectiveness as she had felt towards her younger siblings.

'Oh, my poor head,' her aunt moaned. 'You do not know how lucky you are not to be afflicted with such sensitive nerves, Ellie. Your mother always was more robust than the rest of us and, of course, your father . . .' She gave a faint shudder as though the very act of speaking of Ellie's father was too much for her.

Immediately, Ellie wanted to rush to her father's defence and to tell her aunt how much she wished she was still living in the humble house in Friargate, above her father's shop. She had been so happy then, and had taken that happiness for granted, never dreaming her life would change so drastically.

'The most dreadful thing has happened,' Aunt Lavinia announced theatrically. 'That wretched dressmaker arrived this morning with our outfits for your cousin's wedding, and I cannot believe what she has done. I told her specifically that I wanted the eau-de-Nil silk trimming with matching satin, and the wretched creature has only trimmed it with the most horrid shade of jade imaginable. The gown is completely unwearable and will have to be remade, but now, if you please, she tells me that she is unable to obtain any more of the eau-de-Nil. Your uncle will be furious, as I was to have worn the opals!'

'Perhaps if I were to have a look at it . . .' Ellie suggested, trying to comfort her.

'Well, you are very good with your needle, Ellie,' her aunt allowed, before adding fretfully, 'but I feel so unwell. I really don't feel well enough to go down for dinner tonight. And Mr Parkes is in one of his cross moods.'

Out of the corner of her eye, Ellie saw the looks the women exchanged.

'Perhaps you can coax him round a little, Ellie, my love. He was saying only the other night how well you play the piano, and you are a far better card player than I am,' her aunt began.

'I am sure that Miss Pride will be only too pleased to be able to repay your generosity to her, ma'am,' Wrotham told her aunt, whilst directing a dire look at Ellie herself.

A little uncomfortably, Ellie picked up her cue. 'If Mr Parkes wishes me to play for him then of course I shall be pleased to do so. And if your head is very bad, Aunt, perhaps I could go down to the kitchen and ask Cook to prepare you a tisane,' Ellie offered.

'Oh, that is very kind of you, Ellie, but Wrotham has everything in hand. She is to bring me a light supper, and some of my special restorative tonic.'

'I ordered a fresh supply from the chemist this week, ma'am, as we had almost finished the bottle.'

Ellie's frown deepened. As kind as Mr Parkes was to her, Ellie could not help but notice how very unkind he could sometimes be towards her aunt. She knew that her aunt suffered badly from nervous spasms and intense headaches that prostrated her.

Her sensibilities were easily upset, especially by her husband's often hectoring and critical manner, sometimes so much so that she could be laid low for days and unable either to leave her room or receive anyone. At those times Wrotham virtually stood guard inside the door, insisting that her mistress was not to be disturbed.

Hesitantly, Ellie looked at her aunt. She had been bolstering her courage all week to ask Aunt Lavinia for a very special favour and now was as good a moment as she was likely to get.

It was almost the anniversary of her mother's death, and although Ellie understood that she could not be with her family so that they could all remember Lydia and mourn her loss together, she was desperately hoping that she would be allowed to telephone them all. The telephone was in her uncle's study and the door to the study was kept locked whenever he was away from the house. No one was allowed to use the telephone without her uncle's permission, and Ellie was nervously apprehensive about asking for such a favour.

But it would mean so much to her just to hear the voices of her father, her sister and her brother. Baby Joseph, of course, would not be talking yet.

Ellie had carefully stitched a little lawn gown for his first birthday and only the previous day she had handed it to Mr Parkes and asked him to post it for her, along with her handmade birthday card. She had painstakingly copied from a photograph her mother's features inside the card, her hand trembling so much with emotion that she had been forced to stop several times to wait for it to steady.

Her aunt was moaning softly and Wrotham was giving Ellie a meaningful look. Disheartened, Ellie recognised that this was not a good time to beg for her favour after all.

In her own room, off which she had her own private bathroom – a previously unheard of luxury – Ellie rang for Lizzie, explaining when the maid arrived, 'I am to dine alone with Mr Parkes this evening, since my aunt is not well enough to leave her room. Apparently he wishes me to play the piano for him.'

There was a look in Lizzie's eyes that Ellie did not understand, a combination of pity and anger. But then all the servants were in awe, perhaps even a little afraid, of her formidable uncle.

Very daringly, Ellie wondered if she might actually ask Mr Parkes himself if she could telephone her family.

Kind though her uncle was to her, Ellie could not feel quite comfortable addressing him as 'Uncle Josiah'. Even her aunt referred to him as Mr Parkes. Perhaps tonight, if he was particularly pleased with her playing, she might ask him.

'Which dress will you be wanting to wear, miss?' Lizzie asked, going to the closet.

'I think perhaps the grey silk,' Ellie told her. Her grey silk was amongst some new gowns her aunt had had made for her, its style elegantly plain, showing off her hand-span waist and firm, high breasts.

Thanks to Lizzie's skilled help it didn't take Ellie long to change. Quickly thanking and then dismissing her, Ellie made her way downstairs.

'Ah, Ellie, my dear, how delightful you look.'

Automatically, Ellie got up from the chair where she had been seated; flushing a little self-consciously beneath her uncle's approving scrutiny as he walked into the drawing room.

Every night, no matter that they might be dining alone, her aunt and uncle always changed for dinner. The diamonds in Mr Parkes' shirt cuffs glinted in the light. His dark hair was thinning and, like the King, he sported a full beard. As he came into the room he brought with him the smell of hair oil, male cologne and cigars.

As he spoke he looked fully at Ellie, his gaze not quite resting on her waist and then her breasts. Telling herself that her nervousness was caused by the favour she wanted to ask him, Ellie returned his smile.

'Mr Parkes has a real fondness for you, Ellie,' her aunt had told her not long after she had come to live in Hoylake, and Ellie knew that it was true that her uncle was well disposed towards her. So much so, in fact, that occasionally she felt a little uncomfortable when she compared his jovial manner towards her with the impatient irritation with which he so often addressed his wife!

He removed his pocket-watch from his waist-coat, studied it, replaced it in his pocket, and then announced, 'Time for dinner, if you are ready, my dear,' extending his arm to Ellie.

Ellie found herself hesitating slightly before placing her hand on her uncle's crooked arm. Such formality made her uncomfortable, as if she were on show.

'I am sorry that my aunt is not well enough to come down for dinner,' Ellie commented, as the parlour maid bobbed a brief curtsy before opening the dining-room door for them.

'Are you? I'm not,' her uncle responded, causing Ellie to draw in her breath a little. 'She is much better off remaining in her room until she is feeling better,' he continued smoothly. 'And I would not wish to add to her malaise by constraining her to join us for a meal for which she has no appetite. You, I hope, have a good appetite tonight, Ellie?'

For some reason both his words and the tone of his voice sent a frisson of unease down Ellie's spine.

'I . . . I do not know, sir,' she responded. 'I . . .'

'Sir?' her uncle checked her. 'Come, come, we have already agreed, have we not, that you are to call me "Uncle". For, after all, that is what I am.'

Normally Ellie had a good appetite but tonight she found that she was picking at her food, and feeling very apprehensive. Every time she opened her mouth to introduce the subject of her using the telephone, she somehow found it impossible to actually say the words, and had to close it again. The dining room felt very hot, and her own head was beginning to ache a little. It was foolish of her, Ellie knew, but she did not feel entirely comfortable being alone with her uncle, even though he was obviously doing his best to put her at her ease, and even paying her compliments. However, when she got up, intending to leave her uncle to his port, he stopped her, reaching out and taking hold of her wrist.

'I do not think that tonight I shall need any other intoxication than that of watching you playing the piano for me, Ellie.'

His hand was on her arm, and Ellie felt herself give a little shudder.

'Cold? I shall send for more coals.'

'No, no, it is not that,' Ellie assured him. Surely this was the time to ask for her favour. Before she could lose her courage, she began, 'Mr Parkes – Uncle . . . Josiah,' she corrected herself, stammering nervously, 'Tomorrow is the anniversary of my mother's death, and I . . . I was wondering if you would allow me to use the telephone to speak with my family.'

Immediately the dark eyebrows snapped together and Ellie was treated to a glare every bit as angry and formidable as those normally reserved for her aunt. Her whole body trembled as her uncle's hand tightened on her arm, almost as though he intended to shake her.

'Your family? What is this, Ellie? I thought that you understood that your aunt and I are your family now. Haven't we treated you as our daughter? You have shocked and upset me, Ellie. Naturally you have mourned your mother, as is proper, but as for this request you have made,' he continued sternly, 'you have a new life now, Ellie, and so do your sister and brothers. Do you think it would be fair to them if you, as the eldest of the family, deliberately reminded them of past unhappiness?'

'But my father –' Ellie whispered, her throat dry. 'I have not heard from him, and –'

'Does that in itself not tell you something, Ellie?' Mr Parkes demanded sharply. 'Your father has handed the responsibility of you all into the hands of others now, my dear. Your concern for him does you credit, and I well know that you have a tender heart, but I promise you, the kindest thing you can do for him is to allow him to live his life as he has chosen to live it.'

Ellie could feel a hot ball of pain burning her throat. She longed to cry out against what Mr Parkes was saying to her, but she was afraid to do so. Mr Parkes was telling her that her father had abandoned them, that he no longer considered them to be his concern; his children! Ellie wanted to protest that that was impossible, but then she remembered her father's lack of response to her letters, and her pleas to him to let her know he still loved her.

'There now, Ellie, do not look so distressed. Haven't we made you happy here, Mrs Parkes and myself? I can assure you, my dear, that we wish to do so. Now, why don't you be a good girl and play the piano for me and we shall forget all about this little upset and say no more about it?'

As Ellie battled with her tears she allowed her uncle to guide her into the drawing room. Ellie had always had a good ear for music and normally enjoyed playing the piano but tonight her fingers felt stiff, fumbling over some of the keys.

Her uncle was standing very close to her, leaning over her to turn the pages of the music for her, a kindness that Ellie knew she should thank him for but which, for some silly reason, only added to her discomfort.

'You smell deliciously of violets, Ellie – a young girl's scent,' he told her, his breath hot against the side of her neck.

Ellie could feel herself starting to blush, as she almost missed a note.

'Come, you must not be embarrassed because I pay you a compliment. Surely our young men here in Hoylake have not been slow to notice what a very pretty girl you are?'

Ellie's embarrassment intensified.

'And then, of course, there was that unsuitable young man in Preston. I am sure that he told you how pretty you are, Ellie, and perhaps did more than merely speaking to you of his feelings, eh?'

Ellie was too shocked to speak. It was unbearable to be reminded of Gideon so soon after being told that her father had deserted them. Only she knew of the fierce battle she had fought with herself to put Gideon out of her heart and her thoughts. To be reminded of him now, at a time when she was feeling so vulnerable, filled her with an intense feeling of loss and grief. The scent of her uncle's body so close to her own was suddenly overwhelmingly nauseating. Gideon had smelled of fresh air and youth instead of strong cologne; Gideon's touch on her skin had made her feel happy. Her uncle was stroking her arm, no doubt intending to comfort her, but, to Ellie's relief, she heard the rattle of coffee cups outside the drawing-room door. Her uncle's hand dropped away from her arm, and she was free to stand up.

ELEVEN

Robert Pride stared unseeingly at the table in front of him. The bottle resting on it was nearly empty and so was the glass beside it. Empty just like this parlour . . . just like his life!

Despairingly, Robert got to his feet. Was it really only a year since this room had rung with the voices of his family – his wife, Lyddy, and his children!

But now Lyddy was dead and had been for nearly twelve months, and as for his children . . . Bitterness pulled down Robert's mouth and hardened his eyes. It was his wife's sisters who had robbed him of his children, who had taken from him the only comfort left to him – aye, and it was they who kept them from him too, turning them against him.

He had heard nothing from Ellie, nothing at all. Connie, bless her, had written to him though – but only in the briefest way, and as for John, his son . . .

Robert knew he would never forget the humiliation of taking a hansom out to Hutton Grammar

School, all dressed up in his best clothes, his hair washed and slicked back with brilliantine, wanting to surprise John on his birthday and being forbidden to see his son. He had had news for John as well, news that he knew would gladden his heart.

Gideon Walker had offered to give a home to Rex, the collie pup he had given John, and which John had not been allowed to take to Hutton with him, but Robert's brother-in-law, summoned by his wife, had flatly refused to allow Robert to see his son.

'John's settled with us now. And the baby too,' Emily Jepson said.

Robert had known from the way the other man was looking at him that he believed that John would be as unwilling to see him as they were to allow him to do so.

And as though in confirmation of his fears his brother-in-law declared contemptuously, 'Look at yourself, man. Do you think John will want to see you?'

Suddenly Robert had felt out of place and uncomfortably conscious of the social gulf that existed between his wife's relatives and himself. He had wanted to leave John a few guineas, but the shop hadn't been doing as well as it had formerly, and he had had to lay off one of his young apprentices. There had been a tale put about by a jealous rival butcher that Robert Pride's meat was tainted, and then there had been those days when he had simply not felt able to overcome the black cloud of despair hanging over him and go down and open up the shop, and so he had left it closed and his customers to buy their meat elsewhere. Long black days when he had lain in the bed he had shared with Lyddy and cried out to the Lord to tell him what he had done to be so punished, to have his children taken from him as well as his wife. The baby, Joseph, wouldn't even know that he was his father!

Robert frowned as he heard his brother Will calling up to him as he ascended the stairs. Guiltily he pushed the bottle and the glass out of sight, although they had left telltale marks in the dusty surface of the small table.

'I thought I might find you in the Drover's,' Will commented breezily, 'seeing as you've become a regular down there.'

Robert said nothing. Will would not understand if he told him that it wasn't the drink that took him to the public house, but his desire to escape from the emptiness of his house – the emptiness and the ghosts of his lost family.

Will Pride watched his brother with a mixture of compassion and irritation. Robert had always been the stronger of the two; the more respectable, the one whom the rest of their family held up to Will as a pattern card, but now it seemed that Robert's strength had gone, and Will, who had never felt comfortable dealing in emotions, couldn't understand why a man in his brother's position spent his nights alone in an empty house when he could have spent them in the arms and the bed of any one of a dozen accommodating buxom beauties. Robert was still a well-set-up man, and one who would appear even better if he smiled occasionally instead of looking as though he had lost a guinea and found a sixpence.

After Lyddy's death Robert had poured out his feelings to Will, begging him to tell him that he had done the right thing in allowing his sisters-in-law to take his children.

'Well, wi'out anyone to run this house for you I don't see as how you could have done anything else,' Will had confirmed robustly.

It wasn't his place after all to add to Robert's misery by telling him what he thought of young Ellie for behaving in the way she had. Dropping Gideon who just wasn't the same lad any more – aye, and acting like Preston wasn't good enough for her now! Anyroad, Will knew his brother well enough to know that he would fly to his daughter's defence, just as he had always done to his wife's.

Now, though, Will's forehead crinkled in genuine concern as he looked around the unkempt room. He had been hearing tales about his brother that made him feel it was time he stepped in and did what he could to help.

'Se'thee, our Rob,' he began breezily. 'Why don't you and me go into town and to a music hall this evening? That 'ud cheer you up. Bit of a comedian, and all them pretty lasses?' he encouraged him enthusiastically.

Robert expelled a sigh. He didn't really care what

he did but he knew his brother well enough to know that he would not give up until he got his way.

'Aw, come on, Robert. It's too late to change your mind now! And besides, what harm will it do? It's time you went out and had a bit o' fun. You've mourned your Lyddy for a full twelve-month, as is right and proper, like, and now it's time to get on with living. An evening at the music hall and a bit o' supper. Where's the harm in that?'

'I suppose you're right,' Robert agreed. He noticed that Will was wearing a new suit in honour of the occasion and looked very dapper indeed. There was an eager glint in his eyes that Robert knew of old but it was too late for him to have second thoughts now. Will was already urging him to hurry.

It had been a warm day and the town was busy, the millworkers making the most of their Saturday afternoon off. It brought a wry smile to Robert's lips to notice that on no less than three separate occasions different women made bold attempts to catch the eye of his brother.

'A friend of yours, Will?' Robert teased him, mock innocently, when the third woman had taken umbrage at Will's attempts to pretend not to know her. Lyddy would certainly not have approved of such an enterprise as a music-hall trip, especially in the company of Will.

The market square was still busy with shoppers and the brothers skirted round them.

'Seen anything of young Gideon Walker lately?' Will asked Robert conversationally as they reached the theatre, where a queue had already formed for the next performance.

'He called by the other week,' Robert answered. 'You know he offered to take John's dog when he went off to school and he wanted John's address so that he could let him know how the dog was going on.' Robert's mouth compressed with remembered pain. He hadn't been able to admit to Gideon that he couldn't give him any news of John as he had none.

'Well, seems like he's doing pretty well for himself,' Will commented, pausing to wink at one of the pair of girls standing in the queue in front of them as she turned round.

She responded with a saucy smile, nudging her friend, who also turned round. Tall, with a mop of red curls, she looked past Will to Robert, her eyes widening in recognition as she did so.

'It's Robert Pride, isn't it?' she asked.

Assuming that the young woman must be an occasional customer he could not remember, Robert allowed himself to be drawn into the conversation, which Will had already eagerly instigated with the two girls.

Although, as a married man, he had never indulged in the open flirtatiousness that Will always adopted towards members of the opposite sex, Robert was by no means immune to the charms of a pretty face, especially when its owner was only too happy to make it plain that she was enjoying his company, and, somehow or other, by the time they actually got into the music hall, it had been arranged that the four of them would sit together.

'Perhaps we could even go out and have a bit o' supper together after the show, eh, girls?' Will suggested nonchalantly, throwing Robert a grin as he did so.

Robert could feel the claims of his dead wife tugging at his conscience, but the doors had opened and the crowd swirled forward, catching the red-headed girl off guard and almost unbalancing her. Automatically Robert reached out a protective hand to steady her.

'My, what a gentleman you are, Robert Pride,' she teased him, batting her eyelashes at him and smiling provocatively. They had reached the door now and she grinned up at him. 'Not going to offer me your arm, then?'

Obediently Robert did so.

'That's more like it, our Rob,' Will murmured approvingly behind him, before demanding, 'So what are your names, then, girls?'

'Mine's Maggie,' the redhead responded boldly, whilst the young woman on Will's arm giggled and told him, 'And I'm Daisy.'

Gideon tensed and stopped walking, causing the person behind him in the busy street to curse as he almost bumped into him. His mind had been

175

too busy mentally reckoning up how he was going to pay his suppliers' bills whilst he waited for the money that was owing to him to warn him that he was about to turn into Friargate.

He avoided the street like the plague, although why he should bother to avoid it when Ellie wasn't there any more was unclear.

Ellie. Gideon scowled, angry with himself for even remembering her name, never mind allowing her into his thoughts.

The sun had been dipping, dying into the horizon on a crimson sea, when he had emerged from his workroom to breath the sawdust out of his lungs and some fresh air into them. He had been working night and day for the last three weeks, desperate to finish a contract, which it now looked as though he wasn't going to be paid for in full. And as if that wasn't bad enough, the more senior of the two jobbing carpenters he had taken on had drunk too much one Saturday night a fortnight ago, started a fight and ended up with a broken wrist. Unable to replace him at short notice, Gideon had been forced to do his work as well as his own.

The men who worked for him complained that Gideon drove them too hard, but it was no harder than he drove himself. All they had to worry about was their pay at the end of the week; he had to worry about a hell of a lot more. All the time he was driven by the fear that he could lose everything he was working so hard for. He was earning enough to pay his rent – just – and the men –

most of the time – but he had had to cut his prices to the bone to get in as many orders as he could manage to establish himself, but also to make ends meet.

One of the first jobbing carpenters he had hired had lost his job with him because he had questioned Gideon's pricing, shaking his head as he told him that he was cutting things too close.

'I'll thank you to keep your opinions to yourself,' Gideon had told him angrily. 'I know what I'm doing. That's why I'm the one doing the hiring and you're the one working for me.'

He had to make money; he had to get himself established; he had to prove . . . Gideon froze. He had nothing to prove. Nothing. Especially not to Ellie Pride, damn her. A girl who had deserted her family when they needed her most.

Gideon had one ambition, one goal, and that was to become rich. So rich that when Ellie Pride heard how rich he was she would regret to her dying day that she had rejected him.

The pain inside him was like the dying sun, now painting the river with crimson streaks of light – hot, burning . . .

Gideon's fingers itched for charcoal so that he could capture the scene in front of him. On the rare occasions when he wasn't working, he walked the town, pausing to sketch buildings that caught his eye. Gideon was fascinated by buildings of every kind. Only the previous month, when he had gone to Winckley Square to finish a job for

Miss Isherwood, he had watched from a distance as the young architect she had hired to design a conservatory for her had shown her his drawings.

Later that evening Gideon had got out his own sketchbook and started drafting some ideas of his own, before throwing the pad aside in a gesture of bitter frustration. He was a cabinet-maker and he had better remember it instead of wasting his time on fools' dreams.

The year had driven the last of the youthful softness from his face, carving harsh lines of bitterness from his nose to his mouth. The tender young lover who had walked with Ellie in the spring green of Avenham Park a year ago no longer existed. The man who had taken his place had stamped the tenderness out of his soul and replaced it with pitiless iron bitterness.

He was a man driven in equal measure by pride and pain. A man who had refused to give that broken-wristed workman a halfpenny more than he owed him, and a man who had still been fool enough to hand the carpenter's wife a full guinea when she had come crying at his door, two snotty-nosed brats at her heels.

He looked down at the dog at his feet – John Pride's dog, in reality, and the reason he was out here now, heading for a walk along the river instead of working on his accounts.

A woman with two brats and no money to put food in their mouths, a young boy with a dog he loved to desperation and could not keep – maybe he was soft enough to find compassion in his heart for them, but there would never be any there for Ellie Pride.

TWELVE

It was the week of Cecily's wedding and of Ellie's longed-for opportunity to see her family. Now that she was finally back home in Preston, Ellie could hardly breathe for excitement and anticipation.

'Oh, thank goodness we are arrived. I am exhausted,' Aunt Lavinia announced as she sank down into a chair.

Mr Parkes had hired several rooms at the Bull and Royal Hotel in Preston, where the wedding breakfast was to be held, with dancing in one of its ballrooms afterwards, and they had travelled by train from Liverpool earlier in the day.

Their visit was to last for several days to accommodate not just the wedding celebrations, but also to allow the four remaining Barclay sisters to spend time with one another.

Mr Parkes had not travelled to Preston on the train with them, having announced that he was far too busy to take so much time away from his practice, and would instead motor over to Preston and then return to Hoylake the day after the wedding.

At Aunt Lavinia's insistence, both Wrotham and Lizzie had accompanied them, and Lizzie was now busy unpacking and pressing their gowns whilst Wrotham looked on watchfully. Aunt Lavinia's eau-de-Nil silk gown, which Ellie had painstakingly altered, shimmered as Lizzie carefully removed it from the trunk.

'Wrotham, you have packed my tonic, haven't you?' Lavinia demanded anxiously. 'Perhaps I should have some now just as a precaution . . . Yes, I think I will!'

Surreptitiously Ellie glanced at her watch. All the bridesmaids, of which she and Connie were two, were to change into their dresses at the Gibsons', and she did not want to be late arriving there. Connie and her Aunt and Uncle Simpkins were not staying at the Bull, having made arrangements to stay with another clergyman, whose parish lay within the town.

'Well, of course, my sister's husband does not possess the same financial advantages as Mr Parkes,' had been Lavinia's comment when she had discussed the arrangements for the wedding with Ellie, 'and it will doubtless cost them nothing to stay with a fellow vicar.'

One of the things Ellie had learned during the months she had lived with her Aunt Lavinia was the sometimes amusing rivalry that seemed to exist between the sisters, often manifesting itself in petty jealousies more suited to the schoolroom than the drawing rooms of mature ladies. Although her own mother had refused ever to breathe a word of criticism against any member of her family, no matter how much Ellie and her siblings had sometimes done so in private.

So Ellie now knew that Amelia, the eldest of the sisters, was sometimes considered 'bossy' by the others, and that Jane, who was married to the Reverend Mr Simpkins, was, in Lavinia's opinion, too fond of standing in moral judgement on Lavinia's extravagances, whilst Emily, who was married to the headmaster of John's school, must surely find it dreary having forever to listen to a man who spoke more often in Latin than he did in English.

However, nowhere was the rivalry between the sisters more keenly felt and shown than in social situations – hence Aunt Lavinia's anxiety over her outfit for the wedding. Normally Ellie would have been endlessly entertained and amused by her aunt, but today she was too eager to see Connie to want to listen.

'Ellie! Oh, I have missed you so much.' Connie's eyes filled with tears the minute she saw her elder sister, her determination to ignore her as a punishment for the way she had not written to her forgotten as she rushed towards Ellie.

Despite knowing their Aunt Amelia's disapproving eye was on them, Ellie returned Connie's hug with fierce intensity.

'Ellie, I've got to talk to you,' Connie burst out 'Quick, let's go somewhere that we can talk on our own.'

Ellie shook her head warningly. This was the Connie she remembered, and very definitely not the Connie of those stilted uninformative letters.

'Connie, we can't, not now! Not until after the wedding!'

'Oh, that's typical of you,' Connie protested sulkily, 'Ellie, you have no idea how miserable I have been.' Connie couldn't contain her feelings any longer. 'You are so lucky to be living with our Aunt and Uncle Parkes. Just look at your gown – silk and in the latest style,' she declared enviously. 'Our Aunt Jane considers that it is wickedly sinful to waste money on expensive clothes instead of giving it to the poor! All she and our Uncle Simpkins can think of is religion and good works.' Connie made a face as she glanced over her shoulder in the direction of their aunts.

Worriedly, Ellie studied her sister. She was used, of course, to Connie's theatrical exaggeration, but she could see that her sister was thinner, and there was a look of desperation in her eyes that made Ellie's heart clench in sisterly anxiety. She could well understand that her vain, giddy little sister would not take kindly to being dressed in a gown so plain that it was almost puritan, without so

183

much as a flounce or tuck of lace to break up its severity.

'I hate this dress! It's just horrid,' Connie complained, looking enviously again at Ellie's.

'The colour suits you,' Ellie told her placatingly, 'and if there is time whilst we are here I could trim it a little for you.'

'Oh, Ellie, would you? When? On Monday? We could go to Miller's Arcade and get the trimming. Mama's sewing machine will still be at home. We can go there and . . .' Suddenly her face crumpled. 'Oh, Ellie, I miss home so much. You have no idea how unhappy I have been.'

Her distress caused Ellie's own eyes to prickle a little with threatening tears. In an attempt to comfort her, Ellie whispered quickly to her, 'Oh, Connie, so do I!'

'Why can't we go home, Ellie? I would have written to Father asking him to let us, but it was hard enough sending my letter to you. I was so afraid that the postboy wouldn't take it, and it cost me a whole penny.' She pulled a face. 'I hate those stupid letters they make me write to you. Ellie, they are so unkind to me . . .' Connie whispered, her bottom lip trembling and her eyes dark.

Ellie listened with growing dismay, not least because she had most definitely not received an uncensored letter from Connie. Her heart beat unpleasantly fast, and she felt frightened and distressed. It was a shock to learn how unhappy Connie was, and Ellie was already conscious of the narrow-eyed look their Aunt Jane was giving them. Connie was wilful and headstrong, Ellie knew, but she could see that her sister was genuinely upset.

Connie was her younger sister and it was her duty and her responsibility to take care of her!

'Father has never written to me once, nor come to see me.' Connie was practically wailing. 'If he had done so I would have begged him to take me away. Ellie, you have no idea how unhappy I have been. And cold. I am always cold and hungry . . .'

Now Ellie really was shocked. 'Connie, you are exaggerating,' she began and then stopped as Connie gave her a bleak look.

'No I am not,' Connie replied passionately. 'If you knew half of what I have had to put up with – reading dreary books and being made to sew for the poor . . . and . . . and just not being at home with everyone, with Father and John and you . . . Oh, Ellie!'

Ellie couldn't say anything. The truth was that she longed to return to their old home and their old life just as much as Connie. And now, added to that need, there was also her elder-sister desire to protect her younger siblings. Ellie felt conscience-stricken to discover that Connie was so unhappy, but what could she do about it?

'Ellie, whilst we're here couldn't you go and see Father, and persuade him to let us come home? You could look after us all, and I know he would listen to you because you are the eldest.'

Ellie opened her mouth to tell Connie that they

would never be allowed to do any such thing, and then closed it again. Her heart was racing with nervous excitement. It was a bold plan but maybe she could persuade their father. As her heart leaped again, Ellie realised just how much she longed to return home.

She took a deep breath. 'Very well, Connie, I . . . I will speak to Father at the dance this evening. You are right, I'm sure, that I could manage to run the household at Friargate. Our Aunt Parkes suffers with her nerves, and often deputises me to give the servants their instructions, and besides, Mother taught us both how things should be done. I am older now and I do not believe that Mother would want us all to be separated from one another in the way that we are, especially the poor little baby. He will grow up without knowing us at all. I wrote to Aunt Jepson asking her to send me a photograph of him, but she has not replied.' The subject of their baby brother had been causing Ellie increasing anxiety and guilt. 'I am going to ask our father to change his mind and allow us all to come home, but you are not to say anything until I have spoken with him,' she cautioned her sister.

'But Father will not be at the dance,' Connie told her sharply. 'Did you not know? He has not been invited.'

'Not invited?' Ellie frowned. 'But that's impossible. He is our father, and –'

'Aunt Jane says that Aunt Gibson has said she does not want to take him away from the shop on a busy Saturday,' Connie informed Ellie with a careless shrug.

'Come along, girls, it is time for you to go upstairs and change into your gowns.' Aunt Amelia was now standing in front of the sisters. Ellie knew that she had never approved of their father, but to have excluded him from Cecily's wedding!

'Aunt Amelia, Connie has just told me that our father is not to attend the wedding. Surely that cannot be true?' Ellie demanded, stammering slightly beneath the weight of her shocked disbelief.

A slight tinge of colour betrayed Amelia Gibson's chagrin, as her mouth thinned and she darted Connie a distinctly hostile look.

'Your father has a shop to keep open, Ellie; you know that,' she replied. 'And besides, it is only just twelve months since he lost your mother, and to be amongst us without her would, I am sure, cause him a measure of distress he will be grateful to us for sparing him.'

'But he is our father,' Ellie insisted, her face starting to burn with the intensity of her feelings.

'Ellie, this is neither the time nor the place for a discussion of this nature,' Amelia Gibson reproved her determinedly. 'I hope I do not need to remind you of your mother's dying wishes!'

Suddenly Ellie's face was as pale as it had been flushed.

'Ellie, come on,' Connie urged her sister from halfway up the stairs. Swallowing hard, Ellie followed her whilst Amelia watched her go.

It was her duty to ensure that her sister's wishes were carried out, just as it was Ellie's to remember the promise she had given her mother, and Amelia had very few qualms about deliberately driving a wedge between Robert and his family – and none whatsoever about excluding him from her daughter's wedding! Which was why the sisters had made a pact that the siblings were not to be allowed any unchecked correspondence with one another.

Lavinia had been the hardest to persuade, shrinking from doing as Jane had done and standing over Ellie dictating what she might write to her brother and sister. So instead, Ellie's letters had been handed to Mr Parkes who, for Ellie's own sake and to spare her the pain of keeping in contact with the others, had simply disposed of them.

Ellie gave a small sigh as the congregation emerged from the church and John immediately attached himself to the photographer. No doubt her brother was plaguing the poor man with a dozen or more questions! Ellie frowned as she thought about John. Her young brother seemed so different from the noisy boy she remembered, much quieter and far more withdrawn. When she had rushed to hug him he had stiffened and looked over his shoulder to where their Aunt and Uncle Jepson were watching them, and she was sure she had seen apprehension in his eyes.

She had not as yet seen the baby Joseph, but John, boy-like, had simply shrugged when she had asked about him, telling her, 'I don't see very much of him. Our aunt doesn't like me being with him because she says I wake him up. And he isn't called Joseph any more, he's called Philip.'

Ellie had felt a shock of anger surge through her. It had been their mother's decision to name the baby Joseph. Not only had their aunts taken them away from their father, they had even taken his name away from their baby brother. Disturbed and distressed by her own thoughts, Ellie promised herself that somehow she would make her father see that they all had to come home.

The weather had been kind, with sunshine and the merest light breeze, and Cecily was such a radiantly happy bride that just looking at her caused a lump to fill Ellie's throat.

'And Mr Parkes is thinking of taking on a man-servant to answer the telephone at home as he says it sounds much more businesslike when important clients telephone than merely having one of the maids do so.'

'Really?' Amelia Gibson raised one eyebrow in judicious consideration of her sister's comment, whilst Ellie listened a little impatiently. 'Actually Dr Gibson was saying only the other day that he feels he might employ one of these new telephonist stenographers,' Amelia countered sturdily. 'When he went to consult one of the specialists in Rodney Street about a patient the other week, he discovered that they are all employing these young women now.'

Whilst her Aunt Parkes digested this information, Ellie seized her moment.

'Aunt, I have promised Connie that I will trim one of her gowns for her whilst we are here in Preston and I was thinking that I might walk round to Miller's Arcade and . . . and see what I can find.'

Ellie hated being deceitful. 'And then visit my father in Friargate,' was what she had really wanted to say, but she had quickly discovered over the weekend that any talk of her father or of Friargate was not something that her mother's family had any intentions of encouraging.

As she waited for her aunts' response Ellie held her breath, praying that they would not refuse her request. It was two days after the wedding and Connie was upstairs in the Winckley Square house with her cousins, only Ellie being deemed grown-up enough to be included in the drawing-room conversation of the older generation.

'Walk all that way? On your own?' Aunt Parkes looked concerned and was, Ellie feared, about to refuse her permission to go.

But to her relief her Aunt Gibson pursed her lips and announced, 'I am sure that it will be perfectly safe. Ellie could take her maid with her, perhaps.'

Take Lizzie! Ellie's heart sank as Aunt Parkes signified her approval of this course of action. Ellie had had no idea when her mother had talked to her about the pleasures of being a 'young lady' that those pleasures came laced up with all manner of petty restrictions and loss of freedom!

An hour later, as they stood together at the entrance to Miller's Arcade, Lizzie meticulously standing a couple of paces behind Ellie as she guarded the small package containing the trimming for Connie's dress, Ellie turned to her, her face flushing uncomfortably.

'Lizzie, I don't want to . . . to put you in a difficult position, but I . . . I am going to Friargate to see my father,' she announced defiantly. 'My aunts do not approve of him, I know, but he is my father and I . . . I have to see him because there is something I need to discuss with him. I was wondering . . . if I were to give you a shilling, would you be happy to stay here and perhaps enjoy a cup of tea . . . ?'

Lizzie looked wisely at her. In truth she felt rather sorry for Ellie, although, of course, it was not her place to say so. There had been the usual kind of talk about her amongst the servants at Hoylake and about her background.

'A shilling would buy a good deal more than one cup of tea, miss,' she pointed out drily. 'But I shall take it, for it will add to our fund.'

'Your fund? What is that?'

'It is the money me and my sisters are saving, miss, so that we can rent out a house down by the docks and set up in business as landladies. There's allus a big demand down there for clean rooms and decent food for seafaring men.'

Ellie gazed at her in admiration. 'You will have your own business! Oh, Lizzie, how very brave and daring. But what if one of you should marry?'

'Marry?' Lizzie gave a disparaging sniff. 'Oh, no, us'll not be doing any of that, thank you, miss! Catch me taking on a man! No, thank you.'

'I'll be back as soon as I can, Lizzie,' Ellie promised as she opened her purse and removed a shilling, handing it to Lizzie.

'Don't you worry about me, miss. I shall be fine. Oh, and by the by, should anyone have any cause to ask me about today – well I shall just say that it was a good thing that you decided to check on the trimming whilst you was in the teashop and that you discovered you had been given the wrong one, like, and had to take it back to change it.'

'Oh, Lizzie!'

Ellie gave her a grateful look and then hugged her, much to the maid's obvious bemusement.

She had been away only just over twelve months and surely it was not possible in that short space of time that somehow Friargate could have become narrower and its houses shrunk, but somehow they had, Ellie acknowledged.

Her father's apprentice looked up from serving

the shop's single customer, his mouth agape and his face bright red as Ellie hurried past him.

Since it was a Monday, Ellie was fully expecting the yard to be busy with the bustle of washday, the copper boiling viciously in the outhouse, whilst Jenny kneaded and scrubbed the dirty clothes, but there was no sign of either Jenny or of any activity as Ellie hurried through the yard and into the kitchen. Annie too was absent.

Had her father perhaps taken to sending everything out to the laundry, Ellie wondered absently, as she made her way upstairs, calling out her father's name eagerly as she opened the door into the parlour.

The room was empty, but Ellie could hear muffled sounds from the bedroom above. Picking up her skirts, she hurried upstairs.

Pushing open the door to her father's bedroom, Ellie rushed inside, calling out happily, 'Father, it's me, Ellie, I have –'

Abruptly Ellie stopped speaking, her face turning hot crimson and then milky white as she stared at the scene in front of her.

Her father was lying on his bed – the bed he had shared with her mother – and straddling him was a woman Ellie had never seen before, her untidy red hair hanging round her face, her body, like Ellie's father's, completely naked. Her father's hand was clutching one of her full breasts, and . . .

Ellie's stomach churned nauseously as she tried to look away. But for some reason she could not do so.

Could not speak or move as shock locked her where she was.

The woman was looking at her, a sly smile of smug triumph curling her mouth as she deliberately jiggled her breasts and moved disgustingly on Ellie's father's body whilst saying, 'Why, Robbie, why didn't tha tell us, us 'ud be having company?'

Nausea rose in Ellie's throat, bitter and sour. Somehow she managed to move, managed to turn and run towards the door, her father calling out frantically, 'Ellie! Ellie, lass! Wait . . .'

Ignoring him, Ellie ran full pelt down the stairs and through the parlour, down into the shop and then out into the street, her body heaving with nausea and dry, choking sobs.

How could her father? How could he? How could he sully their mother's memory in such a way? And with such a woman – a woman who had made it plain to Ellie with that sidelong taunting look that she considered herself to be very much in possession of Ellie's father?

Half walking, half running, Ellie discovered that she had almost reached the river. Trying to calm herself, she stopped and drew in deep breaths of air. She was shivering, huge shudders of distress and shock that rocked her whole body.

Her head felt as though it was going to burst with the intensity of her thoughts. Images danced inside her head, tormenting her: her father's face, hot with lust; the woman's eyes, mocking with a knowledge she knew Ellie did not possess; even the smell of the room was in her nostrils, still clinging to her clothes and her skin, the smell of animals on heat! Ellie could still see the beads of perspiration trickling down her father's face and glistening on the thick mat of grey hair on his chest; she could still feel the forbidden excitement in the room.

Anger burst through her. Anger against the woman, for mocking her; against her father, for betraying her mother; against her aunts for their selfishness in breaking up their family; anger against Connie for making her feel so guilty; but, most shockingly of all, anger against her dead mother.

Ellie shuddered and sobbed as she fought to suppress what she was feeling and struggled to remind herself of her duty and her promise, but still her anger would not go away.

The sound of a church bell striking the hour made her realise the time. She had to get back to Miller's Arcade and Lizzie.

THIRTEEN

'Is something wrong, Gideon?' Mary Isherwood asked, walking into the kitchen. She had sent for him to take some measurements for a new china cupboard.

On the point of lying, to his own bemusement Gideon heard himself admitting reluctantly, 'With the business expanding the way it has done these last months, I need larger premises, but property of the type I want – with a storage yard, good light and a couple o' rooms for myself, and at a reasonable rent – is impossible to find.' He reflected wearily on just how many hours he had wasted over the last couple of weeks looking for new accommodation.

'Have you approached the agent you're already renting from?' Mary suggested.

Gideon informed her grimly, 'He's out of town on business, and the clerk in his office told me that they didn't have anything available at the kind of rent I can afford, and even if they did, like as not I'd have to make a good-sized deposit.'

'And you can't afford to do that?' Mary guessed.

Gideon tensed, wary of discussing something so personal with a customer. 'I make a fair living,' he answered guardedly.

Mary acknowledged inwardly that her questions were making Gideon feel uncomfortable, but she had her own reasons for asking them.

'Well, if I were you, Gideon, I think I should insist on seeing the letting agent himself when he returns, and not his clerk. But, of course, you know your own business best . . . Oh!' Mary gave a small exclamation of concern as she accidentally dislodged Gideon's sketchbook from the table. 'You draw?' she questioned him, bending down to pick up the pad before he could stop her. 'May I?' And then without waiting for his reply she looked through the sketches.

Gideon felt both acutely uncomfortable and angry. Those drawings were in many ways his secret dreams – dreams that he knew could never come true. The sketches were not just of buildings that he had seen, but, more privately, of buildings he would like to see, buildings he had conjured up out of his imagination. But his anger turned to guilt when he saw Mary picking up the conservatory sketch he had drawn. He held his breath but, to his relief, she made no comment.

But as she handed the sketchpad back to him, she told him quietly, 'These are very good, Gideon. Have you ever had any proper lessons?'

Her question made Gideon feel vulnerable and

defensive. How did she think someone like him could afford 'proper lessons'? He took the pad from her, and told her stiffly, 'I've measured up for the cupboards you want in here. I'll price them for you and then come back to you.'

He didn't want to talk about his sketches or his dreams, and he certainly didn't want to be patronised by a rich woman who had no idea of the bitterness he felt in his heart.

'Did you see our father, then, Ellie?' Connie demanded eagerly the moment she and Ellie were alone. 'Is everything arranged? When are we to move back to Friargate?'

'I . . . I did see him,' Ellie confirmed, but how could she tell Connie just what she had seen? She couldn't. She had to protect her sister from the sordidness of her discovery, as she now ached to have been protected herself!

There was no way they could return to Friargate now, Ellie knew that. And no way, she suspected, would their father want them back! No, that would spoil the new life he had made for himself. And even if he did, it would be impossible for them to live there whilst he . . . whilst that woman . . . Ellie's eyes burned with shocked, angry tears she could not allow herself to cry, and her throat felt raw and painful. No, they could never return to Friargate. There was no place for them there now.

Ellie could still see inside her head that woman's

smirking look of contempt and triumph. Ellie knew instinctively that they would be enemies. How could it be otherwise? That woman had taken their mother's place; taken their father from them. And what a dreadful example she would be to Connie!

No wonder their father had not replied to her letters, not telephoned her, not come to see her, Ellie reflected bitterly.

'We can't go back, Connie,' she told her sister.

The despair and anger in Connie's eyes echoed Ellie's own feelings, but she told herself that she had to be strong for them both.

'Why not? You promised that we could. You promised,' Connie sobbed furiously.

Biting her lip, Ellie turned her head slightly, fearing that Connie might see the truth in her eyes as she told her quietly, 'I know I did, Connie, but . . .' she searched for the right words, the words that would silence Connie's passionate objections. 'I've changed my mind.' Ellie heard her words fall like stones into a very deep pool.

Connie's mouth opened and stayed open in a round 'O' of silent dismay, her whole body frozen. And then she gave a small shudder.

'I hate you, Ellie Pride,' she burst out furiously. 'You promised . . . you promised.'

Ellie went to hold her and comfort her, but she pulled away, her eyes burning with anger.

'I shall hate you for ever for this!' she cried passionately. 'And I know why you've changed your mind. It's because you don't care about me and John, because everything's all right for you, being spoiled and petted in Hoylake. Well, if you won't help me then I shall just have to find a way to help myself. And I shall do so. Just you wait and see!'

Dully, Ellie listened in silence as Connie bombarded her with insults, pleas and threats, her head bowed beneath the injustice of Connie's fury. Connie's anger and bitterness were so hard to bear but they had to be borne for Connie's own sake.

One day, perhaps when they were both older, she might be able to tell Connie the truth, Ellie thought, as her body shook in response to Connie's cruel words, but not now. She could not tell her now! Connie had been so close to their father. She had worshipped him almost. Now she must never know what Ellie knew.

'I hate you, Ellie,' Connie repeated, her voice trembling. 'It's all right for you, living with Aunt Parkes, with your fine new clothes and your own maid, and now too our cousin Cecily so close at hand! I suppose I should not be surprised that you do not want to return to Friargate.'

'Connie, that is not true. I do,' Ellie protested uneasily.

'No, you don't! You don't care about the rest of us at all! All you care about is yourself! You are comfortable enough in Hoylake! Do you know what I think, Ellie? I think that you believe yourself too good for Friargate now, and that is why you have not done as you promised!' Tears filled Connie's eyes.

'Connie, please,' Ellie begged, but her sister hurried out of the room, letting the door slam behind her.

There! That was Connie's dress finished and only just in time, since she was to return to the vicarage in the morning.

Lizzie would have to take the dress round to Connie for her, Ellie acknowledged, since Mr Parkes had arrived unexpectedly just over an hour ago, to announce that he had a business meeting in Preston and had decided that he would join the family dinner party that the Gibsons were holding that night.

As a special treat for her sister, Ellie had secretly made a new gown, using the dress she was trimming for her as a pattern, but copying a design Connie had been swooning over in a ladies' magazine. She had stayed up late into the night working on it, ignoring the ache behind her eyes as she painstakingly recreated every tiny pintuck and flounce.

Rubbing her aching neck muscles tiredly, Ellie tensed as she suddenly heard raised voices from her aunt's room, followed by the sound of breaking furniture and then a shrill scream followed by silence.

She ran out into the corridor, only to find her way blocked by Wrotham, who was barring the door to her aunt and uncle's room.

'Something has happened to my aunt,' Ellie protested anxiously. 'I must go to her.'

'It's nothing for you to worry about, miss,' Wrotham told Ellie firmly. 'The mistress just had one of her turns, that's all. The master is with her and I am just going to get her tonic for her.'

A little uncertainly Ellie looked past the maid to the closed door.

'You should go back to your own room, miss,' Wrotham insisted.

'Very well,' Ellie agreed, 'but if my aunt should need me . . .'

'You had best be thinking about getting ready for this evening, miss,' Wrotham told her sharply. 'The master will not take too kindly to being kept waiting.'

A little reluctantly Ellie returned to her own room to pick up Connie's gown, which she had thrown down in her anxiety, and to ring for Lizzie.

FOURTEEN

Gideon frowned as Rex the collie began to yip excit-edly, the way he did when he knew and welcomed a caller. Closing the book on architecture which he had been reading, Gideon got up and went to the door. His frown deepened as he recognised his visitor.

'John Pride!' he exclaimed in astonishment. 'What are you doing here?'

John was already down on his knees, hugging the wriggling dog, who had thrown itself at him in excited delight.

'I came to see my dog,' John told him gruffly. 'We are to leave tomorrow and I could not go without doing so.'

'Leave?' Gideon's heart was thudding as though he had run too fast, and a peculiar sensation he didn't want to name was invading his body.

'Yes. We have all been here for our cousin Cecily's wedding – Ellie and Connie and our aunts and uncles. I would have come before, but this is the first opportunity I have had to get away,' John explained.

Ellie was here in Preston! Gideon's chest constricted and he struggled for breath. Anger, that was what he was feeling, anger, he told himself quickly. What did he care where Ellie Pride was? He didn't.

Gideon looked at the down-bent tow head as John stroked the dog, guessing that the child wasn't far from tears. He knew how much the pup had meant to John and how reluctant he had been to part with him – and all so that he could be sent to some damned school. Weren't there schools enough in Preston, without having to send the lad to live miles away and deprive him of the company of his much-loved pet – and so soon after the loss of his mother? But according to Will Pride it had been John's mother's wish that he should go to Hutton.

As John rolled on the floor, playing with the dog, his shirt rode up his back, revealing three angry-looking blood-encrusted weals.

'What the –' Gideon began, and then stopped as John turned round.

'My uncle gave me a whipping for not doing my Latin prep well enough,' he told him gruffly. 'He does not like me very much, I think. But it is not just me he beats,' he added simply. 'My aunt says that he always wanted children of his own, but I do not think that can be true, for he complains every time the baby cries, and my aunt has to keep him shut away whenever my uncle is there.'

Gideon listened to these artless disclosures in angry contemptuous silence.

'Have you seen the notices for the Wild West Show, Gideon?' John demanded eagerly. 'I wish more than anything that I might see it. Will you be going?'

'Perhaps, if I am not too busy.'

'Are you busy?' John enquired. 'I wish I might leave school and come and live here with you, Gideon, and be your apprentice.'

'I thought it was a balloonist or a photographer you wanted to be, not a cabinet-maker,' Gideon reminded him drily.

'It is,' John agreed, unabashed, 'but if I was your apprentice I could live here in Preston. Connie and I wanted Ellie to ask our father if we could come back to live at Friargate, but she doesn't want to. Connie says she likes living in Hoylake and having lots of new dresses and her own maid too much to care about us!' John told him sadly.

Gideon's mouth hardened. He had had a lucky escape when Ellie had rejected his love, that was for sure.

'Well, now that you have seen your dog, don't you think you should be getting back before your family start to miss you, John?' he prompted.

'No.' John's mouth was stubborn, but his eyes were anxious with a fear that aroused all Gideon's protective instincts as well as reinforcing his angry contempt for Ellie. 'No, please don't make me go back, Gideon. Please let me stay here. I won't be any trouble, I promise.'

Gideon sighed. If he hadn't seen those nearly fresh strap marks he might have been more inclined to cuff John's ear and send him straight back where he belonged. As it was . . .

Hunkering down beside him, he said gently, 'You know you can't stay here, John. People are going to miss you and –'

'No they won't,' John insisted. 'Not yet. They – my aunt and uncle and the others – are to go to our Aunt Gibson's for dinner tonight, but I am to stay behind at the Bull.'

Gideon gave another small sigh and caved in. 'I was just about to take Rex for a bit o' a walk,' he told John. 'You could come along with us, if you like, but then it's straight back to the Bull.'

'Connie, if you do know where John has gone then please tell us now,' Ellie begged her younger sister frantically.

They were all in a private salon at the hotel: their Aunt and Uncle Parkes; their Aunt and Uncle Jepson, who had, half an hour ago, discovered that John was missing and raised the alarm; and their Aunt and Uncle Simpkins, summoned from their accommodation to join in the outcry about John's disappearance and to add their own measure of critical disapproval of his behaviour. And, of course, Ellie, torn between anxiety over her missing brother, and her desire to find a way to placate their angry relatives.

Connie, who had been the last person to see John, was tearful but stubbornly refusing to say a single word to indicate whether or not she knew where John might be. Uncle Parkes was coldly grim-faced as he listened to Uncle Jepson's furious tirade against John, whilst Aunt Jepson bemoaned his lack of gratitude for the care they had given him.

Aunt Parkes, in contrast, had said nothing, her fingers tugging anxiously at the collar of pearls covering the whole of her throat from just beneath her chin to her collarbone, along which Ellie could see the beginnings of an angry graze, obviously caused earlier when she had fallen. As she lifted her arm, Ellie also noticed the beginnings of a bruise swelling the pale skin.

'Connie, if you know anything about John's disappearance,' Ellie whispered to her sister, 'then –'

'Do you think I would tell *you* if I did?' Connie whispered back furiously. 'If John wants to see his dog –'

The dog! Of course. Why on earth hadn't she thought of that?

Under cover of their older relatives' angry discussion, Ellie looked at her sister. Connie's defiant expression gave her away immediately.

'Connie, why didn't you tell me?' Ellie demanded.

'Why should I?' Connie hissed back. 'I told John that we can't go back home because of you and he hates you for it as much as I do.'

Ellie could have cried. Torn between a juvenile desire to defend herself and a more mature need to protect her siblings, she felt both deserted and to blame. Bleakly she recognised how alone she was, and how afraid that made her feel. And all the time inside her head there was still that shocking image of her father in bed with that woman!

There was no one she could turn to – no one at all.

But right now what mattered more than her own feelings was getting John back before he got into any more trouble. It was still an hour before they were due to leave for Winckley Square, and so Ellie excused herself and hurried from the room.

There was no time for her to change out of her evening finery – and she had no idea where Gideon Walker was living. Neither could she bring herself to return to Friargate to ask her father, but she suspected that her uncle, Will Pride, would know.

In her bedroom, Ellie pulled on a coat over her gown, and then hurried downstairs, leaving the Bull by a rear entrance. Her uncle lived on the opposite side of the town to the Bull and Royal, and the easiest way to get there, without drawing attention to herself in her finery, would be for her to cut through the park.

Wryly, Gideon slowed his step to match John's dragging feet. It was growing late and Gideon's belly was grumbling with hunger, but he could sense John's reluctance to return to his family.

They had left the river and crossed into the park, somewhere that Gideon avoided whenever he could. For him, the park and Ellie were inextricably linked.

Rex, tired after his walk and content to lollop at Gideon's side, suddenly gave an excited whine and started to run. Up ahead of them a young woman was hurrying in the direction of the park, the thin coat she had on doing little to conceal the expensive elegance of the evening dress she was wearing beneath it, her golden hair framing her face.

As she heard the dog she stopped and turned, stretching out her hands to fend off its enthusiastic greeting.

At Gideon's side, John burst out in a voice of wary dismay, 'Ellie!' But Gideon hadn't needed John's recognition of his sister to tell him who the young woman was.

Across the distance separating them he could sense her stillness, his heart angered by the hauteur of her erect carriage. It was obvious that she considered herself too good to come to them, Gideon seethed, but, even as he formed the thought, suddenly Ellie came hurrying towards them. When she reached them her face was flushed, and Gideon saw how her hand trembled as she reached out to touch John, who immediately stepped back from her.

'John, John, quickly. We must get back. You

are in such trouble,' Ellie told him. 'You should not –'

'You can't tell me what to do, Ellie,' John burst out, knuckling his eyes with his fists in a gesture that betrayed rather than hid his tears, and which tore at Ellie's sensitive heart. She ached to put her arms around him and hug him but sensed that he would reject her if she did.

All the time she was talking to John, Ellie was hideously conscious of Gideon's presence. Her heart had almost burst out of her body when she had seen the dog come racing towards her and had then looked up and seen John and Gideon. When she had hurried out to find John she had not given a thought to how it might affect her to see Gideon! The stays Lizzie had laced in to narrow her waist made it hard enough for her to run and breathe without Gideon adding to her weakness.

Ellie could feel her whole face burning – and not just her face. The imploring hand she had lifted towards John had started to tremble, and quickly she snatched it back.

Ellie looked just as he might have imagined, Gideon decided bitterly. That fancy dress her coat was doing little to conceal must have cost a pretty penny, and probably as much as he earned in a full quarter! Beneath the fine fabric he could see Ellie's breasts rising and falling with the quickness of her breathing, caused no doubt by her temper at being thus put out by her brother. What would she say if he were to pull up young John's shirt and show her the marks on his back? Didn't he already know from John just how little Ellie cared about her siblings? Bitterness hardened his mouth and his eyes, and he was looking at her with contempt, and Ellie, seeing it, felt as though he had struck her.

Gideon had changed, Ellie decided, unable to stop herself from stealing a quick greedy look at him whilst John clung to his dog. His shoulders had broadened and so, surely, had his chest. Ellie blushed at the waywardness of her thoughts. Gideon's body hair would not be grey, it would be dark and silky and . . . Ellie discovered that she was trembling.

'John, come along. We must return,' she insisted, anger quickening her to attack as she saw the contempt with which Gideon was regarding her. 'This is all your fault,' she told him, unable to hold back the words. 'If you had not encouraged him to –'

'Whoa there,' Gideon stopped her, his mouth folding into an angry rebuttal of her accusation. 'This is none of my doing. Young John here took it upon himself to come looking for his pet. Not that I wouldn't have taken the dog to see John myself had I thought we would be welcome,' he added pointedly.

It pleased Gideon to see the way her face burned, and to know too that she needed his co-operation to persuade John, now glued to his side, to go back with her.

With every word Ellie had said John had crept

closer to Gideon, and Ellie felt her heart turn over as she looked at them both.

'John, we must get back,' she repeated. John was just behaving like this because he was missing his dog, Ellie tried to reassure herself. It had always been their mother's intention that he should go to Hutton. All boys hated school.

John was leaning into Gideon's side and Gideon had his hand on John's shoulder in a gesture of comfort and masculine solidarity. Ellie felt a fresh spurt of anger burn through her as she looked pointedly at Gideon, forcing herself to meet his gaze. His eyes were openly mocking her, taunting her, Ellie recognised bitterly. Instinctively she knew that if he chose to do so, Gideon could walk away from her and take John with him, and that her brother would follow him willingly. What would happen if she returned to the Bull and Royal without her brother? She had already been gone far longer than she had intended, and her absence was bound to have been noticed.

In desperation she insisted, 'John, it is already a quarter to the hour and I am to be at our Aunt Gibson's for the hour. We must go.'

'Yes, John, you must not delay your sister in her entertainment,' Gideon cut across her, his mouth twisting unkindly.

But as Ellie stared at him, her face burning beneath his insulting scrutiny, he pushed John towards her, and leashed the dog.

Even through her own disruptive emotions, Ellie

still felt a sharp pang of pain for her brother as he bent to give Rex a fierce hug.

Over John's head, his voice so low that only Ellie could hear, Gideon said softly to her, 'You cannot know how pleased I am to have had this chance of meeting with you. Or how much it means to me,' he added, his voice even lower.

Ellie's emotions were in turmoil. Without knowing she had done so she took a step towards Gideon, driven by something inside her that was beyond her control. 'Gideon . . .' His name whispered past her lips.

'Yes?' Gideon swept her face with an acid look. 'Aye, it's just as I thought! Seeing you like this has made me thank God that you are no longer in my life! In fact, I cannot imagine why I was ever foolish enough to believe I loved you. You are wearing a fine and expensive gown, Miss Pride,' he told her tauntingly, 'but your fine clothes cannot hide your true nature. I am grateful that I have been spared the fate that has been handed to your brother and sister, and that my future happiness does not lie in your hands. Aye, for had it done, I know that there would be no happiness for me.'

Then, without giving Ellie a chance to say anything, he turned round and said firmly to John, 'John, you had best go with your sister, but I promise you that Rex will be safe with me.'

With that he turned on his heel and started to walk away from them, leaving Ellie to stand staring after him, consumed with pain and humiliation.

They had almost reached the Bull and Royal when John burst out, 'Why didn't you marry Gideon, Ellie? If you had done so then we would all have been happy, because Connie and me and the baby could have lived with you.'

And then he ran the rest of the distance to the hotel, leaving her to follow him.

The aunts and uncles were lined up waiting in the private parlour, immediately demanding an explanation for Ellie's absence, whilst her Uncle Jepson had grabbed hold of John by his ear and was loudly berating him.

'How dare you leave this place without my permission? A sound whipping is what you deserve, my lad, and a sound whipping is what you shall get.'

Ellie stiffened, all her protective instincts aroused at this threat to her brother.

'No,' she protested. 'You must not blame John, Uncle. I am the one who is to blame. Until Connie reminded me, I had forgotten that John had asked me if it would be all right for him to go and see his dog.' Ellie could see the fury in her uncle's eyes but she refused to be cowed by it. She would not stand by and see her brother whipped!

'Indeed, and since when have you had the authority to say what anyone should and shouldn't have permission to do, miss?' her Aunt Emily demanded peevishly.

'I am truly sorry, Aunt,' Ellie apologised, hanging her head penitently.

'Whether he had spoken to you about the matter

or not, John still had no right to take himself off anywhere without informing us first,' her husband announced coldly, adding ominously, 'And I intend to ensure that he is punished accordingly.'

'Oh no, please do not punish him,' Ellie begged. 'Truly, it is all my fault.'

The look in their uncle's eyes warned Ellie that she was wasting her time but to her relief her Uncle Parkes, who had made no comment as yet, came over to her and took both her hands in his, giving her an avuncular smile as he did so.

'Come, Jepson,' he smiled, 'you are distressing Ellie and she is far too pretty to be distressed. Will it help if I were to add my pleas to hers that on this occasion young John be spared his undoubtedly rightful punishment?'

Ellie held her breath, waiting for her Uncle Charles's response. She could see from the expression on his face that he was not best pleased by Mr Parkes' interference.

She could see too the Adam's apple in his throat bobbing as he swallowed before responding with obvious reluctance, 'Very well, Mr Parkes, since you are disposed to take such a generous view of the situation I suppose I can hardly do other than follow suit.'

'And you will not punish John?' Ellie pressed him, anxious to have a firm declaration that her brother would not suffer.

'No,' he confirmed curtly, 'I shall not punish him – on this occasion.'

'There now, puss, that should put the pretty smile back on your face,' Uncle Parkes declared indulgently as he pinched Ellie's cheek and laughed.

Grateful though she was to her uncle, his touch made Ellie feel actually uncomfortable. Uneasily, she remembered how she had felt in the drawing room of the Hoylake house the evening she had dined alone with him. For some reason she suddenly had a very clear mental image of Gideon's contemptuous expression when he had thrown his insults at her, and tears burned the backs of her eyes.

FIFTEEN

'Ah, there you are, Ellie my dear. There is something I wish to discuss with you.'

Ellie tried not to flinch as her uncle came up to her and gave her waist a little squeeze.

It was nearly six weeks since their return from Preston – six weeks during which there had not been a single day, indeed not a single hour, when she had not relived over and over again inside her head the events of that brief visit.

At night she was constantly woken from her sleep by nightmares; the sound of Gideon's laughter taunting her as he walked away from her, his arm round the waist of a redheaded woman; Connie's cruel insults; and John's stubborn silence. Even the baby cried whenever she went to cradle him. Shivering in the darkness of her bed Ellie felt as though her whole family hated her – and not just her family. Gideon hated her as well. He had as good as told her so.

Gideon, Gideon, Gideon – why was she wasting

217

her time thinking about him when she had far more pressing problems?

Increasingly, Ellie was feeling uncomfortable and ill at ease whenever she was around her Uncle Josiah. She tried to tell herself that she was being foolish and that her uncle's familiarity towards her was his way of making her feel welcome in his home. Her Uncle Will was another who gave her such physical attention, but somehow with Uncle Josiah it was different, although why it should be so, Ellie could not say. She just knew that the comforting presence of her Uncle Will's arm around her as he gave her a boisterous hug was a world away from the chilling feeling that ran down her spine whenever Uncle Josiah placed his arm around her and drew her close.

But more worrying to Ellie than Uncle Josiah were her sister and brother. Neither of them had written to her since her return to Hoylake, despite the many urgent letters she had sent to them begging them to understand that she was only doing what she believed to be in their best interests. When they had said their goodbyes, John had been sullen with her, refusing to return her hug, whilst Connie had been openly bitter.

Ellie had tried to reason with herself that they were young and did not understand, but still she had been left feeling miserable and isolated.

John's angry comment about her marrying Gideon had lodged in her heart, though, and had refused to go away, and even now, thinking about it made her eyes blur with tears. It had been for her mother's sake that she had sent Gideon away, not for her own. Gideon's contemptuous words had left tiny barbs lodged in her heart, which ached every time she remembered them, no matter how much she tried not to let them do so.

Her aunt had not been at all well since their return from Preston, and increasingly she shut herself away in her room, allowing only Wrotham access to her. Ellie was grateful for the fact that Cecily, newly married and living in Liverpool, had turned to her for companionship, regularly inviting Ellie to visit her, and introducing her to her husband's family, including his sister, Iris, who was studying to become a doctor and, shockingly, as Cecily had confided to Ellie, was a member of the women's movement!

Ellie had expected to find Iris somewhat intimidating, but in fact she had been surprised to discover how much fun she was, and now found that whenever she visited Cecily, or went with her to take afternoon tea with her mother-in-law, she always hoped that Iris might be present.

Now, rather hesitantly, Ellie positioned herself as close to the door as she could whilst Mr Parkes settled himself behind his huge desk. Ellie never felt at ease in the study. Its thick Turkish carpet muffled any sound, and the heavy ruby velvet curtains hanging at the north-facing windows took away the light. Bookcases filled two walls, and even the mantel of the fireplace was dark. The telephone stood on the desk within his reach. But Mr Parkes was not seated behind his desk now. He had got up and was standing with his back to the fire, rocking slightly on his heels.

'Why, Ellie, you look quite frightened. You're not frightened of me, are you?' he demanded genially, whilst Ellie blushed and shook her head in denial, inwardly berating herself for feeling the way she did. No one could have been kinder to her than Mr Parkes. In many ways he concerned himself more about her happiness than her aunt did, and Ellie felt very guilty about how she felt whenever she was in his company.

Ellie did not know why she felt so wary of him, but she did know that her discomfort had increased after her visit to her own father. It was, of course, impossible for her to discuss with anyone what she had witnessed – even Cecily, who was a married woman.

'Ellie, I need your help,' Mr Parkes announced.

Ellie looked at him in surprise.

'As you know, your aunt is not in the best of health at the moment.' His smile was replaced by an angry frown. 'And because of that we have not been entertaining very much of late,' he continued. 'However, I have a duty to my clients, many of whom are extremely wealthy and whose hospitality your aunt and I have enjoyed on many occasions, and I have decided that the best means of repaying them is for us to have a ball here.'

A party! Ellie could not help feeling a small surge

of excitement. For all that Connie believed she lived a giddily exciting life, the truth was that they lived very quietly.

'Ah, I see that you like the idea,' her uncle continued, his smile returning. 'Excellent. Then you will have no hesitation in agreeing to my proposal to you, Ellie, which is that you help me to organise this event.'

Ellie's smile faltered. 'Me? But I do not think –'

'There, there, Ellie. I did not mean to alarm you.'

Somehow or other, Mr Parkes had crossed the Turkish carpet and was holding one of Ellie's hands between his own and patting it reassuringly. 'I have every faith in you. After all, I have seen how competently and discreetly you have taken over many of your aunt's domestic duties.'

'Well, only because she asked that I might,' Ellie stammered.

She wished that she might remove her hand, but it seemed impolite to do so whilst Mr Parkes was still holding on to it and, indeed, squeezing it as though in reassurance.

To be entrusted with the responsibility of organising an important party! Ellie acknowledged that there was a part of her that relished the prospect. But another part of her wondered apprehensively if she was competent to do so. She would hate to disappoint her uncle or let him down.

'I, I . . . will be happy to do everything that I can,' she told him, 'but I do not have the experience . . .'

Something in the way her uncle was looking at her made Ellie stop speaking. He was squeezing her hand quite hard, and she couldn't stop herself from tugging it away.

'You must not worry your pretty head about that, Ellie,' he told her smoothly. 'I have more than enough experience for the two of us.'

Gideon rubbed his hand over the finished surface of the kitchen cupboard. Mary had left an instruction that he was to present himself in her workroom when he had finished. Normally when she had something she wanted to say to him she came and did so whilst he was working. Was the unusual formality because she had a complaint to make about some of his work? He hoped not. She had been a very good customer to him and through her he had secured a great many commissions. What was more, unlike the majority of his customers, she always paid him in full and on time. Gideon wished he might have a dozen customers like her.

He gave the smooth surface another brief check, even though he knew the finish was perfect. He could not delay any longer. Making his way over to the sink, he rolled up his sleeves and washed his hands, too deep in his own thoughts to be aware of the quick look of invitation the tweeny was giving him.

Upstairs in her workroom, Mary straightened the already straight blotter on her desk. She had been putting off this interview for over a week, knowing how Gideon was likely to react. But she had made up her mind, and she was not going to change it!

Gideon knocked on the workroom door and waited to hear Mary's cool 'Come', before opening it.

She was seated behind her desk, and the look she gave him was grave and unsmiling. Gideon felt his heart lurch. He was just about making ends meet and covering all his costs. Mary had already hinted that she had further work for him. If she was displeased with the work he had already done and decided to change her mind . . . Gideon's mouth compressed but he held his head high as he approached her desk.

Mary gave a small sigh as she saw the pride in Gideon's stance. This was not going to be easy!

'Gideon, please sit down,' she invited him, and then fell silent, her fingers toying with her pen for so long that Gideon could feel his apprehension increasing.

At last she put the pen down and looked at him. 'Gideon, do you have your sketchbook with you, the one you dropped in the kitchen a few weeks ago?'

'No, no, I don't,' he told her, wondering why she should ask such a question.

Mary persisted, 'You had a sketch in it as I remember, of a conservatory – my conservatory, in fact.'

Gideon's mouth was dry. He could remember

how Mary had looked at that sketch, and how anxious he had been about her scrutiny of it, fearing that she might demand an explanation for its existence.

'You do remember the sketch I am referring to?' she asked him almost sharply.

'Aye,' Gideon agreed reluctantly.

Mary sat back in her chair and beamed at him. 'Excellent!'

Excellent? Gideon was still pondering her comment when she continued calmly, 'You see it has occurred to me, Gideon, that since your drawing was far superior to that of the young gentleman I had approached to design the conservatory for me, then if you were not only to produce the drawings for my conservatory but also to oversee its construction then I would, no doubt, save myself a good deal of money.'

Mary held her breath as she waited for Gideon's reaction. So much depended on how he reacted; so much that she had not even allowed herself to hope for yet, never mind express to him!

Gideon stared warily at Mary, wondering if he had perhaps misunderstood her. 'But I am not an architect, I am a cabinet-maker,' he reminded her almost angrily, in a tone that could not quite conceal his longing.

'You may not have the training or qualifications of an architect,' Mary corrected him, 'but you most certainly have a good eye for line and design, Gideon. I am not exaggerating when I say that I found your drawing to be far superior to that of Mr Hartman.'

'Why are you saying such things to me?' Gideon challenged her suspiciously.

'Because I mean them,' Mary answered him calmly. 'First and foremost, Gideon, I am a woman who likes to get value for money in her business dealings. You have already proved to me through the work you have done that you are an excellent craftsman who does not overcharge.' Looking away from him, Mary continued, 'I have recently received some rather disquieting reports on Mr Hartman. My chancing to see your sketches merely confirmed what was already in my mind, that being that I should look elsewhere for someone to design and construct my conservatory.'

Would he accept what she had said? Would he guess the real motive behind her suggestion? If only she could tell him what was in her heart. But Mary knew that she could not. If her secret became known she would be risking public censure, not just for herself but for him as well.

Gideon's eyes narrowed. He took a deep breath and repeated slowly, 'You want me to design a conservatory for you and be responsible for its construction?' – just so that he could hear the words again before reality buried them and he was told that he had got it wrong!

'Yes,' Mary repeated firmly. 'I want you to design it, Gideon.'

Somehow Gideon managed to resist the temptation to give a great yell of euphoric excitement!

And somehow he managed to hang on to sanity and reality enough to point out, 'Drawing something is one thing, but I'm not trained and –'

Mary looked at him very directly. 'Do you want the job, Gideon – yes or no?'

SIXTEEN

'Ellie dearest, oh, how pretty you look.'

Ellie laughed as her cousin Cecily hugged her.

'And how kind of Mr Parkes to go out of his way to accompany you.' They watched Mr Parkes driving away. 'You are very fortunate,' Cecily continued, ushering Ellie into her pretty parlour. 'When I was living at home my father never once offered to chauffeur me on my calls.'

Ellie could feel her smile beginning to stiffen but it was impossible for her to inform Cecily just how much she disliked sitting in the rear of the large car with its smell of leather and cigars, with Mr Parkes seated next to her, his thigh pressed close to hers, his hand often reaching out to hold hers. No, Ellie could not tell Cecily just how much she would have preferred to make her own way to her cousin's home in Liverpool for her fortnightly visits.

When Cecily's maid had taken her coat, Cecily rang for tea, demanding, 'Ellie, my mama-in-law has directed me to tell her how you are going on with the preparations for the ball.'

Cecily's mother-in-law, Lady Angela, had come to Ellie's rescue when Ellie had confided to her cousin just how apprehensive she was about the task Mr Parkes had given her, and although Ellie would not have said so to anyone, she had found herself envying Cecily her mama-in-law and, indeed, wishing that not just her Aunt Parkes but all her aunts were more like her.

Ellie had been instructed to visit the Rodney Street mansion where Paul's parents lived, and had listened intently to what Paul's mama had told her.

'You must not be afraid to ask me for whatever help you might need,' Lady Angela had smiled. 'I do not know your aunt very well, of course, but I have heard from Cecily that she is in delicate health.' She had paused, and Ellie was almost tempted to tell her about her poor Aunt Lavinia's dreadful headaches, and how much Ellie herself worried about her.

'However, I can see that you are an excellently sensible young woman, Ellie.' Lady Angela had given her an approving smile. 'Indeed, my daughter, Iris, was most annoyed with me for inviting you on a day when she herself could not be here.'

Ellie was guiltily aware that she too had been hoping to renew her acquaintance with Cecily's sister-in-law.

'The first thing you must do, if you have not already done so, is to find out from Mr Parkes how many people he intends to invite.'

'I have done that,' Ellie had been relieved to assure her.

There would be well over one hundred people attending the ball.

'Oh, Cecily, I do not know what I would have done without your mama-in-law's kind help,' Ellie told her cousin now, pausing whilst the maid wheeled in the tea trolley and then waiting for her to leave to continue. 'Everything is more or less in hand, Cecily – thanks to the kindness of Lady Angela. I have hired the London caterers she recommended to me, and the florist called round the other day, and fortunately our Aunt Parkes was well enough to look over her suggestions. I own, Cecily, that there are times when I feel a little uncomfortable about taking on a role which, in reality, should be our aunt's, but she has been most vehement in her assurances to me that she does not wish to be burdened with the arrangements.'

'Has her health improved at all?' Cecily asked in concern.

'No, it hasn't! In fact, if anything, her headaches are even worse. Her maid has had to go into Liverpool twice in the last month to fetch the special tonic our aunt takes for the pain.'

'Well, such a task can only be good experience for you once you have your own home,' Cecily told Ellie with a dimpling smile.

Ellie managed not to flush. Cecily was determined to see Ellie married.

'Iris has sworn she will never marry, which is a shocking thing, but Paul says she has always been eccentric, and so, my dearest cousin, I am determined that you shall, and that we shall be young wives together.

'I am so excited about this ball. Will there be much room for dancing, Ellie?'

'Oh, yes. Mr Parkes asked me especially to make arrangements for the carpets to be lifted in the large drawing room – which reminds me, I must impose on your mama-in-law again, Cecily, and ask her which band Mr Parkes should hire. She has been so kind and . . .'

'She likes you, Ellie,' Cecily assured her warmly. 'And indeed, why should she not do, for you really are the kindest person.'

Ellie's face fell. 'I do not think that either Connie or John would agree with you about that, Cecily,' she couldn't help revealing.

Cecily looked concerned. 'Have you heard nothing from them yet?'

'No!'

Ellie had admitted to their cousin that she was anxious at the lack of letters from her siblings, but she had not felt able to tell her why. Cecily was a dear, but Ellie knew that she was very much under the influence of her indomitable mother, and Ellie did not want Cecily innocently to inform Aunt Amelia that her nieces and nephew longed to return to their own home.

'I dare say that they are too busy to think of writing to you, Ellie,' Cecily told her sunnily.

Ellie made no reply. She had written to their Aunt

Jepson three times asking her for news of the baby and had still heard nothing.

'I am going to ask our aunt if Connie might be invited to the ball,' Ellie informed her cousin. 'She is sixteen now and old enough.'

'Oh, Ellie, do you think that is wise, especially when, as you have told me, Mr Parkes is most anxious that everything should go well? Mama has said that Connie does not always behave as she should, and that our aunt is often distressed by her wilfulness.'

'She might be high-spirited, but she has never been wilful,' Ellie defended her sister, adding protectively, 'I worry sometimes that our aunt and uncle's household is not a very happy place for her to be. They are very religious and –'

'Ellie, how can you say that?' Cecily looked very shocked. 'They have been generous to give Connie a home, after all.'

Ellie bit her lip, wishing she had remained silent. It was foolish of her to expect Cecily to understand how they all felt.

'What time is Mr Parkes picking you up, Ellie? Only Iris telephoned this morning and when I told her you were to visit she made me promise that I would keep you here so that she could see you.'

Ellie's face lit up. 'Oh, yes, I would love that. Mr Parkes said that I was to telephone him when I am ready to leave.'

*   *   *

'Ellie, how lovely! I have been looking forward to seeing you again,' Iris exclaimed as she hugged Cecily and then Ellie herself.

'Ellie has been so good. She has brought some baby clothes she has sewn for your charity, Iris,' Cecily informed her sister-in-law as she poured her a cup of tea.

'Oh, Ellie, how kind. And how clever of you,' Iris enthused.

There was a tradition of philanthropy in Cecily's husband's family, and Ellie had been only too pleased to do something to help.

'Oh, but these are exquisite,' Iris encouraged, when she had looked at the small garments. 'I dare say if Mother's friends saw these they would all be begging you to sew for them. You could quite easily establish yourself in a little business, I am sure. Not that you need to, I realise,' Iris was quick to add, 'but you know how I feel about women having some financial independence. I have not given up on persuading you both to attend a women's movement meeting with me.'

The three of them talked happily together for a further half-hour, and Ellie listened eagerly whilst Iris regaled them with a droll story of her experiences as a doctor.

Ellie had never met a woman like Iris before, and greatly admired her. She was so strong and independent, and seemed to care not one jot for the fact that at twenty-six she was neither engaged nor married.

'. . . And, of course, Ewan is such a stick in the mud,' Iris was saying.

Ewan Cameron was a close friend of Cecily's husband, Paul, and Cecily had confided to Ellie that Paul very much hoped that his sister and his friend would marry.

'I have borrowed Father's car, since he and Mother are in London, and I have to drive out to Hoylake to see a friend when I leave here, Ellie, so why don't I take you home?' Iris suggested.

'Oh, but Mr Parkes always collects Ellie. All she needs to do is to telephone him and he will drive over to collect her immediately,' Cecily broke in. 'Mr Parkes practically dotes on her, doesn't he, Ellie? Mama says that you have been very fortunate.'

'Indeed?' There was a crispness in Iris's voice that surprised Ellie. 'Well, on this occasion there is no need for Ellie to bother Mr Parkes, since I am to drive to Hoylake anyway.'

Iris had a way of saying things that made it impossible to argue with her, Ellie acknowledged. Not that she minded being driven by her in the least. Thanks to Iris she had laughed more this afternoon than she could remember doing in a long time. Even the air in the sitting room felt different with Iris in it: almost crackling with energy and enthusiasm.

'You know, Ellie, you really should learn to drive yourself,' Iris announced as she turned into the road that led to Ellie's aunt and uncle's house.

'Oh, I don't think my aunt and uncle –' Ellie began, but Iris stopped her.

'I could teach you. In fact, I would enjoy doing so. I love Cecily,' she added, 'and she is the perfect wife for Paul, but,' she paused and gave Ellie a wry look, 'but she is still very much beneath her formidable mama's influence. Whilst in you, Ellie, I detect a certain independence of spirit! You must always be true to yourself, Ellie. That is the most important thing that we, as modern women, can do. We owe it to our mothers and to our daughters,' she added solemnly, expertly bringing the large car to a halt.

After they had exchanged goodbyes, Ellie hurried into the house. Cecily had promised to telephone their uncle to advise him that Ellie was on her way home, and Ellie could see that there was a light on in his study.

Lizzie was waiting for her in the hall, and as Ellie handed her her coat she told her, 'I must just go up to my aunt's room and see how she is. I do wish something could be done about these headaches she has, Lizzie. I –'

'The master said that he wanted to see you the minute you returned, miss,' Lizzie stopped her, woodenly.

A closeness had developed between Ellie and her maid, and Ellie often found herself confiding things to Lizzie that she would normally have told only a sister or close friend. Lizzie knew all about Ellie's concern for her younger sister and her aunt, and now there was a look in Lizzie's eyes that sent a quiver of apprehension down Ellie's spine. Had her aunt's health taken a turn for the worse?

Worriedly, Ellie knocked on the study door and then opened it.

As always the room smelled strongly of her uncle's cigars, and, indeed, a cloud of smoke enveloped the desk, obscuring his expression.

'Lizzie said that you wanted to see me, Uncle,' Ellie began anxiously. 'Is my aunt –'

'Why did you not do as I instructed? Who brought you back to Hoylake? What is his name?'

Completely bemused, Ellie stared at her uncle. 'I . . . I . . .' Ellie gave a small gasp of shock as her uncle stood up and strode towards her. She had never seen him looking so angry, and instinctively she stepped back from him.

'Oh, no you don't.' His hand shot out and grasped Ellie's wrist in a bruising hold.

Ellie could feel the frantic racing of her heart. What had happened to the kind, attentive uncle she was used to? This angrily violent man who had taken his place was frightening her.

'Well, miss?'

The sharp tug her uncle gave her wrist as he shook her made Ellie cry out in pain.

'Why did you not do as I instructed you?'

The pain in her wrist was making Ellie's eyes smart with fear.

'I . . . we didn't think you would mind. Iris had to drive to Hoylake anyway, and I didn't want to offend her by refusing. Her mama has been so kind, helping me with everything for the ball . . .' Ellie could not bring herself to look into her uncle's face. She could feel the sulphurous heat of anger through the thick silence.

'Iris? It was Iris who drove you here?'

'Yes, in her papa's car,' Ellie managed to whisper past the nervously constricted muscles of her throat.

To her disbelief, Mr Parkes started to smile, his anger evaporating as though it had never been.

'Well, I must say that I am surprised that her father should allow her to drive at all, and I am angry with you, Ellie, that you did not obey my wishes. However, I can understand that you would not wish to offend your cousin's family. However, on another occasion I must insist that you do as I tell you.'

His voice had become almost jovial now, and the fingers holding her wrist had slacked their grip, much to Ellie's relief. She could still feel the burn of pain in her tender flesh, though, and now that Mr Parkes' anger had subsided rather like a violent summer storm, Ellie felt so weak that her whole body trembled.

'Poor Ellie, I am sorry if I have distressed you,' her uncle said. 'Why, you are trembling,' he added softly, taking a step towards her and, to Ellie's shock, lifting her wrist to his mouth so that he could kiss the bruised flesh. 'There,' he told her softly. 'That should make your poor wrist feel better.'

Ellie's face burned as much as her wrist. Her

body was shuddering violently with revulsion and disbelief, but her uncle seemed to be unaware of her distress, because he was smiling widely at her, his eyes glittering with a look that Ellie instinctively denied to herself she had seen.

'I have some business to attend to now, Ellie, but this evening after dinner you may tell me what progress you are making with our little venture! Which reminds me – you are a good girl, Ellie, and I think you deserve a small reward. What would you like, eh, my dear? Some pretty little trinket to show off to your cousin? Young ladies always like jewellery, don't they?'

Ellie had to swallow hard on the sick feeling that was clogging her throat. There was a favour she wanted to ask her uncle, she reminded herself, although her stomach churned miserably at the thought of having to do so.

'I . . . it is very kind of you to be so generous, Uncle,' she managed to say shakily. 'But more than anything else I would like it if Connie could be invited to the ball.'

There was a small silence before her uncle said, 'But of course she may come. Indeed, I do not know why I did not think of inviting her myself. Now I shall have the pleasure of enjoying the company of two beautiful nieces.'

In the kitchen Lizzie waited anxiously for Ellie to ring for her.

'What's up with you?' Mrs Foster, the cook, asked her irritably. 'You've done nowt but pace this room for the last half an hour.'

'It's Miss Ellie,' Lizzie answered her, without taking her eyes off the row of bells on the far wall, even though she knew perfectly well she could hear each individual ring from yards away. '*He* wanted to see her "the moment she returns".' She mimicked her employer's sharp voice. Lizzie's mouth compressed. 'I'm worried about her. After all, it's no secret how he treats the mistress, even if Wrotham thinks that none of us knows.'

'That's enough of that,' Mrs Foster reproved her. 'Talking about your betters like that is going to head you into trouble one day, my girl.'

Lizzie gave an impatient snort. 'It's not as though we don't all know what he's like,' she protested. 'I thank the Lord He made me plain every time I look at him, I swear it! And just as soon as I can afford it I'm leaving here. There's many a time I've wanted to warn Miss Ellie to watch out for him.'

'Don't you be doing any such thing,' the cook retorted. 'Like as not she'd never believe you, and if she went telling him what you'd been saying . . .'

But Lizzie wasn't listening. Ellie should have rung for her ages ago. It was almost time for the dinner bell.

'I blame the mistress,' she announced fiercely. 'She should never have left Miss Ellie on her own with the master.'

Mrs Foster gave a small tut of disapproval. 'The

mistress is afeared of him herself! And sickly too. Always ailing . . . !'

'Aye, well, I suppose it's one way to keep him out of her bed,' Lizzie replied bluntly, exhaling in relief as Ellie's bell suddenly started to ring.

SEVENTEEN

'Oh, Ellie, I do hope that everything goes well tonight. Your uncle will be so angry if it doesn't. He's invited everyone of consequence on the Wirral to this ball, and has clients coming from all over the area. If anything should go wrong . . .'

'Nothing will go wrong,' Ellie assured her aunt. 'Aunt, are you all right?' she asked in some concern as her aunt suddenly swayed slightly towards her. Ellie reached out gently to steady her. Aunt Lavinia looked pale and not a little unwell, her face slightly puffy, and Ellie stiffened as the cuff of her aunt's sleeve fell back, revealing a livid bruise.

A feeling like icy water dripping down her spine froze Ellie's body. Immediately in her mind's eye she had an image of her uncle, his face puce with anger, his arm raised. A savage shudder brought her out of her trance as she fought against a knowledge she didn't want to have.

Her aunt's nervousness, the headaches that kept

her to her room with Wrotham beside her, the falls that left her bruised – were they because Mr Parkes ... Panicking, Ellie thrust her thoughts away from her.

Apart from that one incident, her uncle had shown her nothing but kindness and generosity, Ellie reminded herself. And he had gone to a great deal of trouble on her behalf to make sure that Connie could attend the party. She was surely being over-imaginative, letting her fears take control of her.

'I have had some of my tonic,' her aunt was informing her, 'and I should be feeling much better directly.'

Pulling herself together, Ellie asked, 'Would you like to inspect everything, Aunt, just in case I have overlooked something?' She gently took hold of Lavinia's arm to steady her discreetly.

'No, my dear, I have every faith in you, but I wish my sister Amelia would arrive. Mr Parkes will be so cross if they are late.'

Ellie's heart jerked against her ribs. She looked away, not wanting to see what she feared would be in her aunt's eyes. Besides, she was every bit as eager for her Aunt and Uncle Gibson to arrive as her aunt was, but for a very different reason. They were bringing Connie with them!

Ellie couldn't wait to see her sister. There had initially been some doubt as to whether Connie would be permitted to attend the ball, as a punishment for some bad behaviour, but Mr Parkes had prevailed on Uncle Simpkins, who had eventually given his permission.

A pretty evening dress had been ordered for Connie from their Aunt Lavinia's own dressmaker, and Ellie had chosen the fabric and trimmings herself. She couldn't wait to see her sister's face when she saw it.

Aunt and Uncle Gibson had been invited to stay overnight and to attend the lavish dinner party that was to be held for the more favoured guests before the ball.

'At least you will have the opportunity to meet some suitable young men this evening, Ellie,' her aunt was saying. 'We don't want you to end up like that poor sister of Paul's – almost thirty and still unmarried.'

'I do not believe that Iris wants to find a husband,' Ellie informed her.

'Not want to be married? That's impossible!' Aunt Lavinia declared. 'Every woman wants to be married! After all, what else is there for her to do? I feel sorry for her poor mother! How can she face her friends when her daughter cannot find a husband? And as for her not wanting to marry – a very odd creature she must be indeed if that were to be true!'

Ellie wanted to defend Iris but before she could say anything more, an excited bustle of noise informed them that the Gibsons had arrived.

* * *

'And you have this room all to yourself?' Connie demanded enviously when she had finished exploring Ellie's bedroom and bathroom.

At Lizzie's suggestion, the two sisters were to share Ellie's room for the brief duration of Connie's visit. 'It will be company for you, miss, and a good chance to catch up with your sister's news.'

Aunt and Uncle Gibson had not brought Cecily's younger sister, Kitty, with them as she was deemed too young for such a formal affair, but Cecily and Paul were to attend the ball, and Ellie was looking forward to having her cousin's support and company.

For all her excitement, there was a cagey, wary look in Connie's eyes, and she had deliberately stepped back earlier when Ellie had rushed to hug her in greeting. It was plain to Ellie that Connie had still not forgiven her and, in an attempt to win her round, she cajoled, 'Connie, come and look at the gown our aunt has got for you. I chose the colour myself, and the trimmings.'

The eager excitement on Connie's face banished her earlier look as she rushed to the dressing room where Lizzie had already laid out their gowns.

As unmarried young women it was expected that they would wear white gowns, but Ellie had cleverly chosen the softest of topaz-gold underslips for Connie, knowing that the colour would accentuate her sister's warm colouring and golden eyes. The gown was embellished with topaz-gold ribbons. Pretty velvet slippers had been dyed exactly the same colour and Ellie had patiently embroidered a small velvet evening bag in the same fabric. For Connie's blonde hair she had ordered creamy flowers with gold stamens. Indeed, Ellie had spent far more time planning her sister's outfit than she had her own.

Her own dress was underlined with a soft, warm blue to echo the colour of her eyes, but she had had less ornamentation added to it, preferring a plainer look.

'This is my dress?' Eyes shining, Connie whirled round to look at Ellie. 'It is much, much prettier than yours,' Connie crowed unabashed, as she studied her sister's gown. 'I shall outshine you tonight, and our Uncle Parkes will wish that I was the one he had asked to come and live here. I shall have every dance on my card filled,' Connie exulted, twirling round the room as though in the arms of a young man. 'Yes, I shall definitely cast you completely into the shade, Ellie,' she boasted.

Ellie told herself that Connie was not deliberately trying to be hurtful, and tried to smother the sharp stab of unease Connie's high spirits were causing her.

'I must go down and check that everything is in order,' she told Connie. 'The band should have arrived, and –'

'Oh, Ellie, let me come with you,' Connie begged.

A little reluctantly, Ellie agreed.

'Oh, Ellie, you are so lucky to live here,' Connie pouted enviously as she followed Ellie through the drawing room, its carpets removed for dancing and the double doors opened between it and the smaller sitting room.

The air in the large double room was heavy with the scent of the flowers Ellie had chosen. Bearing in mind her mentor's advice, she had opted for simple but opulent arrangements of white and green, and the effect was breathtaking. In the conservatory perfumed candles echoed the scent of the flowers, and beyond the conservatory, further illuminations winked enticingly in the garden.

To Ellie's relief the whole week had been dry and warm, so that those who wished to take a stroll in the garden would be able to do so.

The butler was showing the band to their places, and Ellie hurried over to remind him to make sure refreshments were provided for them.

The band leader, an extremely handsome young man, smiled warmly at Ellie, but before she could say anything Connie had pushed past her and was demanding to know if the band would play her favourite tunes.

'Connie!' Ellie rebuked her sternly. She knew that her sister meant no harm, but she was a young woman now, and must learn to behave accordingly.

Connie tossed her head and threw Ellie a challenging look.

'Ah, Ellie! There you are!'

Ellie tensed as she heard her uncle's voice.

'Oh, Uncle Parkes, I am so grateful to you.' Rushing past Ellie, Connie ran to their uncle and almost threw herself into his arms.

'My, my, that is indeed a warm welcome,' Josiah Parkes smiled, and, as he looked down into Connie's excited face, Ellie felt as though someone had dropped a stone deep down inside her, a cold, icy, hard stone that was sending out painfully sharp ripples of warning.

There was something in the way their Uncle Parkes was looking at Connie that made Ellie want to rush over and wrest her sister from him.

She could hear the panic in her own voice as she demanded, 'Connie, we must go upstairs and get ready.'

Ellie suspected that it was only the thought of being able to parade herself in her finery that made Connie obey her.

They were halfway up the stairs when Connie tossed her head again and announced, 'It isn't fair that you should be able to live here, Ellie, and I should have to live with our horrid and mean Aunt and Uncle Simpkins. I don't see why I shouldn't live here as well. In fact –'

'Connie, if we don't hurry we shall be late,' Ellie warned her. Her heart was thudding painfully. It wasn't just herself she felt afraid for now, she recognised, but her sister as well. Connie was not like her! She had no sense of self-preservation! She was too young to be aware, as Ellie was, of the meaning of that lustful look their uncle had given her.

* * *

'So, Jarvis, have you given further thought to the, er, business opportunity I mentioned to you?' Affably, Josiah Parkes offered his companion a cigar from the box on his desk.

'Well, it certainly sounds tempting,' Jarvis Charnock acknowledged, 'especially if its success can be guaranteed.'

There was a greedy, eager note of oily anticipation in the man's voice that told Josiah Parkes all he needed to know. His fish had taken the bait, now he just had to reel him in and secure his catch!

'My dear sir, there can be no doubt!' Josiah's expression was an artful mixture of gravity, confidence and sincerity. 'I have previously been involved with a consortium of other gentlemen in this kind of business enterprise to our great mutual financial advantage.'

'And there is no question of the insurers not . . . ?'

His catch was growing fearful, wary of the bait and yet still eager to snatch at it!

'The risk is placed only with the most reputable of insurance companies,' Josiah reassured him. 'That, after all, is an essential part of the arrangement. There is no way, my dear sir, that I would recommend that you risk your vessels with an inferior insurer – no way at all. After all, if the unthinkable were to happen and you were to lose one, then naturally you would want to be able to recover the cost of your loss! Not, of course, that that is likely to happen. Not with vessels of the seaworthiness and quality of yours, my dear Charnock!'

He could see the dull, unflattering purple-red surge of colour mottling the other man's face as his gaze slid evasively from his own.

'These insurers are going to require certification regarding my ships.'

'A mere formality, I can assure you, and one which I will be delighted to put in hand on your behalf.'

'Scuttling ships – it's a very risky business, Parkes.'

His tongue wetted his thin lips, and Josiah Parkes could see beads of sweat shining on his forehead. Josiah gave the other man a reassuring smile and raised his eyebrows.

'Risky? Not at all, I do assure you!' Still smiling, he changed the subject.

'I understand that you are currently looking for a suitable wife for your son. My wife's niece is staying with us at present, Charnock,' he commented with apparent casualness. 'My wife and I have a fondness for her, and I should be prepared to settle a handsome dowry on her to see her married to the right young man.'

'Are you suggesting that my son should marry your niece?'

'What could be a happier outcome to our business relationship, my dear Charnock, than to see our young people united in marriage? And as I have already said, I am prepared to settle a handsome sum on the girl.'

It was a business arrangement that he had only just thought of, but which would suit him very well. He congratulated himself on his astuteness. Charnock wouldn't dare renege on their deal once his son was married to Ellie.

'Aye, well, as to that . . .' Jarvis Charnock frowned. It was true that he did want to see Henry married. He had already received a very negative response from the families of the three girls he had decided would make suitable brides for his son.

Anxiously, he returned to their earlier discussion. 'You're sure there won't be any risk of anything going wrong – the insurance company refusing to pay out . . . enquiries being made . . . ?'

Smiling, Josiah lifted his eyebrows in silent confidence, causing Jarvis Charnock's voice to trail away in a fading splutter of anxiety.

'Why should they not pay out? A vessel is attacked by pirates in the South China Sea, an area notorious for such attacks. Your brave captain, whose palm has already been well greased to play his part, testifies to that attack – there can be no question of them not paying out.'

'But as to the matter of changing the bills of loading for the ships, so that –'

'You are worrying unnecessarily, Charnock, I assure you. If I were to whisper in your ear the names of those who have already benefited from such ploys, you would be astonished. Now, as a first step in our shared venture, I would suggest that you extend the company's Board of Directors –'

'To include yourself, I take it?' Jarvis Charnock interrupted him sourly.

'To include myself, yes,' Josiah agreed urbanely.

'It seems you've thought of everything,' Jarvis told him, even more sourly. 'You had best draw up the necessary papers.'

'Excellent. Let us rejoin the others, so that I can introduce my niece to you. I am already looking forward to the felicity of our two families being united. My niece is a comely girl with a sensible head on her shoulders.'

'Comely? Aye, she might be that, but will she be a good breeder?' Jarvis demanded coarsely. 'Grandsons – that's what I want. Grandsons who'll have a deal more of my blood in them than the wheymilk my son inherited from his wretched mother!'

'Ellie, my dear.'

Ellie tried not to flinch as Mr Parkes placed a proprietorial arm around her waist, holding her just a little bit too tight. She could smell the cigar he had been smoking, and the rich aroma of brandy on his breath.

'Come and let me introduce you to Mr Charnock here. He is a client and a business colleague of mine. Charnock, did I not tell you that she was a comely piece?'

Ellie blushed to hear herself so described, looking over her shoulder to where her Aunt Lavinia was seated fanning herself, wanting her to come to her aid and rescue her from her embarrassment and self-consciousness, but her aunt was not looking in her direction.

'Charnock here has a son he would have you meet, Ellie. He is newly returned to Liverpool from Japan, is that not right, Charnock?'

Without being able to specify why, Ellie knew that she did not particularly care for Mr Charnock.

'Come here, Henry, and see if you can manage not to stutter for long enough to speak with Miss Pride,' he was demanding curtly, jerking his head towards the young man standing hesitantly behind him.

Immediately Ellie felt intensely sorry for Henry Charnock. It was obvious to her that he was both uncomfortable with his father's conversation and anxious in his company.

'Miss P-P-P-Pride . . .' There was a slight hesitation in Henry's voice as he bowed jerkily over her hand, but whether it was due to a speech impediment or caused by nervousness Ellie didn't know.

'So you have recently returned from Japan, Mr Charnock?' Ellie enquired politely. 'From what I have read about it in the papers it sounds as though it is a most interesting country.'

Immediately the nervousness left Henry's face, to be replaced with an expression of intense enthusiasm and pleasure.

'Indeed it is, Miss Pride. The country and its people are making such strides into the twentieth century, and when one thinks that until so very recently they were still living in a way that we would consider to be positively medieval, I –'

'Dammit, Henry, don't start boring Miss Pride about Japan.' The angry contempt in Henry's father's voice was clear as he cut across him.

'Come, Charnock, there's someone I want you to meet,' Mr Parkes announced, taking the other man firmly by the arm. 'Young Henry can stay here and talk to Ellie about Japan.'

Ellie could see the relief in Henry Charnock's face as her uncle firmly bore his father away.

'Oh dear, I'm afraid I have rather been wished upon you, Mr Charnock,' Ellie apologised ruefully, once they were on their own.

'No, no, pleasure to have your company. And, please, no need for formality. Always think of m'father when anyone refers to "Mr Charnock".'

'What, even in Japan?' Ellie couldn't help teasing him.

Once again it was as though his whole personality underwent an instantaneous transformation. 'Called me "Henry-san" there,' he explained. 'Wonderful country, Miss Pride, and wonderful people too. Can't speak highly enough of them. Just wish Father would allow me to stay there.'

'Perhaps if, one day, you are to take over his business,' Ellie answered him gently, 'he wishes to ensure that you are familiar with every aspect of it.'

Henry Charnock gave her a half-wry, half-sad look, as he replied, 'My father letting anyone take over the business – that will be the day. It is all down to my mother that he has been able to make it so successful, you know. It was failing when he inherited it from his father and it was my mother's money he used –' He stopped, shaking his head. 'I'm sorry, I'm embarrassing you by speaking so freely and on such short acquaintance. It is just that you are so easy to talk to, Miss Pride. I am not much of a conversationalist and most young ladies find me dull.'

'Oh, no, I am sure that is not true,' Ellie objected.

Already she felt a sense of protectiveness towards him akin to that she felt for her younger siblings. He might be a little awkward and hesitant, but she suspected that most of his nervousness was caused by his father's domineering, hectoring manner towards him.

It was true that he wasn't a strikingly handsome man, like Gideon, and could not even be described, in all honesty, as even a passingly handsome one, having thin hair and pale blue semi-myopic eyes set in an undistinguished-looking face. But his eyes were kind and gentle, and he was tall enough, even if his propensity to stoop bowed his shoulders and made him look both apologetic and somehow older than he was.

Maybe too he was a little on the thin side, and the nervous hesitation in his speech would per-haps make some young women contemptuously dismissive of him, but Ellie was not one of that sort.

'Tell me some more about Japan,' Ellie invited him kind-heartedly.

Shy and unsure of himself Henry might be, but his company was preferable to that of her uncle. Ellie could still feel her flesh burning from the weight of his arm about her waist.

'Yokohama sounds a truly fascinating place, Mr Charnock,' Ellie marvelled.

They were standing in the conservatory, where Henry had been telling her about life as a foreigner in Yokohama, and the foreign trading centre, which was known as 'Ichi Ban'.

'And everyone trades from that place?' Ellie asked him, genuinely interested.

'Virtually. It really is the most fascinating world, Miss Pride. The people and their culture . . . and despite what my father chooses to believe, the business we have there is very profitable. I would like to see us doing more trade with Japan. They are looking to build up their own fleet and to take on Europeans to help them achieve this. I myself –' He broke off as he saw Ellie suddenly turn her head in the direction of a noisy burst of male laughter from the other side of the room. 'I am sorry, I must be boring you.'

'Not at all,' Ellie assured him.

She had thought she had detected Connie's laughter mixed with that of the young men, and as she looked across the room she saw to her dismay that her sister was indeed with them, and behaving in a most indecorous manner. Torn between the good manners that dictated that she remain with Henry, and her concern for her sister, Ellie hesitated and then saw with relief that her cousin Cecily and her husband were making their way to join Connie.

'I'm sorry,' Ellie apologised to Henry. 'You were saying . . . ?' There was, she noticed, virtually no trace at all of his stammer when he was talking about Japan. He even seemed to stand straighter, and to gain in confidence and demeanour.

'I would like to be based out there permanently but I'm afraid my father would never agree.'

Ellie felt very sorry for him. 'Perhaps if you could prove to him just how profitable a connection with Japan could be . . . ?' she suggested.

Henry shook his head. 'He will never allow me to do that because he does not want to have it proved. I have tried to persuade him to have the new ship we are shortly to take delivery of dedicated to the Japanese run, but Father will have none of it! Unfortunately he has a determined ally in my cousin George. In fact,' he continued bitterly, 'I suspect that my father would prefer to have George as his son instead of me and, to be honest, Miss Pride, I sometimes wish that he might be,' he added with a burst of passionate candour. Then, quickly colouring up and apologising, 'I am sorry. I am supposed to be making polite conversation with you, not burdening you with my problems. My father is right: I'm not very skilled at entertaining young ladies, and despite your good manners, I am no doubt boring you.'

'You are not boring me at all!' Ellie denied firmly. 'But I think my aunt will be very cross with me if I continue to monopolise your attention. I see that supper will soon be served, and then afterwards there will be dancing.'

'May I be allowed the privilege of dancing with you, Miss Pride?'

Ellie dimpled a teasing smile at him. 'You fibbed to me, Mr Charnock, when you said that you are not skilled at entertaining my sex,' she laughed as she handed him her dance card.

Iris had said that in some of the more bohemian London circles dance cards were now out of fashion, but her mother had argued judiciously that Hoylake was still conservative enough to expect to see such conventions adhered to, and so Ellie had arranged for every young lady to be presented with one of the specially printed cards. But it wasn't dance cards that were to the forefront of her mind as she hurried away from Henry Charnock, but her sister, Connie.

'Cecily, where has Connie gone?' Ellie asked anxiously, glancing worriedly out into the darkness beyond the conservatory doors. Surely Connie could not have been foolish enough to go out there with the young men Ellie had seen her with.

'My mother has taken her upstairs to talk to her,'

Cecily replied, looking uncomfortable. 'I know that Connie doesn't mean any harm, Ellie, and no doubt the excitement of her first proper ball has overwhelmed her somewhat, but I have to tell you that Mama was very cross with her for her want of conduct.'

'She is high-spirited, I know,' Ellie tried to defend her.

'Oh, Ellie, she was flirting most outrageously with several young men – and, well, her behaviour was quite wild.'

'It isn't your fault, Ellie,' Paul said kindly. 'And you must not blame yourself. If anything, I suspect that it is because your Aunt and Uncle Simpkins have kept Connie so close that tonight's jollities have gone to her head a little.'

It was half an hour before Connie came back downstairs, her expression angrily mutinous.

'Connie . . .' Ellie began, hurrying to her side.

'Oh, don't you start,' Connie stopped her rudely. 'You are just as bad as everyone else! It is all very well for you, Ellie. Our Aunt and Uncle Parkes dote on you whilst our Aunt and Uncle Simpkins hate me.'

'Connie, I'm sure that is not true,' Ellie protested in distress.

'It *is* true,' Connie insisted. 'They hate me and I hate them. It is not fair, Ellie. Why should you be living here with every luxury, whilst I am stuck in that cold miserable house with nothing?'

* * *

257

It was almost four o'clock; the last guests had left, and the evening had been declared an outstanding success.

As Ellie made to climb the stairs Connie came hurrying towards her, her face wreathed in an excited smile.

'Ellie, guess what!' she demanded. 'Uncle Parkes has told me that he thinks I'm a very pretty little puss, and he said that he was going to think about having me here to stay on a long visit, as well as to keep you company! Won't that be wonderful?'

Ellie could feel her heart starting to thud with fear and anxiety. If only Connie were older, or had a different personality, she might be able to confide her fears to her, but she knew her younger sister well enough to realise that that was impossible!

EIGHTEEN

'You bain't no proper architect, and I'm telling you now there bain't no way these drawings of yorn are going to work.'

Scornfully, the builder Mary Isherwood had hired to work on her conservatory threw down Gideon's plan and walked away from him.

Somehow Gideon managed to control his feelings, although his cheekbones burned with the effort of doing so. The builder had made it plain from the start how he felt about working with Gideon, and now, a week later, Gideon fully reciprocated his hostility and dislike – and with interest.

It shamed him to acknowledge that he would have to tell Miss Isherwood what had happened, and that shame made him feel angrily resentful towards the builder and towards Miss Isherwood herself.

*　　*　　*

'What's wrong, Gideon?' Mary asked.

They were in her workroom, and Gideon glowered bitterly before telling her tersely, 'The builder is threatening to walk off the job.'

'Why?'

'He says that since I'm not a proper architect he won't work with me,' Gideon told her curtly, unable to bring himself to look directly at her.

'I see.'

'And he's right, dammit,' Gideon burst out savagely. 'I'm not an architect.'

'But you wish that you were?'

Gideon stared at Mary, his expression giving away his feelings.

'Then why don't you study to become one, Gideon? Think about it,' she told him, striving to sound casual.

'It's impossible,' Gideon burst out.

Mary's eyebrows rose. 'Why?' she challenged him.

Gideon glared at her in furious pride. Wasn't it damn well obvious?

'Anything is possible if you want it to be, Gideon,' Mary told him softly.

Their eyes met and it was Gideon who looked away first.

What she was suggesting was impossible.

But what if it wasn't? What if somehow he could? That would show Ellie Pride! Show her and humble her too, right enough, when he was an architect!

Mary waited until Gideon had gone before she unfolded the hands she had clasped together in her lap. They were trembling wildly. Like her whole body. She had promised herself she would not let herself hope like this, that she wouldn't allow herself to dream impossible dreams, but she had broken those promises, she acknowledged.

She had seen from Gideon's expression just how much he yearned to follow his dream, and she could make that possible for him, if only he would allow her to do so. Already she had arranged for him to have new premises – and at a peppercorn rent – though this was her secret. She must go carefully and slowly, she warned herself. She must not offend his pride or let him guess . . . She pressed one trembling hand to her lips. She longed to be able to tell Gideon the truth, but she was afraid of him rejecting her if she did.

'And there are some more flowers from Mr Charnock, miss . . .'

Ellie gave Lizzie a wan smile. It was nearly a month since the ball, and Henry Charnock had sent her flowers every single day, as well as asking her aunt if he might call on them.

'What is it, Miss Ellie? Is something wrong?' Lizzie asked her in concern.

Ellie felt sharp tears spring to her eyes. Lizzie was the only person who had noticed how unhappy she felt.

'It's my sister, Miss Connie, Lizzie,' Ellie confided, her voice faltering. 'She – she is most unhappy with our aunt and uncle, and she begged me before she left to ask my aunt if she might come to live here.' It was very wrong of her to confide like this in a maid, she knew, but she was so worried!

'It seems to me, miss, that Miss Connie would be best off staying where she is,' Lizzie told Ellie bluntly.

Silently they exchanged looks, and Ellie knew then that Lizzie understood very well the real cause of her concern.

A little later in the day Ellie had a visit from her cousin Cecily.

'Our aunt has told me that Mr Henry Charnock is being most attentive towards you, Ellie,' she commented archly.

'He has been kind enough to send me flowers,' Ellie responded sedately, but she felt herself blushing.

'Do you know what I think, Ellie?' Cecily asked her, continuing without waiting for Ellie to answer her. 'I believe that Mr Charnock has fallen in love with you.'

'Oh, Cecily, I don't think so. He is merely being polite, that's all!' Ellie responded, but she was uncomfortably aware that her aunt had said much the same thing to her, and she had no intention of telling her cousin that, as well as sending her flowers, Henry had called round with another gift for her – a book on Japan, which he had explained earnestly to her was one of his own and which he had thought she would like to read.

She felt no romantic yearnings towards Henry, but she did feel sorry for him.

There was a brief knock on the door and Henry Charnock was shown in.

Cecily immediately got up and announced that she must leave, throwing Ellie a teasingly speaking look as she did so.

'No, Ellie, no need to see me out. Please stay here and entertain Mr Charnock,' she announced, before whisking herself out of the door.

'Would you care for some tea, Mr Charnock?' Ellie invited politely.

'No, no, Miss Pride. I do not wish to put you to any trouble, nor to spoil your visit from your cousin. I just called to see if you had read the book I gave you yet, and if you should like to read another one?'

'I have begun it,' Ellie told him truthfully, 'and it is most interesting.'

Immediately Henry's eyes started to shine, and he launched into an enthusiastic description of the Japanese way of life.

Discreetly Ellie rang for tea, sensing that it would be some time before Henry left.

'You really are the most wonderful girl, Miss Pride,' Henry enthused warmly, as he bit hungrily into the delicate sandwiches whilst Ellie poured him a second cup of tea. 'My father wants me to marry, you know,' he began, and then stopped, going bright red.

'Do try some of the plum cake, Mr Charnock,' Ellie suggested calmly, tactfully ignoring his embarrassment.

Henry was as different from Gideon Walker as it was possible for a man to be, she acknowledged, and then wondered why that knowledge should cause her heart to feel like a lump of stone inside her chest.

'Well now, puss,' Mr Parkes addressed Ellie genially, 'Mrs Parkes tells me that you have an admirer!'

Ellie had been on her own in the drawing room when Mr Parkes had walked in, and now she glanced thankfully towards the still-open door.

'He will make a good match for you!' Mr Parkes approved. 'Although he is not perhaps the strongest of men,' he added, his expression revealing his contempt for Henry. 'You will have to see that you do not frighten him, Ellie, for I dare say he is as virginal as you are yourself.'

Ellie stiffened.

'Why, there is no need for you to look so self-conscious, Ellie. I am your uncle, after all, child! This would be a good marriage for you, as I have already said. I have spoken to Charnock and he is prepared to overlook your father's station in life.'

Ellie had to clench her hands at her sides to prevent herself from protesting. Her father was a Pride of Preston and good enough to stand up in any man's company. Or at least he had been until he had . . . Ellie tried to push away the memory of the last time she had seen her father.

'Aye, a good marriage, but I doubt that young Henry will be man enough for you, Ellie.'

Shocked, Ellie wheeled round and almost ran out of the room, covering her hot face with her hands, her uncle's laughter ringing in her ears. It was wrong that he should speak to her thus, but it was impossible for her to say so to him – or to anyone else!

Upstairs in her room she paced the floor. She felt trapped – weighed down with her fears, her duties, her guilt and her secrets. So much for being true to herself. Her life was getting out of her control and the romantic attentions of Henry were becoming part of the nightmare. Everyone seemed to think she should be delighted and grateful because Henry was showing an interest in her, but how could she marry him when she did not love him? How could she marry him when he was not . . . Gideon?

Abruptly, Ellie stopped pacing, the colour draining from her face.

No, that was not true! She would not allow it to be true!

John tried not to scream as he felt the thin cane slicing into his bare buttocks. The last time he had been whipped so, he had bitten through his bottom lip in his attempts to stifle his fear and pain, and he knew better than to do that again.

'That is five strokes for stealing and five for lying

265

about it,' his uncle said, panting as he wielded the cane with firm vigour.

An hour later John crawled sobbing into his narrow cold bed. Hetty, the maid, had washed his back with salt and water and then rubbed a cream of her own making into the open cuts, and the pain had been numbed a little by the tot of spirits she had given him.

All the boys at Hutton knew about the headmaster's temper and his savage pleasure in caning them, but they, unlike John, were protected from his cruelty to some extent by the fact that they had parents to complain to and a dormitory to sleep in.

John lived with his aunt and uncle, since his uncle refused to pay for him to have a bed with the others. And his aunt and uncle also saved extra money by insisting that John ate at home with them rather than with his schoolmates. Which was why John had come to steal the bun that had earned him his beating. John was tall and broad for his age, with an appetite to match, but his aunt complained that on a headmaster's salary she could not be expected to provide huge meals for a lazy boy, and so John was constantly hungry. He had been walking through the kitchen when he had seen the buns, freshly baked for his aunt's afternoon tea, and he had been unable to resist their temptation. Unfortunately his aunt had come into the kitchen just as he was biting into one, and had set up an angry fuss, sending for his uncle, who had called John a thief and said he had earned a whipping.

Miserably John knuckled his eyes. He considered himself too old to cry; that was for babies and girls.

He heard a small sound and tensed, but it wasn't his aunt or his uncle who had come into his room, but his little brother.

Philip was walking now and beginning to talk too, and in secret John was teaching him all about Friargate and the life he had had there.

Reaching out, he tugged the little boy onto the bed and held him close for comfort.

'Gideon.' Mary approached him, hesitating whilst she considered the best and most productive way of saying what she wanted without alienating him through the fierce pride he wore like armour. 'I had occasion to visit Manchester last week,' she began, 'and whilst I was there I showed your designs for my conservatory to an architect friend of mine.'

Gideon could feel his heart thumping heavily, and there was a raw taste of defensive anxiety in his mouth. He knew what she was going to say. She was going to tell him that she had changed her mind. Rigid with anger, Gideon waited for the blow to fall.

'He was most impressed with your drawings, Gideon,' Mary continued. 'In fact, he was so impressed that he said that he would like to meet you! It seems there could be an opportunity there for you to be articled to him as a sort of apprentice.'

Gideon stared at her in disbelief, unable to comprehend what he had heard.

'Gideon?' Mary prompted.

Frowning, he told her bluntly, 'Apprenticeships cost money, and besides –'

Mary did not allow him to go any further. 'My friend was very impressed with your work, Gideon,' she interrupted him. 'So much so that I am sure he would be prepared to take you on with very little outlay on your behalf, and indeed, I –'

'No.' Gideon's rejection was immediate and harsh, cutting into the eager excitement of Mary's words. 'I know you mean it for the best,' he continued heavily, 'but it would still be charity.' His mouth twisted as he looked at Mary. Her face was flushed and there was a look in her eyes, a woman's look of . . .

'Why should you do such a thing for me?' Gideon demanded hostilely.

'Why should I not?' Mary countered evenly. Outwardly she might look controlled, but inwardly she was not. She was deliberately deceiving Gideon, withholding information from him! She was afraid that otherwise he would start to press on her questions she could not allow herself to answer.

The look Miss Isherwood was giving him now was cool and slightly distant, the regard of a lady for a mere tradesman, Gideon recognised. And, of course, the well-to-do were a law unto themselves.

'It would involve a great deal of hard work and even sacrifice on your part, Gideon. My friend has been kind enough to give me a list of books which he recommends you read prior to meeting him.' Mary prayed that Gideon wouldn't sense her ulterior motives. 'He has to go away on business for some weeks, but once he returns he wishes to see you.'

'Books?'

'Yes, indeed. There is a very long list, I'm afraid, but, as I have already said, Gideon, I am prepared to help you with the expense of your training. You will need somewhere to study, of course, but there is no reason on earth why you should not study here and make use of the library. I certainly never use it, and, for all his faults, my father was an extremely learned man.'

'You mean you'll take me as a charity case?' Gideon demanded truculently.

Immediately Mary recognised her error. That pride of his! 'If I wanted to do good works, Gideon, I'm sure I could employ myself far better visiting the poor than by trying to assist a certain very stubborn young man to make something of himself!' she responded tartly.

'There's any number you could do that for,' Gideon persisted. 'Why should you choose me?'

Mary could feel the furious betraying race of her heart, and she prayed that Gideon might not notice her agitation.

'I can see that you have talent, Gideon, and the kind of stubborn determination you will need if you are to achieve your ambitions,' Mary told him drily. 'But the choice and the decision are yours. Indeed, if you are foolish enough to let your unwarranted suspicion and stubborn pride prevent you from accepting my offer, then perhaps I was wrong about you after all.'

Now there was a certain haughtiness in Mary's voice that checked Gideon. He *was* suspicious about her offer. Life had taught him to be!

'I dunno why you should do such a thing,' he protested, shaking his head.

'Then I suggest that you leave me to worry about my reasoning, Gideon! Now,' she continued, 'is it to be yes or no?'

Mary's stomach cramped as she waited for his answer. Only she knew just how much courage it had taken her to make him this offer, what it would mean to her life if he accepted – and what it would mean if he refused!

He didn't want to be beholden to anyone, but to be offered the chance to train as an architect . . . Gideon could feel his resolve crumbling.

'Aye!' The strangled word echoed round the room. It was too late to take it back. Miss Isherwood was beaming delightedly at him, and he was almost sure he could actually see tears in her eyes.

When she spoke, though, her voice was coolly serious as she warned him, 'It will not be easy for you, and what lies ahead will demand many sacrifices.'

Sacrifices! He would sacrifice his soul to become an architect, Gideon acknowledged inwardly.

'Now,' Mary continued briskly, 'to business! I shall give you the list of books, Gideon, and those you cannot manage to borrow from the library or find here I shall buy myself for you. No, don't look at me like that,' she told him. 'Their cost will be repaid to me along with any other disbursements I may make on your behalf once you are qualified.'

'But that will be years,' Gideon protested.

'Then I shall charge you interest,' Mary returned evenly, her mouth quirking in a brief smile.

She already knew perfectly well that Gideon would find all the books he needed in her library. After all, hadn't she gone to the trouble of making sure she brought them back from Manchester with her? Quite ruthlessly she had removed a whole shelf of her father's first editions so that she might fill it with those she had purchased for Gideon.

Her 'friend' had been well primed by her regarding his benevolent role – and well paid to carry out his part as well. She had done everything she could do, and now she was totally in Gideon's hands. Her whole future, her life, everything depended on his acceptance of her suggestion.

'I may seem to be behaving philanthropically, Gideon,' Mary continued calmly, 'but I assure you I intend to be well reimbursed for my pains.'

Angrily Gideon listened to her. Miss Isherwood always used big words when she wanted to put him in his place. Architecture wasn't the only thing he would be studying in her library, he decided grimly. There were bound to be dictionaries in there!

NINETEEN

'If I might have a word, madam . . . ?'

Mary frowned at her housekeeper. The woman was good enough at her job but Mary had never really taken to her. She could not forget that she had been employed by her father and something of his disapproval and contempt for Mary herself seemed to have rubbed off on the woman.

'Yes indeed, Mrs Jenkins. What is it?' she asked mildly, keeping her feelings to herself. She was, after all, an excellent housekeeper, if given to being over-harsh with the maids.

'Well, it's like this, madam.' Mrs Jenkins had drawn herself up to her full height. A tall, big-boned woman, she stood a good four inches taller than Mary. 'There's goings-on in this house that I cannot approve of and on account o' that I'm handing in me notice. I'm a Christian woman, and I don't hold with . . .' Thin lips folding into a disapproving line, she glared at Mary. 'Your poor dear father would be spinning in his grave if he knew what was going on under this very roof.'

'Going on?'

'Yes, madam, going on! It comes to something when a mere workman feels free to come in and out of decent houses using the front door, just as though he owned it, if you please, and for all the world to see as well. It ain't proper, and I –'

'Mrs Jenkins, are you referring to Mr Walker?'

'Oh, it's *Mr* Walker, is it now?' the housekeeper sniffed angrily. 'Well, you can call him what you like, but it's a pound to a penny that the rest of the street knows the truth of what's going on just as I do myself! Coming and going at all hours, talking like he's one of the gentry. If your father knew –'

'My father is dead, Mrs Jenkins,' Mary told her coldly, 'and I am now the mistress of this house. Mr Walker comes to this house to make use of the library, and he uses the front door because I have instructed him to do so – not that there is any reason why I should explain any of this to you, Mrs Jenkins.'

The housekeeper's face was burning red with moral indignation, and Mary could see that she desperately wanted to give full vent to her feelings.

Betty Jenkins glared angrily at her mistress. Oh, she could stand there looking all hoity-toity, and with that face of hers not so much as marked by a blush, but she knew what was going on, right enough. She'd seen it coming a long way back. Disgraceful it was as well. And not just because the mistress was a good twenty years older than Gideon Walker.

She was ashamed to be working in such a household! Why, she had even seen Gideon in Miss Isherwood's bedroom the previous week. Oh, he had lied and pretended that he was there to measure up for something or other, but the whole street knew the truth!

Well, the mistress might treat him as her equal, but *she* was certainly not going to!

'Not one single day more will I stay in this house,' she told Mary, giving her a disapproving look. 'Not one single day!'

Not one single day, but she certainly intended to go over and share a pot of tea with her closest friend before she left, and tell her just how her brazen-faced mistress had received her declaration.

She would have to contact the employment agency and get them to send her a temporary housekeeper until she could find a suitable replacement for Mrs Jenkins, Mary decided. Perhaps she should have expected there to be gossip about Gideon's regular visits to the house and the instructions she had given on how he was to be treated. She knew how hard he was working during the day whilst studying the books in her library at night, and she had given orders that he was to be provided with a meal, and that a fire was to be kept burning in the library for him.

She tried to limit the number of times she allowed herself the joy of going into the library to see him to just once or twice a week.

Already she was aware of a change in him. He held himself with more confidence; he spoke with more confidence as well, using a far larger vocabulary, experimenting fearlessly with words she suspected he had newly learned. Watching the eager, almost greedy way in which his mind was soaking up the knowledge he was feeding it both touched and excited her.

'Ellie, I have some news for you.'

As she looked at her cousin's happy, glowing face, Ellie couldn't help reflecting how lucky Cecily was to have fallen in love with a man her parents approved of.

'I . . . we . . . I am to have a baby,' Cecily announced, blushing a little and then laughing. 'I am so excited and happy, and so is Paul.'

'Oh, Cecily!' Ellie hugged her cousin, trying to sound as enthusiastic as Cecily obviously expected her to be, but she could only remember the birth of her younger brother and the death of her mother, and to her dismay she heard herself blurting out, 'Cecily, does it not worry you to . . . to be having a child?'

Ellie's face burned with guilty heat as soon as she had asked her unguarded question but, to her relief, Cecily did not chide her for its intimacy, saying calmly, 'You are thinking of your mother, I know, Ellie, and I must admit that I was a little anxious when I first realised, but both Mama and Paul have assured me that I have nothing to worry about and, of course, with my dearest Paul I could not be in safer hands. It is the natural consequence of marriage that a woman should bear children.'

Ellie smiled wanly.

'Mother and Father came over at the weekend, and I told them then,' Cecily continued chattily, before pausing and looking a little uncomfortable. 'There has been . . . Ellie, there is something I think I should tell you, but I don't want . . . It is about Gideon Walker. Oh, Ellie, it is the most shocking thing, but Mama's cook had it from Miss Isherwood's housekeeper – well, she was her house-keeper, but now she has handed in her notice on account of what has been happening.'

With every word Cecily uttered Ellie could feel her tension increase.

'It seems that Miss Isherwood is . . . well, that she . . . there is an involvement between them, Ellie, with Mr Walker calling there every night and staying until the early hours of the morning! Miss Isherwood has given instructions to her staff that he is to be admitted through the front door, and treated like a gentleman!'

Ellie experienced the kind of pain one felt on an icy day when one's fingers and toes burned with cold, only now her pain filled her whole body.

'Ellie?' she heard Cecily asking anxiously.

'Cecily, I . . . I think I have a headache coming on,' Ellie whispered painfully.

It was just because she had not been prepared for it that hearing news of Gideon had affected her so strongly, that was all. Nothing more. How could there be? Gideon was nothing to her now!

'Ellie, I am sorry. I should not have told you. I have upset you,' Cecily apologised unhappily. 'I was not thinking properly.'

'Not at all,' Ellie denied fiercely. 'Mr Walker is of no consequence to me, Cecily. I might have been foolish enough to think myself attracted to him at one time, but it is a foolishness I have long since left behind me.'

If her voice trembled a little it was just because she felt so relieved at her own escape, and so shocked by Cecily's revelations, Ellie told herself determinedly.

Diplomatically Cecily changed the subject. 'Poor Iris is very angry at the moment. You know how passionately she feels about the women's suffrage movement, Ellie, and she has become very involved with it. She says that it is appalling that our sex should be denied the vote, and you should have heard her and Ewan Cameron arguing the other evening. Ewan loves to bait her so. I think he is in love with her, but Paul laughs at me for saying so.'

'I cannot see how the movement will ever be able to persuade Parliament round to their way of thinking,' Ellie responded.

Thanks, in the main, to listening to Iris herself, Ellie had begun to take a lively interest in political affairs, eagerly reading her uncle's newspapers once he had finished with them, and secretly she admired Iris and her friends for their beliefs.

Mary made her way to the front of the crowd gathered to hear Mrs Pankhurst speak. Mary had travelled to Manchester with her fellow activists from Preston.

There was, she knew, a rift developing within the movement between those who supported Mrs Pankhurst and her cry for stronger action, and those who believed that genteel debate was the proper order of things.

'Oh, well said.' As the woman standing next to her broke into applause, Mary turned to look at her, recognising her from previous meetings.

Iris smiled ruefully. 'I'm sorry, did I startle you? It's just that I agree so passionately with everything she's saying. We are never going to make any progress whilst we pathetically wait for men to allow us to have the vote. If necessary we have to take it for ourselves.'

'You sound very militant,' Mary responded, amused.

'I feel very militant,' Iris confessed. 'We are just not making any progress. Whilst we talk amongst ourselves, those who really hold the power are keeping it and laughing at us behind our backs, whilst to our faces they are pretending to consider our claims.'

'I must say, I feel inclined to agree with you,' Mary admitted. 'Have you met Emmeline yet? If not, perhaps you would like me to introduce you?'

'No, and yes, I should very much like to meet her.'

'There is to be a smaller . . . get-together after this meeting,' Mary informed Iris in a low voice. They were having to be so careful. Even within their own ranks there were spies, and worse . . . but she considered herself to be a good judge of character and she sensed both Iris's resolve and commitment. 'If you would care to come to it as my guest . . .'

'Thank you,' Iris responded. 'I should very much like to do so.'

'What do you mean, you want to return to Japan? You are my son, Henry, and your place is here. The Charnock Shipping Line is not the success it is today, Henry, because I have spent the last thirty-odd years doing as I pleased and sailing off to Japan whenever I have felt like it! Have you no sense of duty? No sense of what you owe me?'

Jarvis Charnock's mouth compressed angrily as he looked at his only son, and, seeing the anger and hostility in his father's eyes, Henry felt a familiar sense of anguish beginning to overtake him.

He knew that he was a disappointment to his father. He was too like his mother, both physically and emotionally, ever to have won his father's approval.

'Why should I have been cursed with such a son?' Jarvis demanded. 'Look at your cousin – married and with a fine family of sons, but you . . .'

Henry winced. He knew all about his father's desire to have grandsons he could mould in his own image and to whom he could pass on the business.

'Father . . .' he began unsteadily.

'You will marry, Henry, and soon,' Jarvis announced, making no attempt to conceal his contempt for his son. 'And let me tell you now, if you refuse to do as I wish, and attempt to go against me in this, then you will find yourself disinherited and disgraced. And you can forget all about going back to Japan! I shall see to it that there isn't a shipping line the length and breadth of England that will give you a passage. So if you'll take my advice you'll stop sending the Pride girl milksop bunches of flowers and books, and fix your interest with her, and the sooner the better. Her uncle's a warm man – and well connected. He's willing to give the girl a handsome dowry and . . .'

A little shiftily, Jarvis looked away from his son. He was not prepared to take Henry into his confidence about the special business venture he and Josiah Parkes were planning.

Henry listened to his father in silent despair. He ached and yearned to go back to Japan. It was the only place he had ever felt that he belonged. And there were other reasons.

He so badly wanted to defy his father but he knew too well that he simply did not have the strength. A familiar black pit of despair opened up inside him. If his father had made up his mind Henry was to marry Ellie then that was exactly what would happen!

'Let me look at you, Ellie. Yes, my dear, that gown looks very pretty,' Ellie's aunt approved. 'We must hurry now, for I wouldn't want us to be late.'

Ellie and her Aunt Parkes had been invited to take tea with Mrs George Fazackerly, Henry Charnock's cousin's wife, and Lavinia was in quite a state of agitation about the visit.

'There is no mistaking the seriousness of Henry Charnock's intentions now, Ellie!' she continued, pleased. 'He has not declared himself yet, of course, but his attentiveness towards you and this invitation to visit his cousin makes everything quite clear. Such a marriage is exactly what your dear mama wanted for you, Ellie. I am so pleased for you, my love, but you must remember that Mrs Fazackerly's opinion is very highly regarded by Henry's father.'

Closing her ears to her aunt's voice, with a definite feeling of duty over pleasure, Ellie followed her out to the waiting carriage.

'Now, children, that is enough. I am sure that Miss Pride is quite tired of playing cricket!'

Firmly instructing the hovering maid to take Ellie's place on the makeshift cricket pitch, Elizabeth Fazackerly turned to smile at Ellie.

Why was it that when some people smiled, you were instantly aware that they did not really care for you, Ellie wondered ruefully, as Henry's cousin's wife indicated that Ellie was to take the empty chair next to her own.

'I must admit that I have been intrigued to meet you, Miss Pride,' Elizabeth said. 'Mr Charnock has sung your praises enthusiastically, but then, of course, I have to say that he is bound to look favourably on anyone prepared to take on poor Henry.'

Her disparaging tone immediately made Ellie bristle indignantly on Henry's behalf. It had been easy for Ellie to guess from his conversation how bullied and unvalued by those closest to him Henry Charnock was.

'I have tried to introduce him to any number of suitable young women myself,' Elizabeth complained, 'but he is so lacking in any social graces, so very unlike either his father or my own dear husband, that one wonders sometimes how ... But then Mr Charnock has always maintained that Henry is very much his mother's child. She was a quiet poor thing as well, by all accounts.'

There was no way Ellie intended to allow Elizabeth to speak so unkindly of Henry. Sitting up in her chair she returned crisply, 'Henry may seem a little shy and inarticulate in company, but I can assure you, Mrs Fazackerly, that given the opportunity he is a most entertaining and informed raconteur. One only has to have the privilege of hearing him speak about those matters closest to his heart, such as his travels to Japan, to know that!'

Ellie could see from her hostess's narrow-eyed expression that she had registered Ellie's subtle retaliation.

'Oh, Japan! I pray you will take my advice, Miss Pride, and not mention that country in the presence of my husband's uncle – especially if you wish to retain his goodwill. It is poor Henry's obsession with that country that has been the cause of so much discord between them. Mr Charnock is thoroughly exasperated by Henry's ridiculous insistence on being allowed to return to Yokohama. George, my own dear husband, has tried to speak to Henry – to act as mediator between father and son, as it were – but he has confessed to me that he finds it hard since he totally supports his uncle's point of view. If Henry is to take over the shipping line and maintain its successful operation, then he needs to be here and not in some remote part of the world playing at doing a job he really knows nothing about.

'It was the talk of Liverpool the other year what a fool Henry had made of himself by trying to over-rule a decision of one of his father's shipmasters. Heaven knows how much money his folly might have lost the business if he had been allowed to have his way.'

No, she did not like Elizabeth Fazackerly, Ellie

decided firmly later in the afternoon as she and her aunt were driven back to Hoylake.

'So, Ellie, and how did you find Mrs Fazackerly?'

It was the day after her meeting with Henry's cousin's family, and Ellie was having afternoon tea with Iris in the Palm Court lounge of the Adelphi Hotel.

'She was not really to my taste,' Ellie admitted, wrinkling her nose. 'And I thought that she was very unkind about Henry. She kept referring to him as "poor Henry", and belittling him to such an extent that I own I felt I had to defend him. I cannot think why she was so unkind about him to me!'

'Can't you?' Iris asked her drily. 'It seems to me that Mrs Fazackerly has a good deal to gain by attempting to prevent Henry from marrying. It is no secret that his father has hopes of a grandson to take his place in the business! If Henry were not to marry then Mr George Fazackerly would be the next in line to inherit the shipping line.'

Whilst Ellie digested her comment, Iris calmly changed the subject.

'Such good news about Cecily,' she said. 'Although I do hope that Paul will not allow her to conceive too quickly a second time! I know there are many men who insist that the whole purpose of sex is to produce children, and who refuse to allow their wives to use any form of birth control, but that, as any intelligent person knows, is a canard – otherwise why would there be so many brothels? No, the truth is that far too many men wish to control us in any and every way that they can.'

Ellie stared at Iris. 'Is that true?' she blurted out, pink-cheeked. 'Is it indeed possible for a woman to . . . to have marital relations and not become . . . ?'

Iris frowned. 'Oh, Ellie, I am sorry. I had forgotten how ignorant of such things you will have been kept! And that is yet another reason why it is so important that we women should have the rights that our government continues to deny us. There are means, yes,' she confirmed briskly.

Ellie felt as though an enormous weight had been lifted off her shoulders; a terrible fear pushed away to a safe distance. She longed to question Iris more deeply, but felt too shy to do so, and besides, Iris was now deep in vehement vocal monologue decrying the power and control that men had over their wives.

'You should attend one of our meetings, Ellie. I really wish you would. You would find it most instructive.'

'I can't see Mr Parkes ever allowing any woman living beneath his roof to do that,' Ellie replied wryly.

'No indeed. And that is exactly why we have to succeed in our aims – so that men like your uncle no longer have the right to tell us what to do!'

Ellie listened to her affectionately. Iris didn't know how lucky she was to be financially independent and to have parents whose outlook was so modern, and indulgent. Although Sir James teased Iris for her dedication to her cause, he happily accepted it, and Lady Angela made no secret of the fact that she both supported and applauded her daughter's stance.

Female emancipation was something her Uncle Parkes would certainly not approve of and even less support!

'Oh, that reminds me,' Iris continued, 'I saw a neighbour of Cecily's mama's at the meeting – a Miss Mary Isherwood. She is apparently an old friend of Emmeline Pankhurst's, and was very much a part of their circle when the Pankhursts lived in London. She was there with her young protégé, a Mr Gideon Walker, who is studying to become an architect.'

So it wasn't just gossip Cecily had heard. Iris had seen this Miss Isherwood and Gideon – 'her protégé' – with her own eyes.

Ellie looked away so that Iris would not read the expression she feared was all too plain on her face.

'Gideon, I have to attend a meeting in Manchester tomorrow, but I do not intend to ask you to accompany me there, since I know how busy you are.'

'I don't feel I can leave the workmen to their own devices with the construction of your conservatory at such a delicate stage,' Gideon replied. 'And then I have promised Mrs Edgar she shall have her new library finished for the end of the month.'

On his own insistence, Gideon was still taking on cabinet-making commissions, determined to earn as much as he could to support himself whilst he studied the books Mary's architect friend had set for him to read prior to taking up his place in the practice at the beginning of the new year.

Mary had offered him a room in a boarding house she owned in Manchester, rent-free, but he had refused, insisting that he must pay his own way.

He was glad to be able to avoid going with her to Manchester. Privately Gideon could not agree with the aims of the women's suffrage movement, since he felt that it went against the natural order of things for women to want to take charge of their own lives, but he was loath to expose his views to Mary's criticism, knowing how quickly and incisively she would shred his arguments to nothing. And, secretly, if he was honest with himself, he could not help but admire her financial expertise and the way she had taken control of her life, even if a part of him refused to believe it necessary for a woman to be so skilled in what should be wholly male territory.

Every morning she read the financial papers and

often expressed to him her views and her decisions, explaining to him why she considered this investment to be a sound and potentially profitable one, and the other not.

'Property is the key – the most solid foundation to wealth, Gideon,' she often told him. 'Bricks and mortar.'

'I believe you took tea with my cousin's wife a few days ago, Miss Pride?'

As always, Henry's stilted attempts to make conversation made Ellie feel maternally protective towards him. He developed his slight stammer whenever he was exceptionally nervous, and Ellie always tried to steer him into calmer conversational waters whenever she sensed the onset of one of these small crises. And nothing, she had discovered, increased the likelihood of Henry stammering more than being in other male company, especially, it seemed, that of his father, his cousin and her Uncle Parkes.

On these occasions Ellie skilfully and discreetly managed the conversation so as to shield him from their contempt. He had become to her almost another brother, she recognised, someone with whom she felt comfortable and at ease, and with whom she could talk openly about the newspaper articles she had read, and her growing feeling of confusion about what she herself believed a woman's role should be.

'Indeed, and I also played cricket with Masters Matthew, Godfrey, and Timothy,' Ellie smiled.

'Ah, my cousin's sons.' Henry sighed, and Ellie knew the reason for that sigh. To comfort him, she touched his arm lightly.

They were walking together along the sea front at Parkgate, where they had gone to spend the pleasantly warm late autumn day. Many others had had the same idea and the long narrow road was crowded with people, many of them eating the delicious ice cream for which the small town was famous. From the low sea wall, Ellie could see children shrimping, shrieking with delight when they thought they had caught something.

Henry coughed and cleared his throat a little nervously.

'Miss Pride – Ellie,' he began, 'there is something I wish to say to you . . .'

Sensing what was coming, Ellie strove to remain calm, turning her head to look at him, but as she did so, a piercing scream of distress caused them both to look at the small child who had fallen over in front of them and was bewailing the loss of his ice cream.

Watching the way in which Henry obligingly went to his aid and even promised him a fresh ice cream if he would only stop crying, Ellie was amused to see how firmly masterful he sounded instead of his normal tentative, hesitant self.

A flustered nurse came running up to reclaim her charge, giving him a cross little shake as she did so, for 'bothering the gentleman', until Henry gently reproved her, telling her that he had been no bother at all.

After they had gone Ellie said ruefully, 'Poor little boy, I imagine he must have thought his whole day spoiled by the loss of his ice cream.'

'Indeed. No doubt it was a treat he had been promised and had looked forward to a good long time,' Henry agreed, smiling.

They had reached the end of the waterfront now, but as she made to turn round, Henry stopped her, taking hold of her arm and clearing his throat awkwardly before beginning to stammer.

'Miss P-Pride . . . Ellie . . . there is s-something I wish to say . . . that is, I would like t-to ask if . . . would you do me the honour of c-consenting to be my wife, Ellie?'

She had known, of course, that it would come, and she had thought herself prepared for it – prepared for the final renunciation of the silly, foolish dream she had once had – but to her own distress, Ellie suddenly discovered that instead of receiving Henry's proposal with dignified mature acceptance, what she really wanted to do was to pick up her skirts and run. But where? Friargate?

Sensing her distress, Henry immediately became concerned. 'I have spoken too soon and shocked you, I can see that. My mistake. I should have given you more time. You do not have to answer me, Ellie. Let us say no more about it!'

Tears pricked Ellie's eyes as she recognised his goodness and humility. 'Oh, Henry, you are so kind,' she told him impulsively. 'Too kind,' she added.

But how could she marry a man because he was kind, when deep down inside her a rebellious part of her cried out to love and be loved?

'Ellie, you are back! Well, did Henry say anything?' Aunt Lavinia demanded expectantly.

Ellie had been brought up to be honest and she gave a small sigh. 'Henry has done me the honour of asking me to be his wife, Aunt, but –'

'Oh, I am so pleased. I knew he would, of course. In fact, I was so sure of it that I asked your uncle if we might not have Connie to live here with us once you are married! I am sure that he will agree because he has enjoyed your company as much as I have, Ellie.'

Ice-cold fear for her sister poured through Ellie's veins. She could still see the lascivious look her uncle had given Connie, and Connie was not like her, Ellie admitted wretchedly; she was so head-strong and yet at the same time so unaware, she would not recognise, as Ellie had done, that she might be in danger. But what could she do? How could she protect Connie?

A small voice inside her head suddenly spoke up and told her! If she married Henry she could have Connie to live with her, and John too – there were, after all, excellent schools in Liverpool – and even perhaps the baby.

Without even being aware of it, Ellie had set her foot on the bridge that led from girlhood to womanhood. When Henry called to see her she would tell him that she would marry him, and she would tell him too that she wanted to have her siblings to live with them.

She had made up her mind and she could not allow herself to be swayed from her decision. It was her duty to put the needs of her siblings above her own, but she said nothing of her decision to her aunt.

Instead she said, 'I have asked for a little time to consider and then I will give Henry my answer.'

Three days later, when Henry called to see her, Ellie was ready with her answer.

'I am sorry to press you, Ellie,' Henry began uncomfortably, 'but my father is eager to . . . that is, he . . .' Henry was obviously nervous, his Adam's apple wobbling as he spoke, but Ellie was calm.

'I have made up my mind, Henry, and I am happy to accept your proposal,' she told him sedately. 'Although there is one favour I must ask. Would you be agreeable to my sister and my brothers coming to live with us after we are married?'

Happy to accept? She was accepting him! Henry beamed with relief.

'You don't object, Henry?' Ellie asked him anxiously, when he didn't reply immediately.

'Not at all. If that is what you want, Ellie,' he

assured her, still hardly able to comprehend that she had said yes.

'Oh, Ellie, I am so pleased, and Mr Parkes will be too. We must start making plans. Your betrothal will have to be announced. Oh, what a nuisance it is that your uncle is away on business now,' Aunt Lavinia complained.

Ellie had given her her news as soon as Henry had left, and now she was sitting feeling empty and somehow detached from everything whilst her aunt made excited plans.

'We shall have to let your father know, of course. I shall write to him immediately, and my sisters must be told as well.'

Silently Ellie listened to her. She did not intend to inform her aunt of her plans to have her siblings live with her after her marriage – just in case her uncle somehow managed to thwart them – but she longed to tell Connie. Surely when she did her sister would finally forgive her?

TWENTY

Gideon whistled softly beneath his breath as he put the finishing touches to Mrs Edgar's library bookshelves. He had been up early, making the most of the light in order to finish reading one of the books Toby Mackenzie, the architect to whom he was to be apprenticed, had set him, and then on impulse he had headed for the market where he had eaten a hearty breakfast whilst watching the world go by.

Will Pride, espying him sitting on a bench, his dog at his feet, came across to him.

'Will? How are you and how's Robert?' Gideon asked.

'I'm fair to middlin',' Will responded cheerfully, 'but as for our Robert, got hissel' in a fair old mess, he has! Never thought he'd tek it into his head to take on all serious with that Maggie. Nor her with him, truth to tell. I just thought she was up for a bit o' fun and our Rob certainly needed to have some, but that's women for you! Now it seems she's nagging him to tek her to church. I've told

294

him straight he'd be a fool if he does. After all, he bain't the first she's lifted her petticoats for, if we're speaking man to man, but our Rob allus was a softie, and seems like she's carrying! I never thought 'un should ha' married that uppity piece Lydia, but would he listen – no.' Will shook his head. 'And look what happened there. Lyddy dead and our Rob robbed of his young 'uns by them other Barclay sisters.

'Seems like our Ellie has fallen on feathers, though. She's got some rich young master chasing after her. Maggie was cutting up a fine fuss the last time I called round at Friargate, claiming that if there was to be a wedding there was no way our Rob was going without her, and shaming her in front of the whole town, and no way either she was going with him unchurched or without a fine new outfit. I told our Rob not to let it worry him. Chances are he won't even get a look in at the wedding, not with Ellie being so taken up with rich folk and putting on a grand show.'

After a few more minutes' conversation Will called his dogs to him and went on his way, leaving Gideon to ponder on what he had said.

So Ellie was about to get married. Well, he certainly pitied the poor fool she was planning to wed! He'd had a lucky escape there, he told himself, as he looked at his half-eaten breakfast and realised his appetite had gone.

*   *   *

295

Gideon spent the rest of the morning working furiously on Mrs Edgar's bookshelves, only realising when he stopped to drink a mug of strong tea and eat a ham sandwich that the sketches he had been doodling on his drawing pad were not just of coving details to complete the bookshelves but also included a dozen or more sketches of Ellie!

It was early evening before he had finished his work to his own satisfaction. Packing up his tools, he started to make his way home, choosing to walk through the pleasantness of Avenham Park instead of taking a tramcar, before turning to trudge along the long streets of mills and millworkers' cottages that lay between the park and his destination.

He had just drawn level with one of the older mills when there was a splintering sound, the windows shattered and a loud bang shook the entire building. Then there were screams as the whole side wall started to fall. As millworkers came tumbling out of the huge hole that had appeared, screaming, covered in lint and dust, Gideon reacted instinctively, dropping his tools and hurrying into the tangle of bricks and girders in the direction of agonised cries.

Entering the mill was like stepping into the mouth of hell. Where a ceiling had collapsed above the ground floor, huge pieces of machinery tilted at ominous angles over the hole, threatening to descend at any second, as one of them already had done.

Gideon had to turn his head away and cover his mouth as his stomach heaved at the sight of the broken, mangled flesh of what had once been human beings crushed beneath a weaving frame. The smell of dust and death choked his nostrils and half blinded him. Figures appeared out of the dimness of the mill, hurrying past him in blind panic.

'Get out! Get out! The rest of it's going to come down,' he heard one man screaming as he half-pushed past, dragging a sobbing girl with him.

The carnage was appalling. The sight of young girls who would never reach womanhood lying in indecent untimely death, burned his eyes as much as the acrid unbreathable air.

His draughtsman's eye had already seen a dozen ways in which the building was unsafe, his ears catching the dull roar presaging the total collapse of the entire upper floor.

Gideon turned to leave, and then he heard a faint whimpering sob. 'Oh, please, sir, help me . . .'

It took him several valuable seconds to find her, a tiny slip of a thing, who looked no older than a child, her thin face bloodless, her eyes frantic with fear. She was trapped beneath a heavy piece of wood and, as Gideon looked, he saw sickeningly what he realised were the snapped bones of her thin legs piercing the skin. There was no way he could help her, and no way he could leave her either, he recognised helplessly as he dropped down on the floor beside her and started to try to move the spar trapping her.

The scream she gave as he tried to lift the spar from her nearly amputated legs made him feel sick. Above them dust fell in an ominous waterfall. Gideon could hear the groan of the broken floorboards, and the squeal of the machinery they could no longer support as it rocked above their heads.

Somewhere in the distance there were voices, sounds – a fire engine, running feet. But Gideon knew they would be too late to save them.

As he finally managed to lift the spar a piece of metal dropped from the floor above, slicing down onto his exposed wrist. Gideon screamed as the pain splintered through him, the sound mingling with the agonised animal howl of the injured girl, and with the voices of those who had come too late to rescue them.

Mary heard the news when she got off the train in Preston. Late editions of the local paper had been rushed out, bearing deep bands of black, and a stark empty space to list the as yet unnamed dead. Over fifty were thought to have lost their lives in the collapse of the mill.

The town's angry grief hung over it like a pall, and as she made her way to the hansom cab rank, Mary caught snatches of conversation.

'. . . t' mill weren't safe. Everyone has allus known that.'

'. . . t'owld place should 'a bin pulled down years back.'

'. . . My missus were inside – aye, and m' daughters as well. Lost them all, I have . . .'

By the time the cab had discharged her outside her front door, Mary's face was wet with tears as her shocked senses absorbed the full horror of what had happened.

So many senseless deaths caused by one man's greed. The blame lay totally with the mill owner, who had known that his building wasn't safe; that its floors could not support the machines he had continued to cram into it so that he could wring the last halfpenny of profit out of them and out of his workers.

Tilly, the parlour maid, crept through the hall white-faced and blank-eyed. Mary knew that she had cousins who worked in the mill, and who had considered her foolish for going into service and not following their example. There would scarcely be a working family in the town not affected by the tragedy, Mary acknowledged.

If she had doubted the wisdom of Christabel Pankhurst's desire for more militant action, then she did so no longer, Mary recognised, as she prepared wearily for bed.

Morning dawned grey and bleak, the dust from the destroyed mill hanging thickly over the grieving and unfamiliarly silent town.

Mary was not surprised to learn over breakfast that Tilly could not be found and was thought to have gone home to mourn with what was left of her family.

The papers had been delivered and, contrary to her normal custom, Mary reached first for the local paper instead of *The Times*. News of the terrible disaster was spread all over the front page, which included a photograph of the destroyed building.

Quickly, Mary began to read, and then froze as Gideon's name leaped off the page at her.

She rang at once for Fielding.

'Have the car brought round immediately! At once!' Her hands were trembling so much she had to let her maid help her into her coat. She hadn't felt like this, experienced this degree of fear and pain since ... Quickly, she closed her eyes as tightly as she could, forcing back the acid burn of her tears. That other loss was two decades ago now, and those years had softened its rawness. But she must not think about that now!

'The car's here, madam.'

Taking a deep breath, she opened her eyes.

White-faced, Mary hurried into the chaotic busyness of the infirmary. Everywhere she looked there were people huddled around makeshift beds. The sounds of moans and sobbing filled the air, the full horror of what was happening highlighted by the sudden cries of despair whenever someone realised that they had lost a loved one.

As she stood stock-still, too shocked by the scene before her to move, Mary was conscious of the anguish of those around her: mothers, clutching their shawls and begging every passing nurse if they had seen their daughters; men who should have been young but now looked aged beyond belief, crying out hoarsely for their wives and sweethearts. And lying over everything, infiltrating everywhere, overpowering even the fierce smell of carbolic, lay the stench of blood and death.

A nurse, her starched uniform soiled, hurried down the ward, shaking off all those who tried to reach out to her to beg for news of their loved ones.

As she reached one of her colleagues, Mary heard her saying, 'The morgue is already full and we have nowhere to put any more bodies. And still they are bringing them in – or rather what bits of them they can find.'

Mary's gorge rose, and she turned away, forcing back her nausea.

Somewhere in this carnage lay Gideon. And she intended to find him!

It took her close on an hour, having given up asking the exhausted and impatient medical staff, following instead the example of the other searchers as anxious as herself and examining the occupant of every bed.

Some of the sights she saw were so sickeningly

distressing that she wondered if these victims might not be better dead. A young girl, a child really, with one arm torn off, her face so badly bruised it was impossible to recognise what was really left of it, lay moaning on one bed and, despite her urgent need to find Gideon, Mary had to stop beside her and do what she could to comfort the child. A nun appeared beside her, silent and black-clad, taking the child's hand from Mary and beginning to pray. As the child struggled to breathe, Mary heard the beginnings of the death rattle in her throat.

Getting up she plunged blindly through the ward. Not even Dante himself could have depicted a scene more horrific!

When she couldn't find Gideon amongst those waiting for treatment, she began to fear the worst.

'You could always try the morgue,' one of the nurses told her.

Mary could feel herself dizzying with anguish and despair, and then she overheard someone saying that those who had already received treatment had been removed to another ward. Mary almost ran towards it.

Here, there was some sort of order, although the moans of those who were lying on the neatly made beds were pitiful to hear.

'I am looking for Gideon Walker,' Mary told the nurse, her heart slamming heavily against her ribs as the woman pursed her lips and frowned.

'Who are you?' she demanded brusquely. 'The

next of kin?' Without waiting for Mary to reply, she ordered her curtly, 'Wait here.'

Whilst she waited, the woman sitting at a nearby bed, holding the hand of the girl lying still on it, suddenly gave a keening howl of grief, and burst out, 'My daughter. My baby . . . she's gone . . . she's gone . . .'

Rigid with distress, Mary tried to look away as two nurses tried to pull the woman from the body of her daughter, but found she could not tear her gaze from the haunting scene.

'You are enquiring about Gideon Walker?'

Mary turned to look into the haggard face of the man standing in front of her. She guessed that he was probably only in his early thirties, but right now he looked closer to sixty.

'Yes.' Her throat had gone so dry that her voice was a papery rasp. 'I . . . He . . .'

'He's alive – just,' the doctor told her, 'but he's still unconscious. He lost a lot of blood.'

'Can I . . . can I see him?' Mary whispered.

The doctor gave a tired nod of consent.

Gideon was at the end of the ward, his limbs – or so it seemed to Mary from her anxious glance – still mercifully intact, a bandage pinned round his head and another binding his wrist.

'You said he was unconscious,' she said anxiously.

'He suffered a blow to his head, as well as the damage to his hand.'

'Why isn't someone sitting with him – a nurse?' Mary demanded.

The doctor gave her a grim look. 'Given the numbers of injured we're trying to deal with he's lucky to have a bed, and to have seen a surgeon.'

Mary took a deep breath. 'If he is well enough to be moved, I want to take him home.' As the doctor frowned she told him fiercely, 'He will receive every care, I assure you – the very best of care.'

'I shall have to speak with the chief surgeon,' he told her stiffly.

Mary could see that he did not like her interference, but she could also see how desperately he needed every single bed for more patients, who were even now being brought into the room.

It took Mary over half an hour to get the infirmary's chief surgeon to agree that she could take Gideon home, and then a further two hours to make arrangements for him to be carried there, well protected with blankets and pillows she had had brought from her home, on a flat conveyance, so that he should not be any further hurt.

'He is still unconscious,' Mary had overheard the young doctor protesting to the chief surgeon.

'His lack of consciousness won't kill him, but an infection from his injury very well may, and we already have enough bodies here, don't you think?' had been his senior's cynical reply.

TWENTY-ONE

'Dead? Dozens of people killed? But not Gideon? You did say not Gideon, Cecily?' Ellie could not hide her panic.

'No, no, he's alive. But it was awful, Ellie, truly dreadful.'

Ellie learned of the accident within hours of it happening from her cousin Cecily, who had heard of it from her mother.

'Gideon!' she whispered, pressing her hand to her breast as though to control the furious racing of her heart, and swaying so much that she had to reach for a chair in Cecily's morning room to support herself. 'Gideon has been hurt?'

'Ellie, I'm so sorry,' Cecily tried to comfort her, her own face paling as she recognised the intensity of Ellie's emotions. Ellie had always insisted that Mr Walker no longer meant anything to her, and Cecily had believed her, but now . . . It was too late for her to wish that she had not mentioned his name, Cecily recognised, or to refuse to answer Ellie's frantically anxious questions.

'What has happened? Tell me. I want to know everything. *Tell me*, Cecily,' she demanded fiercely.

Cecily bit her lip, but Ellie would not be denied.

'Tell me,' she insisted.

'Well, it seems that my father saw Mr Walker when he was first taken into hospital,' Cecily informed her reluctantly, 'and –'

'He is in hospital?'

Cecily looked away, her tender heart aching for the anguish she could see in her cousin's eyes.

Then: 'Ellie, Ellie, where are you going?' she called after her worriedly as, without a word, Ellie turned and ran towards the door.

'Cecily, I'm sorry, I have to go,' she told her.

They had planned to go shopping together, but Cecily made no attempt to dissuade her. Nevertheless, just as soon as Ellie had gone she lost no time in telephoning her husband to confide in him her anxieties about her cousin.

'She must still love him, Paul,' she wept. 'And yet she has always denied doing so.'

'She is more than likely suffering from shock,' Paul had comforted her. 'Leave her be for now, Cecily. Ellie is a sensible and very strong young woman. She will soon be her normal self again, you'll see. As to her loving Gideon Walker, it would be unnatural in the circumstances if she were not affected by such dreadful news, but Ellie has accepted Henry's proposal of marriage.'

Ellie wasn't quite sure how she came to be standing on Preston station. She had no recollection of having boarded the train in Liverpool, but obviously she must have done so.

The motion of the hansom cab made her feel sick, its air stale and fetid.

A grim pall of death hung over the infirmary, although its corridors were empty, and there was nothing of the disaster for Ellie to see.

'Gideon Walker?' The exhausted-looking nurse frowned as Ellie gave Gideon's name in a faltering voice. 'Who are you then?'

'I . . . he is a friend of my family,' Ellie managed to respond. She had gone terribly cold and her teeth had started to chatter. She felt sick, dizzy, light-headed, a hundred times worse than she had done when her mother had died. Because this time her fear wasn't for herself but for Gideon? She fought to resist the thought.

The nurse scrutinised her before replying, 'What a shame, duck. You won't be able to see him. You're too late. He's gone!'

Ellie gasped and swayed, her face blenching. Gideon was dead! She would never see him again. Never hear his voice . . . The pain tore at her like nothing she had ever experienced or ever imagined – dark, feral, clawing and ripping at her like a wild animal.

'Aye,' the woman continued, oblivious to Ellie's distress. 'Some fine lady came and took him away. In a fair old state she was too, proper upset! And a grand to-do about her taking 'im away, but they let her in the end.'

Mary Isherwood – that must be who the woman was talking about, Ellie guessed through her blaze of pain. Mary Isherwood had taken Gideon.

Numbly Ellie started to walk away.

'Ellie?'

Ellie stared uncomprehendingly into her Aunt Amelia's stern face as though she were a stranger.

'What are you doing here in Preston? In Winckley Square and on your own?'

'I came to see Gideon,' Ellie told her quietly.

Amelia Gibson frowned, her lips pursing. 'Quite obviously, Ellie, you are not feeling yourself, otherwise you would never have done something so . . . foolish. Does my sister know you are here? No?' she challenged, when Ellie merely shook her head slowly. 'Come with me, Ellie. This sort of behaviour is intolerable and would have deeply shamed your mother.'

'Gideon . . .' Ellie began helplessly, as her aunt took a firm hold of her arm.

'I will not hear that young man's name spoken,' Amelia Gibson told her coldly. 'I am disappointed in you, Ellie. How can you behave so, after everything that has been done for you?'

Ellie gave a deep shudder as her aunt pushed her firmly into her home.

'Have you any idea how shocked I was to look out of my parlour window and see you standing in the square, for all the world . . . ?' Her lips folded into a condemningly hard line. 'I shall telephone my sister immediately and you will be sent back to Liverpool on the first available train, and from there escorted to Hoylake. Whatever can have possessed you?'

Ellie wanted to cry even though her eyes were so dry that she could not do so. She had no more idea than her aunt as to just what had motivated her behaviour, or even of how she came to be in Winckley Square.

'So, miss, what do you have to say for yourself?'

Ellie quailed as she looked into the angry features of her Uncle Parkes. He had sent for her to present herself to him in his study, making her feel like a prisoner as she was firmly escorted there by his manservant.

The air in the room was so thick with cigar smoke that it made her choke a little. A decanter of spirit stood nearly empty on his desk, a half-filled glass beside it.

As he came out from behind his desk and walked towards her, Ellie could smell the overpowering scent of alcohol on his breath.

'I-I can't explain what . . . why . . . my feelings . . .'

Ellie realised immediately that she had said the wrong thing as his face darkened and he took a step towards her.

'Your feelings. Aye, well, we all know now what those are, don't we?' he raged. 'Just as we all know what you are! Bringing disgrace upon yourself and upon my house by . . .' Reaching for his glass, he took a deep swallow, almost emptying it, whilst Ellie trembled in distress.

'You are an ungrateful little harlot – a whore. And it is my duty to castigate and punish you for your sinfulness.'

Ellie was beginning to feel frightened. Her uncle's face was a dark red colour, and tiny specks of spittle flew from his mouth as he raged at her, calling her all manner of horrible things, using words she had never heard before but which she knew instinctively were degrading and disgusting. Shock piled up on top of shock, fear upon fear, until they lay suffocatingly heavy over her, choking, smothering her ability to protest.

She felt numbed, as though what was happening around her could not possibly be real, and yet at the same time her senses were somehow heightened so that she could feel the sharp, savage bite of her own fear so intensely that it was magnified a hundred times. She was afraid of the intensity of his anger, which was totally outside her experience but, more than that, she was desperately afraid of the danger she could sense closing around her, a danger that had its roots in the sickening look she could see in his eyes, the hot feral smell he was generating in the air around her, the deep inner awareness she suddenly had that made her want to turn and run, and yet held her immobile where she stood.

'Engaged to a decent, respectable young man, and yet you go whoring with your lover – well, I fully intend to put an end to that. You will marry Henry Charnock, miss, without delay, and just to make sure you understand what I am saying to you . . .'

To Ellie's terror he removed a thick heavy leather belt studded with brass from his desk drawer, wrapping it slowly and almost caressingly around his hand as he stared at her, transfixing her with the intensity of his gaze.

'There is only one way to punish females like you!'

Terrified, Ellie turned and ran blindly towards the door, but Josiah reached it before her, barring her exit, his lips parting in a hot panting breath of pleasure as he saw her fear and heard her small anguished cry of despair.

'Seeking to evade your deserved punishment. For that you will get double rations.'

He was insane, Ellie decided frantically. He had to be. Just the sight of the hot, gloating look in his eyes made her feel sick and faint. She could not believe that this was happening. Her own father had never once whipped either her or her sister in all their lives, and he was a mere butcher, whilst her uncle was a gentleman. Then she remembered the bruises she had seen on her aunt's body, and the haunting look of fear Ellie had so often seen in her eyes as she looked at her husband.

Later Ellie was to acknowledge that it was in those seconds, trapped in that room, that she had undergone the fiercely swift and ferociously painful metamorphosis from which she emerged as a very different person. Panic shocked through her. Helplessly she looked towards the curtained window, but even if she could reach it before her uncle she knew she could not escape through it.

As she looked at him the plea she had been about to make to him to reconsider his actions died unspoken. He was licking his lips lasciviously and, as he smiled coldly at her, Ellie saw the way his hand strayed to his own body.

Her face burning with outrage and shame, she looked away from him, her stomach heaving.

'Little whore.' He said it almost tenderly, but his grip on her shoulder was anything but tender, making her cry out in pain. 'You should be thankful to me that I am providing you with the respectability of a husband; protecting you from your own sinfulness! Slut . . . harlot . . .' He ground out the words in her face, covering her skin in spittle as he lowered his mouth towards hers.

Nauseous, Ellie managed to turn her face aside as she frantically begged him to stop.

'Stop? Why? Do not pretend that you are not enjoying it,' he taunted her. 'A slut like you – how many times have you done it? Tell me . . .'

Sobbing, Ellie tried desperately to pull away, gasping in terror as she felt the sleeve of her gown tear beneath his grip.

'Defy me, would you?' Josiah challenged her savagely.

His hand was on her bare arm, his nails digging into her flesh. Revulsion jolted through her, a hot lava-flow of disgust. His hand moved from her arm to the bodice of her dress, his fingers clawing at her breast.

A strength she hadn't known she possessed came to her rescue, and she shoved him aside with all her might.

Caught off guard he staggered but still retained his hold on her.

'Now you will be punished,' he told her, and Ellie could see the anticipatory pleasure in his eyes.

As he spoke he reached for the front of her gown, tearing at it, his nails sharp against her skin. Ellie screamed as she felt his hot breath against her semi-exposed breasts as his fingers tugged and pinched at them.

Her shock and fear, the heat, the stench of alcohol and male sexual aggression were overwhelming her. She could feel her senses starting to slip away. Frantically she fought to remain conscious.

He was tearing at her skirts now, and reaching for the leather belt. Terror-stricken, Ellie screamed again. She could see him raising his arm, the light glinting off the brass studs on the belt. She was

doomed. He would beat her senseless and then . . .
She dare not even think of it.

Desperately she tried to pull away from him,
but the pain of his fingers squeezing tightly into
her breast was agonising. As the reality of what
was happening to her crashed down on her, Ellie
instinctively prayed to her mother.

'Stop fighting me and take your punishment,
little whore . . .'

'Josiah, let her go at once!'

Ellie wasn't sure which of them was the more
shocked by the coldly demanding sound of her
aunt's voice, her uncle or herself.

The library door was open and her aunt stood
just within it, flanked by Wrotham and Lizzie.

'Get out of here,' Josiah said thickly, slurring his
words slightly, 'otherwise you will get the same.'

'If you do not let her go this instant, Josiah,
I promise you you will regret it,' her aunt persisted doggedly, though Ellie could see the fear in
her eyes.

Perhaps more out of disbelief than anything else,
her uncle had relaxed his grip. Seizing her opportunity, Ellie ran for the door and was half pulled
through it by Lizzie, whilst Wrotham slammed it
firmly and quickly turned the key, leaving Josiah
locked inside.

Ellie could hear the sound of her uncle's fists
pounding against it as he demanded to be let out.

'It is all right, Ellie. You will be safe now,'
her aunt told her. 'Your uncle will be sober in

the morning and then the monster you have seen tonight will be safely leashed.'

Safely leashed . . . Ellie stared at her, unable to say a word.

'Come on, miss, let's get you to your room.'

Staring unseeingly ahead, Ellie allowed Lizzie to guide her across the hallway.

TWENTY-TWO

It was almost lunchtime when Ellie woke, her mouth dry and her head still muzzy from the sleeping draught her aunt and Wrotham had insisted she was to take.

A brief knock on her bedroom door threw her into panic, her heart racing frantically until the door opened and she saw that the person entering her room was not, as she had feared, her uncle, but Lizzie.

'I've been up a few times, miss,' Lizzie informed her, 'but you was still asleep and the mistress said I was to let you be.'

'Oh, Lizzie!' The intensity of her emotions choked Ellie's voice, her hand gripping Lizzie's wrist as she clung to her maid.

'It's all right, miss,' Lizzie tried to reassure her. 'It seems Mr Parkes was called away on some urgent business this morning.'

The very mention of her uncle's name was enough to make Ellie tremble violently. 'Oh, Lizzie,'

Ellie wept. 'What am I to do? My aunt insists that . . . that I must not think about last night, that it is to be forgotten, but I am so afraid.'

'With good reason, miss,' Lizzie told her fiercely. 'I blame myself. All us servants know what the master can be like. You bain't the first, miss, not by a long chalk. Us 'ave all seen the way he's been eyeing you but none of us thought that he'd actually dare.'

'Oh, Lizzie, what am I to do?' Ellie wept. 'I cannot stay here now, but there is nowhere else I can go!'

'If you want my advice, miss,' Lizzie told her firmly, 'the best thing you can do now is to marry Mr Henry just as quick as it can be arranged.'

Ashen-faced, Ellie listened.

The sleeping draught she had been given was clogging her brain, whilst her fear was driving her heart to beat so fast it was making her feel dizzy. Her skin was bruised and scratched just like her aunt's. Closing her eyes, Ellie shuddered. For as long as she lived she would remember those fear-filled minutes during which she had had to endure Josiah's touch.

'He won't leave you alone, miss, not now,' Lizzie was insisting. 'Doesn't like not getting what he wants.'

Ellie's stomach churned nauseously as she recognised the truth of Lizzie's words.

'I . . . I must get up, Lizzie,' she told her maid.

'Aye, and we'll have to find something that will

317

cover those bruises, miss,' Lizzie advised her as she helped Ellie to get out of bed.

'Ellie, my dear, you are looking a little pale. Now you must not take Mr Parkes' crossness of last night too much to heart. You must own that he had every reason to be displeased with you after your behaviour! My sister Gibson was most shocked to find you in Winckley Square, and we must hope that no one outside the family will discover just why you went there. Such unacceptable behaviour, Ellie – I'm sure if your Aunt Gibson had not seen you, you would have been completely disgraced. It is no wonder that your uncle was so annoyed. Your poor dear mother would have been so very upset. However, I am sure you now realise the error of your ways, and we need say no more about the subject. Had you been Mr Parkes' own daughter he could not be more fond of you, Ellie, and . . . and that is why –'

'Why he tried to rape me,' Ellie supplied quietly for her.

'Ellie!'

Her aunt had placed her hand to her heart, and Ellie could see how agitated and upset she was, even without Wrotham moving protectively to her mistress's side, whilst glaring warningly at Ellie.

'You must never ever say such a thing again, Ellie,' her aunt told her, white-faced. 'Never! Mr Parkes is a man of probity and family – a man whom other men respect and trust. And you are a very fortunate woman to have been given a home beneath his roof. There will scarcely be a mother of daughters in this city, Ellie, who will not feel that Mr Parkes had every right to chastise you for your disgraceful behaviour – and for you to make such ... such accusations against him ... I have to confess I do not understand you, Ellie! I am very disappointed in you. It is to be hoped that what you did does not become public knowledge. If it did, Mr Henry Charnock would have every reason to end his engagement to you.'

Ellie could feel her throat locking with grief and disbelief as she listened to her aunt.

She ached to confront her with the reality of what had happened, but she could see that there was no point; that her aunt had simply closed her mind to that reality, and that nothing and no one, least of all Ellie herself, was going to change that!

TWENTY-THREE

In the crush of the crowd that had gathered to watch the launching of the new liner, Ellie felt herself being pushed closer to Henry's side. On her left hand, beneath the softness of her fur-trimmed leather gloves, she could feel the diamond engagement ring he had given her.

They were to be married the Saturday before Christmas, and for Ellie that day could not come soon enough.

Several yards away Ellie could see Josiah Parkes standing next to Henry's father. Immediately, she stiffened. Since his attack on her she had taken great care never to be alone in his company.

A good stout bolt now secured her bedroom door from the inside, and Ellie suspected she owed its welcome appearance to Lizzie, although her maid had never openly said so.

In order to defeat the chill of the damp November day, Ellie was wearing a new winter walking dress, over which she was wearing a matching coat, and over that she was wearing the sable furs her aunt had recently insisted on having remodelled for her. They were beautiful and expensive clothes – the pretty leather boots she was wearing with them handmade, just as her gloves were, cut from the finest leather, but Ellie was chokingly conscious of the fact that every stitch she had on had been paid for with Josiah Parkes' money, like all her other clothes, and the food she ate, and the roof over her head.

'Ellie, I do not understand you,' her aunt had complained when Ellie had insisted that she did not want or need any more new clothes. 'You cannot shame your uncle by appearing at such an important occasion in last winter's things.'

A brisk wind was blowing in off the sea, and Ellie burrowed deeper into her furs, unaware of how stunningly pretty she looked with her new hat framing the delicacy of her face, and the wind bringing some much-needed pink to her cheeks.

'Those are fine furs you are wearing, Miss Pride. Sables, are they not?'

What was it about Elizabeth Fazackerly that jarred against her so, Ellie wondered guiltily as she forced herself to smile and respond as politely as she could, and not to pull away as Elizabeth leaned forward and removed her glove, stroking her fingertips over the soft fur, a look of such open acquisitiveness in her eyes that Ellie felt repelled.

It had been her aunt who had insisted on giving Ellie the furs, even though she had tried to refuse.

'Look, Ellie,' Henry was commending her urgently, 'she is about to be launched.'

Obediently Ellie turned her attention to the huge ship in front of them, a frisson of emotion shivering down her spine at the awesome spectacle.

Henry's eyes were shining, his whole expression animated.

'You cannot know how much I long to be back at sea . . . to return to Japan,' he breathed as they watched the vessel released from her moorings. 'Oh, Ellie, I'm sorry,' he checked himself, his face flushing. 'I did not mean –'

'It's all right, Henry,' Ellie assured him.

'You are the best of girls,' Henry told her simply, 'and I am the luckiest of fellows to be marrying you, Ellie.'

'I'm sorry,' the eminent surgeon Mary had begged to travel from London to Preston to examine Gideon's injury began, 'but I'm afraid that whilst the wound has healed well, the tendons are irreparably damaged, and Mr Walker's hand –'

'Is useless!' Gideon supplied bitterly for him, raising himself up on his pillows, whilst Mary looked on in silent helplessness. 'I am useless! Better that I had died than been left like this!'

'Gideon, no, you must not say that,' Mary protested, white-faced. She understood his pain, and the frustration he must be feeling, the apparent destruction of his dreams, but to wish away his life . . .

'Must I not? Why, when it is the truth? What is the point in my being alive now?'

Pleadingly, Mary turned to Sir Gregory, the surgeon. 'Surely it is too soon yet to be so sure. There could be much improvement . . . and . . .' Her voice trailed away as he shook his head.

'I wish I could be more optimistic, but I would not be doing my duty were I to offer you false hope. The tendons are severed; the damage is total.'

Five minutes later, as Mary escorted Sir Gregory down the stairs, she pressed him again.

'Surely there is something that could be done.'

'I'm afraid not. I wish I could tell you differently. I am sorry to be the bearer of such sad news about your . . .'

As he paused, Mary's face pinkened slightly. 'Mr Walker is not actually related to me . . . as . . . as such,' she explained self-consciously.

'Indeed? Then all the more credit to you for your concern for him. He is a most fortunate young man.'

'I doubt that he thinks so. He has lost the use of his right hand, after all,' Mary said sadly.

'A sad business, I agree, but it does not do to dwell on such things. And Mr Walker has survived a tragedy in which many unfortunate souls lost their lives,' Sir Gregory returned loftily. 'As I have already said, Mr Walker will, with perseverance, regain some limited use of his hand and, thanks to your splendid nursing, ma'am, he has recovered marvellously in every other way. There are those who would consider that he has been very fortunate,' he repeated.

Sensing Sir Gregory's disapproval of Gideon's bitterness, Mary explained gently, 'Mr Walker was hoping to begin his formal training as an architect and he has been working very hard towards that goal. However, now –'

'An architect!' The surgeon shook his head. 'No, I'm afraid that is totally out of the question, in view of the injury to his right hand.'

Mary waited until he had stepped into the hansom cab that was to take him to his train, before going back upstairs to Gideon.

It was almost a fortnight now since she had first brought him here unconscious to Winckley Square, and from the moment he had first recovered full consciousness he had demanded to know how badly injured his hand was.

The surgeon from Preston's infirmary had been blunt and to the point. Gideon's tendons had been severed by the accident, and he was lucky that, thanks to Mary's devoted nursing, he did not have to lose the hand itself. As to the fact that it had set stiff like a claw, the surgeon was sorry, but there was nothing that could be done.

In desperation Mary had set about finding out the name of the most experienced and knowledgeable surgeon in the country in the hope of getting a more optimistic opinion, and although he had refused to let her see it, she knew just how much Gideon had been hoping that Sir Gregory would be able to tell him that he could regain the use of his hand.

She could well understand how sharply bitter his disappointment must be. She felt it for him herself.

From the moment he had been well enough to do so, Gideon had railed about being there. Soon he would be insisting that he was going to leave – unless she could find a good reason for making him stay . . .

Upstairs in the large airy room Mary had brought him to, Gideon lay on his bed, staring with burning eyes up at the ceiling. So now it was final, incontestable. He was to be a cripple. Not an architect. A cripple. Why had he ever been fool enough to listen to Mary, to believe that he might realise his dream?

What future was there for him now? He couldn't even work as a bloody cabinet-maker any more, never mind anything else. No, he would end up like the poor legless rag-dressed war veteran sitting in the marketplace selling matches!

When he heard Mary coming back upstairs he deliberately turned his head away from the door, feigning sleep, but in the darkness behind his shuttered eyelids all he could see was his clawlike hand and the broken shards of his shattered dreams, and beyond them, in the shadows, the careless, uncaring, taunting face of Ellie Pride.

*   *   *

'Ah, Mary!' Edith Rigby smiled at her neighbour as Mary was shown into her drawing room where several women were already gathered. 'I am so glad you could make it. I was a little concerned when you weren't able to attend our last meeting, especially since you have always been such a stalwart supporter of our cause. Christabel Pankhurst gave a very lively talk.'

'Yes, I heard about it,' Mary agreed. 'It seems we are becoming increasingly militant.'

'And you do not approve?' Edith questioned her.

Mary gave a small sigh. 'It is not a matter of approving or disapproving, Edith. I am just concerned for the success of our cause.'

'As indeed are we all,' Edith agreed firmly.

There was a lot of news to be exchanged and plans to be made, and it was early evening before the meeting finally broke up.

Mary, who was one of the last to leave, was just on the point of doing so, when Edith said quietly to her, 'Mary, please don't go yet. There is something I wish to discuss with you. Of . . . of a private nature.'

Doubtless Edith was going to ask her if she was able to make an increased donation to their cause, Mary reflected as she waited discreetly whilst Edith said farewell to the last of her guests.

'Mary, come back into the drawing room. I shall ring for fresh tea,' Edith told her.

Following the other woman back into the room,

Mary tried not to look impatient. The meeting had taken longer than she had anticipated and she was anxious to return home to see how Gideon was. He had, understandably, been very low following the surgeon's visit.

'No, thank you, do not trouble to order tea for me,' she told her hostess.

'Mary, this is not an easy subject for me to raise,' Edith began, looking acutely uncomfortable as she folded her hands neatly together on her lap. 'However, I have been asked to raise it by . . . by your concerned friends. We . . . we all appreciate that you have an interest in Mr Gideon Walker and his wellbeing, but . . . well, to be frank, my dear, there is some concern that you should have this young man living beneath your roof with you. I mean, it is not as though he is related to you in any way, and you are a single woman and . . .'

As Edith's voice trailed lamely away, Mary could feel her face starting to burn.

'Gideon is the son of an old . . . friend of mine,' she announced firmly. 'Naturally I feel that I have a duty to her and to him to do whatever I can to help him. His injuries are such that he is no longer able to begin the . . . the studies he had planned to take up, and –'

'Mary, my dear, we are simply thinking of your welfare. There is already talk in the town.'

'Talk? What kind of talk?' Mary challenged her.

Unable to meet her gaze or answer her, Edith Rigby looked away.

'If I am not permitted to show Gideon the ... the natural affection and concern of ... of a god-mother, because –'

'A godmother? You are his godmother,' Edith pronounced in relief. 'Oh, well, in that case ... No one realised that that was the relationship between you.'

A little guiltily Mary acknowledged that she ought immediately to have corrected Edith's mis-understanding, but now unfortunately it was too late! And besides, there was no way she wanted anyone to guess what her real feelings for Gideon were. How shocked they would be. How shamed she would be! Not even Gideon himself could be allowed to know. If he did, she had little doubt that he would reject her, and she didn't think she could bear that. No, better to have what little she did have of him in her life and her home than to have nothing of him at all, even if their relationship was not and could never be what she really secretly yearned for.

'So, Gideon, how are you feeling today?' Mary asked warmly as she walked into his room.

When he got up from the chair where he had been sitting she could see how thin and drawn he looked.

'How do you think I'm feeling?' he challenged

her acidly. 'I can't use my bloody right hand, and no amount of pills or potions will ever change that!'

'No, I'm afraid it won't,' Mary agreed calmly, taking advantage of his momentary silence to continue, 'I have a proposition I wish to put to you, Gideon. It has long been my desire to visit Florence, but up until now I have been hesitant to go because of the lack of a suitable male travelling companion to accompany me.' She could see that Gideon had started to frown. 'Since, as you have said yourself, you are no longer able to pursue your studies or return to your work, it occurs to me that you would be the ideal person to accompany me. I would pay you, of course, and everything would be done in a proper businesslike way. You would be *chef d'affaires*, so to speak, the comptroller of my travelling household and responsible for the safe conduct not only of myself but also of my luggage.'

Gideon was openly glowering now.

'I have told you before,' he burst out angrily, 'I do not want your charity.'

'Indeed not!' Mary returned smartly. 'And I'm afraid that I must correct your misapprehension that you are about to be offered it. Charity in the form of engineering for your benefit a job that does not exist is simply a luxury I cannot afford, Gideon! This is not charity. It is a genuine offer of a job, and your acceptance of it would not only benefit you, it would benefit me as well.' Emotion filling her voice, she whispered, 'You cannot know how much it would mean to me to go to Florence. It would be a pleasure beyond any price.'

Her use of the word 'pleasure' made Gideon's mouth twist with cynical contempt. 'Pleasure' was not something he was ever likely to experience now, was it? The damage to his hand had destroyed for ever all his hopes for the future, all his plans.

'I shall leave you to think about it,' Mary told him gently. 'I have to go out for a few hours, but on my return we can discuss it again.'

Mary's step quickened as she hurried into the house and out of the raw November wind. By now, she hoped, Gideon would have had time to calm down. She was eager to talk to him about her plans for them both. They would use Mr Thomas Cook's services to organise their journey . . .

Mary hurried across the landing at the top of the stairs and pushed open the door to Gideon's room.

Empty!

Gideon could not have gone! But as she stared around the room Mary knew that he had.

TWENTY-FOUR

Bitterly, Connie hunched her shoulders against the cold and cast an angry look towards her aunt. They were going to visit the parish poor, a task Connie loathed.

Shivering she pulled her thin, shabby coat closer to her. Only the previous day a large parcel had arrived from Hoylake, containing some of Ellie's clothes that she had sent for Connie. But after taking one look at them, Aunt Simpkins had declared that they were far too good for a wicked girl like Connie to be permitted to wear, and had refused to allow her to have them.

Connie longed to cry, but she was not going to give her aunt the satisfaction of seeing her do so. The coat Ellie had sent had been in the prettiest colour and had had a thick fur collar. Connie's eyes ached with the pressure of her forced-back tears.

In another few weeks Ellie would be getting married and she, Connie, was to be her bridesmaid. Her Aunt Parkes was having her dress made for her.

Lucky Ellie. Enviously Connie kicked out at a stone in the road. Why couldn't she have been the one to go to Hoylake and Ellie be forced to live here with horrid Aunt Simpkins?

Connie had decided that she was going to use the opportunity of the wedding to beg her Aunt Lavinia to let her take Ellie's place and live with her. Connie soon became lost in a wonderful daydream in which she was the spoiled and pampered niece of the Parkeses.

Ellie was the meanest sister anyone could have! Had she been in Ellie's shoes she would immediately have sent for her sister to be at her side whilst she prepared for her wedding, Connie told herself virtuously, but, of course, Ellie was far too selfish to think of her!

Nauseously, Gideon leaned against the wall of his cold bedroom. His whole body ached, not just his injured hand. It even hurt him to breathe, the cold raw air burning his lungs.

He had not thought of pain or discomfort, though, when he had dragged himself down the stairs and out of Mary Isherwood's house, determined only to reject her charity.

The damp air in his lodgings, left empty and unheated for weeks, made him shiver. He looked at the empty grate, but he felt too ill to go down and get sticks and coal to light it.

He was shivering violently now, his teeth chattering

audibly, whilst the inside of his head felt as though it were on fire, clouding his thinking.

Somehow he managed to find the strength to crawl into his bed, pulling the damp bedding around himself, and then lying there, half in and half out of consciousness, whilst John's dog, who had been at Mary's with him and whom he had collected before leaving, jumped up onto the bed and curled up next to him.

When Gideon woke up it was light. He was shivering and there was frost on the window, his breath vaporising in the icy cold. Rex was still curled up around his feet. Gideon's whole body felt stiff, and his hand ached and throbbed. He threw back the bedclothes and frowned to realise he had gone to bed in his clothes.

His head throbbed with fever, but he ignored both it and the pain in his body as he forced himself to go downstairs into the yard. The fire had to be lit and he had a business to run, although God alone knew how the hell he was going to do it.

Reaching for the shovel, he winced as he automatically tried to use his right hand and the shovel fell uselessly to the floor. Cursing savagely he tried again, clumsily attempting to use his left hand.

Half an hour later, in a raging temper, his face as burning hot as his body was freezing cold, Gideon gave up any attempt to use the shovel and instead started to pick up individual pieces of coal with his left hand.

*　*　*

'Morning, Gideon. How's thee hand this morning? T'usual, is it?'

Ignoring the landlord's cheery enquiry, Gideon nodded his head, picking up his gin as soon as it was poured and demanding another before heading for the seat that had become his. It was over a week since he had left Mary Isherwood's.

Will Pride, coming into the pub and seeing him, frowned a little.

'In here every day he is,' the landlord told Will as he saw the direction in which he was looking. 'Standing outside waiting for me to open this morning, he were. Aye, and back again come tonight, he'll be.'

Picking up his glass, Will made his way over to where Gideon was sitting.

'Let me get thee a drink, lad. What'll it be?' he asked amiably.

'Gin,' Gideon told him curtly.

'You don't want to be drinking spirits,' Will told him warningly. 'If tha wants a drink –'

'If you don't want to buy me a drink, Will, then I'll get my own,' Gideon retorted, struggling to his feet.

'Nay, lad, I didn't mean that!' Will told him, also hastily getting to his own feet. 'Sit thee down whilst I go to the bar.'

When Will returned with their drinks Gideon picked his up with his left hand and took a large swallow.

'I'd ha' thought thee'd be working this time of day, lad,' Will told Gideon.

'Working?' Gideon shot him a mirthless look. 'Oh aye, I'm in fine fettle to do that, Will Pride. See this?' He held up his right hand. 'Watch,' he commanded, and reached for his glass.

'Nay, lad,' Will stopped him pityingly, as Gideon failed to grasp the glass. 'But thee could still oversee apprentices and such,' Will suggested.

Gideon looked at him scathingly. 'Aye, I'm sure,' he sneered, his voice starting to slur as the gin took effect. 'Who the hell is going to want to be apprenticed to a crippled cabinet-maker? Have some sense, Will.'

'But thee could tek on other men to do the work for 'e, Gideon,' Will insisted.

Moodily Gideon refused to answer him. What craftsman worthy of the name was going to work for a crippled wreck like him when he could just as easily work on his own behalf? And besides, Gideon didn't want to work building cabinets and the like any more; he wanted to be an architect. Somehow, through the foggy blanket of the gin the pain still managed to slice into him.

He emptied the glass and staggered to his feet, demanding, 'What's yours, Will, another bitter?'

'Nay, lad, I've not finished this one yet,' Will protested. 'Wait up a bit.'

But Gideon wasn't listening.

When he came back, the glass he was holding in his left hand held a double measure, and Will looked at him anxiously.

'Look, lad, if it's money thee needs, well, I'm

335

allus looking for an extra drover, thee knows that.'

Gideon gave a harsh bitter laugh. 'Droving!' His face contorted. 'Aye, happen that's all I'm fit for now, Will, but no thanks. The rent's paid up until quarter day and I've got a bit put by.'

The bit put by was the money he had been saving towards his studies.

Gideon was still drinking when the landlord rang time. Staggering drunkenly to his feet, he finished his drink and called to Rex, who had been waiting patiently beneath the table.

The dog at his side, Gideon lurched out into the cold November air.

'Ellie, there is a letter for you from your father. I expect he has written to congratulate you on your engagement.'

Beaming, Ellie took the letter from her aunt and opened it. Mr Parkes had left early to go to the city and the post had only just arrived.

'Dear Ellie,' her father had written,

I have had your letter informing me of your engagement, and I have some news of my own for you.

I am to be married this Saturday to Miss Margaret Chadwell, who you have met. I know you will wish me happy, and I wish that to you as well.

Yrs, your loving father, Robert Pride.

Ellie read the letter again, her hand trembling, tears blurring her eyes. Saturday, he had written, and today was Monday, which meant that he was already married!

'Ellie, what is it?' her aunt asked, seeing her distress.

Too upset to speak, Ellie handed her the letter so that she could read it for herself, which she did very speedily, putting it down on the table and saying wrathfully, 'Well, I must say that I am shocked that your father has so quickly overcome his grief and found himself a new wife!'

Ellie wasn't listening. Miss Margaret Chadwell – was she the redheaded woman Ellie had seen in his bed? Was that what he had meant by writing that she had met her?

'I . . . I would like to telephone my father, if I may?' she told her aunt.

'Well, you know that Mr Parkes does not –' Lavinia began, and then stopped, saying instead, 'But perhaps in the circumstances he will not mind, Ellie.'

Ellie was trembling as she picked up the telephone, and gave the telephonist her father's number. It was several minutes before she was connected and heard not her father's voice but that of a woman, demanding to know who she was.

'Ellie Pride,' Ellie answered. 'I . . . I would like to speak with my father, please.'

'Oh, you would, would you?' came back the truculent response. 'Well, I'm afraid that won't be possible, seeing as your pa is still sleeping off celebrating our marriage!'

The moment she had heard her voice Ellie had known that the woman her father had married was the redhead. Her stomach churning sickly, she put down the receiver. How could her father have put someone like that in her mother's place?

TWENTY-FIVE

'Oh, Ellie, you look beautiful. Your Aunt Simpkins says that in view of Connie's wilfulness and head-strong ways, the sooner a husband is found for her the better, and, in fact, she and your Aunt Gibson both agree that an older gentleman would be the best kind of husband for Connie – a gentleman who knows how to be firm with her. But no matter who she may marry she will not make as beautiful a bride as you.'

Ignoring her aunt's compliment, Ellie exclaimed, distressed, 'Aunt, surely Connie is far too young for my aunts to be thinking of seeing her married! I know she can be headstrong, but that is just because she is not yet mature. And an older husband – I cannot –'

'Ellie, you must leave these matters to those who know best,' her aunt stopped her sternly. 'Remember, we only want for you what we know your dear mama would have wanted. Ah, if only your dead mother were here today, Ellie.'

Ellie's eyes misted as she saw the tears in her aunt's. On her right hand she was wearing the ring her mother had left her, and she touched it gently, and then suddenly remembered, 'Aunt Lavinia, has my father arrived yet, only –'

'Ellie,' immediately her aunt's expression changed, and she touched Ellie's arm as she told her firmly, 'your other aunts and I decided . . . that is, we felt that under the circumstances . . . I mean in view of his recent marriage and . . . well, we felt that it would not be appropriate to invite your father to the wedding.'

Ellie stared at her aunt in shocked disbelief. 'Not invite him? But he must be here: he is my father!' she exclaimed in bewilderment.

'Mr Pride has recently remarried, Ellie, and neither I nor my sisters could endure to see him – not when our precious sister . . .' her aunt trailed off, biting her lip.

Pain and misery filled Ellie. 'But if my father is not to be here then who is to give me away?' she asked slowly, still trying to comprehend what her aunt had told her.

'Why Mr Parkes, of course. Who else should do so? He is, after all, paying for your wedding, Ellie.'

Mr Parkes! Mr Parkes was to give her away! Ellie threw down her bouquet, her hands trembling.

'No, no, he cannot . . . I cannot . . .' she began, and then stopped. What was the use of her saying anything, she asked herself bitterly. Silently, she reached for her flowers. 'I wish you had not done this, Aunt,' she whispered despairingly. 'I wanted my father to give me away.'

Lifting to his lips the bottle of gin he had bought as he left the station, and taking a deep swig, Gideon stared at the church.

Flowers and white silk ribbons had been tied to the gate and the ribbons tangled in the cold December breeze.

He had heard about Ellie's wedding from her father, drowning his sorrows as he told Gideon, 'Our Ellie don't even want me there. Her own father . . . Wants her uncle to give her away. I'm not good enough for her any more, seemingly! Our Connie's to be a bridesmaid but she's not even thought o' asking our Will's lasses! Our John's been invited, and the babby is going to be a pageboy, along o' some of her fine new relatives' young 'uns,' he'd hiccuped as he'd ordered them both another drink.

The wedding guests were arriving: fancy folk in fancy clothes, Gideon noted bitterly as he concealed himself behind one of the churchyard yew trees.

Ellie had been obliged by Elizabeth Fazackerly's heavy hints to ask her children to be her attendants, and Connie, who was in charge of the little bridesmaid and the pageboys, gave Godfrey Fazackerly a sharp nip on his velvet-clad upper arm when she caught him aiming a kick at little Timothy.

'Ow!' he bawled. 'I'm going to tell my mother of you.'

Connie pulled the kind of horrid face at him that she had once used to terrify John, enjoying his instant silence.

Kitty, Cecily's younger sister, was also a bridesmaid, but since Connie was in a bad mood and had resolved not to enjoy herself one little bit, she ignored her cousin's attempts to make conversation with her, turning her back when Kitty complained, 'Brrr, it is so cold. I wish we could go inside.'

Henry had already arrived, and was inside the church.

An elegant carriage, drawn by matching greys, was sweeping down the road towards the church. Sulkily, Connie refused to look.

From his vantage point, Gideon had an excellent view of Ellie as she was handed out of the carriage and given her uncle's arm. Her veil covered her face, but Gideon could still see her lips part and her small teeth clench on her bottom lip as she stood still for a moment, almost as though she was reluctant to move.

Reluctant – that would be the day when Ellie Pride was reluctant to do something to her own advantage, Gideon thought bitterly. If he was lucky he should be able to slip into the church behind all the guests without anyone seeing him.

Ellie could feel Henry trembling as they walked together back up the aisle, now man and wife. He had been ashen-faced all through the ceremony, and twice had had to be prompted with his words by the bishop.

Ellie blinked fiercely. His wedding ring felt cold and heavy on her finger. Then she tensed and missed a step as a movement in the shadows beyond the congregation caught her eye. Abruptly she stopped walking.

Gideon! But it couldn't be! Not here. Her aching heart was playing cruel tricks on her. She looked again, but there was nothing . . . no one.

Behind her she heard Connie hissing fiercely, 'Ellie, do get a move on, otherwise I shall be treading on your train.' And automatically she responded, her movements jerky and uncoordinated as though she were a clockwork doll.

Gideon – a trick of the light, Ellie decided. Yet he had looked so real. She was married now and she should make the best of her new life with Henry. She must put all thoughts of Gideon Walker out of her head.

But even as she made her resolve, Ellie admitted to herself that once before she had decided to do exactly that – and had utterly failed.

TWENTY-SIX

Tiredly, Ellie looked at her new husband. They had arrived just over an hour ago at the small hotel in the Lake District where they were to spend their honeymoon. As they sat silently, picking at the meal that had been served to them, Ellie reflected that Henry looked as apprehensive and ill at ease as she felt. Ellie pushed her plate away.

'It has been a long day. If you should wish to retire . . .' Henry began, and then stopped, his face going brick red.

'I-I am tired,' Ellie admitted, unable to bring herself to look properly at him.

Coughing nervously and then clearing his throat, Henry stuttered, 'Thought I-I might take a turn around the g-gardens before turning in. That is, unless you –'

'No, no,' Ellie assured him quickly, her own voice as constrained as his. 'I will go and ring for Lizzie. She can . . .' Biting her lip, she stopped.

Only just over a week ago, Cecily had been

with her when the final items of her trousseau arrived. Examining the pretty ribbon-decorated stays, Cecily had commented ruefully that Ellie was so slender she barely needed them.

'I was so nervous on my wedding night, worrying about how I would manage, since Evans was Mama's maid, and I was not sure how I would go on with the servants in the hotel. But in the end it was my own darling Paul who unfastened them for me. One of the advantages of having a husband I had not looked for!' Cecily had exclaimed, dimpling Ellie a conspiratorial smile.

Ellie knew that Cecily had been seeking to reassure her, as well as drop her a delicate hint of what to expect, but the truth was that Cecily's words had only intensified her anxiety and apprehension. To her relief, though, her aunt had seemed to take it for granted that Lizzie would accompany her on her honeymoon.

Ellie had received rather more essential practical advice from Iris. Since Iris had spoken of marital relations not solely to conceive children, Ellie had wondered if Iris, who was, after all, training to be a doctor, would be able to advise her. She had eventually plucked up the courage to ask Iris how she might avoid conceiving a child on her wedding night. Iris had been so sensible and so kind, and now, putting into use the little sponge and bottle of vinegar her friend had recommended, Ellie felt a little more ready to face her ordeal.

'Why, you're chilled to the bone, miss,' Lizzie

remarked, bustling into the hotel bedroom in response to Ellie's summons, and immediately adding extra coals to the small fire. 'I've had them put hot bricks and a warming pan over the bed, but I could swear the sheets are damp. It will be a mercy if you don't catch a cold sleeping in them. What Mr Charnock was thinking of, bringing you to such a place for your honeymoon, and over Christmas too, I do not know.'

'The Lake District is reputed to be exceedingly beautiful, Lizzie,' Ellie told her.

'Beautiful!' Lizzie gave a disparaging snort. 'Aye, well, as to that, it may well be on a fine summer's day when the sun is shining!'

Ellie had to hide a small smile. Lizzie was a city girl at heart, who constantly grumbled that even Hoylake was too 'countrified' for her.

'Goodness, miss,' Lizzie exclaimed as she removed Ellie's dress. 'If you lose any more weight we shall have to be padding you out and not lacing you in.'

The very thought of having to wear the horsehair pads some ladies used to enhance their figures into the S-shaped curve dictated by fashion made Ellie shudder.

'There . . .' Lizzie helped Ellie into her satin *peignoir* and waited for her to sit down at the dressing table before beginning to brush her hair.

The brand-new travelling case, with its silver and tortoiseshell bottles and brushes, had been a special wedding gift to Ellie from Cecily, who had given it to her with a whispered, 'I found mine so useful when I was on my own honeymoon, Ellie dearest.'

'Not like home, this isn't, miss,' Lizzie informed her with a disparaging sniff as she finished brushing Ellie's hair and then helped her into the double bed with its brass bedstead. 'They've no proper bathroom to speak of – leastways not what I would call one – but I've arranged that hot water will be brought up to you in the morning, and I dare say that Mr Henry will need some as well so as he can have a shave –' She broke off as they both heard a discreet knock on the door. 'That will be Mr Henry now,' Lizzie guessed, giving the covers a final pat, and going towards the door.

'Lizzie . . .' Ellie began, and then stopped as the maid turned to look at her. She felt cold and sick, and wished passionately that she had not married Henry. Guilt and shame that she should feel so, added to her distress, so that the set look on her face as Henry walked into the room and saw her lying stiffly beneath the bedclothes brought him up short, his face betraying his own discomfort and uncertainty.

Whisking herself through the open door, Lizzie closed it firmly behind her.

Despairingly Ellie closed her eyes as Henry began to undress behind the heavy dressing screen, but although she could blot out the sight of what he was doing she could not escape from the sounds: the thud of boots hitting the floor; the stiff squeak

347

of buttons forced through new buttonholes; the alien jarring noise of male clothing.

Henry was not Josiah Parkes, Ellie reminded herself over and over again, repeating the words inside her head as though they were some magic charm that had the power to transform what she was feeling – the fear, the embarrassment, the sheer sickening, loathsomeness of the thought of what was to come, what had to be. He was her husband . . . and a husband had rights . . . expectations . . . a husband . . .

Ellie shuddered, her eyes snapping open as she felt the other side of the bed depress. The only other men she had seen in their night attire were her father and her brother, and Henry, with his thin legs in his thick winter combinations, emphasised how very different a husband was to a father or a brother.

She could see the agitated movement of his Adam's apple, and the slight tremble of his hand as he edged back the bedcovers, and suddenly her fear began to relax its savage grip on her. Poor Henry was as apprehensive as she was herself!

Clearing his throat, he told her hoarsely, 'You looked very lovely today, Ellie, and I-I-I want you to know how proud I am to have you as my wife.'

His wife! Ellie's fear returned. She knew perfectly well what the act of consummating their marriage entailed – in theory – but the experience of it . . . the result of it, should she conceive Henry's child, as eventually she must, these were the things that were making her whole body quake with dread.

She held her breath as Henry snuffed out the candle. Only the dying glow of the sea-coals in the fireplace illuminated the room now.

She tensed as she felt the dry tremor of Henry's lips against her cheek as he turned his head to kiss her, and a huge aching swell of anguished misery broke inside her.

Somehow, as perfect in every detail as though it had been a photograph, she could see the day she had spent in Avenham Park with Gideon. With her senses she could relive the touch and feel of him, the scent of his skin, the taste of his mouth. She knew that her body would never, ever ache for Henry in the way it had ached for Gideon, in the way it was aching right now, just at the thought of all she had lost.

She could feel Henry's hands moving awkwardly over her body, his breathing becoming heavier, and she closed her eyes.

Henry was fumbling beneath her nightgown, his hands so cold that his touch made her shiver. Resigned, Ellie waited, the bright shiny hopes of her youth draining from her in a slow flood of misery. When Henry's hand touched her breast she squeezed her eyes as tightly closed as she could, turning her head away so that his clumsy kiss reached her cheek and not her lips. The hand he had placed on her breast felt damp and soft. A huge wave of despair engulfed her, but she made no sound of protest when Henry heaved up his own nightshirt, and removed his combinations.

In the end it wasn't as bad as Ellie had dreaded. True, Henry had panted and moaned in a way that had chilled her body, his breathing hot and hard in her ear as he thrust against her and into her, in unrhythmic bursts of energy that caused her more distaste than pain, until at last he lay gasping for breath on top of her.

Mindful of Iris's careful instructions, Ellie got up quickly and hurried behind the screen, carefully removing the little sponge she had soaked in vinegar, and then washing it out.

When Ellie climbed back into the bed, Henry was fast asleep, lying on his back, his mouth agape.

Blankly Ellie looked at him as though he was a stranger, someone she didn't know . . . someone she didn't want to know?

Her eyes dry with the painful weight of her misery, Ellie clung to her side of the bed, keeping her body as far away from Henry's as she could.

Gideon gave a moan as he woke. His head felt as though it was about to split apart with pain, and he could hear Rex whining close by. As he looked round he realised that he was lying out in the freezing cold yard. Groaning, he pulled himself to his feet, the shock of discovering where he was making him suddenly stone-cold sober. If the dog hadn't woken him, he would more than likely have frozen to death, he recognised, as he stumbled on numb legs towards the door.

He had no recollection of returning home from Liverpool – from Ellie's wedding – and no idea how long he had been lying outside in the hard frost. He cursed at the pain that shot through his limbs as circulation returned to them.

In the clear, cold air he could smell the scent of the gin on his own breath, and his stomach heaved with nausea.

He only just made it to the privy, retching until his stomach was sore.

Bitterly Gideon made his way inside the house. There was no point in trying to relight the fire. Calling the dog to him, he curled up on the sofa, dragging the dusty rug from the floor on top of him to keep himself warm.

He was still lying there, deep in an alcohol-induced sleep, when Will Pride, finding the door open, walked in and woke him.

'What the . . . ?'

'Door were open, lad, and so I thought I'd best come in,' Will told him, giving an unhappy look at the chaos of the cold room, the empty gin bottles on the floor, and the state of Gideon himself. The lad was obviously finding it hard to manage – and no wonder with no work.

Will had always had a soft spot for Gideon, and it led him to say sorrowfully now, 'Nay, lad, tha' canna go on like this.' Nodding towards Rex he added, 'T' pair of you are as thin as whippets! I know thee've paid t' rent until quarter day but that's not that far off now, and then what'll 'e do? Bloody landlords,' he cursed. 'Money for nowt it is, if you ask me, letting out a house.'

Whilst Will was talking, Gideon had sat up, grimacing at the sour taste in his mouth.

'What you need, lad, is some food in your belly,' Will told him, nodding towards the empty bottles as he added firmly, 'and a bit less of that! I'm a drinking man mesel' but I would never touch spirits, Gideon! Gut rot, that stuff is. You and our Robert are as bad as one another . . . and likely to be in the poorhouse, the pair of you, if you don't mend your ways.'

With that piece of advice, Will went over to the fire and started to wriggle the ashes. John's dog, Rex, pushed his cold nose into Gideon's hand. Frowning, Gideon looked at him. He was thin, Will was right. Guilt filled him. He ached from head to foot, and as for his hand . . . How on earth could he drag himself out of the mess his life had become?

TWENTY-SEVEN

A little nervously Ellie stared up at the stark façade
of her new home. It was late in the afternoon
and they had brought snow back with them from
the Lake District. Small white flakes of it dusted
Ellie's shoulders as she shivered in the fading winter
afternoon light.

Naturally, prior to her marriage she had never
visited the mistress-less Charnock house, a large,
well-proportioned villa with a big garden, set in a
row of similar properties, and now she stared at it
curiously.

Henry had come to stand at her side, whilst
the hackney driver took their bags round to the
servants' entrance.

Henry had to bang on the front door, and Ellie's
eyes rounded in surprise when she saw the grubby,
waiflike scullery maid who opened it. Surely her
father-in-law employed a housekeeper.

A gust of cold air rattled through the dark
hallway, making Ellie shiver and quickly close the

front door, whilst the maid stared open-mouthed at her. Gaslight flickered in the old-fashioned light fittings, revealing an unpolished floor and a shabby Turkish rug.

'Thank you, Maisie,' Ellie heard Henry saying. 'Is my father –'

'The master isn't home yet, sir, and he said you was to go straight down to the office the minute you got back,' the girl told him, bobbing him an uncoordinated curtsy before starting to back away.

Ellie couldn't believe her eyes! It was four o'clock in the afternoon and they had been travelling all day. She was freezing cold and tired, and she had expected to be welcomed to her new home by a competent housekeeper, who would show her to her room and provide her with some much-needed afternoon tea, instead of which she was faced with a grubby untrained maid, who, she suspected, would not even be able to boil a kettle of water!

Turning to her husband, she began, 'Henry –'

'Maisie will show you to our room, Ellie,' Henry told her, looking uncomfortable. 'I had best obey my father, but I shouldn't be too long.'

He was gone before Ellie could object, leaving her alone with the maid.

'Will I show you to yer room then, miss?' she asked.

'Thank you, but I should like to speak with the housekeeper first,' Ellie responded firmly.

'The housekeeper?' The girl's eyes rounded. 'There

354

bain't no housekeeper here. There's no one here but me and Cook.'

Ellie was too tired to query her statement and said wearily instead, 'Very well, then I think you had better show me round the house, if you please.'

An hour later Ellie stood in the large but damp and grubby bedroom she had been told was to be hers and Henry's, and wondered how on earth her husband and her father-in-law could bear to live in such a cold, uncared for and frankly dirty house.

When Ellie asked Maisie to bring up sticks and coal so that she could light the bedroom fire, the maid looked nervously at her and told her, 'Begging your pardon, madam, but Mr Charnock, he don't allow no fires in the bedrooms.'

No fires? Ellie was dumbstruck. The maid could not possibly be right!

'Perhaps you will ask Cook to send me up something to eat then,' she suggested, trying to remain calm.

Maisie looked terrified. 'Cook's asleep and I durstn't wake 'er.'

Ellie took a deep breath. 'Very well then, Maisie, I shall go down to the kitchen and see Cook myself,' she said as pleasantly as she could.

Ellie discovered that Cook was indeed sound asleep – and in a drunken sleep too, she suspected.

The further discovery that the only food available for her supper was some cold meat and the kind of bread her mother would have refused to give her children to feed to Avenham Park's wildlife left her virtually speechless.

When Henry returned he found her on her hands and knees, scrubbing the kitchen, whilst Maisie, whom Ellie had quickly realised was a little 'simple', stood by, open-mouthed, watching her, and the cook snored loudly in her chair.

'Ellie –' Henry protested, red-faced.

'This kitchen is a health hazard, Henry,' Ellie cut him off. 'I must speak with your father. He –'

'No, Ellie. I . . . it's late and you should be in bed . . . and besides, my father is not in at present.'

As she followed him out of the kitchen, Ellie told him worriedly, 'I am sure that your cook is drunk, Henry. She should be turned out immediately. I am surprised that your father doesn't have a housekeeper, by the way. Oh, and Maisie said that your father would not allow me to have a fire in the bedroom. I am sure she must be mistaken.'

When Henry stopped walking and turned round to face her, Ellie almost bumped into him.

'I realise that things here are not . . . what you are used to, Ellie,' he told her unhappily. 'But my father –'

'I do understand, Henry,' Ellie tried to reassure him. 'The house has not had a mistress for a long time, I know. Even the sheets on the bed are damp,' she told him, wrinkling her nose. 'If your father will allow me I shall speak with the agency my aunt uses first thing in the morning and ask them to find us a suitable housekeeper and a new cook.'

In the shadows of the stairway, Henry made an unhappy noise in his throat, but Ellie didn't hear it, her mind busy with all that she would have to do.

Ellie was up early in the morning, leaving Henry asleep as she washed in the icy cold bathroom and in equally cold water.

Downstairs she found the cook coughing over a pan she was stirring on the stove.

'Good morning, Mrs Reilly,' Ellie offered.

When her greeting was ignored Ellie felt her face begin to burn. Maisie had appeared from outside the house and was standing, wide-eyed, watching.

'Mrs Reilly, it be Mrs Charnock,' she told the cook in a loud whisper.

'Mr Charnock is master here and it's him as I take me orders from,' the cook announced without looking at either Ellie or Maisie.

Ellie knew that her mother would have dismissed the woman on the instant for such insolence, but of course she had no right to do any such thing.

'There was no hot water this morning, Mrs Reilly, and –'

'If it's 'ot water you want then youse'll have ter come down here and boil it yourself,' came the uncompromising response.

'Surely the furnace heats the water,' Ellie demanded.

'The master won't have it lit, madam,' Maisie hissed. 'Uses too many coals.'

Ellie could not believe her ears.

A smell of burning porridge assaulted her nostrils and she screwed up her nose.

'Tek the master up his jug o' 'ot water, Maisie, and look sharp about it,' Mrs Reilly commanded, still ignoring Ellie as she filled a ewer of water from the large kettle on the range and Maisie rushed to obey her.

The moment Maisie left the room, Mrs Reilly cursed her and said, 'Not right in the head, she is . . . useless article!'

'What time is breakfast served, Mrs Reilly?' Ellie enquired coolly, ignoring her comment.

'Breakfast?' The cook turned round and gave Ellie a glare. 'Hoity-toity, ain't we, to say youse only a butcher's daughter! The master has his tea and toast in his room, and as for anyone else, if they wants breakfast then they comes in here and gets it.'

Ellie was lost for words. What was Mr Charnock thinking of, employing such a person? And as for her comments about Ellie's parentage . . . It was on the tip of Ellie's tongue to tell her that she was very proud of her origins and her father but, reminding herself of her position, she bit back her answer. It would never do for the mistress of the house to lower herself to recognise the cook's insult.

*   *   *

By the end of her first week in her new home, Ellie's hands were red raw from scrubbing the kitchen from top to bottom with strong soap. And Mrs Reilly had handed in her notice. Maisie was incapable of taking any kind of instruction but, tender-heartedly, Ellie had refused to think of having her turned out, knowing that she would be unable to find another place. Instead she had acknowledged that she could only give her the simplest of familiar tasks to do.

By the end of the second week, Ellie had turned out every china and linen cupboard in the house, setting up a flurry of dust and startling disgruntled moths, which had caused both Ellie and Maisie to sneeze violently. The best of the linen Ellie had sent to the laundry, since she had no servants to help her with such a vast amount of washing, and the rest she had repaired, sitting up each night sewing until her eyes ached and then making bags to fill with lavender and rose petals to place in the freshly cleaned cupboards.

Although everyone else kept scrupulously to the unwritten rule that dictated no woman should receive or pay calls during the first month of her marriage, Ellie did have one unexpected, and unwelcome, visitor – Henry's cousin's wife, Elizabeth Fazackerly.

She arrived unannounced one afternoon whilst Ellie was busy upstairs going through the linen cupboards, causing Ellie to have to run down to the hall to find out what all the commotion she could hear was about.

'Ellie, my dear,' Elizabeth gushed, subjecting Ellie to an embrace she did not want. 'I know you will not be receiving callers as yet, but I own I feel we are as close as though we were sisters. Speaking of which, how is your sister? A very spirited girl, is she not? Your aunt confided to me at the wedding that she finds her headstrong wilfulness hard to bear at times.'

Already stiffening in Elizabeth's embrace, Ellie stiffened even more at hearing her sister so criticised, but Elizabeth, oblivious to her reaction, continued, 'You must not hesitate to let me know should you need any help managing such a large house, Ellie.'

Her sharp-eyed look around the hall as she released Ellie and stepped without invitation into the drawing room rendered Ellie speechless with affront – although she had noticed the distinct note of envy in Elizabeth's voice as she commented on the generous size of the large mansion.

'I confess that my dear Uncle Jarvis has complimented me on many occasions for the manner in which I run my own home. He swears he feels more content there than anywhere else, but then I have always felt that a woman should put the comfort of her family before everything. I know that you are used to living a very gay life, Ellie, running around town with your cousin Cecily, and enjoying all manner of treats, but you are a married woman now, my dear, and I hope you will understand when I say that I feel it is my duty to warn you that Uncle Jarvis has already commented to us about your lack of skill in dealing with the servants. Mrs Reilly has left, I understand. That is such a pity. She was devoted to Uncle Jarvis.'

Devoted to her father-in-law she might have been, Ellie decided, but she had certainly not been devoted to the execution of her duties, not if the state Ellie had found the kitchen in was anything to go by!

'I have always prided myself on my choice of servants, Ellie,' Elizabeth informed her. 'Only the other evening, when Uncle Jarvis dined with us, he asked me to convey his compliments to my cook.'

There! The grate was finished. As Ellie stood back to check her handiwork, the drawing-room door opened and Henry came in.

'Ellie, what on earth . . . ?' he began as he looked from his wife's tired face to the immaculate fire grate. 'You should not be doing this,' he announced sternly. 'Maisie –'

'I could not trust her with the blacking, Henry. Poor girl, it is not her fault, but last time she got it everywhere, and it took me an age to get the carpet clean. I'm afraid that dinner will be late this evening.'

Ellie was having to do all the cooking her-self as they had still not got a new cook, her father-in-law having announced that he would deal with the matter of Mrs Reilly's replacement himself.

Unusually, Ellie's father-in-law joined them that evening for dinner.

Since Ellie could not trust Maisie to serve at table, she was obliged to serve the food herself as well as cook it.

'Ellie, this is delicious,' Henry praised her warmly as he started to drink his soup.

Ellie smiled, glad to see that her father-in-law was also emptying his bowl.

'Henry, I should like to write to my aunts soon so that we can make arrangements for my sister and my brothers to come here to live with us –' Ellie began.

'What? What nonsense is this?' Ellie's father-in-law interrupted her harshly. 'No one comes to live in this house without my permission, and as I recollect I have certainly not agreed that you may have the rest of your family here, missie! Nor do I intend to agree to it.'

Shocked, Ellie looked at Henry, expecting him to come to her rescue, but instead he kept his gaze firmly on his soup plate, patting his lips with his napkin.

Bravely, Ellie faced Henry's father. 'Father-in-law, Henry has already agreed that I might –'

'Henry has agreed?' he cut her off angrily. 'Henry

has no right to agree to anything. I am master of this house, not my son! My God, isn't having the two of you living off me enough? Do you really expect me to house and feed the whole of your family as well, miss?'

Ellie went scarlet and then white with embarrassment and shame. Her soup had gone cold but she could not have eaten it anyway.

Dismayed and upset, she pushed back her chair and got to her feet, hurrying from the room.

She was upstairs in their room when Henry came to her.

'Ellie,' he begged her miserably, 'please try to understand.'

'Why didn't you say something to your father, Henry?' Ellie demanded.

'This is my father's home,' Henry told her, avoiding meeting her eyes.

'So they can't come then?' she demanded.

'It isn't my fault, Ellie. I cannot do anything. Once my father has made up his mind about something, it is impossible to sway him. This matter of a grandchild . . .' his voice trailed away uncomfortably.

Ellie was too upset to challenge him further.

'I am so very sorry, but there is nothing I can do. You can see for yourself what my father is like. This is his home. I am dependent upon his goodwill for everything and I cannot –'

'It's all right, Henry,' Ellie told him quietly. 'You do not have to say any more.'

'Ellie, please do not be cross with me,' he pleaded.

The look in his eyes was that of a child rather than a man, Ellie recognised, as she was filled with a mixture of anger and pity.

After he had left her, Ellie went to the window and stared out into the cold February darkness. She was a married woman now, but somehow she felt lonelier in her marriage than she ever had done before. Ellie shivered. She felt somehow that she had nothing – no hope, no joy, no anything!

PART THREE

TWENTY-EIGHT

Gideon pulled his coat a little more warmly around himself as he turned into the dockside street and felt the ice-cold blast of air funnelling down it.

The street, like its fellows, comprised a row of terraced houses, many looking dilapidated and uncared for.

He had visited this particular street three times already in the last month, his stomach clenched with a mixture of anger and determination as he thought about the risk he was thinking of taking.

He hadn't discussed his intentions with anyone – there was no one for him to discuss them with. Mary was the only person who might have understood, and certainly the only person he knew who would have been able to advise him, seeing as she owned a great deal of property herself.

Not property like this, of course – dirty, uncared for, with broken windows – but he had heard that such properties brought in a fair rent, especially if they were let off as single rooms.

If he used all his savings Gideon reckoned he would have just enough to buy himself two, or, if he was very lucky, perhaps three, of the cheapest sort of terraced houses. With all the rooms in each one let, and with no one defaulting on that rent, within twelve months he would be able to . . . But the likelihood was that he would not be able to let every room, and his tenants would default if they thought he might be weak enough to allow them to do so.

Mary had an agent who dealt with the humdrum business of her properties for her, but Gideon would have to take on that role himself.

Bleakly, Gideon turned his back to the whipping arctic wind. It might almost be the end of March but as yet there was no sign that spring had arrived. In the town's parks the daffodils might be in bloom, but here down by the docks everything was grey: grey sky, grey houses, and grey water.

Gideon looked again at the small house in front of him. He knew that what he was planning was the biggest risk of his life, but what alternative did he have, he asked himself bitterly. He was a cripple with no way of earning his own living, save off other people's backs.

Ellie tried not to feel nervous as she stood outside her father-in-law's library door and heard him call out sharply, 'Come.'

As she walked in she reminded herself that she

was Mr Charnock's daughter-in-law and not his servant, and, moreover, that the book she was carrying in her hand and in which she had meticulously listed all her household expenses was as frugal and careful as it was possible to be.

It had come as a shock to Ellie to discover that her father-in-law expected her to render a weekly and detailed list to him of everything she had spent.

'Well, miss,' Mr Charnock greeted her unpleasantly, 'and what falderals have you wasted my money on this week, if you please?'

As he had done right from the first of these unpleasant interviews, Ellie's father-in-law kept her standing whilst he went through her accounts.

Far from welcoming her marriage to Henry, as Henry had informed her his father did, Mr Charnock, Ellie felt, had taken a great dislike to her the moment she had mentioned to him the possibility of having her family to live with them.

Ellie's expression grew sad and forlorn as she thought about her sister. There had been no more talk of Connie coming to Hoylake, and for that Ellie was grateful, but she couldn't help feeling that she'd let her down again.

Ellie waited as Mr Charnock went over and over her figures, holding her breath as he did so, and then tensing as he cried out, 'What is the meaning of this, if you please? You have writ here that you have ordered more coals, but it is still not a month since they were last ordered!'

Ellie tried to remain calm. 'You may remember, Father-in-law, that Henry was not very well two weeks ago, and I lit the fire in the bedroom because I was afraid he might take a chill on the chest.' She could see from Mr Charnock's expression that her explanation had not placated him.

'Not very well? Nonsense! If you didn't namby-pamby him so much he would be a great deal better!' As he was speaking to her Mr Charnock was counting out a small bag of guineas.

'Here,' he told Ellie ungraciously, pushing the bag across the desk. 'I have deducted two guineas this week: one since I consider that your expenditure is excessive, and the other to repay me for the extra coal which has had to be ordered.'

Ellie was nearly in tears when she left the room. The money Mr Charnock gave her was barely enough to cover what she had to buy anyway – and she had already secretly been buying a few extra little delicacies for Henry, whom she had discovered had a delicate stomach, out of the swiftly dwindling money she had been given by her Aunt Parkes on her marriage.

'Ellie, what is it? What's wrong?'

Henry, whom Mr Charnock had told to stay late at the office, had just opened the door, his expression concerned as he saw Ellie's tears.

'I have just come from presenting my accounts to your father, Henry, and he has deducted two guineas from the money he allocates me. There will not be enough for me to pay for everything!'

Ellie only just managed to hold back her distress.

'I hate to see you looking so unhappy,' Henry told her sadly. 'I shall speak to my father on your behalf, Ellie, and ask him if he will not relent and give you a small personal allowance. But I cannot promise that my request will meet with success,' he warned her, looking unhappy and worried.

Although Ellie was appreciative of his support, privately she knew that it was very unlikely that his father would pay any attention to him.

'Father, if I might have a word with you . . . ?'

As he was subjected to his father's hard-edged, almost contemptuous stare, Henry wished desperately that he might be stronger, braver, hardier – much more the kind of man his father would so obviously have preferred him to be – a man such as his cousin George.

Unusually, he could smell spirit on his father's breath, and his heart sank as he recognised the look of ill temper in his eyes, suspecting that he had chosen his moment badly and that his father was not in the best of moods. Had he been approaching him solely on his own behalf, Henry knew that his courage would have deserted him, but he was not here for himself. Every time he pictured Ellie as he had seen her this evening, looking so unhappy, his conscience racked him. He was her husband, her protector, and it was both immoral and ignoble that he should allow her to be treated as a skivvy.

'Father, I am concerned that no provision has been made for giving Ellie an allowance.'

'What? The chit has dared to demand that I pay for her fripperies, when that wretched uncle of hers has not yet handed over to me the dowry he promised?'

The apoplectic manner in which his words had been received confirmed all Henry's worst fears. His father was building himself up into one of his fearsome rages, his face already burning with dark angry colour, his small eyes glittering with hostility.

'If she wants to waste money on falderals then let her waste her uncle's. Tell her to make her demands of him, and –'

'Father, you are not being fair.'

'Oh, I am not, am I? Your wife obviously thinks she has got herself married very well, and into money. I haven't forgotten that she was naught but a butcher's daughter, even if she chooses to do so. Elizabeth has already warned me that she suspects your wife is taking on airs above her station, and is of a dangerously frivolous and wasteful nature. And as to any matter of an allowance –' spite gleamed in the small, mean eyes '– as her husband, that surely is your responsibility.'

Henry went white. 'I wish that it could be, Father, but, as you well know, since you have refused ever to pay me a decent living wage –'

'"A decent living wage",' Jarvis Charnock roared. 'You idle good-for-nothing. I provide you with a roof over your head, clothes to wear, food to eat, and a job for which you are plainly not equipped, and yet you still have the temerity to ask me for more. Are you blind? Can you not see what difficult times the business is in?'

It was infuriating to Jarvis that whilst he had done everything Josiah Parkes had told him to do to put in hand the final stages of their business arrangement, Josiah had told him to wait another week before giving the captain of the *Antareas*, who was waiting in China, the instruction to put their plan into action. Jarvis wasn't sure his bank manager was prepared to wait yet another week, having waited several already, and Jarvis was desperately in need of the money he had expected to gain. And now here was his wretched son, daring to demand that he pay the Parkes girl an allowance to do what she was supposed to do and that was run the house! Well, the pair of them would soon learn that he was not going to be manipulated. No, sir!

Poor Henry, unaware of what was going on inside his father's head, and desperately conscious of his duty to Ellie, protested fatally, 'You say that, Father, and yet only this morning my cousin George told me that you had promised to increase his salary.'

'You dare to question me?'

For a moment Henry thought that his father

373

might actually strike him, such was the intensity of his rage. His face had turned from red to a deeply mottled purple, and a few flecks of spittle foamed from his mouth as he jabbed one finger menacingly at Henry and told him viciously, 'God knows how I ever came to father such a one as you, Henry – if indeed I ever did, and your cursed mother didn't foist some byblow off on me!'

Bitterly Henry wondered what his father would say if he were to tell him that in many ways there was nothing he would like more than to discover that he was not his son were it not for the slur such a discovery would inevitably cast on his mother.

Heavy-hearted, he left his father's office. He had as good as promised Ellie that she should have some more money, and now he was going to have to let her down. Unless there was a way . . .

Ellie was seated in the small parlour sewing when Henry went to her.

'I'm afraid that my father is not in the best of moods at present,' he told her. 'There have been some problems with the business. However, you must not worry, I have money of my own and . . . and I shall provide you with some pin money for yourself, Ellie. The fault is mine in not thinking to do so before!'

Laying aside her sewing, Ellie smiled up at him in pleased relief. 'I am so grateful to you, Henry. I cannot tell you how worried I have been.'

The smile she was giving him made Henry clear his throat and suggest, 'Perhaps we might have an early night, Ellie. You have been working very hard and I should not want you to spoil your pretty eyes by spending so much time sewing.'

Nearly three months of marriage was long enough for Ellie to know what Henry's suggestion of an 'early night' portended. Inside her head she could almost hear her mother's voice reminding her that it was her duty to accede to Henry's intimate marital demands.

Her duty. A small, obstinate thrill of rebellion shot through her. According to Iris, a woman's first and most profound duty was to herself!

TWENTY-NINE

'And so what am I bid for these two dockside ter-races? Three floors, mind, and a fine opportunity to acquire a highly lettable property, which will bring in a tidy income.'

A little hesitantly Gideon waited for the bidding to start before raising his own hand. So much depended on what he was attempting to do. He had decided to use his savings – the money he had originally put aside from his earnings in order to help him finance himself through his architechtural studies – and invest them in some property that would, he hoped, bring him in a good rental income, and to this end he had spent the last month finding out as much as he could about such business, trudging through the town in the raw winter, cold and damp, his muffler pulled up around his face to keep out the icy fog with its taint of factory chimneys; nursing his stiff hand, which, whilst unable to respond to the commands of his brain, somehow managed to react acutely to the cold so that it ached and burned with pain. He had studied various buildings from the outside, and whenever he could from the inside as well, following his nose and his instincts, which had now led him to this auction and the hope that he might be successful in bidding for the two terraced houses of the very cheapest sort by the docks. They could potentially bring him in a tidy sum in rental, provided he was not too fussy about who his tenants might be. Dockside properties were generally occupied by the rougher type of persons: sailors wanting a room in between jobs; drabs and doxies who 'serviced' and 'entertained' them. Such lettings were not for those of high moral tone, nor those who could not, when needed, employ suffi-cient brute force to gain their tenants' respect and ensure that their rents were paid. But the returns were good and the rooms in constant demand, although Gideon had already noted that the most successful landlords were those who insisted on taking a sum in advance of letting a room.

It seemed he was not the only one who had seen the potential of the three-storey properties, but Gideon had set himself a limit beyond which he was not prepared to bid.

As he nodded to signal his intent to go on bidding, Gideon realised that there were only two of them in this auction now: himself, and a swarthy thickset man on the other side of the room, whom Gideon could see quite clearly because of the dis tinct ring of space around him, almost as though someone had drawn an invisible circle into which no one was allowed to intrude.

The auction was being held in the taproom of an out-of-town public house, its floor covered in a greasy film of sawdust and the air thick with a blue haze of coal and cigarette smoke.

Gideon had already reached his personal limit, but something about the look the other man gave him and the lazy, self-confident way he raised his bid challenged him to continue. Three more times they bid against one another, and Gideon could feel himself sweating. He was way above his limit now, and would have to let every single one of the rooms in the properties to recoup his outlay.

As he signalled his final bid, he found that he was half hoping the other man would outbid him, but instead he shook his head.

Gideon could feel the ripple of shock that ran through the room. It seemed that all eyes were on him as the auctioneer raised his gavel and pronounced, 'Going at one hundred and fifty guineas the pair . . . going . . . going . . . gone!'

Caught between euphoria and terror, Gideon saw that his hands were shaking.

'Well, sonny, you made a right fool of yourself there, didn't you, landing yourself with a real pig in a poke – and at a fair bit more than you can afford, I'll wager.'

A large hand clapped him on his shoulder and Gideon discovered that he was being confronted by his rival bidder. He could hear the malice beneath the other's apparent bonhomie – aye, and see it too in his cold, pale eyes.

'You must have thought it worth the money since you kept on bidding,' he pointed out.

The other man laughed. 'You are a novice, aren't you, son? I didn't keep bidding because I wanted the houses, I kept on 'cos I wanted to see how much of a fool you could make of yourself.' Giving Gideon a fake indulgent smile, he added, 'Course, I'd be willing to take them off your hands – at the right price.'

Quick as a flash Gideon retorted, 'I won't be selling. Those properties are a good investment.'

'Aye, in the right hands and at the right price! When you're ready to accept it – and you will be – you can get in touch with me. Connolly's the name – Bill Connolly. Eighty guineas and not a penny more, that's my top offer, and I promise you, lad, you're going to be glad to cut your losses and accept it.'

Giving Gideon another crocodile smile, he stepped back from him and started to walk away. His walk had a distinct swagger to it, Gideon noticed critically, already disliking and distrusting him. He also noticed the way in which people seemed to fall back to let Bill Connolly pass.

Gideon had to wait until the rest of the auction had taken place before presenting himself to the auctioneer to make arrangements to pay for his purchases.

'Well, well, the young man who outbid Bill Connolly . . . That took a fair bit of gumption, lad. Bill had his eye on them houses, that's for sure. Already owns a deal of property down by the docks, he does, and the word is that he's aiming to get his hands on as much as he can. That way he can charge what rent he likes without any fear of anyone undercutting him.'

'He did mention to me that he was willing to buy them off me,' Gideon responded.

'Did he so? Well, in that case, you'd better take care you don't get a visit from Bill's "persuaders", the same ones he uses to make sure that none of his tenants forget to pay him . . . at least not a second time, if you know what I mean!'

For the umpteenth time, Ellie looked anxiously round her spotless drawing room.

She had got up especially early to bake for her 'At Home' – a Victoria sponge, and some orange-flavoured biscuits, as well as making some scones and, of course, there was the fruit cake she had made earlier in the month.

The selection of dainty sandwiches was already arranged on the elegant china she had been given as a wedding present, and the silver teapot, which had been presented to Henry's mother's father by the East India Company and which she had discovered at the back of a cupboard, gleamed from the polishing she had given it. As a back-up she had the silver teapot she and Henry had been given. Since there had been no sign of any homemade jam or preserves in the kitchen cupboard she had had no alternative other than to buy some in, something that her own mother would have deplored – although Ellie had noticed that her Aunt Lavinia had no qualms about purchasing rather than making such things. She had, Ellie admitted, worried about the cost of these items, well aware of her father-in-law's objection to finding anything other than absolute necessities on the household bills, but only last night Henry had unexpectedly handed over to her twenty-five guineas saying that it was to be her pin money and that she may spend it as she wished.

'Henry, I thought you said that your father had refused to –'

'This is my money, Ellie,' Henry had stopped her, ignoring the troubled look she had given him.

'But you don't have much money of your own, you shouldn't . . .' Ellie had told him hesitantly, and then wished she had not when his face had burned with sore pride and chagrin.

'My father does not pay me . . . generously,' Henry had agreed stiffly, turning away from her as he spoke, 'but I-I want you to have this money, Ellie,' he had added simply, and the humbleness in his voice and his face as he turned back towards her had made her eyes smart with tears.

Ellie checked the drawing room yet again. A fire burned brightly in the burnished grate, throwing out a warming heat. By turning down the gas lamps slightly, and thanks to the dullness of the late March afternoon, the shabbiness of the room's drapes and cushions was not immediately apparent. Every piece of furniture in the house shone, her tablecloths were pristinely laundered, and Ellie had spent hours patiently instructing Maisie on just how she was to receive Ellie's visitors.

The doorbell rang, signalling the arrival of the first of her callers. Pink-cheeked, Ellie hurried to the drawing-room door, shooing Maisie towards the front door, gesturing to her to open it.

'Ellie, darling . . .'

Fortunately her first visitor was Cecily, beaming lovingly at her as she embraced her. Her baby was due in just two months but, unlike Ellie's mother, her cousin seemed to be positively enjoying her pregnancy.

'So! Now you are a married woman,' Cecily said archly, adding happily, 'Oh, Ellie, isn't it fun being the mistress of your own home, and having a husband?'

'Let me take your coat,' Ellie offered, as the doorbell rang again and Maisie threw her an anguished look, thankful not to have to reply.

'Is it your maid's day off?' Cecily questioned innocently, as she witnessed Maisie's inexpert

382

attempts to fulfil her duties. 'Oh, I nearly forgot, Iris asks me to give you her apologies. She cannot make it, but she says she will telephone you and arrange to have tea with you. I love that gown, Ellie. It suits you so very well, and that trimming is very pretty. Oh, and I must tell you how much admired that pretty little dress you made for the baby has been! I am the envy of all my friends! Everyone is asking me where I bought it. I dare say if you wanted to you could make yourself a fortune with your needle! Not, of course, that you would ever need to do such a thing!'

The doorbell was ringing again, and Ellie excused herself to her cousin, urging her to go into the drawing room.

'At last, Parkes. I have had a devil of a time getting hold of you. Does that wretched clerk of yours not pass on your messages?'

'I'm afraid the blame lies with me, Jarvis,' Josiah Parkes apologised smoothly, as his visitor immediately made his way over to his office's warm fire. 'I have been very remiss, but pressure of business, you understand.'

'Aye, well, never mind all that. I have a bone to pick with you, Parkes, over the matter of your niece's dowry! Or rather the lack of it!'

The tiniest hint of confusion creased Josiah's forehead. 'I am sorry, Jarvis, but I am afraid I do not follow you. It says quite plainly in the marriage contract that the dowry is to be paid on the first anniversary of the marriage.'

'The devil it does,' Jarvis Charnock spluttered, his eyes bulging hot-temperedly. 'I have no recollection of any such thing ever being discussed between us, and I warn you, Parkes, I have the very best of memories.'

'Indeed, I am sure you do. Perhaps we did not discuss it in so many words. I recall that you were occupied with other matters when the document was drawn up.'

The smooth oily note of satisfaction and amusement in Josiah's voice increased Jarvis Charnock's fury. Not only had the bastard pulled a fast one on him, he was also laughing at him for being fool enough to let him!

'Aye, well, you might think you've outsmarted me, Parkes, but I can tell you I have my own way of dealing with those who would try to cheat me! Your niece is finding out the hard way that I'm a man who likes to see value for his brass. And since she's seen fit to cause my cook to hand in her cards, she's –'

'Come, come, Jarvis, there is no need, surely, for talk such as this. We are both gentlemen, after all,' Josiah intervened jovially, secretly only too delighted to discover how effective his underhand strategies had been. 'So much heat and anger, and for what? I assure you that there was no intent on my part to cheat anyone. No, I thought I had made it clear to you that I could not pay the dowry until

384

our other business had been satisfactorily settled, and that was why I settled on a day one year on from the marriage.'

'Aye, and that is another issue,' Jarvis stormed, refusing to be placated.

'Indeed it is, and it is one we must address without delay,' Josiah cut him off. 'You have your captain standing by, I trust?'

Having the wind taken out of his sails so swiftly and masterfully caused Jarvis to bluster and fume, as he tried to regain control of the argument. 'It is not me who is delaying things,' he denied. 'You –'

'I do understand your impatience, my dear Jarvis, but these things cannot be hurried. However, the time has now come, and you must send word to your captain to act immediately.'

Ellie breathed a tired but very satisfied breath of relief as she carefully returned to the china cabinet the last of the best china.

Her At Home had gone extremely well, and an amused but slightly grim smile touched her mouth as she remembered how she had come upon Elizabeth and the friend she had brought with her upstairs, where Elizabeth had been running a finger over one of the window frames Ellie had spent the previous week cleaning.

At least the friend had had the grace to look ashamed, even if Elizabeth herself had not, re-inforcing Ellie's estimation of Henry's cousin's wife as a woman of very poor upbringing and manners.

Removing her apron, Ellie made her way upstairs.

Henry had come in and gone out again, and she tutted to herself to see the jacket from his suit carelessly discarded across the dressing screen. Automatically she reached for it, neatening it and then bending down to pick up a small folded piece of paper that had fallen from one of the pockets.

Normally Ellie would never have dreamed of reading something that was so obviously personal, but for some reason the minute she saw the pawn-broker's name printed across the front of the paper alongside his immediately recognisable symbol, a horrible feeling of dread crept over her. Her fingers trembling, she slowly unfolded the paper.

It was a receipt from the pawnbroker to say that he had advanced Henry twenty-five guineas against a gold pocket-watch.

Twenty-five guineas – the exact amount of money Henry had given her only recently. Ellie sat down unsteadily on the bed, still holding the pawn-broker's ticket. The gold pocket-watch he had pawned was the one he had once told her proudly was one of his most cherished possessions, and had originally been presented to his maternal grand-father by Her Majesty Queen Victoria. And yet he had obviously pawned it in order to give her money!

Tears blurred Ellie's eyes. Dear sweet Henry! He had done that for her. Ellie's throat ached with pain and despair.

Henry was her husband and the kindest of men, but she already knew that she would never, could never, feel about him as her cousin Cecily did about her Paul – that her love for Henry was born of duty and a protective maternalism rather than passion and desire for him.

As she suddenly heard Henry's footsteps outside the bedroom door, she pushed the ticket into the pocket of her gown.

THIRTY

As she felt the onset of the familiar dragging ache that always preceded her monthly courses, Ellie let out a faint sigh of relief. She had followed the embarrassingly explicit and direct instructions Iris had furnished her with to the letter, and so far, to her relief, it seemed that they were working.

Her winter coat was laid over the back of the bedroom chair, ready for her to put on, and in her bag was the pawnbroker's ticket.

After a night spent barely able to sleep for anxiety and guilt, Ellie had only waited until Henry had left for work before hurrying to re-count the guineas he had given her. Even though she had not as yet spent any of the money she had still needed to reassure herself that she had sufficient for her purpose.

At Cecily's suggestion she was having lunch with her cousin at the Adelphi Hotel – 'My treat,' Cecily had insisted when Ellie had hesitated. Sensitively, Ellie now wondered if her cousin had perhaps guessed just how straitened her and Henry's financial circumstances were.

She shivered a little in the coldness of the house. Only this morning Mr Charnock had announced that he suspected that Ellie was lighting fires in the house against his orders, and that he had therefore reduced the amount of coal to be delivered.

'But if we do not have enough coal to fuel the range then there won't be any hot water,' Ellie had been foolish enough to protest.

'If it's hot water you want, missie, then you can boil up some yourself with the kettle,' he had told Ellie with angry satisfaction.

'Well now, and ain't you a pretty sight for a man's eyes.'

Connie preened beneath the appreciative look she was being given, returning her flatterer's attention with a mock-demure pout, whilst at the same time keeping a sharp eye out for her aunt, who had only brought her to Preston with her because she considered that Connie was not to be trusted left on her own.

Right now, though, her aunt was busily engaged talking to an old acquaintance, her back conveniently turned towards Connie, leaving Connie free to indulge in an exciting flirtation with the young man who had just addressed her.

Approvingly she gave him a quick once-over.

He was tall, with nice, broad shoulders and a

thick shock of ink-black hair. But it was his eyes that really caught and held Connie's attention. As dark as his hair, they had a wicked, dangerous look about them that immediately excited Connie. They were the eyes of the kind of man Connie knew instinctively was her kind of man – bold, flirtatious and exciting – the kind of man her Aunt Simpkins would never approve of in a hundred years.

'From around these parts, are you?' he asked, eyeing her boldly.

'And if I am, what's that to you?' Connie rejoined pertly, her eyes giving away her enjoyment of their flirtatious badinage.

'Well, I was just thinking if you was, and if you wasn't walking out with anyone, then I might think of asking you to come to the picture house wi' me on Saturday afternoon.'

Connie felt a delicious thrill of excitement run right through her all the way down to her toes. It was a brisk March day, the sky grey and overcast, but she felt her cheeks begin to burn as though she were standing in the full heat of the summer sun.

Out of the corner of her eye she saw that her aunt had finished speaking to her friend.

Quickly, before she could turn round and see her, Connie nodded her head and then demanded recklessly, 'Where am I to meet you and what time?'

'In front of the picture house and just before the matinée, say around half past one!' he told her equally as fast, blowing her a cheeky kiss and then melting away into the busy crowd of shoppers.

Saturday! She was going to see him on Saturday! A surge of happiness shot through her, driving out the misery she had been feeling! Giddy with excitement, Connie started to make plans.

As she got off the tram and headed for the pawn-broker's shop, Ellie's stomach fluttered with nerves. To her relief this was at least a reasonably respectable part of the city, but there was no mistaking the meaning of the shop sign, as heavy and threatening as an axe held above her head.

For several nerve-racking minutes she hesitated, walking past the shop and then back again, pausing to look over her shoulder and then into the window, but the ordeal had to be faced.

The inside of the shop was dark and smelled of candle wax and age. The man who shuffled to the counter, peering at her over the top of his spectacles, had a gaze that reminded her of dirty ice.

'I have come about this,' Ellie told him shakily, removing her gloves to open her purse and hand him the ticket.

She could feel him studying her, the silence of the shop almost suffocatingly heavy.

'The watch is my husband's,' she told him, desperate to break the quietness. 'It belonged to his grandfather. I have brought the money – the twenty-five guineas,' she hurried on, gabbling and breathless in her desire to have her ordeal over, as she tipped the guineas onto the counter. 'It is all there, the twenty-five guineas. They are the same ones you gave him. I –'

'Twenty-five guineas? Where is the rest?'

Ellie stared at the pawnbroker, appalled. 'The rest?' she stammered. 'What rest? It is all there . . .'

'The amount advanced against the watch is there, but the fee for the loan is not. The arrangement was that the watch could only be redeemed by a payment of an extra five guineas! Did your husband not tell you this?'

'No . . . that is not possible!' Her head reeled. A charge of five guineas to borrow a sum of twenty-five!

'He . . . I . . . the money has been held for barely a week, and to charge such a sum is . . . is . . . usurious,' she protested shakily.

'Indeed? You may think so but I can assure you that that is the nature of our business.' The look in the dirty-ice eyes was not kind.

Ellie was beginning to feel sick, her breathing rapid and her skin breaking out in a rash of perspiration. But ladies did not perspire, ladies merely glowed! But then ladies did not go into pawnbrokers'! But she wasn't a lady, and she was tired of trying to pretend to be one, of trying to be the person her mother had wanted her to be. Her thoughts, disorientated and muddled, swarmed through her head, making it ache.

'Please, you don't understand, that watch belonged to my husband's grandfather. It is of great senti-mental value to him.'

When the pawnbroker made no response, she protested, 'I do not have five guineas. I do not have –'

'Is there a problem, Father?'

Ellie tensed as a younger man came out from the back of the shop. Taller than his father, he nevertheless possessed the same features.

'My husband pawned his watch here for the sum of twenty-five guineas,' Ellie told him quickly. 'I have come to redeem it but now I am told there is a fee to pay of an additional five guineas, which I do not have. I have no money at all . . .' She felt shamefully close to tears brought on by the sheer misery of what she was enduring.

'No money? I see. Well, in that case . . .' he was shaking his head but then suddenly he stopped. 'I see that you are wearing a pretty little ring.'

Instinctively Ellie covered her left hand and her engagement ring, but to her humiliation he simply laughed and told her, 'No, not that one. It is plain to see that it is merely paste.'

Merely paste! Her engagement ring!

'No, I was meaning the other ring you are wearing.'

The other ring . . . her mother's ring. Ellie felt as though she was going to choke. There was a huge lump in her throat, a huge welling ache of desolation. Silently she slid the ring off and pushed it across the mahogany-topped counter.

Smiling, the young man picked it up. 'It is not a particularly valuable piece but the stone is a pretty one, though small, and the gold of good quality. I am being a fool to myself in doing this, but . . .' He gave a small shrug. 'Give her the watch, Father.'

Dry-eyed, Ellie picked up the watch, carefully checking it to make sure that it was Henry's.

She had no idea how much time she had spent in the pawnbroker's but what she did know was that when she stepped outside it again she was changed for ever.

The last of her girlhood was gone, in every sense. There was a thinness on her right hand where her mother's ring had been, a coldness that matched the tight band of pain around her heart. In half an hour's time she was due to meet Cecily and when she did . . . Ellie took a deep breath. It was no use her having any false pride. She had known this morning, when her housekeeping had been reduced again, what she must say to her cousin, how she must lower her pride and beg Cecily for her help.

'Ellie, what is wrong? You are not yourself at all today,' Cecily complained gently as she broke off her conversation to study her cousin worriedly.

Screwing up her courage, Ellie took a deep breath. 'I . . . Cecily, if that friend of yours should mention again that she likes the dress I made for the baby, would you tell her . . . would you tell her that you can furnish her with my name and that I would be pleased to make up something similar for her – and for any other of your friends who might want any sewing done and are prepared to pay me for it.'

Cecily didn't try to conceal her shock. 'Ellie, what are you saying? What on earth –'

'I need to earn some money, Cecily,' Ellie blurted out, her face burning with embarrassment and shame. 'I . . . Henry . . . Henry's father pays him the merest pittance and . . . and . . .' Tears of anger pricked her eyes.

'Ellie, oh my dear! I had wondered that you did not have proper servants, but I had no idea . . .'

'I hate having to raise such a matter with you, Cecily, but you and Iris have both said that I could earn my living with my needle and now I am very much afraid that I must, for if I do not we shall soon be dressed in rags, as well as having only the poorest food to eat and no coals with which to make a fire.' Ellie caught herself up as she saw how distressed Cecily was looking.

'Oh Ellie, I am so sorry. Of course I shall tell my friends. You may depend upon it.'

Gideon had almost reached his two newly acquired properties when a boy came flying round the corner, running as fast as his thin bare legs could carry him, his head turning to look back in the direction he had just come so that he all but cannoned into Gideon.

Automatically Gideon reached out to steady him,

cursing as he twisted violently in his grip like an eel.

'Hoy there! Hold onto that boy, will you? The young varmint has just stolen a pie from my shop.'

Beneath his grip Gideon could feel the sharp bones, the thin body hunching defensively. The boy was filthy, his clothes little more than rags, his shoes, Gideon realised as he looked down at him, at least a couple of sizes too big and stuffed with newspapers to make them fit and keep out the rain.

Sharp flinty eyes, feral as a wild animal's, savaged him with fury. The small tow head bent towards his wrist, his lips curling back from his teeth. Immediately, Gideon took evasive action. The boy was so thin that even with only one good arm Gideon was able to lift him and swing him off the ground.

'Go on then, hit me,' the boy told him, cursing richly.

The stallholder had reached them now, red-faced and out of breath.

'Little varmint. Deserves to be hanged. This isn't the first time he's stolen off of my stall.'

'Well, you ain't getting it back,' the boy told him unrepentantly. 'Wouldn't have sold it anyway. Off, it was, and you should have the law on you, you should. That's no mutton you've got in them pies – more like rat.'

'Why, you . . . 'Ere, give him to me,' the stallholder demanded.

Without taking his eyes off the boy, Gideon asked the stallholder, 'How much was the pie?'

'Thruppence. No, sixpence!'

'Thruppence. He's lying. Got a big sign up saying they're a penny, four for thruppence. Not that anyone in their right senses 'ud want four!' The boy swore and spat. 'Not worth a farthing, it weren't. Give me gut rot, it will, if it don't kill me altogether.'

Reaching into his trouser pocket, Gideon removed a silver sixpence and gave it to the glowering man.

'You best take it before I change my mind,' he warned him.

Having tested the coin with his teeth to make sure it was real, the man pocketed it and walked away, still muttering under his breath.

'What did you do that for?' the urchin asked Gideon once the stallholder had turned the corner.

'I don't know,' Gideon admitted, and it was the truth. He wasn't normally given to sentimental impulses, and there was nothing about the boy that was remotely deserving of either his protection or his generosity. Quite the opposite.

'Wot's the likes of you doing down here anyway?' the boy challenged him. 'Come whoring, have you? That's wot normally brings you toffs down here. Should'a thought you were more of a stage door Johnny type m'sel', wi' them fine clothes!'

Filthy fingers felt the fabric of Gideon's coat. 'Nice bit o' worsted. Mind you don't take it off. Them girls will have it away and sold before you can say Jack Robinson. But if you're looking for a woman, there's a house three up. Mind you ask for Katie, though; she's clean and young, and don't let them fob you off with Sally. She ain't even got any teeth!'

'I am not looking for a woman,' Gideon told him grimly, releasing him.

'Then wot are you doing down here?'

'I have come to look at some property I have recently acquired. Not that it is any of your business.'

'Property? Down here?' The too-old eyes in the young face suddenly rounded. ''Ere, you ain't the one that's gone and bought them two terraces from under Bill Connolly's nose, are you? You are!' he breathed in wonderment when Gideon made no response. 'Aye, well, no wonder you was fool enough to part with a silver sixpence to old Robber Harry, for a pie you wouldn't give a dog. Bill Connolly 'ull make mincemeat of you – aye, and you'll end up in old Harry's pies like the rats. You'll never keep them houses, Bill Connolly 'ull have 'em off you as fast as a sneak thief could have your watch – no, faster. You watch! Freeze you out, he will; put the frighteners on folk so they won't rent and then put his own rents down. And then, with the places empty, Bill's mob will be round stripping 'em bare. Surprised they haven't been in and done it already. Allus a good market for a bit o' lead flashing . . .'

Gideon listened impassively to him.

'Course, if you wanted, me and a few of the lads could keep an eye on the place for you. Cost yer, mind . . .'

'What about Mr Connolly's men?' Gideon reminded him wryly.

'Oh, they don't give us no trouble,' he boasted, rubbing the side of his nose and giving Gideon a knowing wink. 'Knows a few things about 'em, we do. Think about it, mister,' he urged Gideon.

To his own astonishment Gideon discovered that he was doing. Had he run totally mad? It was obvious that this little varmint would take whatever money he was fool enough to give him and disappear. Narrowing his eyes, Gideon looked at him.

'I'll tell you what I'll do,' he pronounced. 'I'll strike a bargain with you. A week from today, I'll meet you here, and if I find my properties are, er, unmolested, then I shall pay you sixpence.'

'Sixpence?' The boy swore and then spat. 'A shilling 'ud be robbing us. A shilling each that is, mind, and there 'ud be five of us.'

'Five shillings?' Gideon laughed. 'One shilling between the lot of you, and I'll throw in a couple of old Harry's pies apiece!'

'Robbery it is, but go on then!'

Personally Gideon did not think for one moment that the danger to his property was as great as the boy was suggesting, or indeed, if it was, that he would be of any use in deterring the would-be despoilers, but there was something about his sheer dogged opportunism and sang-froid that Gideon found himself admiring. The boy was a survivor. Like him!

THIRTY-ONE

Connie stared excitedly at her reflection in the mirror. The dress she was wearing was one of Ellie's cast-offs, but Connie didn't care, and she didn't care about Ellie any more either! Why should she? Ellie cared nothing for her; living the life of a rich married lady, and indulging in all kinds of entertainment and fun whilst she, Connie, was forced to live here with the hateful and boring Simpkinses! But now Connie had something exciting happening in her life, something much more exciting than Ellie had ever done. But first she had to escape from the vicarage.

Connie had already planned out how to make her escape. Her uncle was in his study, working on his sermon, and she knew that her aunt would be downstairs in the kitchen, giving the cook her instructions for the coming week.

Connie opened her bedroom door and listened. Having satisfied herself that no one was about, she tiptoed hurriedly down the stairs and into the smaller of the vicarage's two drawing rooms, hurriedly unlocking the French windows that gave out onto the garden.

Her uncle's study was on the other side of the house and its window had a view of the front gate, whilst her aunt in the kitchen could easily see her if she attempted to leave by the back, so Connie had decided to make her escape through the garden, avoiding both the gates but making use of a small gap in the hedge, which led directly onto the road.

Once there she could quite easily catch the bus into Preston.

At Ellie's wedding Uncle Parkes had pressed five shiny new guineas into her hands. Connie had one of them now, and was eagerly planning the treats she was going to enjoy in Preston before she met up with her black-haired admirer.

Picking up her skirts, she hurried across the garden and wriggled through the gap in the hedge. A bus was chugging down the road towards her and she hurried to the stop, giving the conductor a flirtatiously innocent look as he helped her on board.

Preston was busy with Saturday bustle and since she had a good two hours to spare, Connie wandered all round the market, enjoying the admiring looks she was getting from young men, and relishing her freedom.

She would be punished for what she had done when she returned, she knew, but what lay before her was so exciting that she hardly cared.

After treating herself to an ice cream, some impulse had her walking into Friargate.

A spotty young apprentice, whom she didn't recognise, was standing idly in her father's shop and Connie frowned to see it so empty of customers. A red-haired woman emerged from the door to the house, her stomach distended, and then, as Connie watched, she saw her father come out to join her.

Connie would have called out to him and run to join him, but for some reason she found that she did not want to.

Her father looked older, and somehow different: his shoulders were hunched and he had a cowed air about him.

When they walked down the street away from her, Connie could hear the woman berating her father. As she turned away from them, tears filled Connie's eyes.

But she didn't stay unhappy for very long. It was almost time for her to meet up with her admirer, and she started to make her way towards the picture house.

To her relief he was standing looking for her, and the black hair was neatly brushed, even if the suit he was wearing looked uncomfortably tight. Connie didn't care. The moment she had seen him her heart had lifted, and she was suffused with joy and excitement; and shyness. She half hesitated, urged by an unfamiliar emotion to turn and quickly walk away, but then he saw her and started to walk towards her, swaggering slightly, a wide grin on his face, and it was too late.

'Came, then? I knew you would,' he announced boldly, the dark eyes approving her in a way that made her feel giddy.

Months of reading the maid Polly's penny-dreadful stories in secret in her bedroom had given Connie a yearning to encounter the same kind of dramatic love experienced by the heroines, the kind of love that would transform her life and rescue her from her misery at the vicarage. And now suddenly Connie knew that she had found it.

'Tell us yer name then?'

'Connie,' she answered, swallowing on the lump in her throat.

'Connie, eh? Well, mine's Kieron, Kieron Connolly,' he told her, adding softly, 'Connie Connolly – got a fine ring to it, hasn't it?'

Connie couldn't speak with the intensity of her emotions. Unable to drag her besotted gaze from Kieron's face, she allowed him to take her hand and lead her into the picture house.

Ellie waited until she and Henry were alone in the privacy of their own room before returning his watch to him. He looked tired and unhappy, and over dinner his father had picked on him constantly, criticising him and comparing him to his cousin.

Ellie had ached to intervene and defend her husband, but of course it was not her place to do so. She was now grimly determined that no way would she give birth to a child – especially a son, to be bullied and tormented in the same way as his poor father by Jarvis Charnock. In her opinion, Elizabeth and George Fazackerly's sons, about whom Ellie's father-in-law spoke in terms of approval, were the most dreadful of children.

'Henry, there is something –' she began, and then stopped, shaking her head a little. 'I have this for you,' she told him gently, handing him the tissue paper in which she had carefully wrapped his watch.

Frowning slightly, he unwrapped it, folding back each leaf of tissue and then standing staring at the watch for what seemed to be the longest amount of time.

She had known that he would be surprised, of course, but the look of bleakness and pain that crossed his face as his hand trembled and he looked away from her shocked her.

'What is it, Henry?' she asked him worriedly. 'I thought you would be pleased. I know how much the watch means to you and when I discovered that you had pawned it to give money to me, I could not rest until I had gone to that dreadful shop and had got it back for you.'

'You are very kind.' His voice was thin and emotionless, a whispery, papery rasp, devoid of life and yet somehow heavy and tortured-sounding in a way that confused her.

'Are you not pleased to have the watch back?' Ellie asked him, upset.

'Yes, yes, of course I am.' His voice was muffled and he kept his back to her as he spoke.

'Henry . . .'

'Oh, Ellie.' As he swung round, his voice was raw and tortured. 'I am such a pathetic, weak apology for a man. My father is right about that! You are worthy of so much more than I am able to give you, and it shames me that I cannot . . . that I am so unworthy of you! You are so strong, Ellie, so much how I wish I might be myself, but know that I am not! Can't you see? I am your husband. It is my duty to provide for you, and what you have done proves that I am not able to do so. I had no other way . . . This was my only way of . . .' He stopped speaking and, to her distress, Ellie saw that he was crying.

A part of her ached to go to him, to comfort him, yet another part of her recoiled from his unmanly vulnerability and pain.

She was sharply aware that her own actions were the cause of his emotional humiliation, and the anguish he was obviously suffering, but she had no idea what to say or do to mend matters.

As though grey clouds had been parted by a sudden frightening zigzag of lightning, Ellie suddenly

405

saw her future. She was destined always to be the stronger partner in their marriage; on her shoulders would fall the onus of protecting Henry – from everything and everyone, for ever.

THIRTY-TWO

It had become a new habit of Gideon's to wander around Preston, keeping an eye on properties that became vacant or were up for sale, and he was on one of these missions when he stopped mid-stride and stiffened as he watched a familiar figure making her way towards the train station.

Miss Isherwood! She looked older and thinner – frailer, somehow – Gideon recognised. A feeling he did not want to acknowledge suddenly struck sharply through him, and before he could stop himself he was calling her name and hurrying towards her.

It shamed him to see the look of joy on her face as she turned and saw him.

'Gideon!' she exclaimed with obvious pleasure. 'How are you?' she asked him warmly. 'I have often thought about you and –' Mary bit her lip, deriding herself mentally for being a fool, and rambling so. But the shock of seeing Gideon when she had least expected to do so had driven rational good sense right out of her head!

'I'm fine,' Gideon told her brusquely.

Mary's evident gladness at seeing him was making him feel guilty. He owed her a great deal, he knew that, but his pride had made it hard for him to admit as much to himself, never mind to her!

'And your hand?' Mary asked him, worriedly. 'You are exercising it as the specialist suggested?'

A brief flare of bitter anger darkened Gideon's eyes. 'No amount of exercising is ever going to make it right,' he told her curtly.

Instantly, Mary's expression shadowed, and Gideon knew that his response had hurt her. Angrily he told himself that it wasn't his fault she was such a daft softie, but then she started to turn away from him and he saw how the small movement caused her to flinch with pain.

'You've hurt yourself.' His statement was both angry and accusing, but it still made Mary smile a little.

'Nothing much. Just a silly twisted ankle,' she declared, not wanting Gideon to ask her any more questions about her ankle, which had been injured at a suffragette meeting when she caught a sharp blow from a policeman's truncheon. Although she had no intention of telling Gideon so, Mary's doctor had told her that she was lucky she had moved quickly enough to avoid the bone being crushed completely.

He had also expressed concern about her lingering cough, but Mary had told him not to fuss.

'I am on my way to Manchester,' she explained

to Gideon instead. 'That's why I'm here. There is an important suffragette meeting there today, and since my chauffeur is sick and I cannot drive the car myself because of this wretched ankle, I have decided to go by train.'

'You're travelling to Manchester on your own?' he demanded, frowning.

'I'm a grown woman, Gideon,' Mary reminded him gently.

'Grown woman or not, with the way you're limping –'

'It's nothing,' Mary tried to assure him, but as she spoke she moved awkwardly and gave an involuntary gasp of pain.

'I'm coming with you,' he announced gruffly, his decision as much a surprise to him as it obviously was to Mary. 'You already know I don't approve of what you're doing, but that doesn't stop me being concerned about the risks you are taking. That ankle –'

'Oh, no, Gideon. I couldn't expect you to do that,' Mary protested, but the expression in her eyes showed her true feelings.

'Aye, well, I owe you a favour or two,' Gideon responded, 'and I'm not one to want to be beholden to anyone.'

He didn't see the sad little smile that touched Mary's mouth as she listened to his defensive speech, but then he insisted, 'I'm going with you and that's an end to it! Let me give you my arm.'

Ten minutes later, as they stood side by side

on the platform, waiting for their train, Mary wondered if this was the moment she had been both longing for and dreading.

Before she could change her mind or lose her courage, she turned to Gideon and began, 'Gideon, there is something I have to tell you. Something very important. I –'

'The train's coming,' Gideon stopped her brusquely, relieved to be able to do so.

If she was thinking of offering him more charity, he was going to tell her that he didn't need it!

As she heard the sound of Iris's motor car drawing up outside the house, Ellie smoothed the skirt of her coat a little nervously. She still wasn't sure she was doing the right thing in agreeing to attend one of the suffrage meetings with Iris, but once Cecily's sister-in-law had set her mind on something, it was virtually impossible to dissuade her.

However, watching discreetly from the drawing-room window whilst Iris stepped out of her newly acquired car, it was hard not to feel her spirits lifting a little, Ellie acknowledged, despite her concern over Henry and the sad moods he seemed to suffer.

These rendered him so miserable and withdrawn that he could not bear any company, even hers, and instead shut himself away for hours on end in his dressing room, reading his Japanese books. Ellie tried not to feel shut out and hurt by his behaviour and was reluctant to discuss it with him in case, by doing so, she made him feel worse.

There was something about Iris, though, that was like a breath of fresh air, and immediately made Ellie feel able to put her concerns to one side for a while.

Maisie, who was totally in awe of Iris, opened the door to her, dumbstruck.

'You are her heroine, Iris, ever since you insisted on driving her in your car.' Ellie laughed as she showed her into the back parlour.

'I have finished altering the tea gown you left with me,' she told her.

'Wonderful. But I am afraid you are going to be very cross with me, Ellie, because I now have a coat that just will not lie right and which desperately needs your magic touch, and I have to admit to telling a few of my friends about you and your sewing skills. I have given them your cards – I did not have any left, but I begged some from Cecily –'

'Oh, Iris!' Ellie stopped her, shaking her head. 'You're too good – too generous.'

'Good? Me?' Iris laughed. 'My dear Ellie, I will have you know that I am anything but! Now please do not put on such a solemn face!'

'Iris, you have done so much to help me, recommending me to so many of your friends, and . . . I am so very grateful to you.'

'Grateful! Ellie, you must not be any such thing,' Iris scolded her. 'And before you accuse me of being charitable or indulging in any other kind of such mawkish foolishness, let me tell you that I should be the one who is grateful to you! I am wholly reformed in the eyes of my friends, who had all but given up on me, claiming that I never cared as I should how I looked. Now, thanks to you, I am a pattern card of elegance. They actually demand to know where I have had my clothes made!'

Ellie smiled, full of gratitude. It was thanks to Iris and her tireless campaigning on Ellie's behalf amongst her friends that Ellie was now earning enough money with her needle to ensure that she and Henry could live in moderate comfort.

Since Iris wanted to show off her latest acquisition, the new Rolls-Royce car she had just bought for herself, she had announced that she would drive them into Manchester where the women's suffrage meeting was to be held.

'Paul will not have it, but I can tell you that I am a far better driver than he,' Iris boasted happily to Ellie as they got into her car.

It was a beautiful late spring day, the leaves newly unfurled in all their fresh greenery, the sky a perfect bowl of blue softened by the merest breath of an occasional fluffy white cloud.

Ellie was delighted to see that Iris was wearing beneath her coat one of the gowns she herself had remodelled for her, removing the fussy trimmings that Iris had allowed the dressmaker to add in a rush of impatience to escape from the boredom of dress fittings, tailoring it into a much more stylish shape to suit Iris's busy life.

Iris worked at Liverpool Hospital, but, of course, there were only certain areas in which, as a woman, she was allowed to practise, and she complained to Ellie about this as she drove them towards Manchester.

'You would think that I had never seen a naked male before – not that in my opinion there is much worth seeing about one – never mind knew anything about the inner workings of the human body to judge from the way some people react,' she snorted acerbically, deftly overtaking a plodding wagoner's cart.

The suffrage meeting was to be held at the Free Trade Hall, and Iris parked her car outside the building, her eyes shining with purpose as she tucked her arm through Ellie's and urged her inside.

'Heavens, what a press of people!' Iris exclaimed. 'So much for Ewan's belief that there would be a poor turnout! The man is a complete bigot!'

'You should not speak so of poor Ewan,' Ellie scolded. 'At heart he is your devoted admirer, Iris.'

'You think so? I don't! He does nothing but criticise me. And besides, I don't wish to have an admirer. I promise you that I feel far more passionate about my medical career and the women's movement than I can ever envisage doing about a mere man!'

Ellie laughed.

'You must see how important our cause is, Ellie,' Iris continued, looking serious. 'For women like dearest Cecily, who are sheltered and shielded from the harsher realities of life, it is perhaps difficult to understand how important our total emancipation is, but in your circumstances . . . I am sorry if I am being tactless, but, my dear, no matter how much you try to shield and protect him it is obvious that your poor Henry is no match for his tyrant of a father, who abuses him dreadfully – and through him, you! To keep you so short of money that you must earn your own living, and yet at the same time be put in a position where you must not be seen to do so, is outrageous.'

'Iris, I know you mean well, but really it is a subject I would rather not discuss,' Ellie stopped her firmly, more out of loyalty to Henry than because she felt she could not talk openly with Iris about her situation.

Fortunately now that they were inside the Free Trade Hall, the noise meant that it was impossible to hold a private conversation anyway.

The meeting was a rousing one, the mood of both the speakers and their audience defiantly militant. A cheer went up when Annie Kenney said that perhaps it would do certain members of their current government good to have the tables turned on them and be forced to live under the

414

same restrictions as women, and denied the right to vote.

After the meeting had broken up some of the women were still passionately expressing their views outside the Free Trade Hall where a solid phalanx of uniformed policemen had drawn up behind a local politician, who had taken it upon himself to remonstrate with the organisers of the meeting.

Ellie didn't see the throwing of the first egg to splatter his coat, but she and Iris were close enough to the commotion for her to look at Iris with anxiety.

'It is all right,' Iris soothed her. 'One cannot blame them. We have tried again and again to use reason and logic but it seems the government is determined not to give us a fair hearing.'

Ellie gasped as she saw a woman detach herself from the crowd in front of her and confront the politician, waving a placard demanding 'Votes for Women'.

The politician, red-faced and spluttering, turned to say something to the police lined up behind him, and then to Ellie's horror she saw the police break ranks and advance on the women at the front of the crowd, their truncheons raised.

Gideon had been listening to the uproar around the politician with one ear whilst reading the newspaper. Despite Mary's protests he had insisted on remaining outside the Free Trade Hall to wait for her. Even if his male ego could not wholly approve of women's suffrage he had a reluctant and secret admiration for Mary in her belief in her cause.

The sight of her pale face when he had first seen her today, though, had aroused within him emotions he was reluctant to acknowledge. It irked him that he should feel so protective towards her, so outraged and antagonistic towards his own sex on her behalf. And now, even though he would never have admitted it, a part of him was alert to any sign that she might be in danger.

The moment he heard a woman's scream piercing the general sounds of chants and protests, he dropped the paper and hurried across the road. At least two thousand women were milling about outside the Free Trade Hall, but amongst those on the crowd's outer edges there was no sign of Mary at all.

Knowing that she was well acquainted with the Pankhurst family, Gideon guessed that she would be at the forefront of the crowd – from where the screams and cries of pain were emanating.

Determinedly he started to push his way through the crowd, but the women, believing he was another of the enemy, refused to make way for him.

By the time he had fought his way through to the front it was too late: Mary was already standing handcuffed to a burly police officer and, to Gideon's anguish and despair, as he tried to reach her, the officer marched her away to the waiting police van.

'Poor sods, I hope they've all got full stomachs, because they'll be on hunger strike once they're in prison,' Gideon heard one woman say as she watched Mary and several others being pushed into the waiting van.

It was accepted practice now amongst those suffragettes imprisoned to refuse to eat any food, Gideon knew, and he also knew that in retaliation the women were being force-fed, often with even greater brutality than was necessary. The thought of Mary undergoing such degradation made him want to break open the police van and secure her freedom, but it was already driving away and a second van taking its place, disgorging a fresh avalanche of uniformed men, who were pushing their way into the crowd and laying about themselves with their truncheons in a way that filled Gideon with disgust and fury.

He tried to remonstrate with one officer.

'Look, mate,' the man snarled at him, 'these bitches are breaking the law, and we've got orders to break them. What kind of man are you, anyway, taking their side?'

Before Gideon could reply the officer had plunged into the crowd of slogan-chanting women.

Tight-lipped, Gideon turned away. Mary's solicitor needed to be told what had happened to her. Gideon wasn't sure of how things would proceed, but there would have to be a court appearance and maybe she would be remanded on bail.

'Quick, Ellie, come this way,' Iris urged as she realised the situation was getting out of control. The arrival of the second vanload of policemen had increased the women's sense of ill-usage, and it seemed the vocalisation of it was causing the new police arrivals to lash out even more violently than before.

To Ellie's shock, right in front of her eyes, a small, shabbily dressed elderly woman, who had done no more than chant a protest, was suddenly seized by a policeman twice her size and dragged away.

'Ellie! This way!' Iris repeated, her experience judging how perilous their position was as she saw just how close to a particularly militant group of women they were.

Ellie turned to follow her, only too glad to leave. The violence that had suddenly erupted out of nowhere had shocked her, but as she turned to obey Iris, Ellie saw a police officer suddenly seize hold of a young girl, who immediately burst into tears and started to cry for her mother.

'Let her go, you bully,' Ellie demanded, her protective instincts to the fore.

His mind on Mary's plight, at first Gideon only vaguely registered the commotion in front of him: the young girl, the police officer, and the young woman pummelling him with her fists, but as he hurried past, something made him stop and look back, his heart turning over as he recognised Ellie.

'Ellie.' He had said her name without even knowing it, just as he had equally unknowingly taken a step back towards her.

'Why, you . . .' The policeman was already making a grab for Ellie when Gideon took a firm hold of her, telling him, 'It's all right, officer, I'll take charge of this one.'

For a second he thought the officer was going to challenge his assumption of authority, but before he could, one of his colleagues called him urgently to assist him, and he turned away, leaving Gideon still holding Ellie.

Silently they stared at one another. Ellie's hair had been dragged from its pins when the policeman had first made a lunge for her. There was a scratch on her cheek and a dirty smudge, but all Gideon could see was the heart-aching delicacy of her face with its huge eyes and soft mouth. Her skin was still as creamy pale as he remembered – and oh, how he did remember.

Ellie couldn't believe her eyes. Gideon. Gideon here. Gideon rescuing her; protecting her!

Silently she greedily absorbed every visual detail of him: the familiar features of his face; the new mature breadth of his shoulders. If she hadn't known, looking at Gideon now she would have assumed that he came from a class well above her own. A class to which he had been elevated via his relationship with Mary Isherwood?

'Ellie . . . oh, thank goodness!' Ellie heard Iris exclaiming, as she took hold of her and bestowed her warm thanks on a still-silent Gideon.

'It was nothing,' he said tersely when Iris continued to thank him.

'On the contrary, it was very much an act of nobility and humanity,' Iris protested warmly. 'Poor Ellie, I am so sorry –'

'If I were you I would make all haste to leave whilst you still can,' Gideon broke in brusquely. 'The police officers are obviously not in any mood to show leniency.'

Ellie noticed that as Gideon spoke he was looking towards the front of the Free Trade Hall where the violence had first broken out, and she could sense that his thoughts and attention were elsewhere. He had obviously not noticed her when he had stepped in to help her. Had he done so, would he still have intervened or would he have left her to her fate?

As he turned to walk away, Ellie saw him glance down at her left hand. Without knowing why she instinctively covered her wedding and engagement ring with her right hand.

One of the first things she had done with the money she had earned from her sewing had been to repossess her mother's ring, and the small stone glinted in the warm sunlight.

420

THIRTY-THREE

Ellie looked up in surprise as she saw Henry coming up the front path. His head was down and his expression concealed from her, but instinctively she knew that he was upset. It was only three o'clock in the afternoon, and he normally did not arrive home until at least seven in the evening. Feeling alarmed, Ellie put down the dress she was altering for one of Iris's friends and went to greet him.

'Henry, is everything all right, only –'

'Ellie, I have just discovered the most dreadful thing.' Henry interrupted her, his voice shaking. 'My father has . . . oh God, Ellie, he has committed the most horrible crime.' And to Ellie's dismay, Henry began to cry, huge dry sobs convulsing his body.

'Henry, please, come and sit down and let me get you something to calm you a little – a cup of tea, perhaps,' she offered soothingly, though her alarm had now turned to sharp fear.

She had been married to Henry for long enough

to recognise that her husband was given to frightening bouts of depression, when he became convinced that the whole world had turned against him. Now, inwardly dreading the thought of Henry sinking into another of his sad moods, she began gently, 'I know how much your father upsets you, Henry. But you –'

'No, you do not understand,' Henry stopped her hoarsely. 'It is not me, Ellie, it is them.'

The wild look in his eyes was increasing her fear. His movements had become agitated and uncoordinated, and he was obviously very disturbed. His face, which had been unnaturally pale, was now burning bright red.

'Henry . . .' she began.

But he refused to listen, crying out despairingly, 'Ellie, my father is a murderer and I cannot bear to know that I am his son . . . that I carry his evil in my blood. Because of him there are women who have been widowed, children who have been orphaned, men who have died the most terrible deaths.' Flinging himself into a chair, Henry buried his face in his hands. 'It is the truth, Ellie. I found out about it today. I had been on an errand and when I returned my father and George were in my father's office. The door was open and . . .'

Blenching, Henry covered his face with his hands and rocked his body to and fro in a state of obvious mental agony. Eventually he calmed sufficiently to explain.

'My father gave orders that one of our ships, the

Antareas, was to be scuttled in the South China Sea, in order that he could claim the insurance monies. News had just come through that the ship had gone down, and my father and my cousin were laughing, boasting about how easy it had been for the captain to do their dirty work for them and pretend to the authorities that the ship had been boarded by pirates and then sunk.

'I knew the second officer on the *Antareas*, and many of the ordinary seamen, and my father has murdered them,' Henry told her brokenly, 'sent them to their deaths for money.'

'Henry, please, you must not upset yourself like this,' Ellie tried to comfort him, but in truth she was as shocked by what Henry had told her as he was himself. 'Are you sure you did not misunderstand your father,' she asked him gently.

Henry sprang up, almost throwing off the caring hand she had placed on his shoulder. 'No. My father convicted himself with his own words. I wish to God he had not.'

Worriedly Ellie asked him, 'Henry, do you think you ought to tell someone? I mean, if your father has –'

'Of course I should!' he responded savagely. 'But how can I? The deed is done and all my reporting the truth of it will do is destroy the business, and us with it, Ellie. I can do nothing, other than suffer the burden of knowing the truth.'

As Henry railed and wept, Ellie tried to make sense of what he was saying.

'I shall sleep in the dressing room for the time being, Ellie,' Henry announced. 'I cannot think of sleeping soundly, knowing what my father has done.' He gave a deep shudder. 'And I do not want to disturb you.'

Silently digesting his statement Ellie knew that she ought to mind more than she actually did.

'And as for my father's desire for a future heir,' Henry continued bitterly, 'let him find himself one amongst my cousin's brats, for he has always considered George to be closer to him than I am. They are two of a kind, and I thank God that I do not have a son to be corrupted into their darkness and greed. A blood sacrifice! Although no sacrifice could ever wash away my father's guilt, not if the South China Sea were a hundred times the size it is.'

Ellie looked a little anxiously over her shoulder for Henry, whilst trying to listen politely to the conversation of her hostess Lady Brocklebank. She and her husband, Sir Aubrey Brocklebank, had invited a large company of their fellow Liverpool shipping line owners to their Cheshire country estate at Nunesmere Hall, ostensibly in order to celebrate the completion of their new home and Sir Aubrey's birthday, but in reality, as Ellie had discovered, so that the gentlemen could discuss the increasing possibility of war with Germany and just how it would affect their business.

'Such a pretty gown, Mrs Charnock,' Grace Brocklebank complimented Ellie with a warm smile, as she admired the dress that, had she but known it, had originally been Cecily's, re-trimmed and altered by Ellie. Thinking of Cecily made Ellie smile as she remembered her visit the previous week to see Cecily and her new baby daughter.

The baby had been so pretty and so sweet that Ellie had not been able to resist picking her up, and when she had, the most unexpected surge of tender maternal love had swept over her.

Not that she was likely to have a child, even if she hadn't taken measures against conceiving. For over a month now, Henry had been sleeping in his dressing room.

Henry – where was he? Ellie's anxiety returned. Her husband had been behaving so oddly lately, alternating between outbursts of truly terrible rage, when he railed furiously against his father, and periods of deep withdrawal, when he refused to speak to anyone.

'Ellie, my love . . .'

Ellie smiled as her hostess moved away to talk to her other guests, to be replaced by her Aunt Parkes. Was it her imagination or was her aunt looking even frailer and less of this world than ever, Ellie wondered worriedly.

She had heard and seen nothing of her Uncle Parkes, and had been too relieved to question why, but then she had learned from Elizabeth Fazackerly, who had quite obviously delighted in passing on the information to her, that her uncle was reported to be spending far more time than his professional services necessitated with a newly widowed client.

For her own sake Ellie was glad that she was no longer the focus of her uncle's unwanted attentions, but at the same time she was forced to acknowledge how unpleasant and humiliating the situation must be for her aunt.

'Really, Ellie, in many ways I am glad that your poor mother is not here to see how ungrateful her children have been – apart from you, of course,' her aunt smiled, patting Ellie's arm fondly. 'According to your Aunt Simpkins, Connie is behaving disgracefully!'

Ellie flushed with a mixture of pain and guilt at the mention of Connie. Connie was still refusing to have anything whatsoever to do with Ellie, despite the many pleading letters she had sent to her, and only Ellie knew how much the gulf between them was hurting her.

'At least *you* have done as your mama would have wished, Ellie, and made an advantageous marriage,' her aunt approved.

Just for a minute Ellie wondered what her aunt would say if she were to tell her just what that advantageous marriage entailed: the hours Ellie had to sit sewing, just to earn enough so-called 'pin money' to keep herself clothed and decently fed – and not just herself. Maisie was also now her responsibility, Mr Charnock having flatly refused to pay her wages any more, claiming that she was useless and should be turned out.

'Have you seen your uncle, by the way, Ellie?'

'I believe that he and the other gentlemen have adjourned to the billiard room,' Ellie replied diplomatically.

She knew that Henry, his father and cousin had accompanied their host and the other shipping magnates to discuss the current political situation, but Ellie was only assuming that Mr Parkes had gone with them, and was not escorting Mrs Nathan Withington, his widowed client and apparently the object of his current attentions, on an exploratory walk of some secluded part of Nunesmere's gardens.

'Oh yes, of course.' Her aunt looked pathetically relieved. 'The gentlemen have much to discuss, I expect.'

'So you think it will definitely come to war, then? I read in *The Times* that Germany is rapidly preparing for war with us. But –'

'There is no doubt about it,' Sir Aubrey confirmed. 'I have it on good authority that it is no longer a matter of *if*, merely *when*, and that is why I have asked you to join me here today, gentlemen. I think I am not exaggerating in saying that between us we represent the pride of Liverpool's mercantile shipping lines.'

There was a chorus of 'Aye's.

'And that being the case, I know you will share with me my concern to protect not just our interests, but also those of our country and our countrymen in the coming confrontation,' he continued sternly. 'That is our duty and it must be our guiding belief!'

'I have heard that you have already secured verbal commitment from those in authority for Brocklebank's to keep essential food supply lines open, if it should ultimately come to war,' one of the other shipowners challenged their host.

'That is indeed so, and I congratulate you on being so well informed. But my endeavours have not been just for my own shipping line, my dear sir, but for all of us. It is important that we all play our roles in this war, gentlemen.'

'Aye, and even more important that we make a good profit from it!' someone else chipped in.

Another rash of handclapping and cheers greeted this comment, quickly shushed by the stern look their host gave them.

'It is all very well to speak amongst ourselves in such terms and, of course, in jest,' he told them, 'but in the eyes of the world it is our patriotism we will want to stress and to be remembered by.'

'Aye, but patriotism is all very well, just so long as it pays,' someone cut in.

'Oh, there is no doubt about that,' Josiah Parkes commented smoothly, 'and I am sure Sir Aubrey will be the first to acknowledge it.'

'Negotiated a good few fat contracts for him,

have you, Parkes?' someone else chuckled knowingly.

'Mr Parkes is not, in actual fact, my solicitor,' Sir Aubrey broke in calmly, 'although he is someone I always prefer to have on my side of the table!'

Everyone laughed, all of them familiar with Josiah's reputation for being an extremely shrewd negotiator.

'But it is true, is it not, Brocklebank,' Jarvis Charnock demanded, 'that you have secured certain promises of contracts to ship necessary food supplies into the country in the event of war being declared? There is a good deal of talk –'

'There is always talk,' Sir Aubrey stopped him.

'Talk, aye,' Jarvis told him aggressively, 'but if there is a profit to be made then it seems only fair to me that we should all have a share in it.'

'It seems to me that there is no reason why we should not combine both our duty to our country and our duty to ourselves and our shareholders to run a profitable business,' Sir Aubrey soothed.

'Well, just so long as we all get a chance to get a slice of the pie, Brocklebank, and it isn't just sliced up between a favoured few . . .' Jarvis Charnock replied belligerently.

THIRTY-FOUR

Gideon cursed as he lost his grip of the pencil he was holding awkwardly in his left hand.

He was working on his accounts and wondering anxiously if he had overstretched himself. The rental income from his properties had turned out to be less than he had anticipated.

His left hand ached from the unfamiliar exercise of writing, but Gideon had no option other than to do his own bookwork. Unlike Mary, he was not in the position to pay someone else to do it for him.

Thinking of Mary caused him to stop work and frown. He had heard that she had been released from prison and that she had returned home in very poor health.

He tried to ignore the unwanted thought that it would cost him nothing to go to see how she did. Why should he, he asked himself irritably, but somehow he found himself pushing his books to one side and standing up.

It was a Saturday evening and already there was

a certain rowdiness about the crowds gathered outside the public houses.

The air was full of summer sunshine and the talk of labour problems and strike action. Men weren't earning enough to keep their families fed, and Gideon had every sympathy with them!

He cut through the market, where they were loading the last of the unsold cheeses onto carts, and then through the streets, past the Co-operative Society's shop, where they were pulling closed the shutters as the final customers left, shawls pulled around their heads despite the heat, clogs clattering on the cobbles. Only the working classes shopped at the Co-operative Society. 'Ladies', like Mary, bought their provisions from Heaney's on the corner of Fishergate and Chapel Street, and Gregson's of Hope Street, famous for its cured hams.

According to Will Pride there had been a falling-off in his brother's business since his marriage to Maggie.

'Too sharp by half, she is – argy-bargied with half of our Rob's customers or more, and fell out wi' 'em!

'Have ye heard about our John?' he had asked Gideon. 'Left Hutton, he has, and gone and got hisself apprenticed to some photographer. Caused a right to-do with Lyddy's stuck-up family! Wanted him to go to be a schoolteacher, they did!'

Will had given an amused snort!

*　　*　　*

Gideon arrived at the house just as the doctor was leaving, and when Mary saw him her pale face lit up immediately.

'I won't stay,' Gideon began.

But Mary overruled him, insisting, 'I have been thinking about you such a lot lately, Gideon, and I am so pleased that you are here. Let's go into my sitting room. I'll ring for tea.'

A little uncomfortably Gideon followed her, noticing as he did so how much weight she had lost since he had last seen her, and how very frail she looked.

Once they reached the sitting room, she sat down, her hand going to her mouth as she began to cough.

'Look, I can see that you aren't well,' Gideon began gruffly. 'I'll leave now and perhaps come back another time.'

'No, Gideon!' Mary protested.

The arrival of the tea tray kept them both silent then, but once the maid had gone, Mary begged him, 'Gideon, please don't go. You don't know . . . I can't tell you how much it means to me to have you here.' To Gideon's embarrassment, tears filled her eyes, and she had to put down the teapot as her hand started to shake.

'Miss Isherwood,' he began awkwardly, 'I –'

'No, please don't call me that,' Mary stopped him fiercely.

She was so obviously overwrought and upset that Gideon's anxiety for her increased, but before he could tell her that he thought she ought to rest, she announced abruptly, 'Gideon, there is something I must tell you. I have tried so many times to do this,' she continued in a low nervous voice. 'I have lain awake at night, rehearsing the words I must say, and trying to imagine –' She stopped and bit her lip, her eyes bright with tears. 'If I don't tell you now, Gideon, it may soon be too late. My doctor has told me that . . . that he believes the weakness in my chest has been exacerbated by my confinement in prison and that there is nothing he can do . . .' Turning her head slightly away from him so that her voice was muffled, she whispered, 'My condition is terminal.'

Gideon couldn't believe what he was hearing. Mary was telling him that she was going to die! A huge surge of angry denial swept over him. But before he could voice it, she was continuing.

'I grew up as a very lonely young woman.' She spoke slowly as though even the effort of talking was tiring for her. 'I was under the rule of an extremely strict and unpleasant father, who made no secret of the fact that he considered me to be a poor substitute for the son he had wished to have.'

She paused, and Gideon's chest tightened as he witnessed her exhaustion. 'You should be resting,' he began.

'No, Gideon, please. I must do this. I have to tell you! My father was a very successful businessman but he was also very suspicious of others. He was

433

a man who could not abide to be outdone by anyone in any way. When one of his fellow mill owners boasted about the portrait he had painted of himself, my father sent for the young artist who had painted it and told him that he wanted him to paint one of him, but, of course, bigger and better than his rival's. The portraitist's name was Richard Warrender.' Mary gave a sad sigh, her mouth trembling.

'I cannot go into details, Gideon. Even now, the pain of speaking about him . . . But he was the most . . . Predictably, I suppose, I fell in love with him, but, not so predictably, he returned my love. I knew, of course, that my father would never agree to us marrying and so we made plans to run away together. I had my mother's jewellery and a small amount of money, and . . . but . . .'

Gideon could hear the emotion in her voice as she pressed her handkerchief to her mouth.

'He deserted you, is that what you are trying to tell me?' he demanded.

The look of anguish in Mary's eyes made him catch his breath.

'In one sense, yes, I suppose you could say that,' she acknowledged. 'You see, there was an accident and Richard was killed. Or at least I was told by my father that there had been an accident.' Her voice shook. 'I have always feared that my father guessed how we felt about one another, and that he was implicated in Richard's death but, of course, I could never have dared to say so, especially when . . . I

434

was so afraid, so alone. I had no one to turn to other than my nurse. She herself was due to be married and was going to leave my father's employ. With her connivance I . . . I managed to escape from this house, and go to London to seek the protection of a great-aunt who lived there.'

'Surely if this Richard was already dead, there was no point in you leaving?' Gideon questioned her bluntly.

Mary lifted her head and looked at him. 'On the contrary, Gideon, there was every point,' she told him quietly. 'You see, I was carrying Richard's child.'

Now she had shocked him and his expression betrayed that shock. But Mary ignored it, pressing on determinedly, 'You were that child, Gideon. My child.'

'No, that's impossible.' Gideon got to his feet, almost overturning his chair in his furious denial of her words. 'My mother . . .'

'Was my nurse,' Mary told him simply. 'When I told my great-aunt of my condition, she suggested that we approach her and ask her and her new husband to accept you as their own. Do not look at me like that, Gideon,' Mary pleaded. 'I had no other option!

'You cannot know how much it hurt me to have to part with you – my child, Richard's son, all that I had left of him – but I was so afraid for you, so afraid from the moment I knew that my father had arranged the death of my beloved Richard, so afraid that he would find out that I was carrying you and that you would be destroyed in turn, either whilst you were still within my body or afterwards, when you had been taken from me at the moment of birth, and I was unable to protect you. I do not exaggerate, Gideon,' she warned him starkly. 'My father was more than capable of such an action. To him you would have been a disgrace, a slur on his public image he could not tolerate.'

Mary stopped speaking, too overcome with emotion to continue, turning her head away from him and, against his will, Gideon felt the sharp burgeoning of an unfamiliar emotion. Not pity, and certainly not understanding, but something sweet and piercing that pushed through the darkness of his furious anger like the green stalks of spring flowers pushing through the winter frost. 'That first time you came here, I so wanted to tell you everything, Gideon, and to claim you as my son, but I was afraid that you would reject me and that if the scandal of our true relationship became public, it would drive us even further apart. You can't know how many times I . . .' she stopped to cough again, but Gideon was oblivious to her distress.

Standing up, he told her violently, 'I do not believe you. How can you be my mother? It is all a lie.' Then, before Mary could say anything further, he wrenched open the door and left.

An hour later Will Pride saw him in The Fleece,

staring bitterly into his empty glass and obviously the worse for wear.

'Eh, Gideon, lad, I thought thee'd given up drinking. In fact, I heard thee 'as become a man o' property,' he added jovially.

Ignoring him, Gideon went up to the bar and bought himself another drink.

Mary Isherwood was not his mother and that tale she had told him was just a pack of lies.

He was drunk when he crawled into his bed two hours later, and he remained drunk for the following three days, whilst war raged inside his head and his heart.

'Henry, please will you try to eat something?' Ellie begged her husband. 'You have barely touched a meal these last three days.' She bit her lip as she looked anxiously at Henry's gaunt face.

'How can I eat,' Henry responded wildly, 'when the men of the *Antareas* are lying dead at the bottom of the sea?'

Ellie put her hand on his arm and asked him, 'Henry, would it not be better if you were to confide in some person, someone of authority your . . . your fears regarding the *Antareas*? If indeed you are right and your father has –'

'If? Do you not believe me then?' Henry raged bitterly. 'If you do not, then why should anyone else? No, I cannot tell anyone. And you must not either, Ellie. You must promise me that. You must speak to no one of what I have told you. No one at all! Do you promise?'

Reluctantly Ellie did as he was insisting, fearing that she might agitate him further if she refused.

'You think that I am deluded,' Henry told her morosely, 'and sometimes I wonder if I am myself. I feel that there is a curse on me at times, Ellie, and that I must pay for the sins of my father.'

'Please don't talk like this, Henry,' Ellie begged him, wishing she had not given him her promise and wishing also that she might confide in Iris and seek her opinion.

Sighing, Ellie broached a subject she had not yet had time to discuss with him.

'Cecily telephoned me today. Her mama-in-law is hiring a house in the Lake District for the rest of the summer, and Cecily is going to go up there with the baby. Iris will go too when she has time and Cecily has invited me to join them. It is to be arranged that the gentlemen, including you, Henry, will drive up to join us when they can –'

'No, no, Ellie, you must not leave me. You cannot. If you do –'

'But, Henry, it will only be for a few days. And –'

'No, no, you must not go.' Henry began to pace the room in agitation, wringing his hands. 'You cannot go, Ellie. Please, I beg you, do not leave me. I cannot bear this house if you are not here. You cannot go and leave me here. You must not. I shall not allow it.'

He started to cry and, suppressing her own disappointment, Ellie went to comfort him, assuring him that she would not accept her cousin's invitation.

It didn't take Gideon very long to walk to Winckley Square, Rex trotting busily at his heels. The maid who answered the door to his knock looked at him in bemusement, but he ignored her flustered response to his arrival, and asked for Mary.

'Miss Isherwood's in her room,' the maid responded unhappily. 'Doctor's orders and . . .' His heart pounding, Gideon told Rex to 'stay' and took the stairs two at a time, rapping briefly on Mary's bedroom door, his stomach clenching as he had to strain to hear her feeble 'Come.'

The look of disbelief and joy suffusing her face when she saw him made him stiffen warily.

'Oh, it's you, Gideon. I thought you must be the doctor. He said he would call this morning. I am so pleased to see you!' Tears filled her eyes and shimmered like rainbows before falling to run down her sunken face.

It shocked Gideon to see how much she had deteriorated in the three days since he was last here, and something twisted painfully round his heart at the thought that he might have been too late. Somehow he found he was standing beside the bed, taking the hand she reached out towards him.

As her thin fingers curled round his, she exclaimed softly, 'You are so like your father, Gideon. Your

439

hands . . .' Her face clouded as she touched his damaged hand. 'I would not have had this happen to you for all the world!' Before he could stop her, she raised his hand to her lips and pressed a maternal kiss against it. 'You have your father's gift, and I wish so much that you and he . . . I have kept all the little drawings you have done for me and put them with your father's sketches. I must show you those . . .' Her eyes misted and Gideon felt his heart lurch against his ribs as her breathing became shallow and laboured.

There was a rap on the door and the maid came in, announcing quietly, 'The doctor is here.'

When the doctor had finished his examination Gideon was waiting downstairs for him.

'Miss Isherwood – how is she?' he demanded.

'Not good, I'm afraid. The damage caused by the force-feeding, combined with an existing weakness . . .' He paused, aware of the tension emanating from Gideon. He had been a doctor for twenty-five years, and this was a part of his job that never got any easier.

'The situation has, I fear, gone too far for an operation, and besides . . .' He looked away from Gideon. Mary had been very specific about her wishes.

There was a small pause in which the ticking of the clock had such a sharp distinctiveness that Gideon wanted to pick it up and hurl it across the room to silence it ticking away the seconds of Mary's life.

'She really is dying, isn't she?' Gideon burst out harshly.

The doctor inclined his head in a brief nod of assent.

'How much . . . how long . . . ?'

'It is hard to say. A week at most, I suspect.'

'A week!' Gideon went grey.

After the doctor had taken his formal leave of him, Gideon made his way upstairs. There was something he had to say to Mary, a decision he had made, which nothing and no one could change.

She was propped up against her pillows, a tiny shrunken figure whose flesh clung tight to the bones of her face. Only her eyes were still her, still Mary.

'You've seen the doctor?' she asked him.

Gideon nodded.

'He says I shall have a week, maybe more, but he is over-optimistic,' Mary told him, giving a small gasp as a rigor of pain shook her body, and she reached for a handkerchief, holding it pressed tight to her mouth as she tried not to cough.

'You must not talk. You must save your strength,' Gideon said, with the gentleness of a son. 'I will stay with you now – until you don't need me any more.'

*   *   *

'Gideon.'

Even though it was almost two o'clock in the morning, Gideon was awake immediately, getting up from the chair where he had been sleeping, to go to Mary's bedside.

Automatically he took the hand she lifted towards him and held it in his own, trying to warm its coldness.

'It's time now, Gideon,' Mary told him softly. 'I can feel it.' Her voice was little more than a breathy whisper, each word a painful effort.

Over these few final shared days she had talked to him continuously, even when he had urged her to save her strength.

'I want to do this, Gideon,' she had told him softly. 'I want to share with you my precious memories of your father and our love, the plans we made.'

Her voice paper thin, she told him now, 'I have made you the main beneficiary of my estate, Gideon. No,' she stopped him when he began to object. 'You do not know how it grieves me even now not to be able to acknowledge you publicly as my son, but I have made a statement to my lawyer telling him of the true relationship between us and of your true parentage. When the time comes and you meet, as I hope you will, the woman you can love as I loved your father, I want you to tell her that I was your mother and that I loved you dearly – so dearly that, for your sake, I chose to give birth to you in secret and hardship instead of taking my own life and yours with it so that I could be with your father. At last I can soon be with him, Gideon. I wonder if he will recognise me, grown old whilst he still has his young handsomeness – and he was so handsome, so gifted. You have his gifts. I have seen it in your drawings . . .

'I pray that when you have a son, Gideon, he will inherit that gift and that you will cherish it in him for your own sake and for your father's.'

She died ten minutes later, her hand clasped between Gideon's, shocking him as she suddenly sat upright in her bed, her whole face transformed with joy, transfixed on something, someone beyond his sight. She trembled as though her whole body was reaching out to a waiting lover.

He saw her great joy as she said his father's name, spending her last breath on it. But he could not see whoever it was she had looked past him to smile at with so much love.

Stiffly Gideon closed her eyes, and kissed her still-warm lips, his voice thick with tears as he whispered to her, 'Goodbye, Mother.'

THIRTY-FIVE

'What a pity it is that Henry will not change his mind and allow you to go and stay with Cecily and my mother,' Iris commented as Ellie kneeled at her feet, pinning the hem of her gown. Iris had brought it round to Ellie announcing that she had torn the hem whilst riding her bicycle.

'I attended a lecture by Annie Kenney this week, Ellie. It made me realise how much has changed in the way we live our lives, even in the short time we have known one another,' Iris commented, adding with candour, 'and you have changed a great deal yourself! You have become a very independent and strong-minded woman, whom I am proud to call my friend, Ellie, and whose opinion in all things I value – especially,' she added with a rueful smile, 'in matters of dress!'

Ellie laughed. 'Well, I am certainly not the same girl who left Preston,' she acknowledged.

'Preston! Oh, I knew there was something I

meant to tell you! How could I have overlooked it? Ellie, the saddest news. You remember Mary Isherwood? She has been one of the movement's longest-standing supporters. I've heard that she has died. She was a neighbour of Cecily's mother's, I know, and Cecily said that according to her mother, the funeral was very quiet, at her own request, and it seems that she has left everything to that young man – what was his name?'

'Gideon Walker,' Ellie told her mechanically.

Her pale face and set expression caused Iris to look queryingly at her, but Ellie ignored the question in her eyes and said expressionlessly, 'I have repinned the hem, Iris, and it shouldn't take me long to repair the tear.'

Once Iris had gone, though, all the emotion Ellie had been forced to suppress surged up inside her. Gideon had, it seemed, been well rewarded for the role he had played in Mary Isherwood's life. An acid feeling of helplessness swirled through Ellie. Gideon . . . Had he ever thought of her when he held Mary in his arms? Had he ever wondered, wanted . . . ? An ache so fierce and sharp that it caught her breath arced through her, a tormenting, fierce thrust of hot female need, unfamiliar and shocking.

Where had that come from – and why? Panic brought tiny beads of perspiration up along her forehead and beneath her breasts.

*   *   *

Gideon stared blindly out of the window and into the garden beyond. It was over. Everything had been done as Mary had desired. Everything! Mary . . . In his thoughts even now she was still Mary, and not . . .

He swallowed and turned and walked up the stairs, pausing before turning the handle of the bedroom that had been hers.

Gideon's hand lay on the bed, flat now without the thinness of Mary's body beneath its covers.

Of course, there had been talk once the news of his inheritance had become public, but he had never once wavered in his determination to keep the truth of their relationship private.

Only he knew how rawly it had rubbed his emotions to open the albums she had left for him, albums that, he realised, she must have taxed herself to prepare during the last months of her illness – filled with her mementoes of his father, his letters to her declaring his love, the little sketches he had drawn for her and which she had treasured, a lock of his hair, as night-dark as his own. He had also discovered, with a surge of shock that had caught his emotions in dragons' teeth of pain, the small baby gown she had given them to dress him in after his birth, a book of prayer in which she had written his name and a blessing for him, and, most painful of all, some rough work sketches he had done for her at various times, on which she had written, obviously for herself and not for him, alongside their date, 'Our son has your gift, my darling one – I pray he may achieve his ambitions, for his sake and for the sake of my own unbearable guilt.'

His ambitions! Well, he would never be an architect, but he was wealthy – extremely wealthy, in fact.

But his wealth was not a ripe juicy fruit whose flavour one wanted to linger on the tongue. Instead it held a tainting bitterness.

It was too soon yet for him to admit to himself how much he yearned for Mary, how much he yearned to be able to share with her the relationship they had both been denied, and so instead he directed his pain towards that segment of the town's matrons, especially those with marriageable daughters, who had suddenly decided that he was now socially worthy of their recognition.

He would never find the love Mary had told him she wanted him to have; he would never find it because he did not believe it existed! One day, no doubt, he would marry – he was now a man of property and means, after all, and as such it behoved him to provide himself with a son or two to pass it on to – but his wife, when he came to choose one, would be picked as carefully and clinically as a shepherd choosing his breeding stock. Of course, there were those who deliberately shunned him, despite his newly acquired wealth, and one of them was Mary's neighbour Dr Gibson's wife, and Ellie Pride's aunt.

Gideon wondered what it was that gave the Barclay sisters such an elevated idea of themselves.

In the town's social pecking order, Mary had ranked a good couple of rungs higher up the ladder than Amelia Gibson. However, there was no disgrace greater than that of a young woman bearing an illegitimate child, and he, as that child, must carry the same stigma! In the eyes of the town's matrons it was better that he should be thought of as Mary's secret lover than her son, and he knew that if Amelia knew the truth she would consider that she had even more reason to shun and ostracise him!

'Henry, please try to understand I have to go and see Connie,' Ellie pleaded across the dining-room table. She had had to wait until Henry had returned from business to tell him of her shock at receiving a tear-stained letter from Connie, begging her sister to help her, and to send her some money, and going on to give her the even more shocking news that she had left their aunt and uncle's home and was presently living in rented accommodation secured for her by 'a friend'.

'Connie would not have written to me if she was not in the direst of circumstances. I have let her down so badly in the past, Henry, I cannot do so again.'

'Ellie, you must not go. You must not leave me here alone with my father. I cannot bear it if you do,' he told her wildly.

'Henry, it will not be for very long,' Ellie soothed

him. 'I shall get the train in the morning and I shall be back before dinner. You will be working, and I shall be home before you return. I must see Connie, Henry,' Ellie told him desperately. 'She needs my help.'

Henry was giving her a peevish look that made her heart sink.

'Henry, I *must* go to Connie,' Ellie persisted pleadingly. 'I cannot let her down again.'

Henry was refusing to answer her, and had not asked her one single thing about Connie or what had happened.

Of course, the moment she had read Connie's letter Ellie had telephoned her Aunt Simpkins, and received the angry disclosure that Connie's 'friend' was probably the most unsuitable young man she had been seeing in direct disregard of her aunt and uncle's wishes.

'He is a young Irishman of the wildest kind of reputation, and a Catholic!'

Ellie's heart had sunk. Whilst, in the main, Catholic and Protestant families in Preston lived amicably with one another, the two religions were strictly segregated and their respective clergy frowned upon them leaving their own faith to marry members of the other, and for Connie, from a strict High Church Protestant family, to have anything whatsoever to do with a young man who was a Catholic was extremely shocking. Protestant girls knew that the only thing Catholic boys wanted from them was the sex they would never be allowed with good Catholic girls, and, because of that, good Protestant girls naturally refused to have anything to do with Catholic boys.

Unhappily Ellie studied her husband's hunched back. She had to help Connie. And, if necessary, she would go to Preston to see her without Henry's permission!

Ellie's head was aching when she got off the train in Preston. Henry had refused to speak to her over breakfast, and had left for the office in a huff.

They were having the hottest August Ellie could remember, and she could feel the perspiration trickling between her breasts as she hurried through the dusty heat of Preston's streets.

All the newspapers were carrying warnings that there were soon to be strikes, and she could see the sombre groups of men huddled together here and there, obviously deep in serious discussion. Ellie had every sympathy with the men, although she would never have dared say so in her father-in-law's presence.

As she hurried through the streets, Ellie recognised that the town had a sullen, sulphurous atmosphere about it which, at any other time, would have alarmed her. This was not the Preston she knew and loved. Trickles of angry-eyed, grim-faced men and women had begun to percolate through the streets, and a crowd was gathering in the market area, but Ellie was too concerned about Connie to pay them much attention. Ellie skirted past the market as she headed for the area close to the docks where Connie had written that she was now living.

As she drew closer to the docks area, Ellie wrinkled her nose fastidiously at the pungent smell wafting along the street, and then gathered her skirt close in to her body with a small gasp as she saw the grey shadow running along the gutter. A rat!

It couldn't be much further now, surely. The streets had become narrow and more squalid-looking, and as she walked past a group of children squatting on the pavement, she heard the clatter of the handful of small stones one of them had thrown after her. Children's foolishness, that was all, and yet suddenly she felt threatened and vulnerable. Deliberately she refused to quicken her pace or show any panic. Preston was her home. She had grown up, if not in these particular streets, then those of Friargate and Fishergate and the market area. She was a Prestonian through and through, just the same as those urchins glowering sullenly at her, and proud to be one!

Grimly, Gideon looked at the faces of the two young people standing in front of him. The last person he had expected to see when he had called at the property his mother had rented out, to find out why the rent had not been paid, was Ellie Pride's sister Connie, and still less had he expected to see her with Bill Connolly's nephew Kieron.

451

Connie's face was streaked with tears, her expression one of fear and defiance, her hands wrapped possessively and determinedly around Kieron's broad forearm as she stood close to him.

Kieron, on the other hand, a sturdy six-footer with a shock of overlong dull black hair, a stubborn jaw and a dangerous temper, looked uncomfortable and ill at ease.

'Look, Mr Walker, don't say anything to me uncle, will ye? I mean about us being here, like.'

'It won't need me to tell him, for him to find out that you're shacked up here with a Protestant, will it, Kieron?' Gideon pointed out bluntly. 'And when he does find out . . .'

It was no secret that Bill Connolly ruled his children and those of his brothers with his belt, and that no child of his or theirs was too big or too old to feel it against their backsides if he felt that they deserved it.

Gideon had walked into the Connollys' kitchen one night to talk business with Bill only to find his eldest daughter bent over a chair, her naked buttocks exposed and already livid with bruises and stained with blood, screaming her head off whilst Bill wiped his belt clean and cuffed her head, whilst telling her not unaffectionately, 'Ah, stop yer noise now, our Maureen. Sure, and you know you had it coming to ye, and ye got off lightly 'cos I've got a soft spot for ye, God help me. But when the priest comes round and tells me that he's heard a rumour that a daughter of mine has been fornicating . . .'

'I wasn'a, Da. I wasn'a,' Maureen had sobbed. 'He's telling lies. He's a dirty rotten liar, that Father O' Malley. All the girls know what he's like, always slipping his hand up their skirts, and –'

A sharp scream had splintered the air as Bill had brought his belt down across her buttocks again.

'Go and wash your mouth out wi' soap, girl,' he had roared. 'No way will a daughter of mine speak so disrespectfully of a man of the cloth!'

Oh yes, Bill Connolly had very strong views about how his family ought to conduct themselves, and no way would he allow one of its members to live over the broomstick with a Protestant girl.

But it was Connie's behaviour that had really surprised Gideon. For a girl of her upbringing and family to do what she had done meant that their reputation was completely ruined.

How were Ellie and her hoity-toity family going to feel when they discovered that Connie had been thrown out into the gutter for not paying her rent, and by him?

However, he gave no hint of the cynical delight he was feeling, the pleasurable sense of antici-pation, as he removed some papers from his pocket and said curtly, 'Well, well, if it isn't Miss Connie Pride. I take it it is still Miss Connie Pride and not –' he began.

But Connie stopped him, her face on fire as she burst out angrily, 'Kieron and I are to be wed just as soon as it can be arranged.'

'Really?' Gideon turned enquiringly towards Kieron. 'Is this true, Kieron?'

'Of course it's true,' Connie stormed, stamping her foot. 'You don't think for one minute that I would be living here if it wasn't, do you?'

'Well, as to that, your morals are not my concern, Miss Connie, but according to my records this house is let to a Miss Byerly, a respectable schoolteacher.'

Immediately, Connie's chin tilted, her eyes darkening with defiance. Tossing her head she told him, 'Miss Byerly was the name of a teacher at my school. I borrowed it when I rented this house.'

'You borrowed it? Well, you might have been better employed "borrowing" enough money to pay your rent,' Gideon told her pithily. 'You do realise that it is three weeks behind, don't you?'

'Three weeks? I have only been here a week!'

'The rent agreement calls for an advance payment of two weeks' rent, which has not yet been paid according to my reckoning, and although I might not have had the advantages of your posh schooling, Miss Pride, I can still reckon up. It means that you owe me three weeks' rent.'

'You aren't my landlord,' Connie objected. 'I have rented this house from Florentine Estates,' she told him, tossing her head again.

'Aye, so you have, and for your information I am now Florentine Estates. But enough of this. Either you pay me the rent you owe me, or you pack your things and leave.'

'I can't pay you – not now. I don't have the money, but I shall have it . . . soon. Can't you give me another couple of days? I promise you I shall have the money.'

Gideon's eyes narrowed. He had heard enough liars to know when he was being told the truth. Connie obviously believed that she was going to be able to pay the rent, even if he had serious doubts.

Mary would, in such circumstances, he suspected, have done her utmost to return Connie to her family, with discretion so her reputation remained unstained, and no more said about the matter, other than reminding Kieron Connolly that it was something far more punishing than his uncle's belt about his backside he was likely to feel if he continued to behave as he was doing. The Connollys married amongst themselves, and Gideon suspected that a suitable Catholic wife would already have been picked out for Kieron, and Connie's association with him, however far it had gone, could only lead to disgrace and shame for her.

But Gideon was not his mother, and there was a certain sweet satisfaction in looking into Connie's undeniably pretty but sullen face and visualising inside his head the haughty expression on the face of her sister and her mother when they had both rejected him.

'Very well then,' he agreed. 'I'll give you another two days, but if you can't pay the rent by then,

Connie, don't ask me for any further licence, for there won't be any.'

Ellie gave a small overheated sigh of relief as she finally turned into the street where her sister was living. Number sixteen – that would be on the opposite side to where she was standing and down a way . . .

Gideon didn't know why he should suddenly feel impelled to turn round and retrace his steps. It certainly wasn't out of any charitable desire to help the young couple he had just left, but something made him do it, and as he did he suddenly froze as he saw Ellie.

She hadn't seen him, and he intended to make sure she did not do so as he fell back into the shadows and watched her hurry towards the house he had just left.

Anxiously, Ellie knocked on the door, surprised to find it suddenly flung open and to hear her sister crying, 'You promised you would give me more time,' before Connie realised that it was Ellie who was standing there and flung herself into Ellie's arms in a flood of tears.

'Connie, Connie, what on earth is going on?' Ellie demanded when she had managed to calm her down a little, stopping speaking abruptly when the parlour door opened and she saw Kieron.

'Ellie, don't look like that,' Connie begged her. 'Kieron and I are engaged. We are to be married.' She gabbled the words as she made a grab for Kieron's hand and held it tightly.

Like Gideon, Ellie was immediately aware of Kieron's discomfort and her heart sank.

'Connie, you made no mention of any plans to marry in the letter you sent me,' she reminded her sister. 'You said –'

'I know what I said, Ellie, but that was because I knew what you would think! Ellie, please, you've got to help us. There's no one else we can turn to. Our aunt and uncle just don't understand. They have forbidden me to see Kieron and –'

'Yes, I know. I have spoken to our aunt.'

The situation was every bit as Aunt Simpkins had predicted, Ellie recognised, if not even worse! Cravenly, she tried to avoid looking at the young man standing at Connie's side, but of course his presence could not be ignored.

A little nervously she began, 'Connie, your friend –'

'Kieron is not my friend,' Connie stopped her immediately. 'He is my fiancé. We are in love with one another, Ellie, and we are determined to be married, no matter what our families say!' She added fiercely, 'And his family are every bit as bad as my aunt and uncle. We love one another! Why should we be forced apart just because of some stupid old religion? I don't care what religion

Kieron is. I love him and I will die if I can't be with him, Ellie.'

It was all very well for Connie to say how she felt, Ellie reflected unhappily. She could see plainly enough that her sister was besotted with her young man, but Ellie was disquietingly aware that he had said nothing to indicate that he shared the intensity of her feelings. Had he been the one to suggest that Connie left home or had it all been Connie's idea?

'Is what Connie says true, Kieron?' Ellie asked him quietly. She might merely be Connie's sister, rather than her parent, but right now it behoved her to take on the role of her protector as well.

'Well, I am very fond of her, of course –' he began uncomfortably.

Ellie stopped him. 'No, actually, Kieron, what I meant was, do your parents also disapprove of the . . . friendship between the two of you, as Connie has already implied?'

A dark guilty colour burned up over his face. 'Well, they would do, that's for sure, if I were to tell 'em, especially my Uncle Bill. Oh Lord, Connie, if Gideon Walker should tell my uncle or my da, I shall be in for it good and proper,' he suddenly burst out, ignoring Ellie to turn towards Connie.

Gideon Walker! Ellie froze. She told herself it was the heat and the lack of air in the small stuffy parlour that caused her to lift her hand to her throat, but in reality she knew her sudden rush of dizziness had a very different cause.

'Ellie, you must help us. You must,' Connie was pleading, thankfully too wrapped up in her own emotions to be aware of Ellie's reaction. 'Gideon has threatened to throw me out in the street if I do not pay the rent. I did have the money but someone stole it from me and Kieron has none. I can't go back to our aunt and uncle . . . I can't!'

'Oh Connie!' Ellie lifted her hand to her head, too distressed to know what to say. 'If Mama could see or hear you now –' she murmured.

'Mama?' Connie cut her off with a bitter laugh. 'Well, you might let Mama rule your life from the grave, Ellie, but I am not so stupid. Mama had her life and made her own choices. She wanted to marry our father, and so she did. Well, I want to marry Kieron and that is exactly what I intend to do, and no one is going to stop me! No one!'

Ellie was too shocked to speak for a few seconds. 'Connie, you cannot stay here,' she protested, when she felt able to do so. 'Not on your own, and most certainly not with . . . with anyone else,' she finished stiffly. Why should she feel embarrassed? She was the one who was a married woman, not Connie, who was standing there looking at her as bold as brass.

Was it already too late? Had Connie already given herself to this young man she claimed to be in love with? If she had, then surely for Connie's sake they should be insisting that Kieron Connolly married her as soon as decently possible. If only things were different and she could take Connie back to Liverpool with her, but Ellie knew how her father-in-law would react if she did so! If only Iris was not in the Lake District and she could seek her wise counsel.

Ellie took a deep breath and then said firmly, 'Connie, you cannot stay here. It isn't fitting. I will take you to Friargate and ask our father if you can stay there until some other arrangements can be made. And as for you, young man,' she continued, turning to Kieron and catching the look of relief on his face that made her heart ache for her vulnerable sister, 'I suggest that before involving my sister in any further underhand deceit you seek the permission of both your own family and hers to pay your addresses to her!'

'Pay his addresses? Ellie, you sound like a stuffy, starchy old book,' Connie burst out. 'Kieron and I are in love, did you not listen to me? We do not need the approval of either our families or our Churches to be together,' she continued wildly. 'And neither you nor anyone else can part us! We shall run away together to Gretna Green and get married.'

'Connie,' Ellie protested, shocked, 'I realise that you are distressed, but you cannot mean what you are saying.'

'I do mean it. I do,' Connie wept. 'And I hate you, Ellie. I hate you. I thought you would help me and all you're doing is lecturing me and being horrid.'

Her sister, Ellie recognised, was working herself up into one of her tantrums.

Firmly Ellie reached for her arm. 'Connie, please stop this nonsense immediately. You are over-wrought, and –'

Ellie gasped as Connie pulled away from her and ran up the stairs before Ellie could stop her, locking herself in one of the bedrooms.

'Connie, please,' Ellie protested.

'Go away, Ellie. I'm not coming with you!' Connie screamed. 'I'm staying here and I shan't come out until you leave. You can't make me go with you. You are only my sister. And, any-way, Kieron and I are already as good as man and wife.'

Shocked, Ellie turned to look at Kieron Connolly. He could not meet her eyes, and Ellie's stomach lurched.

'I think you had best leave,' Kieron told her uncomfortably. 'I'll speak to her; try to persuade her to go to her da's.'

'She cannot stay here,' Ellie told him fiercely, adding bitterly, 'How could you have done this to her?'

'It was not all my doing,' Kieron told her wood-enly. 'I tried to tell her that this wasn't a good idea, but she wouldn't listen. She'll be much better off wi' her da, but she'll still have to pay the rent here. Gideon Walker has already been round demanding it. He's given her two days to find it.'

'How much is it?' Ellie asked.

When he told her she opened her purse and counted out the exact money, and then took it

461

upstairs and pushed it under the locked bedroom door, along with a few extra shillings.

'This is the money for your rent, Connie,' she told her sister through the closed door. 'And a little extra for some food.'

There was no answer. Back downstairs, she begged Kieron, 'Promise me you will persuade her to go to our father's? It's plain she will not listen to me, but you must know she cannot stay here. If you will take my advice you will end this relationship whilst it can still be ended – unless, of course, I have misunderstood the situation and you do really want to marry my sister, in the face of both your families' disapproval?'

'I canna marry to disoblige me uncle. 'Tis himself who gives us all work – me, me da and the others. I never said nothing about marriage to Connie,' he whispered angrily. ''Twas all her idea and doing, that. All I wanted was just a bit o' fun. Connie's up to all the tricks; she knows what life's all about. We were having a grand time until she got this idea that she was in love with us,' he complained.

Ellie closed her eyes, torn between wanting to stay to provide her sister with the comfort she knew she was going to need, and fearing that if she did, she would only provoke Connie into even more indiscretion. Ellie had every confidence that Kieron Connolly would persuade Connie to go to Friargate, even if it would be more for his own sake than poor Connie's.

And right now she needed some far wiser counsel than her own to decide what was the best course of action to protect her sister from her own recklessness. As she glanced up the stairs, Ellie acknowledged how helpless she felt and how much she longed for the strong support of the kind of husband she could turn to in such a crisis, in the way that Cecily would have been able to turn to Paul, were she in such a position.

'I'm going now, Connie,' she called, hesitating in the hope that her sister might see sense and agree to leave with her, but knowing Connie as she did, Ellie was not really surprised when she made no reply.

THIRTY-SIX

Gideon watched as Ellie left the house and started to walk up the street. She still had that same proud air about her, her nose stuck in the air as though she thought herself better than anyone else, and her with a sister living over the brush with a man who would desert her the minute his uncle told him to!

He hadn't intended to wait for her to leave, never mind to follow her. It was simply that she was walking in the same direction as he himself had planned to go.

There was a sultriness in the air now, a brassy sulphurousness that made the tiny hairs at the nape of Ellie's neck prickle as she made her way along the deserted streets.

At least they were deserted until she turned a corner and saw up in front of her how the street ahead was blocked by a huge press of people making their way towards the marketplace. Some of them were carrying placards protesting about working conditions, and some were simply chanting slogans about better pay, but it was obvious that their mood was one of angry defiance.

As Ellie hesitated, she was jostled from behind by a group of millworkers, the women dressed in clogs and shawls, the looks they gave Ellie, in her summer walking dress, ones of open hostility.

Apprehensively, Ellie looked for a means of discreet escape, but the street was becoming even more crowded.

'Watch out, they've sent up to the barracks for some troopers,' Ellie heard someone call out, and suddenly there was a stampede of people hurrying past her, a huge surge of humanity that threatened to overwhelm her. Suddenly she was sixteen again, terrified of being trampled by the crowd of sightseers out to watch the Guild procession. The same unreasoning panic filled her – and then the same strong arm was reaching out to pluck her from danger.

Gideon! Dazed, Ellie stared up at him, unable to drag her gaze away from his face.

'Gideon . . .' She breathed his name and swayed.

'Damn you, Ellie, you can't faint now,' Gideon ground out. 'If you do we'll both be trampled underfoot. Didn't you hear the warning? They've sent for the troopers, and they won't stop to recognise Miss Ellie Pride amongst all this lot. Come on, hurry up, we've got to get out of here whilst we still can.'

Grabbing hold of her arm, he started to force a

way through the angry crowd, dragging Ellie with him. Somewhere behind them she could hear what at first she thought was thunder, and then realised was the sound of horses' hoofs, followed by shouts and screams and then a burst of gunfire.

'Down here.'

Ellie almost lost her balance as Gideon tugged her down a narrow ginnel filled with evil-smelling rubbish so acrid that the stench made her stomach heave. A filthy clutter of broken-down hovels, another back entry, and they were out into Fishergate, and somehow Gideon was battling a way through the panic-stricken crowd, now a seething mass of people all trying to move in different directions to escape from the police and the troopers.

The angry roar of the crowd faded as Gideon ducked into a narrow alleyway, and Ellie drew a sobbing breath of relief as she recognised where she was and knew that they were in a cut-through that eventually would take them to Winckley Square.

In the distance she could hear again the sound of gunfire and she winced. Despite her fear, her sympathy lay entirely with the crowd. Her cheekbone stung from an accidental blow, and the hem of her dress was dusty, her sleeve torn.

As Gideon bundled her through the alleyway he was standing so close to her she could smell the hot male scent of him. Henry always seemed to smell of dry, papery air as dried out as their sexless marriage, an empty husk within which her own femaleness had withered. Gideon, on the other hand, smelled of heat and life and . . .

Ellie closed her eyes and valiantly fought off what she was feeling.

At last they were in Winckley Square.

'Thank you for . . . for helping me,' she began primly. 'I shall make my way to the station now, for my train and –'

'Are you mad?' Gideon stopped her harshly. 'There is no way you can do any such thing right now. It's far too dangerous. I reckon it will be morning before the streets are quiet and safe enough for you to leave.'

'Morning . . . ? But I can't stay here. My aunt is away and the house is closed up, and even if I could get back there, I somehow doubt that Connie would give me a bed for the night. She told me that you are her landlord, by the way.'

'She rented the place under a false name, and from my . . . from Mary Isherwood's landlord, and not from me,' Gideon told her tersely.

Mary . . . Ellie bit her lip and lowered her head. 'I was sorry to hear about her death,' she said awkwardly, her face flushing as she tried not to think about the relationship that gossip said had existed between Gideon and the older woman. 'My friend Iris greatly admired Miss Isherwood for her work for the suffragette movement.'

'Your friend – would that be the woman you were with in Manchester?'

'Yes,' Ellie acknowledged. It seemed so odd in

one way to be talking to him like this, and yet in another it seemed so natural ... so right. 'She is Cecily's sister-in-law. What was that?' she demanded, jumping as she heard a sudden crash close at hand.

'By the sound of it a stone being thrown through a window,' Gideon responded tersely.

Ellie gasped as an unruly mob burst into the square.

'Quick. This way,' Gideon commanded, hurrying her across the road.

For a moment Ellie held back, but the press of people pouring into the square was frightening; the noise they were making drowning out whatever it was Gideon was trying to say to her, and instinctively Ellie moved closer to him. In the distance she could hear artillery fire. Gideon was unlocking the door of a house and urging her inside.

As Ellie hesitated, half a dozen troopers rode into the square in pursuit of the mob, who retaliated by throwing stones. As Ellie heard the retaliatory sound of their artillery fire, she acknowledged unwillingly that Gideon was right. It wasn't safe for her to be on the streets. The mood of the demonstrators had turned ugly.

He took the decision out of her hands by slamming the door shut, enclosing them both in the heavy silence of the house.

'I'm afraid I can't offer you anything much by way of refreshment,' Gideon was saying to her, suddenly very much the formal host.

His manner made her aware of how much more sophisticated and cultured a man he now was, compared to the one she had fallen in love with.

'It's rent-collecting day,' he continued, 'and I've given everyone the day off. There's no point in having half a dozen servants rattling around here with nothing to do, but I dare say I could rustle up a cheese sandwich and a cup of tea, if you could bring yourself to eat such lowly fare. I suppose it's all mulligatawny soup and champagne for you these days . . . Mrs Charnock,' he taunted her, suddenly reviving the enmity between them.

Ellie almost laughed out loud. The soup served in the Charnock household was homemade by herself from her own vegetables, and as for champagne . . .

This house, although perhaps not much larger than the Charnock mansion, was so much more elegantly appointed and decorated, so much more refined and tasteful. It was a woman's house, though, Ellie recognised, decorated and furnished with a woman's delicate eye.

'I'll show you into the drawing room,' Gideon said, and then as she turned away from him he exclaimed sharply, 'What the devil . . . ?' and his left hand was on her face, turning it into the light whilst he frowned down at her swollen cheekbone.

'It is just a bruise, nothing more,' Ellie told him lightly, trying to pull away.

'It is not just a bruise,' Gideon corrected her grimly. 'The skin is broken and the wound has to be cleaned, unless, of course, you wish to risk it becoming infected. It needs to be attended to immediately. Come with me, please . . .'

Ellie lifted her hand to her cheek, dismayed to see blood on her fingertips when she removed them. She had been aware of her face stinging, but she had not realised the extent of the injury. She had listened to Iris enough to know the dangers of heat and unsanitary conditions on open wounds. Apprehensively, she followed Gideon up the stairs.

He showed her into a bedroom and instructed her curtly to wait whilst he brought a basin of water and a medical chest.

Left on her own, Ellie studied her surroundings. The bedroom was obviously a guest room and simply but elegantly furnished. Every surface shone with cleanness and polish, and if she hadn't grown as fond of Maisie as she had, and as defensively protective of her, Ellie suspected she could well have cried to compare the standard of Gideon's servants' abilities with that of her own. This room revealed a house that breathed care and attention, and as Ellie had learned both from living with her aunt and uncle, and from her own marriage, in a house of this size, that meant one simple thing: it was owned by a person of considerable means.

Mary's means.

Which were now Gideon's means.

Ellie could feel the turmoil and agitation of her emotions and thoughts driving her into feverish distress.

Her Uncle Parkes kept as a mistress a woman

who, despite being a widow, was many years younger than he was himself, and the situation was not just tolerated but accepted by his peers. And by her aunt, if she was honest, Ellie admitted, since it meant that he no longer besieged her, but the thought that Mary, a woman who had been born around the same time as her own mother, Ellie had concluded from what she had heard, should take as her lover a man of Gideon's age filled Ellie with such feelings that she was pacing the bedroom floor, hardly able to contain them. Any man of Gideon's age – or were her feelings just restricted to Gideon himself?

'I have found some salve for the cut and some arnica, which should ease the bruising.'

The sound of Gideon's voice had Ellie turning round to face him.

He had removed his jacket and his collar. The top button of his shirt was unfastened and the sleeves rolled back.

A bewildering feeling of agonising longing and bleakness engulfed her, dizzying her, and automatically Ellie put her hand to the bed behind her to steady herself.

As she did so, there was a loud burst of artillery fire from the top end of the square, and even though it wasn't possible for her to see it from the window, she looked automatically towards it, her whole body suddenly starting to shake.

It had been a day of distressing realisations, and they weren't over yet. Although she had chastised

Connie for her behaviour, wasn't there a part of her that secretly envied her sister her boldness; her strength of will when it came to laying claim to her right to be with the man she loved?

A day? Hadn't she had weeks, months, a marriage of unsettling and depressing discoveries, Ellie asked herself miserably, lifting her hand to her pounding head as she tried to ease the dizziness swelling inside it. She was too hot, her body suddenly drenched in perspiration. Her hand went automatically to the tightly closed neck of her gown, her eyes closing as she moaned and swayed slightly.

'Ellie!' Putting down the bowl and the unguents he was carrying, Gideon went immediately to her.

Her face had completely lost its colour, the sharp delicate line of her high cheekbones almost cutting through the fine skin, whilst a dew of dampness lay around her forehead, tightening the soft curls of her hair.

Her face had lost its youthful plumpness, Gideon told himself critically as he reached her, but against his will he was forced to acknowledge that its loss had added to rather than taken away from her beauty.

As she sagged towards the bed he could see the soft dark sweep of her lashes, and the mauve shadows beneath them.

She must not, she would not faint, Ellie told herself dizzily, but already she could hear the roaring

472

in her ears and feel the blackness rushing to suck her into it.

Ellie could hear something thudding, the noise reverberating through her body. It took her several seconds to realise that the sound was her own heartbeat.

She was crying, she recognised, as she lifted her hand to her face to check the source of the slow seep of moisture she could feel against her skin, but not with physical pain! No, her tears were for . . . were because . . .

A sound – a breath, no more, but somehow enough to shock right through her body – had her struggling to sit up as full consciousness came flooding back to her. Gideon was standing beside the bed, frowning down at her, in one hand a glass of water, which he put down on the night stand.

'Don't move,' he warned her tersely.

'I'm perfectly all right,' she snapped back at him. And to prove her point, she sat bolt upright, then froze as she realised that Gideon had released the tightly buttoned neck of her gown right down to her chemise.

'How dare you? You had no right,' she began, her voice trembling. So too were her hands as she tried and failed to refasten the buttons.

'What would you have preferred me to do?' Gideon challenged her sharply. 'You needed air. I can never understand why females insist on wearing clothes that –'

He broke off, a dark surge of colour seeping up along his jaw and burning his cheekbones. The same way that the smouldering heat of how he was looking at her semi-naked breasts was burning her skin, Ellie recognised.

'Don't . . .' Don't look at me like that, she had been about to say, but the words were trapped in her throat, and as though in a dream she watched as Gideon reached out towards her.

His fingertips brushed the buttons of her gown. Ellie held her breath. She was shivering, despite the heat, her whole body a mass of tiny quaking movements, little rigors of sensation and expression.

'Ellie . . .'

Gideon ground out her name as though his throat was being tortured by a million shards of broken glass. The side of his thumb touched her breast – an accident surely, and not a caress, and then suddenly – so suddenly that she couldn't have moved away even if she had wanted to – his hands were on her waist and his head was bent over her, the dark hair she remembered so well brushing her throat and the tip of her chin as she bent her head in silent anguish whilst his lips pressed a kiss that was a mixture of violent anger and sensuality against the exposed curve of her breast.

Her hands lifted to his shoulders. His muscles felt solid and thick, and the flesh covering them hot and firm beneath the thinness of his shirt, burning her fingers as she curled them into it, to push him away.

Jarvis Charnock, returning from work, stared in loathing and contempt at his son, who had come out into the heat, seemingly to confront him.

'What ails you, or do I need to ask? God damn you, Henry, you are no son of my getting, I'll swear to it. You are your wretched mother's son through and through! Every time I look at you I am reminded of her. God knows why I ever married her in the first place.'

'I know what you did, Father,' Henry burst out passionately. 'I know that you arranged the deaths of all those men on the *Antareas*. And because of that, because of you, I have their blood on my hands too. I can never wash it away . . . never. Never be free of its taint . . .'

As he started to weep in great choking sobs, holding up his hands in front of himself as though he could actually see blood on them, Jarvis looked at him in disgust.

'Do you know what I think, Henry?' He leaned closer to him, jabbing his forefinger in his son's face to emphasise his hatred of him as he spoke. 'I think it's a great pity that you weren't on that ship with the rest of that worthless scum, because if you had been, by now your bones would be lying bleached clean on the bottom of the South China Sea. And I wish to God they were!'

Henry groaned. He was a failure, as a man and as a husband. He had done so much that was weak and wrong, and left undone so much that he should have done. Slowly, he started to make his way back to the house. Bleak despair filled him. He knew what he had to do.

THIRTY-SEVEN

Ellie breathed in and her senses swam under the power of Gideon's proximity. How was it possible with just one breath to be transported back to a time – a feeling – she had long ago believed she had completely obliterated from her memory?

To stop them from trembling she pressed her fingertips hard into his flesh, but that only made the tremors race down her arms, then along her veins and the innermost pathways of her body like molten heat.

She felt the brush of his hair against her oversensitive flesh as he raised his head. He was looking at her, and somehow she felt compelled to look back, their gazes meshing.

'Gideon,' she whispered, her voice laden with longing.

She was looking at him as though no other man had ever touched her, Gideon acknowledged dizzily, as though she had longed and hungered for him, as though he was the only man . . .

Anger licked searingly through him. Did she think she was deceiving him? Was it amusing her to look at him so, her eyes all wanton, hungry need, whilst her mouth trembled for his kiss, as though she was afraid of her own reaction?

His little actress friend, a woman he'd been seeing for a few months now, could never rival such a performance.

She had to leave this house, to escape whilst she was still capable of leaving – Ellie knew that. How could she face Connie, or herself, if she did not? But instead of obeying the frantic urgency of her thoughts, her fingers were instead curling into Gideon's shirt, clutching at him to draw him closer instead of thrusting him away. She drew a deep breath that exposed the slender column of her throat and lifted her breasts against the thinness of her chemise.

Gideon's gaze was drawn to her body, along the tender white exposed line of flesh, down to where the dark flush of her nipple was a tormenting shadow just discernible beneath the fine fabric. He wanted to reach out and touch it, pluck at it and feel it swell and harden between his fingertips. He wanted to roll it between his finger and thumb, and to ease her breasts free of her gown so that he could feast his eyes on them – his eyes and his lips; his tongue, savouring their texture, their tenderness, their responsiveness to him as he slowly sucked them into his mouth.

Beneath the thin covering of her chemise Ellie

could feel her nipples swelling and aching, hard eager nubs of longing, filled with a wantonness, a knowing that shook her and shocked her. It was as though a fire, a fever, had suddenly spilled through her, licking along her body like wine, lapping at every most sensitive part of it.

Reality faded and time rolled back to a summer's day on the river, and the exciting, dangerous intimacy that had followed it, the discovery of her womanhood, the sharing of their feelings for one another and the declaration of their love.

Somehow she was that girl again, and Gideon that young man, only now a part of her recognised that she was also a woman – a woman who out of duty and love for her mother had cheated herself – her senses, her emotions, her body, her very womanhood – of experiencing fulfilment, of meeting a need so strongly rooted within her and so ferociously suppressed that, now it had turned the tide on her, she was overwhelmed with its intensity.

Gideon – his scent, his feel, his reality – was all the more dangerous because of her own denial.

She wanted him, Ellie recognised, with all the youthful passion of the girl she had been, and she wanted him too with the hungry intensity of the woman she had become – whose marriage was based on compassion and pride and duty.

'Gideon!'

When she said his name he lifted his head to look at her, his eyes darkening as he recognised the desire in hers. Her mouth was soft, her lips parted and inviting. Anger and longing twisted together inside him, a hot, acid-tipped bayonet that tore at his guts.

He wanted her and yet at the same time he hated her and wanted to punish her. She was a married woman and he wanted to throw that fact at her, but instead he took hold of her, demanding thickly, 'What is it you want, Ellie? Me? This?' And he bent his head and took her mouth in a savage kiss, grinding her lips beneath his own.

Ellie shuddered, her senses whipped by pleasure and pain, her body so acutely sensitised that the ferocious passion of his kiss sent sweet darts of aching heat all through her body, making the most intimate female heart of her tighten and coil; awakening sensations so unexpected and unknown that she cried out, recoiling from them.

Gideon tensed as Ellie cried out, pulling back from her.

'No,' Ellie told him fiercely, reaching out to draw him back to her, her lips brushing his chin and then finding his. 'Kiss me, Gideon,' she pleaded softly against his mouth.

She was begging him to kiss her! Now was his moment to reject her as she had rejected him, but instead Gideon opened his mouth to hers, exploring its softness with his tongue until Ellie moaned and clutched at him.

'What is it?' he demanded, lifting his mouth from hers, his hand meshing into the thickness of her hair so that she couldn't escape. 'You said you wanted me to kiss you.'

'I do,' Ellie responded passionately, 'Gideon, I do.'

It was his mouth that found hers this time, his tongue thrusting into its softness in fierce male triumph and possession. Hungrily, Ellie responded, shuddering in mute delight as she felt Gideon slowly ease her gown away from her body.

'Look!' Gideon demanded thickly, as his hands cupped her almost-naked breasts, lifting them free of her chemise. 'They're perfect. They fit my hands perfectly, Ellie, as though they were made for me to hold, as though you were made for me. But you married someone else, didn't you?' he demanded, his mood suddenly changing, anger taking the place of passion. 'Do his hands fit your breasts perfectly, Ellie? Does he –'

'Stop it!' Ellie begged him. 'Stop it!'

'Stop what?' Gideon challenged her. 'Stop this?'

Ellie could feel his thumbs circling her nipples as he bent his head to kiss her mouth – not savagely this time, but with a slow, aching sweetness that turned her bones to soft melting honey. His tongue-tip stroked her lips and she tried to capture it, closing them around it, shuddering to feel him thrusting it between her lips, the friction setting off a thousand tiny quivering darts of longing.

'Well?' he whispered tauntingly. 'Does he make you feel like this, Ellie? Does he make you want like this?'

Wordlessly Ellie shook her head, tears flooding her eyes.

'You're crying,' Gideon mocked her, lifting his left hand to her face, his fingertips on her tears. 'Why?'

'Because I want you,' Ellie told him, lifting her hands to his face and cupping it to prolong the kiss.

'Your mother wouldn't approve of you doing this,' Gideon warned her when he finally lifted his mouth from hers.

'I don't care,' Ellie answered recklessly. 'I don't care about anything or anyone now, Gideon, other than this and you.'

Surely she deserved this brief moment of pleasure, of knowing how it felt to be a woman with a man. The man.

She trembled as Gideon pushed her dress further down her body, revealing its pale purity, yearning for the feel of his hands on her naked flesh. In the streets beyond the closed windows, the sounds of rioting and disorder had already faded, but Ellie never even registered that fact. All she was aware of was Gideon and how much she wanted him.

In the rose-gold glow of the dipping sun, Gideon stared absorbed at the naked beauty of Ellie's body, the soft peachy flush of her skin, its warmth to his touch, its softness and responsiveness. Just by looking at her he could make her tremble, her nipples harden and flaunt themselves for his attention whilst her belly tightened.

He wanted to absorb every bit of her, to drink in through each of his senses the 'Ellieness' of her, the reality of her.

As Gideon lifted her body free of her clothing, Ellie reached out instinctively to cover the soft curls protecting her sex with her hand. In all the months she and Henry had been married he had never seen her naked. And he had certainly never looked at her with the hungry male need with which Gideon was now looking at her.

Getting up, he took a few paces and, keeping his back towards her, hurriedly pulled off his own clothes.

Enthralled Ellie watched him – the breadth of his shoulders, the strength of his arms, the solid muscles of his thighs – her hungry gaze drank them all in. She stared boldly, refusing to look away, her bottom lip caught between her small white teeth as her breasts rose and fell with the sudden agitation of her breathing.

'What is it?' Gideon demanded mockingly. 'You've seen a man before, haven't you, Ellie? After all, you're a married woman!'

The ugly note in his voice was lost on her. She just said wonderingly, 'Oh, Gideon, you are so very, very beautiful.'

Once, hearing those words, seeing her look at him the way she was doing now, would have made him feel like a king, but now . . .

Unable to stop herself, Ellie went to him, reaching out and touching him, just with her fingertips, letting them tremble in awed pleasure against his arm and then his chest, and then Ellie could feel his stomach tensing as she touched it, her fingers moving lower, delicately and uncertainly drawn to the hard jut of his sex.

Gideon had thought that he was immune to anything she could do, but now he realised just how wrong he had been. He heard himself moan beneath her touch, a shudder ripping through him that set off an answering surge of sensation within Ellie's own flesh.

Gideon picked her up and placed her on the bed, leaning over her. Ellie reached up and traced the shape of his face with one fingertip and then took it to her lips and placed a kiss on it, which she carried to him.

When Gideon's lips opened over her finger and sucked fiercely on it, Ellie felt the contraction of pleasure inside her body.

'You want this, Ellie?' Gideon demanded as his hand parted her thighs. 'You want me?'

'Yes,' Ellie whispered. 'Oh yes! Gideon, yes . . .'

Her answer set off a reaction as incendiary as a match struck against the sharpest tinder, fuelling an explosion that gripped them both, fusing them together in the same ricochet of hot urgency.

The sweet savagery of the way she felt when Gideon touched her, entered her, took her, was, Ellie decided, enraptured, the culmination of the aching wasted years of wanting, and denying that wanting. This was what she had been born for; Gideon was who her body had been made for.

As her flesh tightened and closed around him, holding him, urging him, she had no thought of anyone other than him.

Her body tightened and surged, fiercely urgent in its desire, climbing, climbing, urging her further and further into the intimacy of their togetherness. Her nails dug into the sweat-slicked flesh of his back whilst she wrapped herself tightly around him, the harshness of their mutual breathing filling the room with a rhythmic crescendo of sound, punctuated by Ellie's sharp cries of anguished pleasure and Gideon's deeper guttural sounds of male urgency.

Ellie felt her body surge and teeter, clinging, wanting and yet apprehensive, and then Gideon moved within her and the feel of him pushed her over the edge, into the spinning, dizzying freefall of pleasure that rushed up to embrace her.

She heard herself cry out a sob of disbelieving awed pleasure, and she heard too Gideon's raw shout of triumph.

It was over. She was clinging to him, her hot face pressed into his shoulder whilst she sobbed tears of release into his skin and felt as though she had somehow touched a miraculous place, as though she had been granted a glimpse into a special kind of heaven. Her body still trembled in small aftershocks. The scent of Gideon, his maleness, his mastery of her, and of their shared desire, his release within her, filled her, and she knew it was a scent that would stay with her for the rest of her life.

The rest of her life . . . which she was committed to living out as the wife of another man! Henry, who was not and never could be a man in any of the ways that Gideon was. Henry, to whom she had sold herself in marriage for a dozen different reasons, every single one of which was a betrayal of, a desecration of what she now knew a relationship between a man and a woman should be.

Gideon lay on his back, fighting to control his breath. No woman had ever affected him the way Ellie had just done. No woman had ever made him feel, made him want, made him give so much of himself in so many intensely intimate ways. He had wanted to lay his mark upon her, his personal stamp of possession, in the most primitive of ways. He had wanted to take his revenge on her, he reminded himself fiercely – to right the wrong she had done him! And he had done so!

Instinctively, Ellie reached for his hand to hold it in her own, and then for the first time looked properly at it.

'Oh, Gideon . . .' she whispered. All the pain she felt for him and for herself, and for all that they had both lost filled her eyes with tears of anguish.

'Repulsive, isn't it?' Gideon gritted his teeth, wrenching it away from her. He had seen the look of shock in her eyes and he hated her for it. 'I don't need your pity, Ellie,' he told her acidly.

'Keep it and give it to the husband you have just cuckolded, along with mine!'

His cruel words hit her like blows, the pain too intense for Ellie to be able to say or do anything to defend herself.

Turning his head Gideon told her softly, 'Remember all that time ago when you told me you didn't want me, Ellie?'

Ellie closed her eyes. It would be such a sweet relief, telling him now that she had never wanted to say that to him; that she had forced herself to do it, that she had realised a hundred times and more since, just how foolish she had been to want to protect her mother and to think that it was more important to do as she wanted than to follow her own heart.

'Yes,' she began shakily, but before she could continue, Gideon leaned over her, his face a rictus of bitterness and anger.

'Well, you damn well wanted me just now, didn't you? And do you know what, Ellie Pride? In the end you were no better than any cheap little whore I could have bought for the night. In fact, you were a hell of a lot worse!'

White-faced, Ellie stared up at him. She thought she had known pain before – thought indeed that she had known it very well – but she had been wrong. Nothing she had experienced before came anywhere near this sharp, tearing, ripping agony.

Whilst she lay on the bed, too afraid to move in case she cried out with the agony of what she was feeling, Gideon rolled away from her and stood up, keeping his back to her as he reached for his clothes.

Ellie could feel her stomach clenching with misery and guilt as the hansom cab approached the house. She hated herself for what she had done and she hated Gideon even more – hated him. Dry-eyed, she managed to stifle the sob that threatened to betray her. She had caught the last train from Preston to Liverpool, and had telephoned Henry to explain that the reason she was late was because of the riots, but Henry had not answered her call.

The cab stopped and she got out and paid the driver.

Maisie let her in and told her that her father-in-law had not come home for dinner.

'S'pose he's gone to that Mrs Fazackerly's,' she pronounced darkly.

'Where is Henry, Maisie?' Ellie asked.

All the way home, all she had been able to think about was what she had done and how she had betrayed her husband and her marriage vows, and for what? Not for love, as she had so foolishly believed, but so that Gideon could be revenged on her.

'He's upstairs. Bin there all afternoon, he has. Not even had any dinner!'

Reluctantly, Ellie went upstairs.

Would Henry be able to tell what she had done? Would he look at her and know?

Outside the bedroom door she took a deep breath and then opened it, calling out, 'Henry, I'm so sorry, I'm later than I said. I tried to telephone. There were riots and . . .' Her voice trailed away as she realised the bedroom was empty, and the door to Henry's dressing room slightly ajar. And then she noticed the note prominently displayed on her dressing table, her name written on it in Henry's handwriting.

As she picked it up and opened it, Ellie's hands were trembling. She read it quickly, barely able to comprehend its meaning, and then again more slowly.

'My dearest wife,' Henry had written,

I am writing to say goodbye to you.

You have been the kindest wife any man could want, Ellie, and I want you to know how much I bless you every day for being you, but I cannot continue as I have done, living with the terrible burden of guilt my father has forced upon me so I am tainted by his crime. At night I cannot sleep for seeing the dead faces of those murdered seamen, nor from hearing their screams. What I am doing is for the best, Ellie.

I am your devoted husband, Henry Johnson.

Ellie frowned in bewilderment to see that Henry had signed his name with his mother's surname and not his father's. Where was he? What did his letter mean? Why had he . . . ?

A creak from the dressing-room door caught her attention. Putting down the letter Ellie went towards it.

Pushing the door open she stepped inside and then froze as she saw the inert body of her husband swaying gently from the makeshift gibbet he had set up in the corner of the room, a noose around his neck.

Clumsily Ellie ran towards him, unable to accept what she could see, crying out as she did so.

'Henry, no! Please God, no! No! Oh, no, no, no . . .'

PART FOUR

THIRTY-EIGHT

Ellie stared blankly at the breakfast table. There was a newspaper lying there neatly folded, which, for some reason, was trembling violently.

The newspaper, *The Times*, pristine and ironed, couldn't possibly own its presence to Maisie, whom she had never been able to teach that a newspaper was to be read before being used in lighting fires. No, it must have been put there by the awesomely efficient retired butler, whom Iris, in her usual fashion, had managed to find and had immediately dispatched to the Charnock household, and the trembling, Ellie recognised numbly, was generated by her and not the newspaper.

Wilson, the temporary butler, came in bearing fresh tea and toast. Ellie felt her stomach heave, but she forced herself to thank him. After all, it wasn't his fault that she felt the way she did; that she was gripped in this appalling vice of disbelief and pain and anger.

Oh, such dreadful anger. There was so much of

it that her very skin felt tight against her bones with the pressure of it, not allowing her even to think. She knew its taste – heavy, sour, bitter. It burned inside her like acid, eating away at her. Anger against Gideon, against Henry, against his father and her own mother, against Connie, but most of all anger against herself.

Anger and guilt.

The hand she had reached out to pick up her cup of tea started to tremble so violently she had to pull it back.

Her whole body was trembling wretchedly now, her teeth chattering. It had been months now, but inside her head, everything was as horribly fresh as though it had happened yesterday.

Ellie stood up, her stomach heaving with nausea.

She knew she must have run to find someone, to tell them what had happened, but she had no clear memory of having done so, only of finding that the house was suddenly full of people: her father-in-law; Henry's cousin, George, and his wife; her own cousin Cecily's husband, Paul, looking grave and professional; and Iris, equally professional but somehow managing to stop Maisie's noisy sobbing, and to produce cups of tea for everyone.

That had been three months ago. And since then . . .

Ellie closed her eyes.

From the moment he had learned that Henry had taken his own life, Jarvis Charnock had done everything he could to dissociate himself from his son. Henry was a weakling, whom Jarvis had always privately doubted that he had sired – a weakling who had inherited his mental instability from his mother. That's what he had told everyone who would listen. And according to him Henry had been mentally unstable. What other possible explanation could there be for him taking his own life?

Ellie had shown her father-in-law Henry's letter but he had torn it up and thrown it on the fire, forbidding Ellie ever to mention its contents to anyone!

'I thank God that I have been spared the calamity of him providing me with grandsons who might well have been infected with his own madness,' he had told Ellie viciously.

And that had been the line that he and George had stuck to unyieldingly. With pious sighs and shaken heads, with sombre looks and in hushed whispers, they had let it be known that they had been concerned for Henry's mental health for some time; that they had tried to help and protect him, but that it had proved an impossible task.

'Really, Ellie, I am surprised you felt able to leave poor Henry on his own so much when you must have known how delicate his state of health was,' Elizabeth had chided her loftily. 'Dearest Uncle Charnock had already told me how concerned he was about the amount of time you spent away from the house with your friends, and how worried he was about the effect it was having on Henry. But then you have always been such a very social crea-ture, haven't you? I, on the other hand, have always been content to be at home with my family.'

Her smugness had jarred on Ellie's shredded sensibilities. Useless to try to defend herself by pointing out that her 'socialising with her friends' had, in fact, been her visits to her clients, and that she had been obliged to make such visits in order to provide herself and Henry with an income.

But she had not been working on the day that Henry had taken his own life, had she? She had been in Preston.

She had gone to see Connie, she reminded herself fiercely. But there was no escape from her guilt, no appeasement.

There had been no formal funeral, of course. Instead, Henry had had to be buried in unhallowed ground, his burial attended by the merest handful of mourners: herself, Cecily, Paul and Iris, along with one or two others.

Acquaintances now ignored her in the street, crossing over to the other side of the road in order to avoid her, as though somehow Henry's suicide had tainted her, and even though they were now well into the autumn, she had had hardly any orders from the ladies who, only months earlier, had enthused about her work and insisted that they wanted her to make their winter wardrobes for them.

She was a social pariah. Her Aunt Parkes had telephoned her and begged her in a flustered voice not to telephone her or call on her, since she had been forbidden to have anything to do with her by her husband.

'Oh, Ellie, how could you let poor Henry do such a thing?' she had wailed. 'You cannot know how ashamed I feel. Everyone is asking me why you were not more vigilant, especially when Mr Jarvis Charnock has made it plain that he holds you responsible and that he had actually warned you about Henry's weakness and asked you to take special care not to do or say anything that might provoke it.'

'Ellie, you cannot say that,' Iris had told her firmly when, in a low moment, Ellie had admitted to her friend that she felt she had failed Henry by being in Preston at the time of his death. 'You had no option but to go and see Connie, and once you were there, you could not return whilst the disorder and looting were at their height. And besides, why should you consider yourself to be Henry's guardian?'

Even now, Ellie could not think about that time with Gideon without mentally whipping herself for her behaviour. How foolish she had been to think, to believe . . . All Gideon had wanted was to have his revenge on her, to humiliate and scorn her. Well, he had certainly done so!

She looked at the now cold toast. She knew she should eat something, but she felt so constantly nauseous.

Cecily had promised to call round and see her

this morning. Iris had telephoned to say she would not be able to come with her. Ellie knew how busy Iris was, as she was on the point of leaving the country for an extended visit to Switzerland with a group of friends and colleagues. Another member of the party was to be Ewan Cameron, and Paul had already teased his sister that Ewan was secretly the reason she was going, rather than any fabled views of the Swiss Alps and lakes.

Iris had, of course, determinedly denied any such partiality.

'I wish that Iris would marry Ewan,' Cecily had told Ellie. 'They are so well suited for one another, and although Iris states that she is perfectly happy as she is, I cannot see how any woman can be happy when she is not married.'

And Ellie had other problems to contend with in addition to those surrounding Henry's suicide.

Connie and her young man had disappeared, much to the furious outrage of both families, and because she had appeared to have been the last person to see Connie, the blame for this had been laid at Ellie's door. She had tried to protest that she knew nothing about the whereabouts of the miscreants. It seemed now that in the eyes of her mother's sisters, she and Connie were outcasts to the family.

Ellie stood up. There were things she had to do and one of them was to explain to Iris that she could not allow her to supply her with a servant for any longer, and she certainly could not afford to pay Wilson's wages herself.

Predictably, Henry had not made a will, and even if he had done so, he had had nothing to leave. The sum total of his personal possessions had been the contents of the old leather trunk he had kept in his room, and which Ellie had only managed to force herself to go through three days ago. In it she had found a few cherished memories of Henry's mother, a young boy's treasures, which had torn at her heart, and some photographs he had obviously taken whilst he had been in Japan. She had studied these slowly, trying to see the scenes depicted in them through Henry's eyes. One of them had been of a delicately beautiful Japanese girl who had looked out of the photograph with shy, almond-shaped eyes. Ellie had carefully replaced everything in the trunk and locked it. Everything – including the small hoard of just over one hundred guineas that she had found inside it.

Cecily arrived shortly after lunch – a lunch that Ellie had felt too nauseous to eat.

After they had embraced, Cecily told her that she could not stay for very long.

'Mama has telephoned to say that she wants me to have my sister, Kitty, to stay with me, Ellie.' Flushing a little, she explained, 'She is concerned that her connection with Constance will reflect badly on her at home, and now that she is sixteen, Mama has said that Kitty must come to me, just for a few months. Apparently, Mr Connolly has put it all around Preston that Connie is the one to blame for what has happened and Mama says her reputation is totally ruined. She has said too that I am not to bring Kitty to visit you, Ellie, and that, as well, I am to ask you not to visit me whilst she is here.'

Biting her lip, Cecily continued, 'I have told her that it is very unfair of her and the others to blame you for what Constance has done, but I am afraid . . .'

Cecily looked so unhappy that Ellie didn't have the heart to protest or defend herself.

'I am almost certain that I am to have another child, Ellie,' Cecily continued. 'I have done nothing but be sick for the past week. Which is exactly the way I was with baby. Paul is a little shocked, since we had not planned . . .' She broke off, looking flustered. 'I must say I do not know how I am to entertain Kitty whilst I am feeling so out of sorts.'

A fierce shock of terror surged through Ellie's body, followed by an ice-cold wash of certainty, as she heard Cecily innocently describe the early symptoms of her pregnancy . . . the very same symptoms that Ellie herself was experiencing.

But she could not be having a child – she *must* not! She half stood, her forehead beaded with sweat, her stomach churning, and then had to grip the back of her chair to control her own betraying weakness. Immediately she looked anxiously at her cousin, but, fortunately, Cecily was too busy gathering her belongings about her and preparing for her departure to notice anything amiss. As soon as Cecily had gone, Ellie went upstairs. In her bedroom she leaned against the door, her head pounding.

The unpalatable, irrefutable truth had to be faced. If she was pregnant it was impossible for the child to be Henry's.

But she could not have Gideon Walker's child. She did not want to have a child at all. Childbirth had always terrified her, but oddly, right now it was not the fear of giving birth that was twisting her stomach with dread, but her fear of how on earth she could possibly endure to give birth to a child given to her as an act of vengeance.

Frantically, she wondered how she could bring up such a child when she was penniless and dependent on her father-in-law for a roof over her head and her own skills as a needlewoman in order to make a living!

Dizzily, Ellie tried to think. Only recently Iris had been talking about the various advertisements appearing in women's periodicals, advertising certain medicines to help restore women to 'full health'.

'They are nothing more than aids which purport to bring unwanted pregnancies to an end,' she had continued, disapprovingly.

Aids to bring unwanted pregnancies to an end! Feverishly Ellie started to make plans.

'Ah, Ellie. Good . . . I have come to see you at the express wish of dearest Mr Charnock. He feels it is

501

best if I relay his plans to you woman to woman, so to speak! Goodness, I must say I think it very wasteful of you to be sitting here in this huge room, Ellie, using up coals on just one person, and reading magazines. I should have thought your household duties and your moral duty to Mr Charnock would have ensured that you had plenty to keep you busy!'

Elizabeth, who had arrived unannounced, and whose presence was the last thing Ellie wanted, pursed her lips disapprovingly.

'I am afraid that once my dearest husband and myself move in here, there will have to be a great many changes made.'

As the content of her little speech sank in, Ellie stared at her, a huge sense of foreboding clamping hold of her.

'I'm sorry, Elizabeth,' she stopped her. 'I don't think I understand. What do you mean, when you and George move in here?'

'That is what I am come to tell you, Ellie. Mr Charnock has decided that since George is now his official heir and partner in the business, it would be far better if we were to move in here and live with him. And I must say, I do feel that he is right. Which reminds me, whilst I am here I had best look around the bedrooms. George and I shall probably be best occupying the suite of rooms that was yours and Henry's. After all, they will be far too large for just you, and I know that you would feel uncomfortable occupying them now anyway.

I was saying to George that I am sure you would be much more comfortable in one of the smaller rooms on the attic floor.

'Naturally that dreadful want-wit you have working here will have to go. I couldn't possibly have her answering the door to my callers, nor going anywhere near my precious boys! Fortunately, Mr Charnock has been generous enough to say that he is going to increase George's salary, in view of the extra costs our position will entail. He has promised, too, to pay for the boys' education at Hutton and to make available a housekeeping allowance.'

Like tiny drops of poison polluting clear water, the words fell devastatingly from Elizabeth's thin lips – on and on, remorselessly, spreading and choking the life out of Ellie's own future.

'This could be a lovely home, Ellie. I have never understood why you have not made it so, but then I suppose you are just not a natural homemaker. As I said to Mr Charnock myself, it is all very well for a woman to waste time wandering around her garden and visiting her friends when she has her house in order, but when she has not . . . ! I must say, Ellie, I was a little bit surprised that you chose to stay here anyway. I should have thought in your circumstances you would have felt much happier returning to your own family, your Aunt and Uncle Parkes, perhaps, or maybe even your father in Preston. Mr Charnock has confided to me how relieved he is that your marriage to Henry was without issue, and, of course, you must be too. To bear a child who might inherit Henry's mental weaknesses . . .' she gave a shudder, 'I could never endure that!'

'Henry was not mentally weak,' Ellie protested immediately, 'he was simply bullied and . . . and made to feel so unhappy by his father that –'

Elizabeth's eyes narrowed. 'I shall be magnanimous and pretend that I have not heard you speak so disrespectfully of dear Mr Charnock, Ellie. In your shoes I would have thought you would have had more care. After all, you are totally dependent on Mr Charnock's goodwill, aren't you? With Henry dead, he has no legal reason to continue to support you. Indeed, I confess that I am a little surprised that Mr Parkes has not offered to have you back, especially in view of the fragile health of his own wife. I believe she lives very quietly these days.'

If Elizabeth was hoping to trick her into an indiscreet outburst regarding Mr Parkes' relationship with his mistress then she was going to be disappointed, Ellie decided grimly.

'I must say, though, Ellie that I am a little surprised myself. I own that in your shoes I doubt that I would feel I could continue to stay here, especially in view of the embarrassment any connection to you must cause us now, having regard to the behaviour of a certain member of your family – I shall not sully my lips with her name!

'However, Mr Charnock is the most generous of

504

men and none of us has any wish that you should feel that you are being pushed out of what has been your home, Ellie. Of course, you will be welcome to stay, if you wish, and I have suggested to Mr Charnock that if you do you would probably welcome the chance to repay his kindness to you by taking on the role of housekeeper. With all this talk of war and the increase in the line's business, it is more than likely that I shall have to do a great deal more entertaining here than you have been used to doing. Of course, I have the experience for that sort of thing, which I know that you do not. When Mr Charnock complained to me that you were not running the house as he wished, I did tell him that it was perhaps because you simply did not know how to do so. You will feel much more comfortable working under my direction, Ellie. Oh, and my dear mother-in-law is likely to be moving in with us as well. She is not in the best of health, I am afraid . . .'

Numbly, Ellie listened to her. She had known that her father-in-law intended to appoint his nephew as his heir, but it had never occurred to her that he would invite George and Elizabeth to move into the house, nor that he would give Elizabeth the authority to tell her that she intended to move her into the attic . . . like a servant. A pregnant servant – and everyone knew what happened to them! They were dismissed without references or character and forced to go into the workhouse.

*　　*　　*

The shop, which she had chosen because it was on the other side of the city, was tucked away down a narrow maze of streets. Ellie had taken Maisie with her for moral support, but she left the tweeny outside whilst she went into the chemist's trying to hold her head up high as she showed him the advertisement she had cut from the magazine.

She could feel her face burning as the shopkeeper looked at her, whilst she stammeringly told him that she had come in search of the potion on behalf of a friend.

Without a word he disappeared into the back of the shop, returning within minutes with a small dark-coloured bottle.

Ellie's hand was shaking as she handed over the money and took the bottle from him.

Just in case the one dose should not be sufficient, Ellie gritted her teeth and set herself the task of acquiring two more.

Maisie clung nervously to her arm when she emerged from the final shop. Maisie had been increasingly attached to her and increasingly dependent on her, Ellie recognised as she gently reassured her. Her learning abilities were severely limited and, like the young child she mentally was, she tended to grow extremely fearful whenever she was parted from what was familiar to her.

As they walked home Ellie acknowledged that there was no way any employment agency would take Maisie onto its books, and she doubted that

even her soft-hearted cousin would be persuaded
to find a place in her own household for her.

Ellie had no illusions about her own future.
Apart from the guineas she had found amongst
Henry's things, and the jewellery she had been
given by Mr Parkes, she had no assets of any
value. She could earn herself a modest living with
her needle, of course, provided she could find
enough customers, and providing that she was
allowed enough time off from her 'housekeeping'
duties to do so.

The unpalatable truth was that she was all too
likely to end up as an unpaid drudge in the household where she had been mistress.

But her first and most pressing task now was to
read and then follow the instructions she had been
given with her bottles of 'health restoring' potion,
and it was to that end that she was hurrying Maisie
back to the house she no longer felt she could
call home.

THIRTY-NINE

'Well now, if it in't young Gideon.'

Gideon gave Will Pride a wry look as Will slapped him heartily on the back. He had just been walking past The Fleece public house when Will had come out – staggered out was perhaps a more appropriate description, Gideon recognised.

'Heard how well you've been doing, young 'un. Inheriting all that money, aye, and getting yoursel' a fine business going too by all accounts. Who wud ha' thought it? By, I remember when you first come to me looking for work. Nowt to you then, there wasn't, lad. Aye, I remember too the way our Robert's Lyddy turned her nose up at you, and wouldn't countenance you walking out with her Ellie. Always was stuck up, was Lyddy. Mind, she would ha' had her comeuppance now with all this to-do with their Connie! Run off with one of the Connolly lads, she has, and set the whole town by the ears, no mistake! They're saying that the Barclays have cut themselves right off from all of their Lyddy's young 'uns on account of Connie's disgrace.

'As I heard it, Bill Connolly has said he'll break every bone in young Kieron's body when he catches up with him – aye, and that our Connie wants shutting up in t' workhouse. A fine to-do it's caused, and no mistake, and still no one the wiser as to where the pair of them have gone.

'And then there's poor Ellie, in mourning for that husband o' hers. Topped hissel' . . .' Will shook his head.

Gideon's mouth compressed. He had heard all about Henry's suicide, and Ellie's 'bravery' in coping with her widowhood.

As he took his leave of Will Pride, he told himself sourly that Ellie had no more business being in his thoughts. He had had his revenge on her, and now he had written her out of his life.

So why did he continue to dream so vividly about her, about being with her? So his body remembered her pleasurably! Well, it didn't know her as well as he did, and anyway, wasn't one woman very much like another when you got down to it – and in more ways than one? He had had to make it plain to his actress friend that her none-too-subtle suggestions that he should marry her were a waste of time. She had been happy enough merely to share his bed when he had had precious little else to share with her, but now that the whole town knew just how warm a man he was, she was more interested in having access to his bank account than his body.

A woman might claim that she loved you, but in the end, money and social position were what she loved more. He had seen that proved over and over again.

Of course, there were exceptions – foolish women like his true mother and Connie, who threw their futures away for the sake of some man. Had Ellie been more like her sister, then maybe things would have been different.

From upstairs on the tram where they were sitting, since Maisie had a childlike delight in riding up there, Ellie could see the top of the Royal Liver Building, and the pierhead beyond it, thronged with people. One of the Cunarders was in, and Ellie could see the gaggles of cleaning women making their way towards the vessel.

The business of cleaning out the liners when they arrived in port was very much sought after, and said to be under the control of a handful of Liverpool families all based around the same few streets. Whilst the tram pulled into a stop Ellie glanced out to see a ship of the Elder Dempster Line tied up in Toxteth Dock. One could walk by the docks and hear the imported African grey parrots calling out all manner of pleasantries (and unpleasantries) at the command of the seamen who brought and trained them for sale.

Even Maisie had stopped staring and pointing in excitement now at the sight of so many people from so many different cultures. The docks area, as always, was a hum of activity. From her seat Ellie could just about see the building that housed the offices of the Charnock Shipping Line. Instinctively her hand went to her thankfully still flat stomach. In different circumstances, should she have borne a son, the business would one day be his.

But the child she was carrying, were it to be born, would have no rights to any part of Henry's 'estate', since it was not his child. And even if it had been . . . Tiredly Ellie acknowledged that she would never want her child to be subjected to the same kind of upbringing that had so destroyed poor Henry's spirit and self-confidence.

The dreadful outbreak of strike action, which had paralysed so much of the country and brought so much hardship to its working people, was now thankfully coming to an end, although the poor miners in Wales were still being subjected to the most harsh kind of treatment by the government, and Ellie had noticed that there was an atmosphere of brooding hostility in the city between working men and their employers. And whilst Liverpool's docks and sea lanes were filled with merchant vessels flying the Red Ensign, proving the business and wealth of the city and its shipping lines, wages were still low, and in the lines of men waiting to be taken on they still grumbled amongst themselves about their pay.

The *Liverpool Review* was constantly running

articles about the shameful nature of certain parts of the city to which, unknowingly, seamen were lured and taken advantage of, often left drunk and destitute in the street, an abhorrence that persevered and prospered, despite all the attempts of those worthies who ran the Sailors' Homes, which were supposed to provide them with a decent, respectable place to sleep.

Out in the sea lane a liner was waiting for its pilot boat. What would it be like to board her and sail away to a new country and a new life? Ellie shivered as the tram lurched into life and moved on. A new life? And what exactly was she to live on, pray?

Twenty minutes later, the tram reached their stop and Ellie chivied Maisie downstairs. The maid never wanted the ride to be over and always resisted getting off. Though outwardly patient, inwardly Ellie was in turmoil. She was praying that tonight would be one of the nights when her father-in-law remained away from home so that she could spend the evening completing the task she had set herself.

She wished desperately that Iris was not away. She could not have told her what she planned, of course – it was both illegal and a mortal sin – but she could at least perhaps have asked a few pertinent questions of her so that she might know what to expect.

Women often miscarried children in the early months of their pregnancies, she knew, but what exactly was going to happen? As she hurried Maisie, Ellie felt a sharp resurgence of her long-buried fear of childbirth. She had no alternative than to do what she was going to do. She did not want this child, Gideon's child. How could she, after what he had done; after what he had said to her? And if Mr Charnock should think that she had conceived Henry's child, from what Elizabeth had said to her he was probably likely to render her homeless straight away!

And if that were to happen, where could she go? Not to her Aunt and Uncle Parkes, nor to any other of her late mother's relations. Cecily, always soft-hearted, would be bound to want to help her, but Ellie knew that Cecily's mother would not allow her to do so.

Iris might have helped had she been here, but it was going to be the New Year before she returned from her holiday.

There was a stitch in Ellie's side well before she and Maisie had reached the Charnock house. Partially because of the long walk from the tram stop, and partially because of the sharply cold November wind, Ellie was forced to stop to catch her breath. Several yards away she could see a newspaper vendor. Absently she glanced at the headline written on the board, and then froze as she read 'Murderer to Hang Before the Month is Out!'

Her stomach churned. Quickly she turned away, urging Maisie to walk faster.

Never ever would she forget discovering Henry's body. Never, ever would she forget the mixture of anguish, guilt and grief that had filled her. How could she endure to bear a child conceived in such a way. And at such a time!

Gripped by her own unhappy thoughts, at first Ellie didn't see the hackney carriage pulled up on their carriageway, but she could see the open front door and she could hear too the loud furious voice of her father-in-law.

Quickly dispatching Maisie to the kitchen entrance, Ellie hurried inside the house and then came to an abrupt stop.

There, in the middle of the hall, was the most extraordinary and unexpected sight: a tiny dark-haired lady, who was obviously Japanese from her costume, her hands folded and her head bowed as she listened to Jarvis Charnock's furious raging, and a small girl, no more than three years old at best, Ellie guessed, standing equally still at her side, and dressed in a matching costume.

Elizabeth stood next to Ellie's father-in-law, her mouth compressed with distaste.

'You dare to come here and claim some acquaintance with my son, telling me that this child you have brought with you was fathered by him?'

'Do not listen to her, Mr Charnock,' Elizabeth was demanding. 'Look how well she speaks English. She has never come all the way from Japan, no matter what she says. You may depend on it she is out of some dreadful unspeakable place down by the docks and is trying to lay claim to poor Henry as a father for her wretched child because she knows he is dead.'

'Dead? My Henry-san is dead? No! That cannot be.'

The soft voice was filled with a pain of such intensity that Ellie's eyes immediately filled with sympathetic tears.

The young woman had lifted her head as she spoke, and now that Ellie could see her face properly she recognised her immediately as the figure in the photograph she had found with Henry's things.

Immediately, she stepped forward and said firmly,

'Father-in-law . . . Elizabeth . . . I think you may be misjudging this young woman. At all events, let us at least show her hospitality and good manners by offering her something to eat and drink.'

The small white face turned towards Ellie, the dark eyes burning with an intensity that made her ache with sympathy.

'I am – was Henry's wife,' Ellie explained gently to her.

'You are my Henry-san's wife?' The girl, for she was little more than that, Ellie recognised, looked searchingly at her. 'You were fortunate to have such a brave husband as my Henry-san,' she told Ellie gravely.

'Brave?' Jarvis Charnock repeated scornfully.

'Yes, he was very brave,' she insisted fiercely. 'For did he not rescue me with his own hands and take me from that dreadful ship I was to be sent away on!'

Ellie frowned as she listened to her, remembering the passion with which Henry had denounced to her the fate of innocent young girls sent by their parents to work abroad, but in reality destined to end up in brothels.

'You must know how kind a man he was,' she appealed to Ellie, 'for did you not have the good fortune to be his wife?'

She was trembling as she spoke, huge tears filling the slanting dark eyes, the small rosebud mouth stiff with distress. At her side the little girl, whom Ellie saw was definitely of mixed blood, having much rounder European eyes and softer hair of a different texture from her mother's, as well as paler skin, clung despairingly to her. The combination of East and West was an exotic one, Ellie recognised, and when the child grew up she would be very beautiful. For now, though, she was clinging in mute exhaustion to her mother's robe, her little face tight with fear.

'Oh, I do not think I can endure any more of this,' Elizabeth suddenly exclaimed, expressing her hand to her forehead in a theatrical fashion. 'The shame of such a thing happening – the brazenness of it!' She gave a deep shudder, closing her eyes, and then opening them again to turn to Henry's father and demand, 'You must send this woman away, Mr Charnock. I cannot bring my innocent children under the same roof as this kind of woman. To brazenly seek out Henry, and to bring her . . . the results of her sinful relationship with her . . .'

'Henry-san told me he would come back for me, and when he did not I knew he would want me to come to him!' the Japanese woman burst out frantically. 'Oh, my beloved Henry, I cannot believe that he is dead!'

'Let me take you and the child down to the kitchen where you can have something to eat,' Ellie suggested gently.

'No! I forbid it,' Elizabeth announced dramatically. 'That woman shall not be allowed to stay a single minute longer beneath this roof. You must send her away immediately, Mr Charnock,' she repeated.

'Elizabeth, you cannot mean that,' Ellie protested, genuinely shocked at the other woman's lack of compassion. 'Whatever the rights and wrongs of the situation, we should at least offer Henry's . . . friend a bed for the night, and then –'

'Well, of course, you would say that, wouldn't you?' Elizabeth sneered. 'After all, what difference is there really between this . . . this creature and your own sister? The woman must go.' As she spoke, Elizabeth was sweeping towards the front door.

Outraged, Ellie picked up her skirts and followed her, reaching the door and barring it.

'Step out of my way this instant,' Elizabeth demanded furiously. 'I am the mistress of this house now, Ellie.' As she spoke she turned to Jarvis

517

Charnock for support and immediately he gave it, inclining his head in a nod of agreement.

Triumph glittered malevolently in Elizabeth's blue eyes.

'The woman must leave – and now. I will not have my home, the home to which I shall be bringing my children, sullied by the presence of such as her, and the . . . the fruits of her illicit union. Of course, if you wish to do so, Ellie, you could always leave with her.'

Ellie stared at her, but there was no mistaking the intention in Elizabeth's challenge. She wanted her to leave, Ellie recognised, and she would go on wanting her to, until she finally did so. A shiver of fear went through her. And if she felt fear then how on earth must this poor woman in front of her be feeling, Ellie wondered.

'Very well then, I shall leave. I would far rather be rendered homeless than live amongst people who are so lacking in human Christian charity,' Ellie declared bravely, whilst inwardly she wondered just what she was doing. It was too late to call back the words, though. She could see the smugness of victory on Elizabeth's face.

'We shall all leave,' she continued coolly, lifting her chin as she added challengingly, 'But not until tomorrow morning, since it will take me some time to collect my belongings together and to make alternative arrangements for – to make alternative arrangements.'

For a dreadful moment Ellie thought that Elizabeth

was actually going to demand that she left immediately, but to her relief the other woman's gaze flickered and she looked away.

'Very well then, but if this woman is to remain overnight it must be in your room, Ellie, and the child with her.'

Not bothering to make any reply, Ellie shepherded the Japanese lady and her child towards the kitchen. Tonight the three of them would have to share the bed she had shared with Henry, and then tomorrow . . .

There was only one place she could go now, Ellie recognised. Only one person she could turn to.

It was only when she was on the verge of falling asleep that she remembered the potions she had been at such pains to buy. She would worry about them tomorrow, she told herself wearily, as she tried to close her ears to the muffled sobbing of the woman curled up on the other side of the bed, the woman who was mourning Henry in a way that a woman mourns the loss of the man to whom she had committed her life and her love. After all, what possible difference could one more day make?

'But why do they have to come with us, miss?' Maisie demanded sulkily as Ellie settled her three charges as comfortably as she could in their carriage. There was no way she could leave Maisie behind to fend for herself, and Ellie hoped her father would understand why it had been necessary for her to bring three unrelated people home with her. She had decided against telephoning him with any advance warning of her arrival, and instead planned to plead her case with him once she had arrived. The Friargate house may not be large but it did have extra bedroom space on its third and attic floors, and Ellie wasn't too proud to occupy one of them, nor to set about getting herself some work in order to contribute to the household expenses, both for herself and for her newly acquired responsibilities – because Maisie, the Japanese girl, whose name was Minaco, and the little girl, whom she had named Henrietta in honour of her father, were now her responsibilities, Ellie recognised.

She had arranged that the trunks she had packed so speedily this morning with all her belongings would be collected from the house and then transported to her in Preston.

She had already learned from Minaco that it was Henry who had taught her to speak English and that on his departure she had found herself a job as a translator in order to support herself once the money Henry had left for her had run out.

'He promised me that he would send me more, and that he would come back to me,' she had told Ellie, with eyes full of tears.

Ellie's heart had ached for her, despite her shock.

Preston would always be her home, Ellie acknowledged, as she guided her charges through its streets. It was market day, and the town was busy. Several people recognised her and stopped to talk to her whilst looking curiously at her small entourage.

At last they reached Friargate, and Ellie was relieved to see that the shop was empty of customers and that only her father was standing behind the counter.

'Ellie!' He looked older and somehow smaller as he hurried over to hug her. 'Me and Maggie were both sorry to hear about your Henry. A sad business, that was, lass. Suicide.' He shook his head, as Ellie stepped back from him.

'It's because of Henry's death that I . . . we are here, Father,' she began quietly. 'Henry's father does not . . . will not . . .' Ellie could hear someone passing outside, and, not wanting to have their conversation overheard, she reached out and touched her father's arm, begging him, 'Can we not go upstairs? This is not the place to discuss what I have to say to you.'

Her father frowned. 'Well, I'm not sure as Maggie would like that, Ellie. You see –'

'What are you saying I would not like? Oh, it's you,' Maggie announced as she suddenly appeared in the shop, carrying her baby daughter. Giving Ellie a sharply disagreeable look, she demanded, 'And who might this lot be?'

Ignoring her stepmother Ellie turned in desperation to her father. 'Father, please, I must speak with you. Henry's father has refused to take in Minaco and her child, despite the fact that they are both morally Henry's responsibility, and since my role within the household has been taken over

521

by Henry's cousin's wife, I have had no option but to leave myself. Father, please, may we stay here with you?'

'Stay here?' Maggie interrupted sharply, jiggling her baby on her hip. 'I'd like to know where, seeing as there's a houseful here already.'

'A houseful?' Ellie queried, looking in bewilderment from Maggie and the baby to her father.

'Maggie's mother and her brother and sister are currently living with us, Ellie,' her father told her uncomfortably, avoiding meeting Ellie's eyes.

Ellie could feel frightened tears burning the backs of her eyes. Did Maggie's relatives have more claim on him now than his own flesh and blood?

'Father, please,' she begged.

'Don't you go giving in to her, Robert Pride,' Maggie warned him angrily. 'It's hard enough trying to feed the mouths we've already got wi'out tekin' any more in, thanks to you letting the business go to rack and ruin.'

Ellie felt for her father as she heard the angry contempt in Maggie's voice.

'Not more'n half a dozen customers you've had in all week,' she continued, glowering at Ellie. 'Only last night you was saying business was so bad that you wanted me to try to get m'sel' summat at one o' t' mills whilst Ma looked after the babby!'

Ellie ached for the misery and shame she could see in her father's eyes as he looked at Maggie.

'If your mother had young Andy and Susan in

her room with her, Ellie could have those two attic rooms, and –' he ploughed on.

'What, you would turn my family out of their rooms to house this lot? Over my dead body,' Maggie announced.

With every word her father and his second wife exchanged, Ellie's hopes faded. It was obvious to her that even if Maggie were persuaded to make room for them in the house, there was simply not enough money coming in from the shop to keep them all. The shop-front windows, like those of the house, had their paint peeling from them, an air of shabbiness surrounding them.

Even without the enmity towards her that she could see in Maggie's eyes, Ellie recognised that it would be impossible for her to move back home.

She felt sorry for her father. Rather than distress him any further it was best that they left, she acknowledged wearily.

'Very well then,' she announced quietly, clamping down on the weakening feeling of panic churning her insides. 'If we can't stay here then I had best go and find somewhere we can stay!'

'Try down by the docks,' Maggie suggested, her face flushed. 'There's places there that take in the likes of her,' she added, nodding in Minaco's direction. 'Seems like some of them sailors have a liking for her sort!'

'Maggie!' Ellie heard her father object, but Ellie didn't lower herself to make any response. She just hoped that Minaco had not understood what

Maggie was referring to! Gathering together her small flock she shepherded them out into Friargate. She had no idea what on earth she was going to do or how she was going to put a roof over all their heads, but somehow she would, she promised herself grimly.

They were halfway down Friargate when Ellie heard her father calling her name. Turning round, she saw him hurrying towards her.

'Don't take what Maggie said too much to heart, lass,' he told her awkwardly. 'She doesn't mean any harm. Here . . . take this . . .' Even more uncomfortably he thrust five guineas into Ellie's hand. ''T isn't much, I know, but it's all I can spare right now, lass. And look, I've written down our John's address for you. Happen them as he lodges with might be able to recommend somewhere for you to rent until you get yourself sorted out. Ellie love, I wish I could do summat to help you, but you can see how things are,' he continued miserably. 'Business hasn't been so good just recently: there's men out of work and everyone is tightening their belts. If I was you I'd go back to Liverpool. It's the best place for you, lass. Maggie doesn't mean any harm. I know she's got a sharp tongue, but if things were different . . .'

Ellie couldn't bear the look of defeated misery in her father's eyes. Throwing her arms around him she whispered emotionally, 'It's all right. I understand.'

*　　*　　*

Ellie looked at the money her father had given her. Five guineas! She felt guilty about taking it, but what choice did she have? She needed it to buy them all a roof over their heads tonight. At least tomorrow she could ring the carter and once her things had been delivered – Henry's precious cache of guineas, her sewing machine and the pieces of fabric she had stocked up, as well as the medicine she had been at such pains to buy – then somehow she would have to find a way of making a new life for them all.

Soberly she looked at the other three.

Maisie was red-nosed and sniffling, round-eyed with misery and fear; Minaco's eyes held their own anxiety and also a heart-aching depth of pain; whilst her little girl stood stoically at her side, too young perhaps to understand what was happening to them all, or perhaps too accustomed already to dramatic changes in her life.

'Oh, miss, what's going to happen to us?' Maisie wailed. 'I'm hungry. Me belly's that empty it's fair growling.' As though to underline her point she pressed her hands to her stomach.

'We'll soon all have something to eat, Maisie,' Ellie promised with more conviction than she was feeling, 'but first we need to find somewhere to stay.'

Preston had a good number of inns and hotels, but Ellie had no intention of wasting money on them. No, what they needed was a cheap, clean boarding house where they could all stay until she could find somewhere more permanent for them to rent.

She would need a property in a decent part of town, of course, especially since the only way she could support them all was with her needle. The kind of clients she had sewed for in Liverpool were never going to employ someone who lived in one of the poorer parts of the town!

Wearily Ellie acknowledged that she had been hoping to gain clients by word of mouth – the wives of her father's friends; her late mother's friends. Well, she had best accustom herself to the fact that that was not going to happen, she told herself briskly. Instead she would have to advertise for business – perhaps in the very paper that John's patron sometimes worked for. Every cloud has its silver lining, she reminded herself sternly, and she must just look for hers!

'Miss, why can't we go home?'

It was three hours since they had left Friargate. Maisie's face was smudged with dirt where she had rubbed a grubby hand through her tears. Ellie's own legs ached from all the walking they had done, from street to street, and up and down them, whilst she knocked at every door that displayed a 'Rooms to let' sign.

But on each doorstep she had received the same response. After one look at Minaco and then another at Maisie, their prospective landlady had given a grim shake of her head and told them that she had no spare rooms.

'Miss, I'm hungry,' Maisie wailed as they walked through the market. Many of the stallholders were closing up for the day, and out of the corner of her eye Ellie saw a shabbily dressed young urchin dodging a cuff from one of them as he snatched a piece of cheese from the stall.

As a girl – a lifetime ago now, or so it seemed – Ellie could remember watching round-eyed as the poor people of the town clustered round the closing stalls, begging for spoiled pies, some of them even retrieving food that had fallen from them onto the floor.

Her own stomach was growling emptily. Automatically she covered it with her hand. It was still flat. Her heart started to beat faster. The sooner her trunk arrived and she could follow the instructions on those bottles she had purchased, the better. For a moment, as she contemplated the situation she was in, tears burned her eyes. Fiercely she blinked them away. She was the leader of their small group; the others were dependent on her. She had to be strong for their sakes.

'Quick, Maisie,' she instructed the serving girl. 'Over here . . .' Hurrying them over to a bread stall, she dug into her pocket for some farthings, offering them to the harassed woman packing everything up.

'Those rolls over there – I'll give you a halfpenny for them,' she offered. There were six rolls left in a basket.

The woman scowled at her. 'Oh, you will, will you? Well, I'll have you know them is a farthing each.'

Ellie stood her ground. 'A halfpenny for four of them,' she persisted.

At her side Maisie began to sob noisily. And Ellie's heart sank as she saw from the woman's expression that she wasn't going to give way, but then suddenly half a dozen young boys came rushing past, bumping into the stall and sending the basket flying.

Before Ellie could stop her, Maisie had pounced on one of the rolls and was stuffing it into her mouth. Quickly snatching up another three, Ellie dropped her halfpenny down on the stall, and hurried them all away.

What she had done was as good as stealing, she told herself, as she handed Minaco and Henrietta a roll each, waiting until her own heart had stopped pounding before beginning to eat her own.

It was almost evening and they still hadn't found anywhere to stay. She had tried John's address, but the family were away and the house closed up. The sky had clouded over and it was beginning to rain. Wearily, Ellie hurried towards yet another door.

The woman who opened it to her knock was wearing clogs and her hair was tied up in rag curlers. A smell of grease and cabbage wafted down the hallway and Ellie's stomach heaved.

'What is it you want? If you're after selling summat you're wasting your time.'

'We're looking for a room,' Ellie explained.

Immediately, the woman's expression hardened. 'Oh, ye are, are ye? Well, you won't find one here! This is a respectable house, not one where we take in heathen savages,' she announced, looking at Minaco. 'It's down by the docks for the likes of you, where they don't mind what they take in.'

Ellie could feel her face burning with resentment and shame.

The street was busy with workers from the mills and Dick Kerr's, the tram factory, making their way home. Ellie envied them for having homes to go to; for having lives in which they felt safe and secure.

Perhaps her father was right. Perhaps she should go back to Liverpool. But if she did, what would happen to Minaco and her child? Elizabeth would refuse to house them and they would end up in the workhouse – if they were lucky – and as for Maisie . . .

Grimly Ellie stepped back, just as the door was slammed in her face.

The closer they got to the docks, the meaner the streets became. Ellie shuddered, remembering how she had felt the day she had come looking for Connie.

As they walked past a public house, a group of men standing by the doorway called out to them.

Protectively, Ellie hurried her charges past, her face flaming as she heard the men's coarse comments.

It took her four attempts before she finally found a landlady who was prepared to offer them a room.

'You get all sorts down here,' she told Ellie laconically, staring at Minaco, 'but it's not often you get one like her. I run a respectable house, mind, and if any of you is working girls . . .'

It took several seconds for Ellie to grasp what she meant. Affronted, she shook her head. She was, it seemed, obliged to pay for the room for a full week and in advance, but she prayed they would not have to spend more than one night beneath this roof. Tomorrow she would ring the carter and ask him to deliver her trunk to Friargate, and once it was there, if necessary she would use Henry's money to buy herself a small house. Once they had the security of a roof over their heads she could then set about looking for clients.

The room they were shown to was cold and dirty. The one bed looked as though the sheets had been on it through several occupancies, and her stomach heaved at the sour old smell of the air in the room.

'Thank you,' she told the landlady when she had shown them upstairs. 'If you would just tell us where the bathroom is . . .'

'The bathroom?' The woman burst out laughing. 'Lord, where have you come from? There ain't no bathroom here! There's a privy out in the back yard; if ye want water for washing it's a shilling a week extra and there's the public baths. And any funny stuff and you're out, the lot of yer. There's a house down the street for the likes of that. Aye, and she's got room to spare. One of her girls was taken bad the other night and taken off to the hospital. Got herself in the family way and tried to get rid of it. Summat went wrong and, by the sounds of it, she's like to have killed herself as well as the brat she was carrying.'

Ellie stared at her, her face going white. Her head ached and she felt so tired . . . so afraid. How could this be happening to her? How could she be in such a place?

The woman had left the door open and as Ellie glanced towards it she saw a man standing outside, staring in. The look on his face made her shudder. It was exactly the same kind of look she had once seen on her Uncle Parkes' face.

As soon as the landlady had gone, Ellie hurried to the door and closed and bolted it.

'Miss, I need a wee,' Maisie started to wail.

The thought of escorting her downstairs and outside to the privy and then waiting there for her made Ellie quail.

She could see the jerry sticking out from under the bed, and directed Maisie to use it.

It was impossible to avoid the unwanted intimacy of hearing her using the pot. Ellie closed her eyes, trying not to think about the house that had been her home, with the privacy of its bathrooms.

This was, after all, only for tonight. Tomorrow things would be better.

They had to be!

FORTY

Their return to Friargate the next morning was not well received by Maggie, especially when Maisie announced that they had not had any breakfast.

'Well, if you've come here thinking that we're going to feed you –'

'We haven't,' Ellie stopped her quietly. Turning to her father, she said, 'I just want to telephone the carter, Father, to tell him to deliver my things here. I'm going to find us a house I can buy.' Her chin tilted at the look on Maggie's face. 'Henry left me a . . . a little money – enough, I think, to buy somewhere.'

'Oh, aye, and has he left you enough to live on as well? Because if so, what was you doing coming round here wanting charity?'

Continuing to ignore Maggie, Ellie continued, 'I can work. I was already working in Liverpool.'

'Working? A fine lady like you?' Maggie mocked. 'Fie, what would your mama have said? Well, don't expect to get teken on by any o' t' mills round here.'

'I . . . I take in private sewing,' Ellie explained to her father. 'In Liverpool, Cecily and her family were kind enough to recommend me to their friends and –'

'Aw, Ellie, lass! If Lyddy had heard you saying that . . . !' He shook his head whilst Maggie glared at Ellie, obviously not liking to be reminded of his first wife.

'Aye, well, that was all right when you'd got your fine friends, but they won't want to know you now, will they?' Maggie sneered.

'Maggie, there's no call to speak like that,' Ellie's father chastised.

'Oh, that's right! Didn't care about you, this 'un didn't, when she went off wi' 'er fine relatives, wi' not a care about her father, but now she's back you're acting like –'

'No! That isn't true!' Ellie interrupted Maggie passionately. 'Father, I never wanted to go to Hoylake. I wanted to stay here with you!' Tears stood out in her eyes. 'I hated being there and I hoped you would come for me and bring me home, but –'

'Aw, Ellie.' Suddenly her father's arms were round her and he was holding her. 'Eh, lass, I thought you wanted to be there. I thought it were for the best for you. If I'd known . . .' he told her as he let her go.

Struggling to compose herself, Ellie gave Maisie the last of her coppers to send her down the street with Minaco and Henrietta to a pie shop to get themselves something to eat. For herself she felt too queasy. The landlady's comments about the girl from the whorehouse had preyed on her mind all night.

'Come on in, lass, and make your telephone call,' her father was urging her, whilst Maggie looked on surlily.

Ellie could hardly bear to see the changes in her old home, and she deliberately shut out of her mind the last time she had been there, as she asked to be put through to the carter's number.

'Your trunk? No, miss, I can't deliver it for you.'

'What? What do you mean?' Ellie demanded anxiously.

On the other end of the line she could hear the carter explaining to her that he had been refused permission to collect her trunk by Elizabeth, who had told him that Ellie had no right to remove anything from the house.

'But the things in that trunk were mine,' she protested shakily.

'I'm right sorry, miss, but the missus wouldn't let me take 'un,' the carter repeated. 'Said it would be thievery if I did. Very definite about it, she were. Said you was to have nothing but what you had already got. Aye, and Mr Charnock – he was there with her and said the same. Said the trunk belonged to his son and that everything that was in it was family stuff and to stay with him.'

Somewhere in the distance, Ellie heard someone moan – a wretched despairing sound like that of an animal. The room had gone numbingly cold, and yet she felt so dreadfully hot! She could hear Maggie's screechy angry voice somewhere in the distance, and also her father's – louder; urgent. She tried to concentrate on what he was saying but somehow she couldn't. The world had become a whirling, rushing black whirligig of dizziness, sucking her down into its depths.

Reluctantly Ellie opened her eyes. She felt sick, the air around her was pungent with the smell of burned feathers.

She was lying on the floor in the parlour of the Friargate house and her father and Maggie were standing over her, the former looking harried and anxious, and the latter purse-lipped and angry.

'Didn't tell us you was in the family way, did you?' Maggie announced accusingly.

'Ellie, I don't understand what's going on. Surely in view of your condition your father-in-law . . . ?' her own father was asking.

'Henry's father isn't to know,' Ellie protested, sitting up – too quickly, she realised as nausea overwhelmed her.

The speculative look Maggie was giving her filled her with anxiety. 'Mr Charnock has made it clear that he doesn't . . . that is he feels Henry had a . . . a weakness that a child of his might well inherit.'

Her father, Ellie saw, was looking both shocked and uncomfortable.

'So that's five of you you was expecting us to house and feed,' Maggie accused her sharply. 'Well, don't think this changes anything. It don't. We've got more than enough mouths to feed with us own, without taking on someone who by rights ought to be the responsibility of someone else. How far gone are you, anyway?' she demanded.

'About four months,' Ellie told her wearily.

'It's well and truly fixed there, then,' Maggie informed her grimly. 'No use hoping you'll lose it!'

'Maggie,' Robert Pride interrupted grimly, 'that's enough. There's no call for that kind of talk. Ellie, love, the best thing really would be for you to go back to Liverpool. I wish I could do more for thee, lass, but . . .'

Ellie hated to see him looking so unhappy.

'I can't go back,' Ellie told him quietly, 'but it's all right, Father. Don't worry about me. I'll manage.'

Giddily she struggled to stand. She felt so ill and weak, and she longed to be offered a comfortable clean bed to lie on, but her pride wouldn't let her betray as much in front of Maggie. As to her claim that she could manage, Ellie tried to suppress the panic bubbling inside her.

She had in her purse the five guineas her father had given her yesterday, that was all. She had been relying on the money she had tucked away in the trunk, and not just that but on her sewing machine and the fabrics she had put there as well. And what about her clothes? All she had – all any of them had – was what they had on. And the medicine that was to have rid her of the unwanted child she was carrying was also in the trunk. It was obviously too late for that now, even if she could have afforded to replace it. Maggie's eyes were far too sharp.

The thought of another night in the boarding house down by the docks made Ellie feel sick. This morning they had all been scratching, and Ellie was sure she had seen something moving in the landlady's hair when she had stood at the bottom of the stairs watching them leave.

The hallway had smelled of urine, and one of the two men who had come out of the privy whilst Ellie had been waiting her turn to go in had not bothered to button his flies.

In Liverpool the busy life of the dock area had seemed exciting and romantic when viewed from the safety of her own secure life, but here in Preston, living amongst the detritus washed up by the sluggish tide, Ellie had very quickly become aware that the reality of dockside life was very different: the sailors they had walked past this morning on their way to Friargate, still drunk from the night before, lying in their own vomit; the whorehouse at the end of the street, where in the daylight it was easy to see the running sores on the women's faces, despite their youth.

They had walked past a sailors' mission, with its sad huddle of derelicts standing outside, Ellie freezing in affront as a man had swaggered past her and then turned round and come back offering her half a crown – 'Double that if I can have the both of you,' he had added, nodding in Minaco's direction.

The last thing she wanted was to have to return there, but she knew she had no alternative.

Collecting Maisie, Minaco and Henrietta, she walked them back via the town centre, pausing outside the offices of an employment agency. If she couldn't earn any money from her sewing then she would have to find other employment, but prudently she recognised that turning up to be interviewed whilst she was accompanied by her dependants was not perhaps a wise idea. She paused a little longer outside the window of a house-letting agency. A little further down the street she could see the familiar pawnbroker's sign. A bitter smile twisted her mouth. She didn't even have anything she could pawn, other than her wedding ring. Blankly she looked at it.

'Stay here,' she commanded the others.

Inside the shop she tugged off her ring and put it down on the counter.

The man behind it was brisk. 'Two guineas. And I'm being generous at that!' he told her. Shrugging his shoulders: 'Take it or leave it.'

'I need more than that,' Ellie told him. She felt as though she was choking on her own saliva as the despair welled inside her.

'Well, it's a decent enough gown you're wearing,' he began, 'and the brooch is probably worth a crown. 'Course, you could always sell your hair if it's long and thick enough. There's a place down off the market – allus on the lookout, she is, for good-quality hair. Use it for wigs, they do. I can give you a note for her.'

Her hair! Ellie looked at him in distress, hating the sudden memory she had of Gideon's hands in her hair as he kissed her.

'Thank you, but I'll just take the two guineas,' she told him numbly.

Once outside she wondered angrily why on earth she had not taken him up on his offer. The way she felt about Gideon surely she should have wanted to be rid of her hair, and with it her memory of him touching it!

She took her charges back via the alleys that led past a bakery, remembering that they sold off misshaped teacakes at the back door as well as the previous day's stale unsold bread.

She could remember how scornfully her mother had described those so poor that they had to stand in line waiting to buy up such offerings. Now, like them, she was standing there, her face averted as she hoped that she wouldn't be recognised.

The way in which Maisie and Henrietta fell on the hard pieces of bread, tearing into it, filled her with shame and guilt. Ellie broke one of them open and shuddered as she saw the weevil inside it, her gorge rising. Minaco hadn't eaten anything all day. Ellie had woken up in the night to find her sitting on the floor rocking back and forth, holding onto her photograph of Henry.

*   *   *

The smell of urine, stronger than ever, hit her as soon as they walked into the boarding house. Maisie wrinkled up her nose and exclaimed, 'Stinks!' Mixed with it was another smell, sharp and more acrid, and Ellie's body tensed as she recognised it. The whorehouse might officially be at the end of the street, but that smell!

Quickly she bundled the others up the stairs, reaching for the key to unlock their room.

Instinctively she knew that someone had been in it, and obviously not to change the bedding or do any cleaning. Even the chamber pot was still full!

Well, if they had been looking for something to steal they would have been out of luck. All she had in the world was with her!

Henrietta had begun to grizzle. Ellie waited for Minaco to go to her and comfort her, but the Japanese girl was ignoring her. Gently, Ellie went over to her and bent down so that they were on a similar level. There was a solemnness and wariness about the little girl that made Ellie's heart ache for her. When she picked her up she felt as frail as a small bird, her bones tiny and fragile. Beneath her clothes she was frighteningly thin with none of the soft plumpness Ellie remembered from her own siblings and her relatives' small children.

She should not be living here like this, Ellie acknowledged despairingly. She needed food and warmth, and a proper decent home. Giving her a quick cuddle, Ellie put her down again.

Minaco was curled up on the bed, clutching Henry's photograph and staring into space. It was as though she had somehow gone somewhere else.

'Don't like it here,' Maisie was sobbing, her bottom lip jutting out.

'Well, we won't be here much longer,' Ellie promised.

'Are we going back to Liverpool?' Maisie asked eagerly.

Ellie shook her head. It was impossible to explain to her why they could not return to the Charnock house.

Half an hour after they had returned to the house, a fight broke out in the street below. Maisie rushed excitedly to the window to watch, despite Ellie's instructions to her to come away.

Yells and curses filled the air, and some of the girls from the whorehouse had come to watch the proceedings, Ellie saw, as she went to the window to tug Maisie back.

She had planned to walk up to the marketplace as the stallholders were packing up for the day to see what she could scavenge for them all to eat, but there was no way she dared risk going out now!

Her stomach had started to rumble. Putting her hand on it she wondered bitterly if the unwanted life she was carrying inside her might be extinguished through starvation. Her body started to shake but

541

Ellie gritted her teeth against giving in to the temptation to think about the full horror of what was to come. She couldn't afford to!

Ellie woke abruptly, wondering at first where on earth she was. And then she remembered!

The noise that had woken her was someone trying the locked door to their room. She lay frozen with fear beneath the bedclothes as she watched the handle twist to and fro as whoever was outside turned it impatiently. Her heart was thumping as though it was going to break through her chest wall. She felt more alone and afraid than she had ever imagined it was possible to feel.

At Ellie's insistence they had visited the privy together, Ellie insisting that they all stood guard for one another, and then she had ushered them back upstairs to wash as best they could in the bowl of cold and soon scummy water their landlady had reluctantly provided.

Breakfast had been the last of the now very stale bread, and some watery milk Ellie had bought from the landlady.

Ellie wished that she could have left Minaco in charge of Maisie and Henrietta whilst she went alone to find them new lodgings, but the Japanese girl had retreated even further into herself and, pathetically, little Henrietta was now turning to

Ellie with her arms held out for help instead of her mother, snuggling contently onto Ellie's lap when she dressed her, babbling away in a mixture of Japanese and English.

The thought of trudging the streets all day in the damp December air, searching for somewhere to rent, sent Ellie's spirits plummeting, but she knew she could not stay another night in this house.

She had just finished buttoning Henrietta's shoes when she heard someone rattling the doorknob.

'No!' she called out fiercely to Maisie, who was running towards the door obviously intending to open it, but as Maisie's face started to pucker in distress Ellie suddenly heard a voice calling out to her from the other side of the door.

'Ellie, are you in there? It's me, John!'

John! Relief flooded her. Quickly she went to unlock the door.

It had been some time since she had last seen her brother and she was bemused to see how tall he had grown – taller than their father, but still thin and awkward with his new height in the way that very young men were.

'Dad told me you were here. I know all about what's been happening,' John explained as he came into the room, his nose wrinkling in disgust. 'This whole place stinks, Ellie. It isn't fitting that you should be living here. The whole area's got the worst kind of reputation,' he added reprovingly.

Ellie grimaced.

'I'm not here by choice, John,' she pointed out. 'I

543

had hoped that Dad would let me have a couple of the attic rooms until I got myself sorted out.'

'Oh, Maggie would never allow that! Mind, things aren't going very well with the shop, by all accounts – at least not according to Uncle Will.

'Dad asked me to have a word with Mrs Kershaw about you finding somewhere to live and about getting you some sewing work,' he told her awkwardly. 'She's the wife of Mr Kershaw, the photographer I work for. She says that there's some decent houses to be rented up near Horrocks' mill. She's had a word with a friend of hers who rents one, and she's given her the address of the agent who lets them out. They aren't much,' John warned her, 'nothing like what you'll be used to, Ellie, but she says if you like she'll pass the word around amongst her friends that you're looking for sewing work. You know, you might be better off getting a job in one of the mills.' John avoided meeting her eyes. 'Horrocks pays pretty well. Of course, there's always office work,' he continued in a rush when she didn't respond, 'but you'd need to get some training on one of those typewriting machines first. Look,' he added when Ellie still made no response, 'I know it's not much, but Dad has sent you this . . . and . . . and there's a couple of guineas there from me as well, Ellie.'

Hot tears burned Ellie's eyes as he handed her the money: another five guineas from her father, and two guineas from John. Along with what she had, at least she would be able to rent somewhere to live.

'What's the matter with her?' he asked, nodding his head in Minaco's direction. Throughout his visit she had simply sat on the bed, staring into space, clutching Henry's photograph.

'I think it must be her way of grieving,' Ellie told him quietly.

'You know, Ellie, you'd do much better if you only had yourself to support. I mean . . .' he looked uncomfortable again, 'that is, Maggie said there was to be a child!'

Ellie's heart was beating fast, and she could feel the angry panic building up inside her. The more people who knew about her pregnancy, the harder it was getting for her to ignore it and pretend that it wasn't happening. Didn't she already have enough problems?

'Henrietta is Henry's child,' she told John sharply, trying to hide her own sense of despair and dread. 'If I don't take responsibility for her you know what will happen to her? She'll end up in the workhouse orphanage. She's not much older than Philip. How is he, John? No matter how often I have written to ask her, our aunt will never tell me how he does.'

John's expression hardened. 'He's a champion little lad, Ellie, bright as a button! I've told him all about you – aye, and our Connie and Dad as well, and all about Friargate, but I dare say he'll forget it all now. They're bringing him up as if he were their own. He's our brother, Ellie, not their son. I wish Ma had never died, Ellie!'

'So do I, John,' Ellie said sadly.

'Mr Kershaw has given me the day off to give you a hand,' John told her. 'I'll go round to the agents with you, if you like. They'll pay a bit more mind to you when they see you've got a man with you,' he told her, puffing out his chest.

'Oh John!' He was only thirteen, yet here he was for all the world acting as though he was already a man!

Again Ellie felt tears pricking her eyes as she accepted his offer gratefully, and gave him a fierce hug.

Ellie heaved a sigh of relief. The house in Newall Street was hers! It had been touch and go whether or not the agent would rent the house out to her at first, and in the end she had had to pay a full three months' rent up front before he had reluctantly given in.

'And there's to be no subletting of rooms, unless you consult us about it first,' he warned her grimly. 'We've had tenants before who've thought they could take advantage in that way! And no gentlemen callers staying overnight or calling after dark! It's all here in the lease,' he added.

Like the house they had just left, the one they were to rent on Newall Street had no indoor sanitation. There was a privy in the back yard, and the house was apparently equipped with a tin bath in the kitchen.

'A full check will be made at the end of your

tenancy, and if anything is missing you will be held responsible and will have to pay for it,' the agent told her warningly. 'The rent collector will call round every Friday night for the rent, starting from this week.'

'But I've just paid three months' rent,' Ellie protested.

'That's our surety that you'll be a good tenant. Any losses for breakages will be taken out of that at the end of your tenancy and the remainder handed back to you.'

Wearily, Ellie gave in. Her situation was too desperate for her to be able to argue.

It was mid-December; the shops were filled with Christmas cheer of every sort. Grimly, Ellie hurried past their tempting displays, trying not to think about past Christmases or to compare them with the life that now lay ahead of her!

If only she was not carrying the extra burden of this unwanted child. Ellie trembled at the thought of what lay ahead of her.

FORTY-ONE

Nervously, Ellie hurried down the street, shivering as she felt the cold wind against the back of her neck. Outside the shop she had been looking for, she hesitated, and then, taking a deep breath, went in.

'Yes?' the woman inside asked her.

'I-I believe that you . . . that you buy hair,' Ellie told her firmly, removing her hat as she did so.

Ten minutes later, standing in a small icy-cold back room, trying not to shiver whilst she endured the humiliation of having her hair inspected, Ellie reminded herself just why she was here.

It was nearly a month now since she had first returned to Preston, and she was constantly worrying about how little she was earning. She no longer had the kind of customers who were willing to pay a lot of money for hand-smocked baby dresses and the like. If she was to earn anything like enough to keep them all, she needed to have a sewing machine.

Ellie had scoured the town's second-hand shops, looking for something suitable, and two days ago she found a machine in excellent condition, the only problem being she did not have the money to buy it. And then she had remembered being told she could sell her hair. She had lain awake each night since, remembering how her mother used to brush it for her, and how Gideon had said it was the most beautiful hair he had ever seen.

But beautiful hair didn't put food in their mouths, she told herself now as the woman finally delivered an approving nod of her head.

Ellie shivered the whole time the woman was cutting the hair off, unable to bring herself to look at the swathes of corn-gold hair being carefully put on a clean piece of cloth, and she shivered even more when she left the shop!

She had asked John to meet her at the sewing-machine shop so that he might help her get the machine home. The shop owner had promised her the loan of a small handcart providing she paid a deposit on it.

John was waiting for her when she reached the shop, blowing on his cold hands as she hurried up to him.

Inside the shop she dealt briskly with the owner, and watched whilst he and John carefully man-handled the machine into the cart.

Half an hour later, John was puffing with pride as he finally assembled the machine for her and stood back to admire his handiwork.

'Ellie,' he called out, 'come and look. It's working a treat!'

Hesitantly Ellie went into the parlour.

'It's running fine and I've checked –' John began, and then broke off as he finally noticed Ellie's hair.

'Ellie . . . what's happened to your hair?'

'I sold it to pay for the sewing machine,' Ellie told him simply.

The look on his face hurt her.

'I need it so that I can earn more money, John,' she added quickly. 'My hair will grow again, but little Henrietta won't, nor this baby, if there isn't any food for us to eat!'

Ellie blinked her burning eyes as she tried to focus on her sewing. It was gone midnight and she had been working since two o'clock in the afternoon, only breaking off with a bite of something to eat at teatime.

The dress she was making had to be finished by tomorrow. The woman she was making it for had given her the work with that proviso. In Liverpool Ellie would have turned down such work, as much for the fact that she was being underpaid for it as for the ridiculously short time-limit, but the woman had hinted that if Ellie completed this work to her satisfaction she would provide her with more, and Ellie could not afford to turn down that kind of opportunity, no matter how tired her eyes were.

Her short hair tickled the back of her neck; there

was nothing left for Gideon to run his fingers through now! Her eyes blurred again and the needle she was using to hand-sew the ruffles to the hem of the dress slipped and stabbed her finger.

Suddenly everything was too much for her. Dropping the dress, Ellie covered her face with her hands and wept with misery and despair.

A small sound caught her attention, and a small hand touched her knee. Uncovering her face, Ellie looked down. Little Henrietta was standing beside her, looking at her with solemn eyes.

Immediately, Ellie picked her up and settled her on her knee, ignoring the swift objecting kick she felt in her belly.

'Don't cry,' Henrietta told her, patting her face.

'Ellie!'

Ellie smiled gratefully as John hurried across the icy marketplace to where she was standing and took her heavy basket from her.

'This basket is far too heavy for you in your condition,' he told her sternly.

Ellie gave him a wry look. 'It's the end of the day and if I don't take advantage of what materials the stallholders are selling off cheap then we don't get to eat next week.'

She was just about managing to earn enough to pay the rent and feed them all – thanks to the work she was now receiving from the woman whose dress she had sat up all night to finish – although sometimes their diet was made up of little more than bread and soup – a soup cooked up out of cheap vegetables, with a handful of bones from her father's shop thrown in to give it a bit of extra thickness.

It angered Ellie to know that Hilda Brewer, the woman she now sewed for, was selling on what Ellie made at a profit to herself, for which she did nothing, whilst paying Ellie a mere pittance, but she knew that she was not in a position to complain, because she needed the money.

Cecily had sent her several imploring letters to her father's Friargate address, begging her to visit her, but Ellie had too much pride to allow Cecily to see what she had descended to. Cecily's mother would never allow her daughter to 'know' her now, Ellie was aware.

'You should get that girl of yours to do more,' John told her forthrightly. He had assumed a protective manner towards her that both amused and touched Ellie. 'Aye, an' that Minaco as well.'

Ellie sighed. 'You know that Maisie can't be trusted to run errands unsupervised, John, and as for Minaco . . .' She frowned.

The Japanese girl rarely spoke and barely ate, and sometimes Ellie felt that she was deliberately grieving herself to death; that without Henry she felt there was no purpose to her life. Of course, that made her feel guilty, since as Henry's wife, in the eyes of the world she should be the one who was grieving.

'Perhaps I should think about putting a notice in my window, saying, "Sailors' washing taken in" like they do down by the dock,' she sighed, as John took her arm to help her over the icy cobbles.

'What!' His face turned an embarrassed red. 'Ellie, surely you know what that means?' he protested, shaking his head when she looked enquiringly at him. 'It's a notice put in their windows by a . . . a certain class of female who . . . who offer their services to men and . . .'

'Oh!' Ellie's own face crimsoned as she realised what he was trying to say.

'It's all wrong that you should be living like this,' John told her angrily. 'By rights you should be in Liverpool, in the Charnock house. This child you're carrying –'

'I've already told you, John, Mr Charnock has made it plain that . . . well, I know that neither I nor my child would be welcome or wanted.'

Her child. Ellie grimaced to herself. For weeks she had tried her best to ignore the fact that she was pregnant, hoping that somehow if she did not acknowledge it the life within her would magically wither away, but of course it had not done so. No, it had its father's obstinacy, that was for sure!

Sometimes in the night she woke up streaming with sweat, terrified by her own nightmares of giving birth, but a new steely Ellie had metamorphosed from the old Ellie, forced into existence by necessity and the grim daily fight for survival. Her girlhood fear of giving birth was a luxury she could no longer indulge in! She had other, larger fears now, fears brought about by the heavy responsibilities she carried. If she should die, what would happen to those who were dependent upon her?

'Have you heard anything yet from Connie?' Ellie asked her brother anxiously.

'Nope. I reckon she's too ashamed of herself to get in touch or to come back. She was full of wild talk at one stage about going to America.'

'Oh, John, I wish so much that she would let us know where she is. I am so worried about her!'

They had reached Newall Street now, and Ellie's pace quickened. She was always anxious about what might be waiting for her when she had been away. Minaco had retreated completely into herself now, and refused to have anything to do with any of them, including her own daughter; and Maisie, who had become jealous of Henrietta's growing attachment to Ellie, often pinched and bullied the little girl behind Ellie's back. As Ellie went inside she stamped the cold out of her feet, blowing on her almost numb fingers.

Maisie and Henrietta were in the kitchen, playing with a pair of rag dolls Ellie had made them.

'Her ma's gone,' Maisie informed Ellie, jerking her head in Henrietta's direction. 'Took off, she did. Should ha' taken her with her.'

Ellie frowned, pausing in the act of removing her outdoor clothes, thinking Maisie must be mistaken since Minaco never left the house, but after she had gone upstairs and checked the rooms she realised that Maisie was right.

'Where has she gone, Maisie, did she say?' Ellie questioned anxiously.

Maisie gave a dismissive shrug, frowning as Henrietta reached for the doll she had been playing with, then smacking the little girl's hand with a petulant expression.

'Maisie?' Ellie pressed.

'Never said nothing. Just gave a loud cry and picked up that picture she's allus got and ran to the door.'

Ellie looked at her brother. 'John, what on earth could have made her do such a thing? She never goes out,' Ellie told him, her frown changing to a warm smile as Henrietta came and wrapped her arms around her legs. Since Ellie was unable to move, John obligingly unwrapped the little girl's arms and picked her up, tickling her beneath her chin until she giggled.

She really was the prettiest child, Ellie reflected, as she took her from him, watching her eyes sparkle with delight at the attention she was getting. And bright too. Ellie was already starting to teach her her letters, much to Maisie's annoyance.

'She won't have gone far,' John comforted her. 'After all, she doesn't really know her way around Preston, does she? Perhaps she just fancied some fresh air.'

Ellie shook her head decisively. 'No, she won't have done that.'

Whenever she could, weather and her workload permitting, Ellie made a point of taking Maisie and Henrietta to Avenham Park, remembering how much she had enjoyed her own visits there as a child, but after the first visit Minaco had refused to go with them.

'John, I feel really worried about her.' Instinctively as she spoke, Ellie rubbed her side to soothe the small nagging ache there.

Automatically John's attention was caught by her action. It was his opinion that Ellie had more than enough to worry about without the Japanese woman she had taken responsibility for adding to her problems.

'Depend on it, Ellie, she will simply have slipped out on some errand or for some fresh air.'

'But if she hasn't, if something has befallen her . . .' Ellie protested.

'Well, let's wait for now and see if she returns. With temperatures as low as the ones we are currently suffering, she is bound not to want to stay out too long.'

'And if she doesn't return?' Ellie pressed him, unable to feel reassured. She was shivering herself, despite the many layers of clothing she was wearing. February was turning out to be as intensely cold as August had been unusually hot.

John shook his head. 'You are worrying too much, Ellie. She will. After all, where else is there for her to go?'

But despite his attempts to reassure her, Ellie could not shake off her own sense of foreboding.

In truth she was feeling far more despairing than she wanted John to know. Mature as he had grown, he was still only a boy and her younger brother. She should be looking after him, she acknowledged ruefully, not the other way round! The coming birth of her baby loomed over her like an oppressive shadow, her fear of what might befall her streaking her dreams and filling her with acute dread that if she should die she would leave behind her not only her orphaned child, but also Henrietta, whom she had come to love very much, and Maisie, for whom she felt an admittedly sometimes irritated sense of responsibility. What would happen to them if she was not there to care for them?

The thought of the loss of her own life no longer haunted her in the way that it had once done, but the consequences of her death tormented her far more. She now had first-hand knowledge, after all, of just what could happen to a child wrenched from the loving comfort and security of its mother's protection.

Somewhere at the back of her mind she knew that she had been holding onto the reassuring belief that Iris would return home to Liverpool and insist on seeking her out, and that having done so, she would somehow, in her no-nonsense way, wave her version of a magic wand and rescue them all from the life they were currently living. But earlier that week she had received a letter from Iris, sent to her father's address, informing her that she and her companions were enjoying their travels so much that they had decided to extend them and that she now did not expect to be home for at least another three months.

She had also received a letter from Cecily in which she had mentioned the fact that she had seen Elizabeth Fazackerly in Liverpool, wearing what she was sure had been 'our Aunt Parkes' sables, Ellie, remember – the ones she gave to you? I must say that I was both shocked and surprised, and can only assume that you must have grown tired of them. I know my own sister would have dearly loved to have had them and I have to say I think they ought to have remained in the family instead of being passed onto someone who is of no real consequence to us, especially since we are having such a very cold winter. Aunt Parkes has complained that you do not write to her very often. She has become very reclusive, and Mr Parkes seems to spend a great deal of time away on business.'

Ellie had sighed as she had put Cecily's letter down. There was such a gulf between them now.

'Got to go,' John announced, leaning down to kiss her cheek. 'Mr Kershaw wants some photographs taking of the millworkers out on strike, and the ice on the Ribble.'

'John, if Minaco doesn't come back soon –' Ellie persisted, unable to stop herself from expressing her illogical concern.

'She will,' he interrupted, 'otherwise she is likely to freeze to death in this cold,' he added carelessly.

'But if it makes you feel any better I shall call round later tonight, just to make sure.'

'If she hasn't returned by then we shall have to inform the authorities,' Ellie insisted.

'I wish you would not upset yourself so, especially when . . .' John told her gruffly, looking uncomfortably away from her.

As mature as he had become, Ellie reminded herself that he was still little more than a boy, and it was obvious at times that the sight of her swollen belly discomforted him a little.

'Mrs Kershaw said I was to tell you that she knows of a good midwife, when . . . when the time comes, although I would have thought perhaps our Uncle Gibson —'

Ellie shook her head. 'I couldn't afford his fees,' she told him simply, 'and I very much doubt that our Aunt Gibson would want him to attend me anyway. I saw her in town the other day. She was going into Booths.' Ellie's mouth curled into a wry smile. Shopping at Booths, the town's best grocers, was well beyond her meagre means. 'I know she saw me but she pretended not to do so.'

John gave his sister a sympathetic look.

'Gideon – by, but it's been a fair old time since I've seen thee, lad. Ye look well enough. Mind, so ye should with all that money you've got now,' Will Pride chuckled, nudging Gideon familiarly in the ribs.

Gideon suppressed his impatience to be gone out of the smoky beer-stinking public house where he had gone to pay his men, and to be back in the comfort of his own home.

'It 'ull be a late lambing this year, no doubt about that – aye, and many a flock cut back wi' losses. I've never known it so cold. They say that t' Ribble's froze over up Penwortham way, and that folks are out skating on it! You've just missed our John. Bin taking photographs of t' mills wi' workers out. Bloody government. Criminal the way it's treating the working man. I suppose you'll have heard about our Ellie coming back to town.'

Gideon froze. He had been so busy these last few months attending to his own affairs that he had had no time to listen to gossip.

'Can't help but feel sorry for the lass really. Seems like she never wanted to leave Preston at all really, according to what she's told our Rob,' Will was continuing, beerily unaware of Gideon's stiffening stance and lack of desire to hear what he was saying.

'Aye, the lass is having a bit o' a bad time. That father-in-law of hers has virtually thrown her out, and then Maggie refused to have her back wi' them. O' course, all Lyddy's posh relatives are turning their noses up at Ellie on account of our Constance, and Ellie's having to do the best she can for herself. Rented herself a little house down on Newall Street, and set herself up in a bit o' a sewing business, but it's a right rum do. There she is, going

560

on for seven months gone, and that father-in-law of hers refusing to do anything for her, and her his son's widow and the little 'un she's carrying his grandchild. Must ha' been about the last thing he did, getting her in the family way before he took off and hanged hissel', poor sod. Doesn't make any kind o' sense to me what's going on, but according to our Robert, our Ellie's too proud to go a-begging to her father-in-law, and what with him tekin' against his son on account o' thinking he had summat mental wrong wi' him . . .' Will shook his head. 'There, but these posh folk they have their own way o' doing things.'

Gideon stared at him. Ellie was pregnant? A dozen feelings slammed down on him, all of them unwanted.

Somehow or other he managed to escape from Will Pride, shrugging himself deeper into the cashmere coat he had bought. A real toff's coat, his men had called it, mocking him, and yet at the same time they obviously wanted to remind him that he was still one of them, despite his inheritance. Gideon had also seen the wary respect in their eyes. He was a rich man now – a man who, by virtue of his birth, had no need to ape the manners and customs of a better class because he was in fact a part of it, and subconsciously, although Gideon himself wasn't aware of it, that knowledge showed in all manner of subtle ways. The ease with which he wore the cashmere coat was simply one small outward manifestation of the man he had become.

Ellie pregnant! Nearly seven months, Will Pride had said, implying with his usual coarseness of manner that her impregnation had been perhaps the last act of her dead husband.

Nearly seven months. Abruptly Gideon stopped walking, suddenly oblivious to the freezing cold. A sweat heated and then chilled his skin as he did some mental arithmetic. By God, but what he was thinking had to be wrong! If it wasn't, there was no way that she would not have let him know, and come knocking on his door demanding her due. Widowed and virtually destitute, according to Will, she would never have passed up on the opportunity to feather her nest at his expense. That was the kind of woman she was, he knew that! Angrily he reached into his pocket for his cigarette case. As he opened it his hands were shaking.

FORTY-TWO

White-faced, Ellie looked at her brother. John had, as he had promised, come back to find out if Minaco had returned.

'John, something has to have happened to Minaco,' she insisted. 'It's nearly midnight. She would never stay out this long.'

John looked away from her, feeling uncomfortable. Ellie, despite the fact that she had been a wife and was soon to be a mother, was sometimes surprisingly naïve. John might be younger than Ellie but he recognised that he knew a great deal more about the world than she did. The Japanese girl had been her husband's mistress, a girl who, according to Ellie, Henry had rescued from being sold into prostitution. She was a pretty little thing, with her exotic features and her tiny delicate body. John had seen the way men looked at her when she was out with Ellie, and the way she had looked back at them, searchingly, hungrily, somehow. But he still couldn't bring himself to suggest to Ellie that she

563

might simply have taken up with some man, leaving Ellie to be responsible for bringing up the bastard child she had had by Ellie's dead husband.

'Look, I know you're concerned, but let's wait and see what morning brings,' he suggested.

'John!' The look Ellie gave him reminded him sharply that she was his elder sister. 'It's below freezing outside. There isn't any way . . . We have to inform the police,' Ellie told him firmly.

John heaved a small sigh. 'Ellie, it's close on midnight. Most sensible people will be in their beds.'

'I know that, but Sergeant Johnson lives six doors down, and I'm sure he'd understand if you went round and explained to him what has happened.'

John knew when he was beaten.

After he had gone, complaining that Sergeant Johnson might understand, but that he feared that Mrs Johnson, his formidable wife, might not be best pleased at being woken at such an ungodly hour and on such a cold night, Ellie went upstairs to check on the children, pausing halfway to ease her aching back and get her breath.

Maisie was fast asleep in the bed she and Henrietta supposedly shared, snoring slightly. Henrietta, as Ellie had known she would, had crept out of her own bed and was curled up under the covers of Ellie's, lying there so still that Ellie knew immediately that she was awake.

Helplessly, Ellie gathered her into her arms and held her tight, sitting on the bed and rocking her to and fro. There was such a bond between them,

not because she was Henry's child but because of
her circumstances, Ellie suspected. She could see so
often in Henrietta's too knowing and worried eyes
the same fears and miseries she knew she herself
would have felt in her position. Ellie ached to be
able to protect her from every harm that could
befall her – as she had not been able to protect
either herself or her own sister and brothers.

Her own child, unwanted and burdensome, moved
in her womb as though resenting the attention she
was paying Henrietta.

Ellie didn't need to read the newspapers to know
that hard times lay ahead. Evidence of the financial
hardship caused by the long summer of strikes was
all around them: the crowd of women waiting to
buy up the unwanted food from the closing market
stalls grew larger every week, and Ellie had overheard several groups of mill girls discussing whether
or not they would be better off moving to Liverpool,
where at least the docks were still bringing money
into the city.

Once this so wrongfully conceived child had been
born she was seriously contemplating approaching
one of the town's employment agencies to see
if there was any casual domestic work going.
Her Barclay aunts would love that – their sister's
daughter scrubbing other people's floors – but Ellie
knew she would rather do that than beg them for
the charity they were obviously bitterly reluctant to
give her.

Something had hardened in Ellie over the last

few months, so that, phoenix-like, her spirit had become strong and honed.

'I'm cold,' Henrietta told her, shivering in her arms.

'Yes, so am I,' Ellie agreed, kissing the top of her head. 'Let's go downstairs and sit by the range, shall we?'

What he was doing was crazy, Gideon told himself savagely, and what he was thinking was even crazier. Why the hell should he leap to the conclusion that Ellie Pride's child was his just because of that time . . . ?

He paused before crossing the square to let the horse pulling the milk float plod past him. The beast's breath was a fiery white plume on the frozen air, and he could hear the milkman cursing that the milk had frozen in the churns.

It was too early for any of his neighbours in this wealthy part of town to be abroad, but the town itself, as he crossed it, was shivering into reluctant morning life.

Only the youngsters, predictably, were enjoying the icy conditions, laughing as older people skidded on the frozen slides they had made on the pavements. As he walked through the market he overheard some wag commenting that they would need to bring icebreakers into Preston's dock if the freeze continued.

* * *

566

Shivering, Ellie blew on her numb fingers as she tried to sew. Overnight the temperature had dropped even lower and, despite her best efforts, it was impossible to keep the house warm. All three of them were huddled round the range, which she dare not keep at more than barely alight for fear of running out of fuel completely.

Sergeant Johnson had been round before going on duty this morning and promised to report Minaco's disappearance.

Despite Ellie anxiously pressing him he had refused to say what he thought might have befallen her.

Ellie tensed as someone rapped demandingly on the front door knocker.

The street was clean enough, its houses decently maintained, Gideon acknowledged as he noted the white-stoned steps and polished doorknockers of the houses he had passed, but it was still a mean, narrow little street of poor-quality housing, thrown up to house the millworkers, and without any pretence of being anything other than meanly utilitarian. He could almost feel the cheap lace curtains twitching as he strode past them, and he told himself that he should feel pleased that Ellie was demeaned by having to live in such circumstances.

As he knocked on the door he told himself too, as he had told himself a thousand times since last night, that what he was thinking was impossible, but something had still driven him to come here.

Expecting to see either her brother John or Sergeant Johnson standing on her front doorstep, Ellie stared in silent, shocked disbelief at Gideon, unable to do anything other than simply step back when he walked past her into the narrow hallway, shutting the door firmly behind him.

She could see the way he was looking at the surroundings, her home, and immediately her body tensed in defiant pride.

The door to the kitchen was open and, as though he sensed its relative warmth, he headed for it, coming to an abrupt halt as he walked inside and saw Maisie and Henrietta seated at the kitchen table, eating their thin porridge.

Of the two of them Henrietta was the neater eater, Ellie acknowledged. The little girl was finicky and delicate in her ways, instinctively copying the way Ellie herself ate, whilst Maisie, despite Ellie's exhortations to her not to do so, simply crammed her food into her mouth, uncaring of the mess she made.

Gideon stared at Ellie, unable to stop himself from demanding harshly, 'Your hair – what's happened?'

Instinctively, Ellie's hand went to her shorn locks. 'I sold it – I needed the money,' she told him sharply.

Her beautiful hair – but there was something about the soft way it curled into her neck and those little feathery tendrils that made him want to . . .

Gideon frowned as the child put down her spoon

and climbed down off her stool to go to Ellie's side. Automatically Ellie bent down to pick her up.

'What's this?' he asked her tersely. 'A travelling circus?'

He had a vague memory of Will saying something about Ellie having with her a woman who had been Henry's mistress, along with her child, but he had not paid much heed to that part of his tale, being more concerned with his news of Ellie's pregnancy.

Anger flashed in Ellie's eyes as she held Henrietta tightly. She had become very defensive about people's comments regarding the little girl, whose exotic mixed-race heritage made her the subject of their curiosity.

'No,' she told him sharply, 'this circus, as you so rudely and disparagingly refer to them, are my maid, Maisie, and –'

'Your what? Your maid?' Gideon checked her in grim disbelief. 'My God, now I've heard everything! You're renting just about the cheapest decent house you can find, and you've brought your bloody maid. What's wrong – and don't tell me you need her to fasten your stays?' He gave her a look that made her face burn. 'After all, the whole world can see that you aren't in any need of them.' Out of the corner of her eye Ellie saw that Maisie's bottom lip had begun to quiver. She hated loud male voices, and immediately stopped eating, and burst out, 'Why is that nasty man shouting? I don't like him, make him go away!' And then proceeded to suck her thumb as she always did when she was distressed.

Unable to conceal his surprise, Gideon stepped closer.

Immediately, Ellie moved between him and the table, telling him quietly, 'Please don't do that. You're frightening her.'

The look of realisation in his eyes made her put her arm protectively around Maisie's tense shoulders.

'And the young 'un?' Gideon demanded, nodding in Henrietta's direction, although, of course, he already knew what she was going to say.

'Henry's child,' Ellie told him quietly, lifting her chin.

Gideon could feel his heart starting to pound too heavily. There was something here in this shabby poor room he didn't want to recognise or acknowledge, something that ripped away the tissue he had packed around the wound Ellie had given him and left it raw and exposed. For these – these pathetic pieces of human flotsam, she had love and compassion to give, and to spare. Suddenly he was reminded of his own mother, Mary; suddenly and unwantedly he could see an unmistakable connection between the two women.

'And the one you're carrying?' he asked her savagely, nodding in the direction of her swollen belly. 'Seven months gone, I hear you are, so it must have been conceived in August. Just before your husband killed himself, so they say.'

Something dangerous had entered the room, Ellie recognised, as her body poured with sweaty heat and then shivered in the grip of intense cold, something very dangerous.

'If indeed it is your husband's,' Gideon finished with menacing softness.

Ellie tried to speak; tried to pull her glance away from the compelling hold of his but it was as though, somehow, something beyond her power was stopping her from doing so.

Gideon knew the truth the split second he looked into her eyes and saw the sick despair there. Ellie was carrying his child.

'It isn't his, is it?' he challenged her hoarsely. 'It's mine. My child . . . conceived that night . . . Ellie?' he beseeched her urgently, but it was too late. She had pulled away from him, clutching Henrietta defensively to her.

'You have no right to say such things,' she told him, her voice shaking, 'and no right either to be here. I want you to leave. Now . . . Immediately.'

She had begun to shake, the little girl in her arms clutching at Ellie's gown so that she unintentionally dragged the fabric over the tight swell of her belly.

The small, mean house, its cold air, the pathetic signs of Ellie's attempt to give it some homeliness and comfort, the way both girls were clinging anxiously to her, tore at Gideon. He wanted to hate her, deride her – she deserved that he should – but instead he was overwhelmed by a sickening sense of shocked confusion.

Unable to trust himself to speak he swung round and strode towards the door.

Ellie held her breath until she heard it open and then close behind him as he left.

Henrietta's hand touched her face. 'Mama crying,' she said solemnly.

Ellie felt her whole body shudder. Henrietta had never called her anything other than 'Ellie' before. Still holding her, she sank down into the rocking chair beside the range. Why, oh why hadn't she immediately denied Gideon's challenge?

FORTY-THREE

'Ellie, I know that things don't look good, but try not to give up hope. I mean . . .'

Ellie stared blankly at her brother as his voice faded away uncomfortably. He had arrived less than an hour after Gideon's departure, to tell her that as yet there had been no news about Minaco. As she listened to him Ellie realised guiltily that for the past hour she had barely given the Japanese girl a thought.

That was the effect Gideon had on her. He made her selfish. Her mother had always said so.

'Look, why don't you go upstairs and try to get some rest?' John suggested. 'Mr Kershaw has given me permission to stay with you. He knows how anxious you are about Minaco.'

Silently Ellie headed for the stairs. The child in her womb had been moving vigorously all day as though . . . As though what? As though it sensed the presence of its father? Inwardly deriding herself, Ellie climbed the stairs, and entered the small cold bedroom.

*   *   *

Down by the docks the men surveyed the small pathetic bundle of flesh and bones, frozen stiff in death, the icy fingers clutching the photograph of the man she had loved.

Gideon stared around the elegant silence of the Winckley Square drawing room. Ellie Pride was carrying his child!

He could have other children, he reminded himself angrily. Other children with a wife far more suited to that position than the likes of Ellie Pride! He was a wealthy man now and she was a widow and a social outcast, who didn't have the sense not to burden herself with even more responsibilities than she already had – that exotic-looking child, that girl who quite plainly was not in full possession of her wits.

His child! Gideon thought of his own childhood and of Mary.

A discreet tap on the door caused him to swing round.

'Will you be requiring luncheon today, sir, only Cook . . .'

'No, thank you, Fielding. But . . . No, it's all right,' he told the bemused servant. 'I have to go out and I do not know how long I shall be.'

'Gideon!'

John Pride looked surprised as he opened the

door to him, and Gideon grimaced to himself as he stepped past Ellie's brother. His presence was a complication he had neither expected nor wanted. Now that he had made up his mind he was in a fever of impatience to have the matter settled just as soon as it could be.

He could not, would not, turn his back on his own flesh and blood. His own child! He would talk to Ellie, persuade her to hand the child over to him. He would bring it up himself. He would settle a sum of money on Ellie and she could do what she chose. He could hire servants to take care of his baby – a nursemaid . . . a governess . . .

There was no sign of Ellie in the cold parlour John showed him into, and Gideon was just about to ask for her when there was a loud banging on the front door. Excusing himself, John hurried to answer it, leaving the parlour door open as he did so.

'Sergeant Johnson!' Gideon heard him exclaiming, his voice faltering as he asked, 'Have you found her?'

Found her? Gideon's whole body tensed as he felt the ominous silence.

'It's not . . . not bad news, is it?' he heard John's voice falter whilst his own insides felt as though they were being squeezed in a vice. Something had happened to Ellie!

'I'm afraid it is, John,' the other man confirmed gravely. 'A young woman's body has been found –'

Gideon was through the door before he could stop himself, his face ashen. Ellie dead, and it was his fault! He was to blame. He had driven her, the mother of his child, the love of his life to – The love of his life? In a flash of awareness Gideon recognised that his fear, his despair, his gut-wrenching sense of loss and anguish were not for the child he had come here to take from Ellie into his own protection but for Ellie herself . . . his Ellie.

'John, I heard someone at the door. What has happened? Has Minaco been found?'

As Gideon heard Ellie's voice from the top of the stairs, the blood flowed hotly back into his numbed body as relief flooded over him. It was not Ellie who was dead. It was the poor Japanese girl who had been Henry's mistress. He should have realised that for himself, Gideon acknowledged.

The police sergeant was looking uncomfortable. 'Someone will have to come and identify the . . . ahem . . . the person,' he began apologetically.

'I will do it,' John announced.

'No, John!' Ellie said immediately. 'That wouldn't be right.' She avoided telling him he was far too young to have to undergo such an ordeal if anyone else could do it. Nor could she face going herself – and who would look after Maisie and Henrietta?

John turned to Gideon and requested almost formally, 'Gideon, could I ask you, please, to remain here with my sister until I return? I do not think she should be here on her own at a time like this.'

'John, I do not need Gideon to stay with me,' Ellie began to protest, and then stopped as she saw how strained her brother was looking. He had been such a support to her these last months, and sometimes she forgot how very young he still was. She would not reject his kindness, and when she agreed he left to go to Mr Kershaw with Sergeant Johnson.

Somehow she had known already that Minaco was dead. The Japanese girl could never have survived a night outside in such low temperatures and, more than that, Ellie knew intuitively that Minaco had stopped wanting to live.

A heavy shudder ran through her. She was now the only person who stood between Henrietta and the appalling fate of ending up in the workhouse orphanage. But she herself might easily die in childbed, as her own mother had done. Ellie had never felt more vulnerable or afraid – not for herself but for those who depended on her: Henrietta, Maisie, and even this new baby she had carried so unwillingly.

'Ellie, I am sorry to hear about ... about the child's mother, but you and I have urgent matters of our own we need to discuss.'

Blankly Ellie focused on Gideon.

'You are carrying my child,' Gideon told her.

Ellie opened her mouth to deny his assertion and then discovered that she could not.

'We must be married, and as soon as possible!'

Gideon frowned as he heard his own stern declaration. That was not what he had come here
to say at all, but now the words had been said,
and he discovered he had no intention of calling
them back. In fact, bemusingly, he discovered that
he was extremely glad that he had said them! A
cavalier attitude of reckless determination filled
him, a sense of excitement and hope, almost, of
his life suddenly taking an unexpectedly enticing
and longed-for turn.

'We have no alternative. We must marry for the
sake of our child,' he told Ellie firmly – privately
thinking: for the sake of their child and for the sake
of his love for her as well – but these were words he
could not say to her.

Ellie's eyes were dull and empty. Had she heard
what he had said? Had she registered his words,
Gideon wondered.

'I mean what I am saying, Ellie,' he warned her. 'I
understand now what it is not to know my parents,
and I would not have my child suffer from that
under any circumstances.'

Now she was focusing on him! 'What do you
mean?'

Gideon took a deep breath. 'Mary was my
mother,' he told her simply, so simply that Ellie
knew immediately that he was speaking the truth.
'She only told me herself when she was dying, and
she begged me not to reveal it to anyone . . . other
than the woman I . . . I married.'

Ellie stared at him. The knowledge that Mary had

not been his mistress but his mother was causing her to feel an emotion she was afraid to acknowledge. To prevent herself from having to, she reminded him flatly, 'You hate and despise me.'

Gideon turned his head, unable to meet her eyes. 'I shall hate myself even more if I do not do the right thing by my child,' he told her curtly.

Ellie's pride screamed at her to tell him that she would never marry him, never humiliate herself by joining her life to that of a man who had treated her as he had, who thought about her as he did, but a hardiness had developed in her these last months, a toughness that had no time for the luxury of an emotion such as pride. Every day that brought her closer to the birth of this child she carried brought her closer to her own fear.

'Very well,' she told him quietly, 'but there is a condition I must make.'

Gideon waited, his heart twisting in bitterness, already anticipating what was to come. She would want money, payment for his child and for herself. She would want . . .

'I will only marry you if you will legally adopt Henrietta and swear to me on the Bible that no matter what happens – no matter what – that you will care for her, and for this child,' she added, touching her belly, 'yourself! That you will not send them away from you to be reared by others. Also, I want you to swear that there will always be a place beneath your roof for Maisie.'

He was silent for so long that Ellie thought he

was going to refuse, unaware of the confusion and raw emotion making it impossible for him to say so much as a word.

Her 'condition' was so very different from what he had expected, so revealing of a side of her that he had previously refused to allow himself to see.

'She is nothing to you!' he told Ellie sharply, nodding in Henrietta's direction.

'On the contrary, she is everything to me,' Ellie corrected him fiercely. 'She is everything I should have done for my own brothers and sister and did not. I will not be responsible for another child suffering as they have done, Gideon. Either you give me your promise or I will not marry you.'

Gideon knew that she meant it.

'Very well then,' he agreed tersely.

They were married quietly six weeks later. Ellie had told no one in her family of her plans apart from her brother John, knowing how they were likely to react, and not just to the fact that she was marrying Gideon. She was, after all, officially still in mourning for Henry, but with her baby due in April Gideon had been insistent that there was no time to waste.

As they made their vows, Ellie was conscious of the way Gideon avoided looking at her. This was the second time she had been married, she reflected dully. The first time she had married a man she did not love, and now she was marrying a man who did not love her! Despairing tears pricked her eyes. Why was she so upset? She did not love Gideon, after all! Not any more, even though today, marrying him, was making her remember all those joyous, tender, idealistic, youthful hopes she had once had. All the shining, adoring love she had once had . . .

The fierce kick of her child thankfully distracted her.

The staff of her new home had lined up to welcome Ellie as their mistress. For a moment she had hesitated a little apprehensively on the threshold.

'Ellie, please allow me to present Mrs Harris, our housekeeper, to you.'

Ellie only had a moment to register the warm pressure of Gideon's hand on her arm, as the housekeeper bobbed her a respectful curtsy and announced formally, 'Welcome to your new home, ma'am.'

Her new home. She was now the mistress of this elegant, gracious house, Ellie had to remind herself as she was introduced to the other servants.

Gideon, observing her manner towards them, watched as relief and respect replaced the initial wariness in the servants' eyes. By the time she had finished being introduced to them, and had acquainted herself with a brief history of each and every one of them via her gentle questions, Gideon could see that she was going to have them eating out of her hand, an opinion that was confirmed when his starchy and sometimes formidable housekeeper unbent enough to declare, 'I hope I know my place, Mrs Walker, but may I suggest that you take tea before I show you over the house?' Tactfully the housekeeper made no reference to Ellie's advanced state of pregnancy.

Smiling gratefully, Ellie agreed, and slowly followed Mrs Harris towards the small sitting room overlooking the large garden to the rear of the house.

Ruefully Ellie allowed herself to be seated in a comfortable chair and fussed over by Mrs Harris, thankful that her private worries that the servants might not take to her – or, even worse, might look down on her – had come to nothing.

As soon as Mrs Harris had left, John, who had been holding Henrietta, put her down and the little girl ran immediately to Ellie.

Bending down to lift her onto her lap, Ellie felt her eyes starting to fill with tears. Against her will she found herself thinking of the past, and of things she knew it would be better for her to forget. It was nearly four years since she had first seen Gideon and the woman she was now was a very different person from the girl she had been then, but a part of her couldn't help thinking how different things might have been had she been allowed to follow her own heart.

A heart that Gideon had surely broken with his cruelty to her, Ellie reminded herself, as she hugged Henrietta close.

*　　*　　*

'Let me take Henrietta, Ellie,' John suggested, after the maid had brought in the tea trolley. 'Then you can pour the tea.'

'I'll take her, John,' Gideon intervened, mindful of the new role he was going to have to play in Henrietta's life, but as soon as he approached Ellie, the little girl buried herself as tightly as she could against Ellie, hiding her face from him in a gesture of denial.

'You'll have to give her time, Gideon,' Ellie said calmly, as John stepped in and took the little girl.

Gideon's mouth compressed. These last six weeks had shown him an Ellie who had constantly surprised him with her strength and her maturity. The declaration she made to him regarding the future of those she felt responsible for in the event of her death had shocked him in its bleakness. Now, with his own experience of losing Mary, for the first time he was beginning to question within himself what it must have meant to her to lose her own mother in the way that she had.

'Oh!' Ellie exclaimed as she looked at the tea trolley, which was laden not only with several plates full of deliciously dainty and tempting sandwiches, but also a cake. Not just any cake, she recognised as her face began to glow self-consciously, but a wedding cake!

Following the direction of her gaze, Gideon told her brusquely, 'I asked Mrs Harris to do it. I know you said you didn't want any fuss, but I thought a wedding cake . . .'

For some reason Ellie found she had a huge lump in her throat.

'And this is the master bedroom, ma'am,' Mrs Harris announced proudly, and with good reason, Ellie acknowledged, as she stepped into the elegantly proportioned bedroom. Not the room where she and Gideon . . . where he had . . . not that room, Ellie noted thankfully.

She had been dreading returning to this house, but a little to her own surprise she had discovered that being there was not having the traumatic effect on her she had anticipated.

Her nose twitched as she caught the smell of fresh paint.

As though she had guessed her thoughts the housekeeper said, 'The master has had it specially decorated and refurbished. And a brand-new bathroom put in for you, ma'am. He's designed it himself!'

A little dizzily Ellie followed her across the beautiful Chinese carpet and into the bathroom, unable to stop herself from giving a small gasp of awe.

'Had the porcelain specially brought over from France, Mr Gideon did,' Mrs Harris announced proudly. 'And that door there,' she added, nodding in the direction of a second door in the room, 'goes through into a little nursery he's had made, just until the baby's old enough to go upstairs into the

nursery proper. It's not been furnished yet,' she
added as she showed Ellie the room. 'Mr Gideon
said as how you would want to choose everything
for it yourself!'

As they returned to the bedroom Ellie couldn't
help looking at the huge bed. Was she expected to
share that with Gideon?

'And this is the door to the master's dressing room,
ma'am,' the housekeeper was saying as she showed
Ellie the comfortable-sized room off the bedroom, in
which Ellie was relieved to see there was a bed.

By the time she had finished her tour of the house,
Ellie was tired and longed for nothing so much as to
have a nap. But Maisie and Henrietta both needed
reassuring about their new surroundings, and Ellie
intended to speak to Gideon and insist that a small
bed was put in the nursery for Henrietta, so that
she and the coming baby could move into their new
quarters together!

'You look tired. It's been a long day – why don't
you go to bed?'

Ellie tensed as she heard Gideon's terse words.
She had just come from the kitchen where she
had gone to make sure that Maisie had settled in
happily. Gideon was right, she was tired, but she
was also worried about what married life held in
store for her and what Gideon's expectations were.
She knew that he didn't love her, but he was still a
man and . . .

As though he had guessed her thoughts, he said abruptly, 'I shall be sleeping in my dressing room, but –'

Ellie went white.

'What is it?' Gideon demanded.

Ellie shook her head, unable to tell him that his words had suddenly reminded her painfully of Henry. Instead, she bent to pick up Henrietta, who had refused to be parted from her and who had fallen asleep on the sofa.

'I'll do that,' Gideon told her gruffly, but as he reached for her, Henrietta woke up. Gideon's right hand was on her arm, and as she looked at it he stiffened and snatched it back. 'Better not frighten her with this before she's had time to get used to me,' he announced curtly.

'Frightened? Henrietta won't be frightened, Gideon,' she told him firmly. 'She's already asked me about your hand and I've told her that it is a very special hand that you have because you did a very special brave thing. Indeed, if anyone is frightened by it, I think it is you and not Henrietta,' she added perceptively.

The little girl was still looking at him with huge dark eyes. Grimly Gideon picked her up. That was a fine thing Ellie had said to him after the way she had recoiled from him with such pity!

Henrietta was a soft warm weight in his arms as he carried her upstairs. On the landing, when he would have taken the next flight, Ellie stopped him.

'You cannot expect a child as young as Henrietta to sleep alone in an unfamiliar room, Gideon. I have asked Mrs Harris to put a small bed in the little nursery for Henrietta, and until then she will share the bed with me.'

'Share your bed?' Gideon queried grimly. 'Is that for her sake or for yours, Ellie? If you are thinking that having her in your bed will keep me out of it –'

'I thought no such thing,' Ellie countered sharply.

Hostilely they looked at one another.

FORTY-FOUR

'What about this wallpaper for the nursery, Ellie?'

Despite the nagging ache in the small of her back, Ellie's mouth twitched as she looked at the sample Gideon was showing her. The little trains on it quite plainly revealed his hopes!

'It is very nice, Gideon,' she agreed, 'but if I were to have a little girl . . .'

To her amusement Gideon actually looked slightly shame-faced.

Ellie was surprised at how easily she had settled into the Winckley Square house. And how easily she had settled into marriage with Gideon! Too easily, perhaps, given the real situation! Gideon had married her out of necessity, and despite the taunting comment he had made the first night of their marriage he had made no attempt whatsoever to share either the intimacy of the master bedroom with her, or the intimacy of its bed! Which should not have been a problem – far from it, but . . .

Warily Ellie examined her thoughts. By rights

she ought to feel nothing but anger and bitterness towards Gideon, but somehow, despite all her strenuous efforts to reject it, a tiny tendril of something soft and yearning had begun to bind itself around her heart. She had caught herself studying Gideon when she thought he would not notice, finding heart-aching similarities between the man he was now and the youth he had been.

'I suppose it will have to be this one then.' Gideon's voice broke into her thoughts, as he showed her a wallpaper sample in softest lemon, decorated with little lambs.

Gravely, she agreed, but her eyes were dancing with laughter, and as he closed the book, she couldn't stop herself from teasing his straight face.

'We could always decorate your dressing room, or even the study, with the other wallpaper, if you are so attracted to it, Gideon.'

The look he gave her tore at her heart.

Disbelievingly Gideon looked at Ellie, the amusement in her voice, the playfulness of her manner, the fact that she was treating him as though . . . as though . . . His heart was somersaulting inside his chest and banging so loudly against it that he felt sure Ellie must be able to hear it. Only he knew how difficult he had found these last weeks, and how radically his views, his beliefs and his desires had changed. He was overwhelmed by a sudden urgent need to take hold of Ellie and beg her to give him a second chance, to forgive him for the past, and let him show her just how much . . .

Deriding himself for his impossible hopes, he told her instead, drily, 'The dressing room, maybe, but somehow I doubt it would be a good idea to change the silk panels in the study for it.'

As Ellie laughed, Henrietta came rushing up to them, begging Gideon to pick her up.

'I want to see your special magic hand,' she told him imperiously.

Over her head Gideon looked at Ellie, his heart turning over as he saw the tears shimmering in her eyes. If anything should go wrong – if he should lose her as Ellie herself had lost her mother . . . Suddenly the most terrible fear and pain gripped him. If that should happen his life would not be worth living!

Ellie gave a small sigh. Her back had begun to ache and she reached behind herself to rub the ache.

She had decided to walk round to the Kershaws' to see John and to thank Marianne Kershaw for her recommendation of a good midwife. Gideon had been fussing about getting in a special doctor from London, as well as an expensive monthly nurse. A little bleakly Ellie reflected that by rights she ought to have been looking to the women in her family to support her at this time – her aunts and her cousins, and her sister.

There was still no word from Connie, or about her, and Ellie was becoming increasingly concerned. She had written to Cecily, informing her of her marriage, but as yet she had heard nothing back from her cousin.

The ache in her back had intensified and she decided that perhaps the walk might help to ease it a little. Henrietta was upstairs in the care of the smiling young nursemaid Gideon had insisted on hiring.

As Ellie stepped out into the street she hesitated, realising that their aunt was crossing the square. Ellie had not forgotten the way her Aunt Gibson had ignored her when she had seen her outside Booths. Her chin firmed. Let her Aunt Gibson refuse to acknowledge her if she wished. Ellie did not care.

But instead of walking past her, her aunt came up to her, her face an angry shade of crimson.

'How can you shame us like this, Ellie? Re-marrying before you are out of mourning! What your poor mother would think . . . After all she did for you . . . for all of you.'

'I love Mama and I always will,' Ellie replied fiercely, 'but I am an adult now, Aunt, and not a child, and I can tell you this. Never, ever would I want to inflict on my children the pain my mother has unintentionally inflicted upon us – separating us in the way that she did, taking us away from our father and from each other.' Angry tears filled Ellie's eyes but she dashed them away.

'You dare to question her decision?' her aunt breathed. 'She only wanted what was best for you.'

'Best for me? I have come to believe that my poor

mother was overly influenced by the opinions of her sisters, and that because of that –'

'What! How dare you say such a thing?' her aunt stopped her furiously. 'You should be ashamed of yourself, Ellie, and not just for your criticism of your poor mother! You have not yet been widowed a twelve-month and yet here you are remarried, and to Gideon Walker of all men.'

Neither of them were aware that Gideon, who had been working in his study, had come outside and could hear what they were saying.

'And pray what is wrong with that?' Ellie challenged her aunt. 'I would have you know that I am proud to call myself Gideon's wife, and that I wish more than I can say that I had had the good sense and the strength to follow my own heart years ago, Aunt, and accept his proposal.'

'Oh, how can you be so ungrateful? When I think of the advantages you have had, Ellie. Your Aunt Parkes, my sister, took you into her home and gave you the very best of everything, and her husband, Mr Parkes –'

'Mr Parkes!' Ellie wondered what her aunt would say if she told her the truth about him! 'Gideon is worth a dozen of him – no, a hundred,' Ellie corrected herself passionately. 'And I can tell you this, Aunt, I would far rather have married Gideon when he had nothing and known the happiness of that marriage than been given a hundred times more than my Aunt and Uncle Parkes gave me. And what is more –' Ellie had to stop speaking as a sudden surge of pain caught her unawares, making her gasp and hold her side.

'It is just as I have always thought,' her aunt told her bitterly. 'You and your sister both have no Barclay in you. You are all Pride. And as for Connie –'

'Don't you speak against my sister,' Ellie warned her. 'Foolish she might be, but at least she has had the courage to stand up for her love. You cannot know how much I wish that I had done the same,' she added in a low voice. 'Gideon is –'

As another pain tore at her, she gave a sharp gasp. 'Ellie?'

Gideon could feel his emotions choking his throat. There was so much he wanted to say to her, so much he wanted to show her, but suddenly she gasped and clutched her body, and his longing to tell her how much he loved her was banished by his fear for her.

Relief filled Ellie to find that Gideon was there.

'What is it?' he demanded. 'What's wrong?'

'I don't know. There is a pain in my side and my back.' Beads of sweat had begun to form above her top lip and against her hairline.

Amelia Gibson had already turned her back on them both and walked away.

Anxiously, Gideon reached out to support Ellie, aware of the fierce tremors galvanising her body, and immediately fearful for her. If he should lose her now . . . But no; he must not think like that, even though the fate of her mother was haunting him!

'Gideon, I think it might be the baby,' Ellie told him anxiously. 'Help me inside, please.'

The pains came in waves, sometimes receding but always returning, until her whole world was a fiery red-hot torment of them. She was a girl again, hearing the sounds of her mother giving birth to Connie and then John, and then . . .

Ellie cried out sharply as an extra fierce surge of pain gripped her. What if she should die like her mother? What if . . . ? The pain surged and grew and she cried out against it. Someone stroked her damp hair back from her forehead and tried to soothe her. She could hear the midwife urging her to push.

A primeval urgency gripped her, and she began to pant. Everything was pain; a hot-red mist of it that clawed and tore at her, but something was urging her to keep on, to deliver the new life that was demanding to be born; that need was stronger than her fear, stronger than anything else she had ever experienced.

Downstairs, where he had been banished by the midwife, Gideon paced the floor, praying as he had never prayed in his life – not for himself and not even for his child but for Ellie. Ellie, his beloved Ellie, his love, his life. Please God . . . He tensed as he heard her agonised cries, tears running down his face.

'Ellie . . . Oh, please God, let her be all right.'

* * *

Determinedly Ellie battled with the pain, willing her child to be born. There was a sudden rushing surge of pressure, a pain that gripped and coiled itself around her and then suddenly a swift release.

As she lay drained and exhausted, she could hear the thin newborn cry of her child. Tears of joy and release filled her eyes.

'It's a boy – aye, and a right fine one too,' the midwife was saying.

'Give him to me,' Ellie demanded urgently and possessively, struggling to sit up and take the baby from her as she finished cleaning him.

Unsteadily Ellie reached out and touched him – her son. Gideon's son. A fierce shock of intense maternal love surged through her. He had his father's eyes, and his nose too, and his unnerving, unwavering stare. Her heart jumped and skittered as girlishly as it had done that first time she had seen Gideon himself. A feeling of helpless adoring love filled her. Tears momentarily blinded her as she gently explored the small body.

How could she have ever not wanted this precious wonderful new life, this precious wonderful child? The intensity of her feelings awed her, choking her of breath, filling her with emotions she could barely comprehend.

All the time the midwife was working, Ellie clung to her child, refusing to let him go. The most profound sense of pride and fear consumed her. How could she ever bear to let him out of her sight? He was so precious.

Gideon couldn't endure it any more. The silence after that gut-wrenching cry he had heard Ellie give was killing him. He had to see her, had to be with her.

Taking the stairs two at a time, he thrust open the door, ignoring the indignant cluckings of the midwife.

Over her head Ellie smiled proudly at him, and lifted up the tiny bundle she was cradling as she said softly, 'Gideon, come and see your son.'

She was laughing and crying, and so too, Gideon realised, was he. His hands trembled as he held the baby, but his hungry gaze was for Ellie and not for his son. Still holding the baby, Gideon leaned over and kissed Ellie passionately on the mouth. For a second they looked at one another in silence. Never to him had Ellie looked more beautiful than she did right now, her still-short hair clinging to her face in damp wisps, her eyes brilliant with exhilaration and exhaustion, her lips curving in a warm, proud maternal smile, Gideon decided. The baby cried, and instinctively Ellie took him from Gideon, lifting him to her breast.

The midwife was still tutting but Gideon ignored her. His heart felt as though it would burst with love and pain. He so much wanted to tell Ellie everything but now was not the time.

Ellie's eyes burned with disappointed tears as Gideon got up and left the bedroom. When she had seen that look he had given the baby and then her she had so much hoped . . . How foolish of her. His love for her had died long ago, she knew that.

'We shall have to register the birth.'

Ellie managed to stop gazing adoringly at her son for long enough to look at Gideon's stiff back. He was standing in front of her bedroom window with his back to her. Tenderly she nursed her son, smiling indulgently as he tugged fiercely on her nipple. He had been a good weight and the monthly nurse had told her that she had never seen a healthier male child.

There was no mistaking the resemblance between father and son. The little one was every inch his father's child, and no mistake!

'Yes, we shall,' Ellie agreed.

'We shall name Henry as his father, of course,' Gideon announced curtly.

Ellie froze. 'No,' she told him tersely.

Gideon turned round. 'What are you saying, Ellie? We have no option, not unless we want the whole world to know that –'

'I don't care about the whole world,' Ellie told him. 'What I care about is our son and the fact that I want him to grow up knowing who his father is and not believing . . . He is your son, Gideon, and if you are ashamed of acknowledging him as such –'

'Ashamed! Never. But there will be gossip, Ellie, and –'

'There is always gossip of some sort or another.'

A strange sensation was running through his body, a feeling of weightlessness and joy. 'You are sure about this?' he questioned.

'Yes!' Ellie confirmed vehemently. 'And I thought,' – she hesitated, her skin colouring up – 'I thought we might call him Richard, for your father.'

Gideon discovered that he was looking at her through a haze of tears. Turning away, he wiped his hand across his eyes. 'Aye, if you want to,' he responded, shrugging as though he had no real interest in the matter, but Ellie had seen his quick secret gesture, and her own heart lifted.

'Cecily has sent a lovely dress for the baby,' she told Gideon conversationally, 'and Iris has written me the most cross letter demanding to know why I didn't tell her about the baby so that she could deliver him herself. I should like very much to ask her to be Richard's godmama, Gideon.' Her face clouded. 'I should also have liked to have asked Connie. I am so worried about her. No one knows where she has gone, and John said she and Kieron had talked of emigrating to America!'

'I'll find her for you, Ellie.'

Ellie looked at him. Something seemed to quiver in the air between them, something soft and sweet.

Gideon looked at Ellie. He couldn't find the words to tell her what it had meant to him to hear her saying that she wanted to acknowledge him as Richard's father. He was already fiercely proud of his son and wished passionately that Mary might have lived to see him. And it wasn't just his son who filled his heart with emotion, Gideon acknowledged.

Clearing his throat, he began, 'I heard what you were saying to your aunt the day you went into labour with Richard. Ellie, I own that I have misjudged you – not made allowances for your youth or the pressure your family put on you. There are many wrongs between us that perhaps cannot be righted, but if they could be, is it possible . . . could we . . . You are a very special woman, Ellie Pride. Aye, and you carry that name deservedly, for if ever a woman had the right to be proud, Ellie, it is you. You are a woman it would be very easy for a man to love if he were allowed to do so, Ellie, especially this man! I know I have not always treated you as I should – indeed, I am ashamed that I –'

Ellie didn't want to see him humble himself any further. Instinctively she knew what he was trying to say to her but, like him, she had been hurt and had grown cautious.

'I'll thank you to remember, Gideon Walker,' she announced determinedly, 'that I am not Ellie Pride any longer. I am Mrs Gideon Walker, and proud to be so. Very proud to be so. In fact, I am more proud to be your wife than I am of anything else I have ever done,' she told him softly, whilst tears shimmered in her eyes.

'Ellie!' She heard Gideon's groan and barely had time to put the baby down before she was in Gideon's arms, held fast there whilst he rained eager kisses on her face, before finally taking her mouth in a kiss of fierce possessive passion.

Ellie's lips trembled beneath his, passive and soft, whilst his own hardened in pent-up demand. 'Ellie!'

He breathed her name and suddenly she was a girl again, her body coming alive for him, wanting him, her emotions filled by him.

Her lips parted, and Gideon seized his opportunity. It was only the sudden lusty cry of their son that brought an end to their passionate kiss.

'I love you, Ellie Walker,' Gideon told her softly. 'Before, I loved you with a boy's love, and with a boy's foolish pride, but now I love you with a man's love, and with a man's humble recognition of his good fortune in loving such a special woman.'

'Oh, Gideon, you cannot know what it means to me to hear you say such words. I have been so unhappy without you, even though I would not let myself acknowledge it,' Ellie admitted huskily.

'You will never be unhappy again,' Gideon said to her fiercely. 'I promise you that.'